CULTURE, CLASS AND GENDER
IN THE VICTORIAN NOVEL

Also by Arlene Young

THE ODD WOMEN BY GEORGE GISSING (*editor*)

Culture, Class and Gender in the Victorian Novel

Gentlemen, Gents and Working Women

Arlene Young

First published in Great Britain 1999 by
MACMILLAN PRESS LTD
Houndmills, Basingstoke, Hampshire RG21 6XS and London
Companies and representatives throughout the world

A catalogue record for this book is available from the British Library.

ISBN 0–333–74017–3

 First published in the United States of America 1999 by
ST. MARTIN'S PRESS, INC.,
Scholarly and Reference Division,
175 Fifth Avenue, New York, N.Y. 10010

ISBN 0–312–22346–3

Library of Congress Cataloging-in-Publication Data
Young, Arlene.
Culture, class and gender in the Victorian novel : gentlemen,
gents and working women / Arlene Young.
   p.   cm.
Includes bibliographical references (p.   ) and index.
ISBN 0–312–22346–3
1. English fiction—19th century—History and criticism.
2. Social classes in literature.   3. Literature and society—Great
Britain—History—19th century.   4. Man-woman relationships in
literature.   5. Working class women in literature.   6. Sex role in
literature.   7. Men in literature.   I. Title.
PR878.S6Y68   1999
823'.809355—dc21   99–13785
                                                                CIP

© Arlene Young 1999

All rights reserved. No reproduction, copy or transmission of this publication may be made without written permission.

No paragraph of this publication may be reproduced, copied or transmitted save with written permission or in accordance with the provisions of the Copyright, Designs and Patents Act 1988, or under the terms of any licence permitting limited copying issued by the Copyright Licensing Agency, 90 Tottenham Court Road, London W1P 0LP.

Any person who does any unauthorised act in relation to this publication may be liable to criminal prosecution and civil claims for damages.

The author has asserted her right to be identified as the author of this work in accordance with the Copyright, Designs and Patents Act 1988.

This book is printed on paper suitable for recycling and made from fully managed and sustained forest sources.

10 9   8   7   6   5   4   3   2
08 07 06 05 04 03 02 01 00

Printed and bound in Great Britain by
Antony Rowe Ltd, Chippenham, Wiltshire

For Bob

Contents

Introduction		1
1	'A Kind of a Sort of a Gentleman': the Gentleman's Progress from Sir Charles Grandison to John Halifax	14
2	The Literary Evolution of the Lower Middle Class: *The Natural History of the Gent* to *Little Dorrit*	45
3	Voices from the Margins: Dickens, Wells and Bennett	87
4	Bachelor Girls and Working Women: Women and Independence in Oliphant, Levy, Allen and Gissing	119
5	Modern Prometheus Unbound: May Sinclair and *The Divine Fire*	157
Conclusion		189
Notes		192
Bibliography		213
Index		222

Acknowledgements

I wish to acknowledge the support of the Social Sciences and Humanities Research Council of Canada during the research and preparation of this study. I would also like to thank the many people who have read all or part of the typescript at various stages and who have provided sensitive and insightful criticism – Harry Shaw, Dorothy Mermin, Paul Sawyer, Dan Schwarz, Peter Bailey, Regenia Gagnier and Donald Gray. Special thanks to my daughters, Laurel Jebamani and Jenny O'Kell, for working as research and computer assistants and to my husband, Bob O'Kell, who gave me guidance and support and who smooths out all the rough spots.

Portions of Chapter 2 and Chapter 3 were published in *Victorian Studies* 39:4 (Summer 1996), 483–511 as 'Virtue Domesticated: Dickens and the Lower Middle Class' and are reproduced here with the permission of Indiana University Press.

Introduction

In response to the adverse and in his view sometimes irrelevant criticisms that appeared in early reviews of *The Rise of the Novel*, Ian Watt wrote his own review, in which he identifies what he sees as the shortcomings of his famous book and singles out his 'grossest substantive failure of execution':

> Briefly, through diffuse implication and assumption, rather than through explicit statement, I presented 'the rise of the novel' as though it had been achieved in collusion with various changes in philosophical, moral and psychological outlook, and with something called the rising middle class (that restless bunch). In so doing I tended to make it look as though the novel had emerged in consistent, though largely unconscious, opposition to the traditional social and literary establishment of the time.[1]

I herewith embrace this gross error, in somewhat mutated form, as a basic premise of this study and as a means of contextualizing the emergence of the lower middle class as a social, cultural and literary phenomenon. I shall argue that the middle class, rather than the novel, emerged in consistent, though largely unconscious, opposition to the social and cultural establishment of the time and that the rise of this 'restless bunch' was achieved in collusion, so to speak, with the novel. The novel was the forum in which the rising middle class could imaginatively reshape society and reinterpret cultural symbols, in which it could redefine class relations from its own perspective and disseminate its moral code.[2] This quiet insinuation of its values and perspectives greatly enhanced the middle class in its bid for cultural hegemony for, as Harold Perkin observes, 'whichever class manages to impose its own morality on the rest of the nation will become the ascendant class.'[3] In the mid-nineteenth century, having achieved ascendency, the middle class continued to use the novel as a means of consolidating its social and cultural hegemony and of disseminating its social philosophy.

The major focus of this study is the vital role played by the novel, as well as by other forms of literature, in the evolution of class relations in nineteenth-century England. I am not concerned with the prehistory of either the novel or the middle class, or the pre-existence of elements of each in earlier literary and social forms. It is, rather, 'the moment that ... [the English novel] attains its institutional and canonic identity' – the end point of Michael McKeon's accomplished analysis of its murky beginnings – that marks the initial point of my interest.[4] It was at this point that the novel and the middle class began to form a working relationship, one that fostered the rise to respectability and prominence of both genre and class. The novel accordingly becomes the medium in which the dominant nineteenth-century bourgeois social values and attitudes are formulated and expressed, and this is done largely through the conventions for representing specific classes in literature. These conventions are developed by the middle class as a means of controlling and containing other classes, but are subsequently manipulated, mainly by women and lower-middle-class male writers, as a form of resistance to middle-class patriarchal dominance.

The force of historical development thus brings me to a consideration of the lower middle class as a newly emerging and rapidly growing social group that presented an especially vexed problem in class relations and that has been unjustly neglected both as a literary and as a historical phenomenon. Contemporary portrayals present members of the class as insignificant, ineffectual, and contemptible. But the lower middle class, given its sheer size and its role in manning the service sector of Britain's expanding political and commercial empire, was an important component of the power relations of Victorian England. The insistence of contemporary avowals to the contrary and the intensity of the negative responses to the lower middle class indeed suggest that the bourgeoisie recognized it as a potential threat to class stability. The conventions for representing members of the lower middle class in various forms of literature accordingly become a strategic component of bourgeois power relations. The lower middle class is disempowered by means of persistent disparagement and, more significantly, domestication. Ultimately perceived as essentially domestic entities, lower-middle-class men, like women of all classes, remain socially and culturally marginalized throughout the Victorian period. The conventions thus inadvertently form connections across the barriers of class and gender that eventually lead to an informal alliance between middle-class women and lower-middle-class men in their resistance to cultural and literary marginalization.

In arguing as I do, I am aware of falling prey to the same tendency that made Watt uneasy, the tendency to impute a quasi-self-conscious agency to something as abstract and diffuse as a literary genre or a social class. It is difficult to avoid creating such an impression, however, when assessing the development or influence of a collective body such as a class, and it is no more remiss in scholarly terms than discussing the evolution of political society using the concept of the general will. In reality, the middle class, like society as a whole, has never been a monolith and has never acted with a unanimous will. It is notoriously fragmented, fissured on one plane by gradations of class and divided on an intersecting plane into interest groups that may or may not acknowledge class gradations; it could, indeed, be more accurately called a conglomerate, rather than a class.[5] The members of this conglomerate may not act in common – may, given their diversity, be unable or unwilling to act in common. They nevertheless share certain characteristics and goals which lead them to endorse certain common values, such as individualism, industry, domesticity, and piety.[6] It is through the influence of these values that are more or less shared by its members, rather than through action, that the middle class achieves moral dominance in Victorian culture.

The ideal vehicle for disseminating values and ideas during the last half of the eighteenth century and throughout the nineteenth century was the novel. It was by no means the only vehicle, however, and periodical literature plays a significant part in the reinterpretation of society and of class roles that takes place during this period. But periodicals are a forum for debate, for the presentation of contestable positions on issues of current interest or for more or less didactic expositions that are clearly meant to persuade. Novels are much more insinuating. The values and assumptions that inform a novel are presented indirectly. More significantly, these values and assumptions form an integral part of what purports to be an accurate reflection of the real world. The realism of the novel creates the illusion that the precepts of the novel's imagined world are in fact natural and correct. Finally, people would undoubtedly have approached the reading of a novel – the great new leisure pastime of the period – and the reading of articles in a periodical in very different ways. Readers would have had a greater emotional engagement with the text of a novel and a less consciously intellectual one: they would not have been as alert to the possibilities of a silent debate with the author. Accordingly, the novel fosters consensus rather than resistance.[7] Thus the values and perspectives presented in novels – that is, the values and perspectives of the middle class – insinuated themselves imperceptibly into the minds and hearts of the reading public and eventually became normative.

The novel influences the attitudes and values of its readers most powerfully through the manipulation of cultural symbols. In the determination of class relations during this period, the most significant of such symbols is that of the gentleman. The manipulation of cultural symbols is also used liberally in other forms of literature at this time, as is demonstrated in Mary Poovey's *Uneven Developments* and Nancy Armstrong's *Desire and Domestic Fiction*, two of the most powerful and influential examinations of the relation between English society and literature during the nineteenth century.[8] Both works focus on the symbolic significance of woman in the nineteenth century, either as the subject or the locus of social control or as the symbolic agent through which social control is deployed. While thus highlighting power relations within Victorian society, however, neither study emphasizes issues of class relations as a social process. I am not saying that either of these studies ignores class – far from it. Armstrong, for example, acknowledges that she 'could not detach the issues of gender from those of class' (Armstrong, p. 257). Even to consider the possibility of doing so, however, suggests that Armstrong perceives class as less dynamic, as less a matter of process than it is for analysts of class development like E. P. Thompson and Raymond Williams. Also, male images play no significant role in Armstrong's discussion of the development of interiority and concepts of the self in the novel. An approach to Victorian culture that thus decenters class is perhaps a necessary corrective to those that have been exclusively weighted in favor of economic and class models of social development or to exclusively male-oriented interpretations of the social order. But the concept of woman as symbol and the ideal of the domestic woman have limited meaning when considered in isolation from the idea of the gentleman, arguably the most pervasive, important, and unstable symbol in Victorian culture.

As has long been recognized, the idea of the gentleman was a key concept in the first strategic move on the part of the middle class in its rise to social and cultural dominance – the appropriation of the moral authority that had been the birthright of the aristocracy. Such a move was far more difficult than gaining economic supremacy because moral authority, being an abstract commodity, cannot be evaluated quantitatively nor can its use or power be transferred through legal channels. Moral authority is articulated through the symbolic order and so is not directly subject to physical, political, or economic forces; it can be altered only through the manipulation of images and ideals. Poovey argues that the middle class validated its authority through 'the redefinition and relocation of the idea of virtue', which was accomplished by articulating virtue upon gender rather than upon inherited class position, by situating it within the middle-class domestic sphere and the feminine heart (Poovey, p. 10). Armstrong asserts that 'it was the new domestic woman, rather than her counterpart, the new economic man, who first encroached upon aristocratic culture and seized authority from it' (Armstrong, p. 59). But the counterpart of the new domestic woman was not the new economic man; if it had been, *Robinson Crusoe* would be the prototypical fictional representation of middle-class man. The counterpart of the domestic woman was the new bourgeois gentleman. Moreover, the moral authority of the aristocracy was based on the concept of honor, rather than on virtue, and the embodiment of honor was the gentleman. Accordingly, whatever the shifts in the locus of virtue, moral authority could be appropriated most directly through the manipulation of the image of the gentleman.

Traditionally, the aristocracy as a body is not necessarily associated with virtue but with duties and responsibilities to other ranks in society. As Donna T. Andrew points out, the code of honor that governed the conduct of the aristocratic gentleman was indeed 'the moral code of the often irreligious man of fashion'.[9] On the other hand, the association of woman with virtue is not a nineteenth-century bourgeois innovation: the aristocratic lady as the ideal of beauty and goodness is one of the conventions of courtly love in the Middle Ages. Nineteenth-century formulations of the gentleman and the domestic woman are accordingly middle-class appropriations of the aristocratic roles of the medieval knight and lady. Moreover, the nineteenth-century interest in Medievalism is less an attempt to find a satisfactory model for social relations, as Carlyle would have it, than an attempt to establish the bourgeois gentleman rather than the indolent and luxurious aristocrat as the rightful heir of the medieval knight, the man of action governed by codes of honor and duty. But like the knight in Chaucer's *Book of the Duchess*, the gentleman is the active principle that is given inspiration and direction by the idealized vision of his consort. Virtue is the product of their union. This reconstitution of the knight and the lady as the middle-class gentleman and the domestic woman allows the middle class to present itself imaginatively as the natural leaders of their society.

In the eighteenth century, the same authors who figure prominently in the establishment of the novel, Defoe and Richardson, also begin the process of transforming the gentleman from the embodiment of aristocratic honor into the embodiment of bourgeois respectability. His title notwithstanding, Richardson's Sir Charles Grandison is the archetype of the reformed gentleman, the pattern on which subsequent middle-class variations are based. Though a man of rank, Sir Charles is the exemplar not of the gentleman of birth but of the Christian gentleman, and it is through the concept of the Christian gentleman that virtue becomes one of the necessary attributes of gentlemanly status. For while virtue may be the cardinal attribute of the nineteenth-century domestic woman, as Poovey argues, it is also one of a constellation of sterling qualities that constitute her consort, the bourgeois gentleman.

As the nineteenth century progresses, the gentleman becomes an increasingly unstable symbol; 'gentleman' becomes a value-laden term that is paradoxically empty of meaning. Gentlemanly types proliferate; there is the gentleman of birth, of wealth, of breeding, of religion, or of education, to mention just a few possibilities.[10] At the same time, the essence of what a gentleman is becomes increasingly indefinable, as Anthony Trollope, in the voice of the narrator of *He Knew He Was Right* (published serially in 1868–9), attests. A gentleman is, he writes, 'that thing, so impossible of definition, and so capable of recognition'.[11] A few years later, the worldly Mrs Swancourt in Thomas Hardy's *A Pair of Blue Eyes* (1873), in response to an observation about 'ladies and gentlemen', instructs her artless stepdaughter on the demise of the latter term:

> 'My dear, you mustn't say "gentlemen" nowadays. . . . We have handed over "gentlemen" to the lower middle class, where the

word is still to be heard at tradesmen's balls and provincial tea-parties, I believe. It is done with here.'
'What must I say then?'
'"Ladies and *men*" always.'[12]

It is interesting to note that the term 'lady' apparently remains stable, a result, I would argue, of its relative distance from the symbolic associations with virtue and domesticity that cluster around the figures of the gentleman and the middle-class woman. Moreover, 'lady' remains more firmly grounded as an aristocratic designation because it is also a title. The Angel in the House might be a lady, but she cannot be a Lady, and so the term does not drift down the social scale in the way that 'gentleman' does, as a class-cum-moral designation. The term 'lady' can be directly ironic, as in 'ladies of the night', but it is not problematic in the way that 'gentleman' is.

Mrs Swancourt's assertion that 'gentleman' as a term 'is done with here' (i.e., in polite society, the only place, apparently, that counts) is not entirely accurate. There is overwhelming evidence in late nineteenth-century literature that 'gentleman' was still current as a designation of social distinction. What Mrs Swancourt's statement reveals is the extent to which the term has become problematic. The gentleman may survive as an abstract and indefinable ideal, but in common usage the epithet has lost status; it has been appropriated by the lower middle class. The lower middle class thus erodes the power of the most cherished bourgeois symbol and at the same time invades the territory of the novel. Lower-middle-class authors challenge and resist the class stereotypes that had evolved in the middle-class novel and they strive to establish themselves as fully enfranchised novelistic citizens. In other words, they democratize the novel.

Although I am mostly concerned with the development of class relations in the nineteenth century, this study begins in the eighteenth century and ends in the early years of the twentieth. The first chapter traces the evolution – or devolution – of the concept of the gentleman from *Sir Charles Grandison* to *John Halifax, Gentleman* and the social, political, and literary implications of this development. The second chapter analyzes the conventions for representing specific classes in various forms of nineteenth-century literature, with special emphasis on the development of the conventions for representing the lower middle class and on the associations of these conventions with concepts of gender. In Chapter 3, I examine how lower-middle-class male writers respond to the literary stereotypes by reversing the class attributes of their middle- and lower-middle-class characters. As these writers strive to present their lower-middle-class protagonists as characters worthy of the reader's attention, they exploit the issues of class and gender that have marginalized them – the tendency of other classes to feminize them – to their advantage: they highlight the links between lower-middle-class men and women of higher social standing, an association that eventually benefits both groups. In Chapter 4, I demonstrate how lower-middle-class employment eventually provides an avenue of escape from the cultural and novelistic protocols of femininity that limited the freedom and self-expression of women in the nineteenth century. In the last chapter, I argue that in May Sinclair's *The Divine Fire* (1904) the fictional lady forms a new union, this time not with a knight but with a lower-middle-class man who succeeds in demonstrating his superiority over the gentleman – by now a hollow man – and in establishing himself as a modern hero.

The texts that I examine in this study vary widely from novels to volumes of social analysis like Defoe's *The Complete English Tradesman* (c. 1728) or Walter Gallichan's *The Blight of Respectability* (1897), to articles and comic sketches from periodical literature. The novels range from the canonical, like *Great Expectations* (1860–1), to the now completely obscure, like *Anna St. Ives* (1792), *The Bachelor Girls and their Adventures in Search of Independence* (1907), and *The Divine Fire*. My main criteria for selecting novels were the extent to which they focused on social issues and followed themes like the nature of the gentleman or white-collar work for women and the extent to which they elicited public response, either by being exceptionally popular, like *John Halifax, Gentleman* (1856) and *The Divine Fire*, or by being controversial, like *The Woman Who Did* (1895). My assumption is that such texts struck sensitive social nerves and accordingly are likely to yield important insights into the culture that produced them.

A large portion of this study will be devoted to an examination of Victorian social-problem novels, those self-conscious critiques of society that nevertheless reinforce the status quo. In Foucauldian terms, these novels, as forms of resistance, are in fact part of the systems of power which they are intended to challenge. However, I find Raymond Williams's formulation of how power relations work through hegemony more compelling than Foucault's. In *Marxism and Literature*, Williams, drawing on Gramsci, affirms that hegemony is never complete or 'totalizing', except in abstract formulations, which are necessarily static. In practice, hegemony is an active process and is always challenged by counter-cultures and other forms of resistance:

> A lived hegemony is always a process. It is not, except analytically, a system or a structure.... [I]t does not just passively exist as a form of dominance. It has continually to be renewed, recreated, defended, and modified. It is also continually resisted, limited, altered, challenged by pressures not at all its own. We have then to add to the concept of hegemony the concepts of counter-hegemony and alternative hegemony, which are real and persistent elements of practice.[13]

Thus hegemony and resistance to it exist in a symbiotic and dynamic process in which they affect, control, and disrupt each other. The real interest then lies not in demonstrating that resistance reinscribes the culture that it critiques, but in ascertaining what it is that resistance is able to alter as well as what it reinforces, and in determining how the resultant alterations and continuities then contribute to the stifling or fostering of further resistance. In so far as they affirm class boundaries and the status quo, Victorian social novels lull bourgeois fears about class activism and encourage complacency about class stability. They also map out the territory of the middle-class psyche with which other classes have to contend; they define the extent and limitations of bourgeois understanding and compassion. In other words, these novels help to define what other classes must continue to resist.

Since this study concentrates on the lower middle class, which is notoriously difficult to define, I wish to clarify what and whom I am referring to when I use this term. Arno Mayer characterizes the class as a 'complex and unstable social, political, and cultural compound' and argues that the phrase 'lower middle class' 'can be assigned no fixed meaning for all times and places.'[14] In their historical assessments of the lower middle class, Mayer and Geoffrey Crossick acknowledge that a loose definition would include both artisans and white-collar workers.¹⁵ Mayer refers to the artisans and labor aristocrats as 'the old lower middle class' and urban white-collar workers as 'the new lower middle class', which combined to form 'a syncretic lower middle class, a heterogeneous and often incompatible occupational, economic, social, and ideational mixture.' (Mayer, p. 423) The fundamental differences between the two groups, however, demand that the 'old' and the 'new' be seen as distinct from each other, that the 'heterogeneous' and 'incompatible' elements be separated. In his analysis of the emergence of the lower middle class in Britain, Crossick questions the existence of a single lower middle class, noting that as the class evolved 'the distinction between marginal non-manual groups and labour aristocrats became increasingly important.' (Crossick, p. 13) My focus is on urban white-collar workers who form that distinct lower middle class which George Gissing refers to as being 'a social status so peculiarly English' and which contemporary observers found so contemptible.¹⁶ My analysis accordingly follows Crossick's model, which is based on the British experience, while Mayer's is based on the wider Continental experience.

Although their definitions of the lower middle class differ somewhat, Mayer and Crossick outline many of the same features of the lower-middle-class ethos and style of life. Members of the lower middle class tended to define themselves against the working class and its culture. They rejected both formal and informal collective association, the pub and street life as well as professional organizations, in favor of the ideals of individualism and self-help. Like the middle class, the lower middle class retreated into the cocoon of the highly privatized family, separating life into the two spheres of public and private, work and the sanctuary of home. Unlike manual laborers, members of the lower middle class did not dirty their hands or clothing at work and so could wear, and indeed were expected to wear, the same uniform of a dark coat and white linen that their employers did. His genteel garb indeed became the symbol of his respectability for lower-middle-class man and the focus for much derision from outside the class.

Mayer and Crossick differ slightly in their judgments of where recruits into the growing lower middle class came from. Crossick acknowledges the possibility of movement down from middle-class origins, but favors the interpretation of the lower middle class as comprising former members of the working and artisan classes moving up the social ladder. (Crossick, p. 35) Mayer sees the lower middle class as 'the up-and-down escalator par excellence of societies that are in motion.' (Mayer, p. 433) It is certainly at the points of entry into the class that its definition becomes most problematic. Is the son of a military officer or of an impoverished vicar, for example, lower-middle-class because he is poor and forced to work as a low-level clerk, or will he always remain a true gentleman in the eyes of society because of his origins? Is a shop assistant in a haberdasher's a member of the lower middle class while a butcher is not? Is it the counter he stands behind that determines the butcher's status, or the apron that he wears? The apron certainly carried a social stigma, as an incident in Gissing's *Will Warburton* (1905) illustrates. Rosamund, a romantic young woman from the lower middle class, is captivated by Warburton's quiet and refined manner. She is prepared to find his poverty romantic while she believes him to be a clerk, but she is horrified when she learns his real line of work. 'A grocer – in an apron!' she gasps, and she forthwith rejects him completely.[17]

The literature of the later nineteenth century abounds in examples of such problematic class associations. To complicate matters further, one of the curiosities of representation in this period is that identification with the lower middle class restricts and blights male characters, but not female ones. Will Warburton is something of an exception, but one that more or less proves the rule. At the opening of the novel, Warburton is a middle-class gentleman, but he loses his fortune and is forced to find work. He is less blighted than frustrated by the loss of prestige, however; he retains an essentially middle-class persona, which allows Gissing to use him as a credible commentator on the injustices of social biases against him in his reduced circumstances. A grocer born and bred would never be taken seriously in such a role. The young woman whom Warburton eventually marries, by contrast, *is* lower-middle-class born and bred, but is also represented as having taste and breeding, qualities never assigned to lower-middle-class men. Another of Gissing's lower-middle-class heroines, Nancy Lord (*In the Year of the Jubilee*, 1894), is not only possessed of considerable personal discretion and integrity, but is also clearly superior to Lionel Tarrant, the self-satisfied young gentleman who seduces and then reluctantly marries her. Nancy bears his subsequent neglect and eventual abandonment of her with fortitude and dignity. Tarrant ultimately returns to provide a home for Nancy and their young son, and in the end he acknowledges her worth and his own failings in response to her tentative suggestion that he is ashamed of her:

> 'Are you – ever so little – ashamed of me?'
>   He regarded her steadily, smiling.
> 'Not in the least.'
> 'You were – you used to be?'
> 'Before I knew you; and before I knew myself. When, in fact, *you* were a notable young lady of Camberwell, and *I* –'
> 'And you?'
> 'A notable young fool of nowhere at all.'[18]

By the last decade of the nineteenth century, Camberwell had become the quintessential lower-middle-class suburb, the symbol of all that was narrow and drab and blighted by respectability.[19] If Tarrant had referred to 'a notable young gentleman of Camberwell', the phrase could only be ironic. The blight, however, does not infect Nancy. She is at least free of the middle-class snobbery that made Tarrant a young fool.

However encouraging, in terms of perceptions of the lower middle class, this last vignette may sound, the attitudes of society in general towards the class remained largely negative. Moreover, the line between middle and lower middle class could be disturbingly uncertain for those who were insecure in their position on the social ladder. Another incident from a *fin-de-siècle* novel captures the resulting pervasive sense of social insecurity. The lower-middle-class wife of a middle-class swell (appropriately nicknamed Dandie) listens uncomfortably as her husband's cousin relates a recent conversation at their ladies' club:

> There was a discussion at the club the other day about classes. Women's clubs should never discuss. Some one asked how we could distinguish between the upper middle class and the lower middle class. One said it was whether you kept one servant or two; another if you lived in the suburbs – a house in a row; somebody else said you were ostracised if you had ever done the washing at home, and another one that you were lower middle class without doubt if you had been seen to open your own front door or walk down the street with a market basket.

You should have seen the faces! Why, you are flushing and wriggling yourself. We were all touched in some sensitive spot. . . . I think myself that only an idle woman can be a lady: she has time to cultivate grace. I flared up when a distinction was drawn between trades and professions. Dandie's father and mine were only tradesmen on a magnificent scale.[20]

As these fictional vignettes suggest, the perception and attitudes of observers played as significant a role as any objective criteria in determining who was placed in the lower middle class. Just as an individual could consider himself to be middle-class, as someone once postulated, if his neighbors allowed him to do so, so too an individual must admit to being lower-middle-class if his neighbors did not allow him to think otherwise. The quality of being lower-middle-class, it seems, was almost as impressionistic as that of being a gentleman.

1
'A Kind of a Sort of a Gentleman': the Gentleman's Progress from Sir Charles Grandison to John Halifax

> The idea of *descending* into the middle class does not arise, for obvious reasons, the most important one being that the middle class as a whole is seen as progressive and upwardly mobile.
> Patrick Brantlinger, *The Spirit of Reform*

The year 1856 marks an important point in the evolution of the idea of the gentleman, for it was in that year that Dinah Mulock Craik's *John Halifax, Gentleman* appeared. This stunningly mediocre novel was well received by the mostly middle-class reading public who enthusiastically embraced John Halifax and everything he represents, for he is the embodiment of those qualities most revered by the bourgeoisie: industry, piety, integrity, and business acumen. What made John Halifax not just popular but significant, however, was that he could be accepted as a gentleman without the previously indispensable advantages of rank or inherited wealth. The appearance and public endorsement of *John Halifax, Gentleman* marks the culmination of a process that had begun more than a century earlier: the bourgeois redefinition of the gentleman.

Until the eighteenth century, the term 'gentleman' generally denoted a man of high social station, a member of the gentry or the minor aristocracy. But by extension, 'gentleman' could also refer more generally to a man of distinction or to a man who exhibited the chivalry and refined sensibilities appropriate to a person of gentle birth. This lexical imprecision and the consequent vagueness of the concept of gentility contributed to an anxiety about the possibility of encroachments from social inferiors that dates back at least as far as the Renaissance. In 1583, Sir Thomas Smith defines gentlemen as those of noble blood but also acknowledges that there are other means of acquiring genteel status, observing that 'as for gentlemen they be made good cheap in England. For whosoever studieth the laws of the realm, who studieth in the Universities, who professeth liberal sciences, and to be short, who can live idly and without manual labour, and will bear the port, charge and countenance of a gentleman, he shall be called master . . . and shall be taken for a gentleman.'[1]

Most Renaissance writers, according to Ruth Kelso, deplore the rise of the gentlemen 'made good cheap,' but these 'upstarts' were in fact little threat to social stability because of the rapidity with which they assimilated the customs and manners of the nobility. Moreover, acquired gentility had to be sanctioned by the king, or through his representatives in the form of the College of Heralds, and did not attain the same distinction as noble birth.[2] Nevertheless, the term 'gentleman' encompassed a broad range of connotative possibilities that could be exploited by the rising commercial bourgeoisie as it grew in size and wealth and as its members sought to gain social standing. The imprecision and flexibility of the term allowed the most prosperous of the bourgeoisie to assume genteel status with relative ease. According to Peter Earle, the growth of a new urban culture of affluence in London and the integration of younger sons of the gentry into the world of commerce between 1660 and 1730 contributed to the blurring of class boundaries at the upper reaches of the bourgeoisie and helped temporarily to diminish the barrier between commerce and gentlemanly status.[3]

As the bourgeoisie grew in size and importance, however, it would have been increasingly difficult for its members to be assimilated smoothly into the ranks of the gentry. Moreover, as the importance of trade to England's prosperity and to her international relations increased, the trading classes gained wealth and influence and a sense of identity that was resistant to being effaced. Earle concedes that 'some sort of middle-class culture had long existed, closely allied to the dominant culture of the gentry and aristocracy' but that in the period between 1660 and 1730, 'this culture was transformed by the ambition and thirst for knowledge of the middle station' (Earle, p. 10). The inevitable strain that the increasing assertiveness of bourgeois culture placed on relations between the gentry and the bourgeoisie is reflected in the drama of the early eighteenth century, specifically in the representation of the merchant. 'The many efforts at... [merchants'] social rehabilitation so prominent in early-eighteenth-century drama (in the plays, say, of Steele and Lillo), had their origin in controversy,' according to John Loftis: 'they would not have appeared had there not been an active opposition. The incongruity of the merchants' prominence in the nation's economy compared with the subordinate role to which they had long been assigned provided a tension that dominates the social relationships of comedy.'[4] The merchant Sealand, for example, in Richard Steele's *The Conscious Lovers* (1722), expresses his impatience with aristocratic condescension to Sir John Bevil, observing that 'we Merchants are a Species of Gentry... and are as honourable, and almost as useful, as you landed Folks, that have always thought your selves so much above us.' Sealand continues his mockery of the landed gentry's limited economic scope and its lack of initiative by commenting that trade, for the likes of Bevil and his class, 'is extended no farther, than a Load of Hay, or a fat Ox – You are pleasant People, indeed; because you are generally bred up to be lazy, therefore, I warrant you, Industry is dishonourable.'[5] Sealand's classification of merchants as 'a Species of Gentry' suggests an ambivalence about the aristocratic concept of gentility; he wishes to assume a status equivalent to, but not identical with the landed gentry and he mocks the hauteur of 'landed Folks' by redefining them as an inferior species of merchant.

While the tension between the economic importance of the merchant class and its subordinate social position may have dominated the social relations of comedy, the essentially heroic and aristocratic dramatic conventions of the eighteenth-century stage were, as Laura Brown argues, nevertheless unsuited to the aesthetic expressions of the emerging bourgeois ideology. Thus as drama evolves from an aristocratic to a bourgeois form, 'though the fundamental formal and ideological premises of the plays are radically transformed, the conventions of dramatic representation are passed unchallenged from hand to hand.'[6] The resulting ideological division within protobourgeois drama is well illustrated in what Brown affirms is 'the best, most popular, and most strictly bourgeois' eighteenth-century play of its type (Brown, p. 158) – George Lillo's *The London Merchant* (1731). The play's full title, *The London Merchant; or, The History of George Barnwell*, registers the aesthetic and ideological divisions within the text. The merchant of the title is the wealthy and virtuous Thorowgood, who represents the man of trade as the embodiment of the gentlemanly ideal and presents the relationship between the commercial man and the gentleman as an unproblematic correspondence. 'As the Name of Merchant never degrades the Gentleman,' he claims, 'so by no means does it exclude him.'[7] The play's subtitle refers not to the name of the merchant, as might be expected, but to the name of one of his apprentices, whose tragic story is derived from the seventeenth-century 'Ballad of George Barnwell'. The ballad relates the downfall of a young and inexperienced apprentice who falls prey to the wiles of a grasping and unprincipled woman. The merchant of the main title is barely mentioned in the ballad and his role in the play is not well integrated into the action. The static, flat character of the merchant Thorowgood, with his formulaic perorations and invocations to gods and kings, largely conforms to the conventions of heroic action. And in a play in which the general run of characters are called George, Maria, Millwood, and Lucy, the names of the merchant and of his other apprentice, Trueman, indeed confer upon them the status of allegorical characters who can be expected to utter transcendent truths. They are in fact exemplars of the honorable and refined commercial man, thoroughly good and true men who are inferior to the aristocratic gentleman only in birth. At the same time, however, Thorowgood's ideology subordinates bourgeois culture and values to those of the aristocracy.

The London Merchant was an instant success with its first production in 1731 and remained popular throughout the eighteenth century and well into the nineteenth; it also draws comment in several of Dickens's novels, most notably in *Great Expectations* (1860–1), and turns up in *Punch* in 'Punch's Prize Novelists' as 'George de Barnwell' (1847). As the title of this parody by Thackeray suggests, however, it was not the person of the venerable merchant but the story of his unfortunate apprentice that accounts for the endurance of the play, which was regarded as a suitably moral and instructive form of entertainment for other apprentices, rather than as a manifesto of the bourgeoisie.[8] The characterization of the merchant as a bourgeois version of the gentleman appears to have had little impact, no doubt because both the medium and the characterization were inappropriate for the promulgation of bourgeois values. But while constraints of conventions prevent eighteenth-century dramatists from giving adequate aesthetic expression to bourgeois moral values, the 'generic underdevelopment' of the novel, Brown demonstrates, allows writers like Richardson and Fielding to avoid such limitations (Brown, pp. 185–209). The novel indeed provided the ideal medium in which the middle class could embody its interpretation of society, for the novel was less public and formal than drama and could represent the minutiae of everyday life and of ordinary individual action and personal interaction.

Other early and not entirely successful attempts to associate commercialism and the commercial classes with gentlemanly status coincide with the appearance of early and not entirely successful versions of the novel – and from the hands of the same man, Daniel Defoe.[9] Defoe touches on the appropriate relations between the commercial tradesman and the gentleman in *The Complete English Tradesman* (1727), but his assessment is rife with contradictions. He repeatedly warns those in trade to be satisfied with their class position and not to aspire to rise above it. Nevertheless, he frequently associates trade with aspects of gentlemanliness. The state of apprenticeship is no longer one of servitude, he insists, and the behavior of the apprentice and the man of commerce should accordingly be more like that of gentlemen than of that of tradesmen.[10] Defoe also acknowledges that while the tradesman's place is in his own class, he may 'on occasion keep company with Gentlemen' (I, 39). Tradesmen who rise above their class are presented as the exceptions, but examples of these exceptions recur too persistently in the text to be entirely discouraging. Indeed, the appropriate course of action for the aspiring tradesman eventually emerges as a subtext: establish your merit and superiority within your own class, amass a fortune and the property appropriate to a higher station, raise a family in ease and luxury and your descendants may be among the great families of England.[11] That this kind of social advancement has in fact occurred becomes the proof of the dignity of trade:

> Trade is so far *here* from being inconsistent with a Gentleman, that *in short* trade in *England* makes Gentlemen, and has peopled this nation with Gentlemen; for after a generation or two the tradesmen's children, or at least their grand-children, come to

be as good Gentlemen, Statesmen, Parliament-men, Privy-Counsellors, Judges, Bishops, and Noblemen, as those of the highest birth and the most ancient families; and nothing too high for them: Thus the late Earl of *Haversham* was originally a Merchant, and the late Secretary *Craggs* was the son of a *Barber*; the present Lord *Castlemain*'s father was a Tradesman; the great grandfather of the present Duke of *Bedford* the same, and so of several others. (I, 310–11)

The Complete English Tradesman is a work of mixed genre; it is at once a handbook for trade and a conduct book for tradesmen. It is also an apologia of the commercial man, a rationalization of his values and practices. As such, it is unsuccessful in its attempts to collapse the distance between the man of trade and the gentleman, because the precepts of trade as formulated by Defoe are incompatible with the ethos of the gentleman. Defoe presents his advice as exhortations to honesty and Christian duty, but his basic concerns are how to manage life and business rationally, how to make the most profit, and how to avoid being stung by the sharp practices of others. The rationale for honest business is never a version of *noblesse oblige*; it is always that honesty is safer and ultimately more profitable: honesty is in service to prudence. Accordingly, the most memorable of Defoe's maxims undercut his assertions about the dignity of trade. There is a 'difference between an *honest man*,' he asserts, 'and an *honest Tradesman*' (I, 226; emphasis in the original). In an even more ungentlemanly vein, Defoe maintains that 'he must be a perfect *complete hypocrite*, if he will be a *complete tradesman*,' thus introducing the concept of sham gentility behind the counter that was to plague the lower middle class more than a century later (I, 94; emphasis in the original). The repartee attributed to a wealthy London tradesman – that he may not *be* a gentleman, but that he 'can buy a gentleman' (I, 309) – is more telling than Defoe perhaps recognizes.

The same emphasis on pragmatism over integrity that characterizes Defoe's tradesman also defines his fictional creations. And it is indeed the protagonists' concentration on the husbanding of material resources that makes *Robinson Crusoe* (1719) and *Moll Flanders* (1722) less workable paradigms for the nineteenth-century novel than *Pamela* (1741) or *Clarissa* (1748–9). All four novels deal with the balancing of personal and material well-being, but Defoe's characters, like his tradesman, consistently place material considerations above all others. Thus Moll wishes to be a gentlewoman first and foremost because she wants comfort and security. And while Pamela and Clarissa are willing to risk suffering to preserve their integrity, Moll is willing to repent her misdeeds only when it seems prudent to do so; she sees no virtue in suffering. Thus Moll and the tradesman are unfit paradigms for bourgeois models of gentility and as a consequence they are unfit as subjects for the novel, because they are too true to humanity. In disconcertingly realistic fashion, Moll does not wait, Pamela-like, for fate in the guise of the novelist to save her from ruin; she embraces ruin as salvation from destitution. And Moll, like the model tradesman, unblushingly recognizes that she must sometimes dissemble to survive. Defoe is paradoxically too honest in his portrayals to write the prototypical bourgeois novel, too honest in his forthright admission that the tradesman must be a hypocrite to succeed. For what the middle class and the novel needed were not mundane characters like Moll and Crusoe muddling through fantastic situations, but fantastic characters like Pamela and Clarissa turning the mundane conflicts of ordinary existence into transcendent issues of conscience and spirituality. The middle class and the novel needed not reproductions of reality, but fictional constructions that could alter rather than reproduce the status quo.

That Defoe was aware, consciously or unconsciously, that cultural and social constructions were the key to altering existing perceptions of status and merit is evident in the unfinished manuscript of *The Compleat English Gentleman*. Defoe questions the existing concept of the gentleman as strictly a man of birth, pointing out that the most distinguished of families had its beginnings somewhere in an undistinguished past. The main support of antiquity, he cautions ironically, 'is a tender Point.'[12] The ideology of 'birth' distorts and exaggerates the image of the gentleman, presenting him 'as if he were a different Species from the rest of Mankind, that Nature had cast in another Mould, and either that he was not created at the same time, or not made of the same Materials as the rest of the Species of Men.' (p. 16) Defoe then makes the crucial formulation of gentlemanly status as a social construction, rather than the immutable distinction of nature and birth: 'This exalted Creature *of our own forming* [emphasis added] we are now to set up upon the Stage of Honour, rate him above the ordinary Price, and ranking him in a higher Class than his Neighbours, call him a *Gentleman.*' (pp. 16–17)

Once the gentleman is thus defined as something that has been formed rather than ordained, he can be altered and reconstructed. Defoe initially presents this reconstruction in the most soothingly conservative terms. Even the archaic spelling of 'compleat,' which he did not use in his discussion of the tradesman, suggests a cultivated genealogy for the work itself, placing it in the tradition of such ancient and venerated handbooks for the aristocracy as Henry Peacham's *The Compleat Gentleman* (1622). Claiming to be of gentlemanly rank himself (Defoe intended to publish anonymously), he insists that he wishes to preserve the honor of the born gentleman, and that he is resolved 'to giv[e] antiquity its due homage' (p. 4). Accordingly, he outlines what the true gentleman – the 'compleat gentleman' – should be. The starting point hardly seems radical: the complete gentleman combines attributes of birth and breeding. The elaborations that follow sound surprisingly like the Victorian version of the gentleman, which perhaps explains the appeal of Defoe's unfinished and previously unpublished manuscript for its late nineteenth-century editor and publisher. The true gentleman is a 'Person of Merit and Worth; a Man of Honour, Virtue, Sense, Integrity, Honesty, and Religion, without which he is Nothing at all.' (p. 21) He is also a man of learning and manners. Indeed, learning and manners begin to take precedence over other qualities. Defoe warns against having contempt for the man who lacks inherited status but is nevertheless 'rich, wise, learned, well-educated or religious'. He argues for 'setting up a new Class truly qualify'd to inherit the Title' of gentleman, and warns that 'when Learning, Education, Virtue and good Manners are wanting, or degenerated and corrupted in a Gentleman, he sinks out of the Rank, ceases to be any more a Gentleman.' (pp. 17–18) In the illustrations that follow this admonition, it becomes clear that those who will sink are the boorish men of birth who have not changed with the times, and those who will rise are the refined and educated sons of rich and wise merchants. Clearly, the gentleman that the wealthy tradesman can buy is his own son.

The ideas and issues addressed in *The Compleat English Gentleman* conform with the reformation of male manners during this period as analyzed by historian G. J. Barker-Benfield.[13] *The Compleat*

English Gentleman not only reflects ideas about status and the gentleman that were current in the early eighteenth century, but also demonstrates that the middle class had some awareness that the way to appropriate the status of gentleman was not simply to confer aristocratic attributes upon bourgeois man. The perception of what made a man a gentleman had to be altered to accommodate the middle-class persona, and the best way to do this was to have a gentleman of unquestionable pedigree embrace the values of the bourgeoisie. And thus we have Sir Charles Grandison.

THE GENTLEMAN AND THE CODE OF HONOR: *SIR CHARLES GRANDISON* AND *ANNA ST. IVES*

Samuel Richardson was inspired to create Sir Charles Grandison by the urging of his friends to 'produce into public View the Character and Actions of a Man of TRUE HONOUR.'[14] In thus emphasizing 'true honour' and in subsequently focusing on conflicting notions of honorable conduct in the early part of the novel, Richardson places *Sir Charles Grandison* (1753–4) within the ongoing contemporary debate over the aristocratic code of honor, referred to by its critics as the code of false honor.[15] Opposition to the code of honor centered on the practice of dueling, the highly symbolic and formalized ritual through which the aristocratic gentleman both defined and defended his status. As Donna T. Andrew affirms, 'the willingness to fight a duel, as well as the recognition of being a person who was "challenge-able" defined, in great part, what it meant to be a gentleman.' (Andrew, p. 415) Moreover, the duel carried a significance beyond the resolution of individual disputes and the preservation of individual reputations: the duel was the recurring ritualized enactment of aristocratic superiority as symbolized by military prowess and by courageous disregard for personal safety.[16] Accordingly, as Andrew observes, 'the opposition to duelling was more than just an opposition to an annoying but insignificant custom':

> Those that set their hearts and pens against duelling fought it because of what it represented, because of its symbolic value. In opposing duelling, they opposed themselves to an entire vision of society, of privilege and of civility, and in the process

formulated a new ideal of a society bound together by the equal subordination of individuals to Law and to the market place. Thus the debate about duelling was an important element in the formation of the middle class, and the gestation of middle-class culture. (Andrew, 434)

In having Sir Charles disdain the practice of dueling, Richardson not only 'presents to the Public . . . the Example of a Man acting uniformly well' (p. 4), he also presents to the public the example of such action necessarily being in opposition to the values and practices of aristocratic society.[17] As historian J. C. D. Clark observes, '[t]he practice of duelling . . . was the acid test' for contemporary attempts to reconcile the aristocratic code with Christian morals.[18]

To challenge the existing concept of honor successfully, Sir Charles had to be more than simply moral and upright, however. The code of honor had been surprisingly resistant to onslaughts from the ranks of the just, the reasonable, and the virtuous, as the history of the protracted debate over dueling demonstrates. From as far back as the Renaissance, legislators, clerics, and men of letters had been denouncing the duel.[19] Even in the conduct literature of the sixteenth through eighteenth centuries '[t]he condemnation of duelling is emphatic and universal,' according to John Mason, 'the arguments against it being drawn from prudence and common-sense as well as from patriotism and religion.' (Mason, pp. 294–5) During the eighteenth century, dueling suffered assaults, both through satires and through reasoned argumentation, from such pre-eminent men of letters as Addison, Steele, Swift, Defoe, Berkeley, and Hume.[20] It was, however, a very odd debate, with one side using 'their hearts and pens' to pour forth anti-duelist rhetoric, and the other side using their swords to carry on the grand tradition of the duel. And if the opponents of dueling ultimately triumphed, it was perhaps not because the pen was mightier than the sword, but because it was more persistent.

Pertinacity and commitment were absolute requirements of those who would resist the old code of honor, because the rituals of the duel preserved its mystique and made its symbolic power virtually unassailable. The duel of honor had to be performed privately and secretly because, while it was socially sanctioned, it was legally condemned. (Andrew, p. 410) The duel and the culture it represented accordingly largely existed above and beyond the jurisdiction of law and were governed instead by the elaborate machinery of challenges, seconds, and precise formal rules that defined the ritual itself. Because this ritual was carried out in private, its symbolism was resistant to manipulation. There were no visible public images to reinterpret; the mystique of the duel was almost pure abstraction. Thus while the rhetoric of its opponents could influence public opinion and so erode the social sanctioning of dueling, it had little effect on the symbolic power of the duel. A gentleman was still no gentleman if he refused a challenge. Moreover, he was no man; the bravado of the duel, the flouting of the law and the exercise of military skill, all bespoke manliness. None of this symbolism was subject to the rhetoric of reasoned argumentation, but it could be and was altered through fictional representation. Accordingly, the most significant duel in the eighteenth century was the one fought in the pages of Richardson's last novel, between Sir Charles Grandison and Sir Hargrave Pollexfen.

What is most noteworthy about the confrontation between Sir Charles and Sir Hargrave is, of course, that Sir Charles refuses the challenge without losing face. The significance of Sir Charles's ability to retain his dignity has been overlooked, however, by critics who focus on the moral didacticism of his responses to Sir Hargrave's challenge. Modern critics generally follow the lead of Mrs Barbauld, who objects to the fact that Sir Charles is able to avoid the evils of dueling because of his superior fencing skills, his ability to disarm his opponents without harming them; she questions if 'a man's principles' should 'depend on the science of his fencing-master.'[21] This objection is perhaps valid in the realm of realism but through the character of Sir Charles, Richardson is challenging the symbolic order, the moral authority of the aristocratic version of the gentleman as sustained by the secular and militaristic code of honor. Sir Charles's rejection of the old code can have moral force only if he has the ability, and even the desire, to dominate his adversaries according to the dictates of that code. It is indeed Sir Charles's equivocal position as a potentially swashbuckling paladin that enables him to use anti-dueling rhetoric successfully, because his words are underwritten by latent physical force. As one of the adherents of the old code who is converted by Grandison's performance observes, 'the *doctrine* would have been nothing without the *example*.' (II, 256)

Richardson's working out of the dueling dilemma and its symbolic and ethical implications is protracted and painstakingly meticulous, designed as it is to anticipate all possible objections from the pro-dueling camp. His basic strategy is to have Sir Charles undermine the ritual of the duel at every stage. Sir Charles transforms the issuing and receiving of the challenge into a war of words, in which he engages Sir Hargrave and his second, James Bagenhall. Grandison neither accepts the challenge nor rejects it outright. Rather, he recasts the dispute as one based not on the preservation of personal honor, but on the very principles that define honor. He repeatedly questions Sir Hargrave's concept of honor, manliness, and gentlemanliness. In response to Bagenhall's invocation of the 'Laws of Honour,' Sir Charles declares that he owns 'no Laws, but the Laws of God and ... [his] country'. Ultimately, Grandison identifies Sir Hargrave's notion of honor, rather than his person, as the antagonist, telling Bagenhall, 'I will put Sir Hargrave's Honour to the fullest test.' (II, 242)

Despite his resistance, however, Sir Hargrave's challenge presents Sir Charles with a troubling dilemma, for however firm his Christian principles may be, he is also bound by loyalty to his family and his class to respect the social demands of his status. Grandison's words to Bagenhall betray this divided allegiance. He may 'own no Laws' but those of God and his country, but he nevertheless balks at being dishonored; he high-handedly declares that he will not tolerate being threatened or insulted, even by a prince. Moreover, Sir Charles pays due homage to rank and lineage. As a young man, he never disobeyed his father, no matter how faulty he may have found the principles that motivated Sir Thomas, nor does Sir Charles dishonor him after his death. Just as it was unthinkable for the young Charles Grandison openly to flout his father's authority, so it is unthinkable that Sir Charles Grandison would openly scorn the forms of the code of honor. Such an attitude would not only be an affront to his father's memory and heritage, it would also threaten Sir Charles's status and authority and the status of his dependents within their social milieu. With a 'spirited' sister still to be married off, a ward to be protected, and any number of hangers-on to be considered, Sir Charles cannot risk being branded as dishonorable. He is caught between the dictates of his social position, with its inherent duties and responsibilities, and the dictates of his Christian principles. He may, in Harriet's words, be 'govern'd by another set of principles, than those of false honour' (I, 209), but he is also beholden to that code of honor. So while Sir Charles may deplore the morality – or lack of it – that informs the code, he is bound to respect its cultural and social authority. He cannot, therefore, simply ignore the challenge, nor can he refuse to speak to Sir Hargrave's second, nor can he ultimately refuse to meet his challenger.

The initial rhetorical skirmish does not shake the convictions of Grandison's opponents, although it does frustrate and offend them. It is only when Sir Charles reformulates the ritual of the duel that they take notice. Sir Hargrave and his party of backers are uneasy when Grandison insists on calling at Sir Hargrave's home armed, but alone. Sir Charles thus breaches two of the fundamental rules of the dueling ritual, the engagement of a second and the naming of neutral (usually public) ground for the encounter. These irregularities indeed constitute a severe test of Sir Hargrave's honor, because any breach of the ritual could invalidate a duel as an affair of 'honor'. Moreover, Sir Charles is so adept at keeping the conflict focused on the internal logic of the dueling ritual and so imperturbably self-possessed that he dazzles Sir Hargrave's friends, who repeatedly express their admiration for 'such a noble adversary'. (II, 254) Sir Charles accordingly overmasters Sir Hargrave and the ethical position he represents. All of Sir Hargrave's attempts to engage Sir Charles in actual combat fail, without dishonor to his opponent, and his supporters effectively abandon him in favor of Grandison.

To have Sir Hargrave persist and to go on to present the farcical 'duel' in the garden might therefore seem like a bit of narrative overkill on Richardson's part. But while Sir Charles has undermined the stature of Sir Hargrave and the questionable principles that support his notion of honor, the central act of the dueling ritual – the actual sword fight – has yet to be exposed and discredited. The forms that lead up to the fight itself are only the insulation that preserves the mystique of this central act, its secrecy and its virtual invisibility. To discredit the duel and the 'false' code of honor for which it stands, Richardson must bring Sir Charles and Sir Hargrave together with swords in their hands. It is also essential at this point to present the duel as a visual phenomenon only, to abandon rhetoric, logic, and religion and to concentrate on the act and its visual symbolism.[22] The duel is therefore presented from the perspective of the observers, Sir Hargrave's companions and the secretary who is recording the entire affair, who watch the encounter through the closed windows facing the garden. What they see is, in effect, a distorted remnant of the dueling ritual in pantomime.

Just as he has refused to allow the rituals leading up to the duel to dictate and control his conduct, so Sir Charles refuses to comply with the ceremonial forms of the sword fight. He has worn his sword to the meeting, but he has otherwise come in 'morning-dress' (vol. II, 248) – that is, in informal attire rather than the formal dress of which a gentleman's sword was an integral part. He then removes his sword to go into the garden and only reluctantly takes it up again at Sir Hargrave's insistence, but he carries, rather than wears his weapon. The precision with which these kinds of visual details are recorded in the account of the confrontation in the garden indicates their significance:

> Sir Hargrave threw open his coat and waistcoat, and drew; and seemed, by his motions, to insist upon Sir Charles's drawing likewise. Sir Charles had his sword in one hand; but it was undrawn: the other was stuck in his side: his frock was open. Sir Hargrave seemed still to insist upon his drawing, and put himself into a fencing attitude. Sir Charles then calmly stepping towards him, put down Sir Hargrave's sword with his hand, and put his left-arm under Sir Hargrave's sword-arm. Sir Hargrave lifted up the other arm passionately: But Sir Charles, who was on his guard, immediately laid hold of the other arm, and seemed to say something mildly to him; and letting go his left-hand, led him towards the house; his drawn sword still in his hand. Sir Hargrave seemed to expostulate, and to resist being led, tho' but faintly, and as a man overcome with Sir Charles's behaviour; and they both came up together, Sir Charles's arm still within his sword-arm. (II, 253)

In this pantomime duel, Sir Charles repeatedly parries Sir Hargrave's militaristic posturing with quiet non-compliance and with understated, non-combative defensive tactics. The duel made visible is a farce: the duelist in his fencing attitude appears ludicrous as he is overcome by an opponent who never even draws his sword.

Those critics – and they are legion – who claim that Sir Charles's virtue, unlike Clarissa's, is never really put to a severe test have failed to consider carefully the full implications of the imbroglio over the duel. Terry Eagleton asserts that the 'simplest possible contrast between the two novels [*Clarissa* and *Sir Charles Grandison*] lies in the fact that Grandison cannot be raped.'[23] But the obvious phallic symbolism inherent in dueling – from the weapons used, whether rapiers or pistols, to aspects of the ritual, such as sending the length of one's sword to the opponent – belie the simplicity of this contrast. At stake in both a duel and a rape is 'honor,' as socially constructed; if the significance of the latter is apparent to our modern consciousness, while that of the former seems forced, it is because the link between virginity and female honor has lingered into the twentieth century, while the duel has become an anachronism. The remaining contrast, which is admittedly not insignificant, is that in a rape, one of the parties has no offensive weapon. For Clarissa, as for Pamela, there is only the defensive ploy of unconsciousness, the refusal to be consciously present during the rape or its attempt, an expedient that preserves Pamela's physical and Clarissa's spiritual chastity. But Sir Charles, too, is denied an offensive weapon by his conscience: he will use a sword only for defense. And while a sword in the hand of a fencing expert is undeniably a more satisfactory defense than unconsciousness, it is just as undeniably a double-edged sword. If Sir Charles were forced to use his sword in his duel with Sir Hargrave, he would lose his credibility and the false code would prevail and would continue to assert its symbolic authority.

Sir Charles's credibility, and with it the credibility of his ethical position, is further enhanced by Richardson's canny manipulation of the phallic symbolism of the duel. The sword is double-edged for Sir Hargrave as well as for Sir Charles, and Richardson exploits all the emasculating potential of the duel to undercut the antagonist. Even before taking up his sword, Sir Charles has symbolically deflated his opponent's manhood by discharging the pistols that Sir Hargrave has offered as weapons harmlessly out the window. In the encounter in the garden, the duelist and his drawn sword are rendered impotent by exemplary non-combative conduct. Sir Hargrave's highly significant reaction is to cast away his useless sword and lament that Sir Charles 'has made a mere infant' of him. (II, 253) This reaction constitutes a verbal and symbolic discrediting both of the authority of his 'vulgar notions of honour' (I, 208-9) and of the concept of manliness that supports those 'vulgar notions'. Moral authority now resides in 'Sir Charles's behavior,' in conduct that makes supposedly honorable aggression seem infantile, while the casting away of the sword represents both defeat and emasculation. Sir Hargrave's subsequent behavior and the attitudes he expresses further erode his masculine image. His concern for honor has dwindled into a concern for his looks, for the scars and the lost teeth that proclaim his previous defeat at the hands of Sir Charles. Moreover, Sir Hargrave's inability to win Harriet Byron gives greater relevance to his scars. 'If she will not be mine, these marks shall be *hers*, not *yours*,' he tells Grandison (II, 253). His disfigurement has become the inversion of the deflowering he was prevented from accomplishing; the marks symbolize a violation of his honor that can be remedied only by marriage – if 'Miss Byron consents to wipe out these marks.' (II, 267) The conventional relations of sexual politics are thus also inverted, with Harriet in the position of power and Sir Hargrave assuming the role of victim.

After the pantomime duel, Sir Charles holds the field as the embodiment of honor and of manliness and in the course of the remainder of the novel, these socially constructed values are redefined in keeping with the principles that govern the conduct of their exemplar. Having proved his manliness, the Christian gentleman, in the person of Grandison, can now be domesticated. The man of 'true' honor, the 'true' gentleman, is the man who, like Sir Charles, wisely and profitably manages his estate and finances; Sir Charles is, indeed, a proselytizing manager, converting countless admirers to his prudent ways as he steps in and reorganizes their lives as guardian, executor of wills, or arranger of marriages. Moreover, at the base of most of the reorganization is a bourgeois notion of marriage as an institution that should be in the service of love, rather than of the consolidation of estates and inheritances. Sir Charles accordingly administers the Danby inheritance, as he had his own at his father's death, with a view to providing dowries that will enable the women in the family to marry the suitors of their choice. The independence – relative though it may be – that this affords women suggests a sexual politics very different from that practiced by Sir Hargrave. Even Sir Hargrave's inverted model of sexual politics, in which Harriet has the power to reinstate his violated honor, traps Harriet in an intolerable dyadic relationship with him. Sir Charles, by contrast, rescues her not to seize control of her fate, but to make her mistress of it. 'The Lady must be her own mistress,' he tells Sir Hargrave (II, 253), which as a social statement may in retrospect seem disingenuous, but which mediates a recognition and acceptance of women as psychologically, if not socially or politically, autonomous beings. In the pages of a novel, at least, women are free to think and feel, to love (with certain restrictions) and hate, and to influence the lives and the thinking of those close to them; they are, in other words, launched on their careers as domestic heroines. Through the characterization of Sir Charles, Richardson thus not only dissociates the concept of the gentleman from the cultural symbolism of the aristocracy, he also successfully links the gentleman with bourgeois domestic values.

The influence of *Sir Charles Grandison* on eighteenth-century literature was considerable and such pre-eminent nineteenth-century novelists as Jane Austen and George Eliot read it with enthusiasm. But Richardson's great hero does not inspire the interest and respect in current literary criticism that his heroines do. While Terry Eagleton suggests that the Benjaminian moment of readability has arrived for Richardson's work, that our present historical and cultural position allows readers once again to perceive the relevance of *Pamela* and *Clarissa*, this renewed appreciation does not appear to extend to Richardson's last novel. (Eagleton, p. vii) And Eagleton is certainly not alone in finding *Sir Charles Grandison* weak. Modern critics typically focus on the problem of the characterization of Sir Charles, on the deadening effect of the paragon on the novel's realism and on the reader's patience and sympathy. Gerard Barker goes so far as to attribute *Grandison*'s initial influence to this failure of characterization:

> Richardson's very failure in realizing Sir Charles's character is just what made his subject such an attractive prototype for the burgeoning feminine novel. Frances Sheridan and Fanny Burney found Grandison's ill-defined, idealized character a pliant model for creating an externally conceived, shadowy hero who could be subordinated to their genteel heroines. Elizabeth Inchbald and William Godwin, on the other hand, produced two of the finest novels of the late eighteenth century, *A Simple Story* and *Caleb Williams*, in part because they implicitly questioned Richardson's use of exemplary protagonists in realist fiction. (Barker, p. 9)

But to find in the characterization of Sir Charles only those things that now seem aesthetically unsatisfactory is to read the novel purely as an artifact, divorced from its cultural context, rather then as a social document necessarily embedded in that context.

The appeal of the Grandisonian gentleman for writers like Sheridan and Burney and the implicit questioning of Inchbald and Godwin have less to do with literary models, I would argue, than with social and cultural ones. Sir Charles is not so much an 'externally conceived' hero as he is a character who is forced by the expectations of his culture to demonstrate his inner moral worth externally, through action. In this context, it is important to note that Dorriforth's moderation of his rigid commitment to forms and propriety at the end of *A Simple Story* (1791) concurs with his willingness to consign his daughter's would-be seducer to the law, a shift in attitude that represents his moral regeneration. Although Dorriforth has previously slain his wife's lover in a duel, he disdains sending a challenge to Lord Margrave, in language very reminiscent of that used by Sir Charles in his objections to dueling: 'Would you make me an executioner? The law shall be your only antagonist.'[24] And while the evolution of the Grandisonian hero may indeed represent a refinement in realism, it also mediates the development of the bourgeois gentleman.[25] As the Grandisonian hero evolves through the later eighteenth-century, his moral worth is increasingly internalized as a system of bourgeois or proto-bourgeois values similar to those that guided Sir Charles's actions. Sir Charles has thus freed the men as well as the women of the fictional world to be internalized, psychological beings. Moreover, the invisibility of the hero's worth, like the invisibility of the duel, becomes the source of his quasi-mystical power. The invisibility of moral worth is also what makes it most valuable, what allows it to elude commodification in an increasingly materialist culture. The integrity of the moral hero, the indefinable quality that makes him a gentleman, is then what the heroine must come to recognize and value over the flashier appeal of minor Sir Hargraves in order to prove her own worthiness. Evelina, accordingly, must demonstrate her ability to differentiate between the bravado of Sir Clement Willoughby and the unobtrusive moral depth of Lord Orville; and Emma recognizes her love for Mr Knightley only after realizing the inappropriateness of her flirtation with Frank Churchill.

* * *

Sir Charles is the model for the *embourgeoisement* of upper-class fictional heroes like Dorriforth, Orville or Knightley who, as members of the aristocracy or gentry, would have been considered gentlemen because of their class position. But Sir Charles is also the model for representing characters from other classes, such as Frank Henley in Thomas Holcroft's *Anna St. Ives* (1792), as men of 'true honour'. The plot and themes of *Anna St. Ives* draw heavily on Richardson's last two novels and could indeed be characterized as 'Sir Charles Grandison meets Clarissa'. In Holcroft's novel, Lovelace (Coke Clifton) becomes the approved suitor of Clarissa (Anna), who is also loved by Sir Charles reincarnated as a bailiff's son (Frank Henley). As Anna becomes increasingly doubtful about her suitor's character and suitability as a husband, Coke begins to plot her abduction and rape. Frank, who has long since won her heart, rescues Anna and gains the approval of her aristocratic family as a prospective husband.

Anna St. Ives differs from other early descendants of *Sir Charles Grandison*, especially those written by women, in important ways. Women writers of the period, from Frances Sheridan to Jane Austen, continue to focus the examination of moral worth on that portion of society on the boundary between the minor aristocracy and the upper middle class, a quasi-liminal space in which Lord Orville and Mr Knightley are barely distinguishable from each other or from Mr Gardiner (Mrs Bennet's 'sensible, gentlemanlike' brother in *Pride and Prejudice* [1813][26]) or Frederick Wentworth (in *Persuasion* [1818]). Dueling is no longer an issue in most of these novels, but is replaced by less aggressive demonstrations of old-fashioned chivalry – Willoughby rescues Evelina when she is accosted by a group of men at Vauxhall and Frank Churchill rescues Harriet from the gypsies near the end of *Emma* (1816).[27] Even attenuated aggression, however, no longer makes a man of honor in the post-Grandisonian world; the rescue that counts is the one carried out by Knightley, when he asks Harriet to dance, thus saving her from the mortification of Elton's cruel snub. In *Anna St. Ives*, however, dueling plays as significant a role as it does in *Sir Charles Grandison*, partly because the problematic associations between physical courage and honor would have been more difficult for a male writer to dismiss than it had been for many women writers; but mostly because Holcroft is working towards a far more radical transformation of the idea of the gentleman, a transformation that requires more heavily symbolic and dramatic demonstrations of its validity.

In representing Frank Henley as the quintessential gentleman, Holcroft is in effect challenging the society represented in the novel of manners to accept the implications of the definition of the gentleman it espouses – that the 'true' gentleman is the 'true' man of honor, the man of inner worth as opposed to the man of birth. But in novels of manners like *Evelina*, as in *Sir Charles Grandison*, problematic class issues are mitigated by the elevated social positions of their 'true' gentleman heroes, however bourgeois the sensibilities of those true gentlemen might be. Frank Henley, by contrast, has no claims of any kind to status through birth. Frank's father, Abimelech, is not only a mere bailiff on Anna's father's estate, he is also uneducated, coarse, and underhanded. Any claim that Frank has to gentlemanly status resides in his person alone, and that person is as impressive as Sir Charles's. Frank, as his name implies, is open and honest, as well as physically imposing, refined, and courageous. On what grounds, then, the text of *Anna St. Ives* implicitly but insistently asks, can he be denied the gentlemanly status his person so perfectly embodies? Are the traditional grounds of birth valid? The novel answers these questions by discrediting those characters, most notably Coke Clifton, who would disqualify Frank as a man worthy to be called a gentleman. The conflicting criteria for what constitutes a gentleman are represented by the opposition of Frank and Coke, much as Sir Charles and Sir Hargrave represent opposing codes of honor.

Holcroft exemplifies Frank's moral worth most forcibly through representations of dueling. Holcroft, however, never questions the validity of the assumption that Richardson was at such pains to justify: the assumption that it is more courageous to refuse a challenge than it is to fight, that it is more honorable to prevent than to win a duel. Rather than the exemplary character of the hero turning the 'cowardly' act of refusing a challenge into a courageous one, Frank's refusal to duel and his interventions to restrain others from dueling define his merit. Those who are anxious to duel manifest their moral bankruptcy, their inability to restrain their basest passions. The most avid duelists in the novel are individuals whom contemporary English readers would have regarded with suspicion: French servants who impersonate their aristocratic masters for a lark, the Irish sharper MacFane, and the foppish French Count de Beaunoir. And Coke, who, in the words of Anna, 'has too strongly imbibed high but false notions of honour and revenge,'[28] is eventually drawn into association with all of these sham or flawed 'gentlemen,' either in response to challenges, in the case of the Frenchmen, or through a mutual desire with MacFane to avenge themselves on Frank. Coke is accordingly aligned with spurious gentility against Frank, who stands alone as the epitome of integrity and honor, attributes which Coke pretends to as a birthright but which Frank repeatedly demonstrates through his actions.

In spite of his fine qualities, however, Frank's low birth remains an obstacle to his admission into the ranks of the gentleman. The unfairness and illogicality of this situation and the difficulties inherent in using the increasingly problematic epithet of 'gentleman' are recurring themes in *Anna St. Ives*. When Anna's maid refers to Frank as a gentleman, Coke scoffs: 'The son of a gardener a gentleman?' Laura's response makes clear that moral and social perceptions are at odds. 'Yes, sir. To be sure, sir, among thorough bred quality, though perhaps he may be better than the best of them, he is thought no better than a kind of a sort of a gentleman; being not so high born.' (pp. 76–7) Anna challenges the social definition of gentleman more directly. In response to her father's observation that Coke 'is a gentleman, both by birth and education,' she comments cryptically, 'That I own, sir, may be a great disadvantage.' (p. 223) Later, as Sir Arthur's resistance to Frank as a suitor for his daughter softens, he admits to Anna that Frank 'is a very extraordinary young gentleman.' 'Ah, sir!' Anna responds. 'The word gentleman shews the bent of your thoughts. Can you not perceive it is a word without meaning? Or, if it have a meaning, that he who is the best man is the most a gentleman?' (p. 344)

While Holcroft thus makes a plea, through the text of his novel, for the recognition of gentility as a moral quality rather than as a purely social position, the reconstruction of the gentleman that *Anna St. Ives* mediates is more complex and less sublime than a direct moral/social opposition would sustain. Frank's apparently innate goodness has been refined by education, which, while informal and mainly self-directed, has been fostered by the genteel and generous father of his boyhood friend, Oliver Trenchard. The Trenchards have indeed been like a surrogate family to Frank, providing the nursery for his embryonic gentility. Frank's real father provides the other essential qualification for social mobility – money. And the source of Abimelech's money raises disturbing questions about how society reconstitutes class and status. Abimelech is as much a sharper as the reprehensible MacFane; through speculation, manipulation of the assets and estates in his trust, and exploitation of his employer's gullibility, Aby amasses a fortune and virtually bankrupts Sir Arthur. Moreover, having purchased the mortgages on the St Ives estates, Aby holds Sir Arthur in his power, taunting him with veiled threats of foreclosure. It then becomes impossible to untangle the motives for Sir Arthur's change of heart over Anna's wish to marry Frank. He admires Frank and is clearly disturbed when Anna admits she is prepared to marry Coke out of filial duty and obedience, when it is obvious her heart lies elsewhere. Nevertheless, Sir Arthur continues to fret about the dishonor to his name and the inevitable rift with the higher ranking branches of his family that Anna's marriage to Frank would cause. Aby's willingness to use blackmail, not to mention the £30 000 he has offered to Sir Arthur if he agrees to the marriage, becomes part of a constellation of factors that determine Sir Arthur's ultimate decision. The reader can guess but cannot ultimately prove which factor, if any single one, is decisive.

Anna St. Ives accordingly presents reactions to the reconstructed gentleman from two perspectives – the ideal and the pragmatic – each with its own rationale for endorsing his status. Anna assesses Frank and the acceptability of their union on purely ethical grounds. Reminded by her father that the world will censure her for marrying beneath her station, Anna responds with high moral tone: 'Were I to pay false homage to wealth and rank, because the world tells me it is right that I should do so, and to neglect genius and virtue, which my judgment tells me would be an odious wrong, I should find but little satisfaction in the applause of the world, opposed to self-condemnation.' (p. 343) Anna's sense of honor, like Frank's, is based on internalized virtue rather than on socially endorsed but empty forms. Her father's acceptance of Frank, by contrast, takes into account the social and economic consequences of the union, including the fate of the money and property that Abimelech now controls, which, he points out to Anna 'will all return into the family' if she marries Frank. Anna's reasons for desiring the match may differ from Sir

Arthur's but, he reminds her, they 'answer the same end.' (p. 345) The 'same end' is the conferring of social status on Frank, but his rise in status occurs in conjunction with a comparable recognition of his father's newly acquired social power, represented in the text by Sir Arthur's insistence that Anna must now address Aby 'very respectfully' as Mr Henley and that 'when his name is written, it must be tagged with an esquire.' (p. 366) The joint social ascendance of the Henleys dramatizes the social reality, that the viability of the ideal of the non-aristocratic Christian gentleman and the social mobility of the bourgeois entrepreneur are interdependent and inseparable. The Christian ideal is underwritten by the newly acquired wealth and power of the entrepreneur, whose rising status is in turn validated by the exemplary ideal.

By the beginning of the nineteenth century, the new model gentleman is the established fictional norm, although his social dominance may well have been less secure. The male protagonist need no longer be heroic or aristocratic in order to establish his status; he need only demonstrate his intelligence, sensitivity, and moral rectitude – in other words, his essentially middle-class virtues. Released from the burden of justifying his status through his perfection or his heroism, the middle-class gentleman of nineteenth-century fiction can pursue more mundane ends, such as his own education about and initiation into the domestic realm. Just as an essential part of the preparation of Evelina and Anna – not to mention most of Jane Austen's heroines – for their domestic roles as wives is training in the art of understanding and valuing the qualities of true honor as exemplified by Lord Orville and Frank, so too part of the maturation of the Victorian gentleman, from Pendennis to Pip, is education in the appreciation of what constitutes a worthy (that is, domestic) woman.

However different the typical nineteenth-century story of a young man and that of a young woman may be – and they are very different – they have this in common: that the young man, as surely as the young woman, must come to understand and value the primacy of the domestic relationship. And just what that relationship involved is best exemplified by the title and subtitle of an immensely popular early nineteenth-century novel by Hannah More: *Coelebs in Search of a Wife: Comprehending Observations on Domestic Habits and Manners, Religion and Morals.* As the title indicates, the ostensible mission of the novel's protagonist is to find a wife, but *Coelebs* is in fact a *bildungsroman*, and the search incorporates the imbibing of all the right values and attitudes before making the choice of a mate. The unnamed protagonist indeed has no identity but that of 'Coelebs,' or bachelor, and can resume his proper name only at the end of the narrative, when he assumes his proper role in society as a husband. 'Miss Stanley, when that blessed event takes place,' he says in his anticipation of his marriage, 'will resign her name, and I shall resume mine, and joyfully renounce for ever that of Coelebs.'[29]

SIR CHARLES *REDUX*

The legacy of Sir Charles Grandison to nineteenth-century fiction is, in essence, the social enfranchisement of the bourgeois gentleman, who is finally able to wear his identity with ease and confidence. He no longer has to overwhelm observers with the kind of awful perfection delineated in Henry James's ironic assessment of the nineteenth century's favorite exemplary gentleman:

> We know of no scales that will hold him, and of no unit of length with which to compare him. He is infinite; he outlasts time; he is enshrined in a million innocent breasts; and before his awful perfection and his eternal durability we respectfully lower our lance.[30]

As much as this model of rectitude may sound like Sir Charles, it is in fact an assessment of the eponymous hero of Dinah Mulock Craik's *John Halifax, Gentleman*. This return to vigorous perfection, at a time when the middle-class gentleman had long been permitted blemishes and even warts, is necessitated by John Halifax's complete lack of social standing. As a destitute and vagrant orphan, he exists outside the social order and must strive constantly to earn and maintain the trust and respect of everyone from farm laborers to the local squire. Halifax has neither birth nor wealth to legitimize his claim to social recognition. 'He was indebted to no forefathers for a family history,' his friend Phineas observes; 'the chronicle commenced with himself, and was altogether his own making.'[31] John Halifax is the nineteenth-century self-made man who lays his own claim to status and as such he represents the ultimate victory of manners over lineage as the essential defining quality of gentlemanliness.

The progress of John Halifax to gentlemanly status parallels the rise of the class he represents. His 'achievements and experiences,' Sally Mitchell observes, 'correspond allegorically to the events that transferred power from the aristocracy to the middle class'; he lives from 1780 to 1834, a period that covers enclosure to the Reform Bill.[32] Moreover, as Patrick Brantlinger notes, 'John Halifax takes part in the central events of the age – he introduces steam to the woolen industry, brings peace to the "lower orders," and in general supports all good middle-class causes.'[33] Halifax is also the embodiment of the bourgeois ideal of progress through industry and self-help; his fantastical progress from rags to riches indeed relies on the logic of this ideology to give his meteoric rise in status an aura of credibility, however spurious. At the opening of the narrative he is both destitute and ignorant, but rises to subsistence through his willingness to do the most menial chores in Abel Fletcher's tanning yard. His honesty and diligence win him his employer's respect, and since his thirst for knowledge makes him an autodidact of no small scope, young John is soon promoted to the position of clerk. As he matures, his abilities and virtues blossom and multiply; he has mechanical skills, common sense, business acumen, and a soothing way with those bogged down in the ranks he has so recently risen above. Abel designates John as his business heir-apparent, his son Phineas having neither the physical stamina nor the inclination to succeed his father. John eventually establishes a business of his own, which he administers with all the efficiency and compassion of a model captain of industry, gaining a reputation among his employees as 'the best master in all England'. (p. 274)

As he matures into a consummate entrepreneur, John Halifax also emerges as a consummate gentleman, 'a sort of Sir Charles Grandison of the democracy,' as Henry James puts it, 'faultless in manner and in morals'.[34] His gentlemanly qualities emerge almost imperceptibly. Indeed, by using Phineas Fletcher as the narrator, Craik makes it difficult to represent in her hero the internalized qualities of mind and conscience that characterize the nineteenth-century bourgeois gentlemen. But Phineas, being a sensitive observer, recognizes John's inner worth from the outset, detecting in the ragged boy 'a mind and breeding above his outward condition'. (p. 17) As John is gradually able to shed his rags for 'respectable' garb, his innate grace of figure and bearing make it difficult for other characters to place him in their preconceived notions of rank. When he first appears in a new suit of clothes, the Fletchers' housekeeper momentarily fails to recognize him. 'Easily might Jael or any one else have "mistaken" him, as she cuttingly said, for a young gentleman,' observes Phineas. (p. 46) The genteel Mr March, whom John saves from drowning, also has difficulty reconciling the image of the young man before him with his station as a tan-yard worker. March's companion, Richard Brithwood, identifies John:

> 'I know him, Cousin March. He works in Fletcher the Quaker's tan-yard.'
> 'Nonsense!' cried Mr. March, who had stood looking at the boy with a kindly, even half-sad air. 'Impossible! Young man, will you tell me to whom I am so much obliged?'
> 'My name is John Halifax.'
> 'Yes; but *what* are you?'
> 'What he said. Mr. Brithwood knows me well enough; I work in the tan-yard. (pp. 50–1)

It is not long, however, before his name alone designates *what* John Halifax is, which no association with the tan-yard can tarnish. His inner worth is soon reflected in the deference of the other tan-yard workers, who respectfully call him 'Mr Halifax'. Eventually, his name as its backer is enough to save a failing bank from collapse. The 'humbler ranks' who have gathered outside the bank, fearful of losing their savings, are immediately placated: 'how implicitly they trusted in the mere name of a gentleman who all over the country was known for "his being as good as his bond" – John Halifax.' (p. 343)

John Halifax's gentlemanliness is in part represented by his restraint and understatement – characteristics not always shared by his creator or the narrator in their celebrations of his glory. Even as a youth, he remains calm in the most harrowing situations, such as fires and bread riots. He dresses 'with extreme simplicity,' and is similarly unpretentious in his speech. (p. 104) He is not, according to Phineas, 'one of your showy conversationalists,' but uses the 'simplest and fittest' language to express himself. (p. 131) And in later life, as an established and affluent employer and property owner, he maintains a domestic policy of extending 'liberal hospitalities' but strictly forbids 'outward show'. (p. 325) But John Halifax's real inner worth is most emphatically asserted through his domestic relationships. His innate capacities are only partially realized as a single man; in order to fulfil his potential, to be complete, he must marry the right woman, the kind of woman he sees in Ursula March. The primacy of the bourgeois version of gentility and domesticity is exemplified in John and Ursula's relationship. John initially refrains from courting Ursula not because he feels they are not equals, but because society is not yet ready to recognize their equality. Once they do marry, it is not the limitations of John's social station, but of Ursula's, that must be overcome in order to ensure the viability of the bourgeois domestic idyll.[35] Ursula must learn the skills of housewifery, must learn to administer the domestic sphere, a process which Phineas observes indulgently, observing that 'the young gentlewoman had much to learn, and was not ashamed of it either. She laughed at her own mistakes, and tried again; she never was idle, or dull for a minute.' (p. 213) Disdaining rank, pride, luxury, and ease, the gentlewoman metamorphoses into the domestic woman.

The interdependence of husband and wife in this paradigmatic bourgeois union is a continuing motif throughout the text. They quite literally cannot live without each other, Ursula dying within hours of her husband as she picturesquely expires while mourning over his body on the last page of the novel. In life, John may be the one who must fight 'the hard battle . . . daily, hourly, with the outside world' (p. 224), but it is in their union that their middle-class identity is forged. 'We consider that our respectability lies solely in our two selves', John tells Phineas during their early days of financial struggle. (p. 206) Their middle-class respectability depends not on their former identities, nor is it undermined by the present slimness of their means. It depends rather on their new mutual identity as husband and wife, for Ursula may, like Miss Stanley, have to resign her name but John Halifax, like Coelebs, is not fully himself nor can he be a complete bourgeois gentleman until he is no longer a bachelor.

Bourgeois domestic virtue is further highlighted in *John Halifax, Gentleman* through its stark, indeed exaggerated, contrast with the rampant degeneracy of the aristocracy. The aristocracy is represented by the Earl of Luxmore and his family, whose members are associated with any number of supposed moral failings: Catholicism, Gallic sympathies and sensibilities, debauchery, drunkenness, gambling, and insolvency. The Earl's children, Lady Caroline Brithwood and Lord Ravenel, act as foils to the prudent and virtuous Ursula and John. The youthful promise of the beautiful and vivacious Lady Caroline is destroyed by a loveless marriage of convenience to the boorish Richard Brithwood. The solace and adventure she finds in adulterous liaisons with French lovers of questionable pedigree inevitably lead to mental and physical disintegration. Lady Caroline's demise is thus the inevitable result of the aristocracy's corrupt values and practices regarding marriage. Lady Caroline's half-brother, Lord Ravenel, represents another aspect of aristocratic degeneracy. Although more virtuous than Lady Caroline, Ravenel is less energetic; he is the soft and indolent aristocrat, weak and easily led. Even his virtue is vitiated by his Catholicism. In his weakness, Ravenel also becomes the emasculated aristocrat, whose delicate effeminacy – represented by his timidity, his soft voice, his 'delicate ringed hands' and feminine handwriting, and his protective attachment to the Halifax's blind and sickly eldest daughter – contrasts sharply with the strength and virility of John Halifax in his youth, when '[m]anhood had come to him . . . as a rightful inheritance.' (p. 57) In failing to be manly Ravenel has, according to the bourgeois ethos, betrayed a sacred trust. 'Do you recognise what you were born to be?' Halifax demands of him. 'Not only a nobleman, but a gentleman; not only a gentleman, but a man – man, made in the image of God. How can you, how dare you, give the lie to your Creator?' (p. 401) True nobility, in other words, is founded on true gentility and true gentility on the manliness ordained by God. In failing to be manly, Ravenel and the degenerate aristocracy he represents have relinquished their responsibility and consequently their right to leadership and social dominance.

The ascendency of the middle class and its values is made explicit when the unthinkable happens – Lord Ravenel asks John and Ursula for the hand of their second daughter, Maud. He reassures them about the 'disparity' between Maud and himself, only to be told how insignificant they find any disparity 'supposed to exist between the son of the Earl of Luxmore and the daughter of John Halifax.' (p. 399) But they do in fact feel the disparity, and it is not in favor of the noble lord. 'Would it be so great a misfortune to your daughter,' Ravenel inquires of them, 'if I made her Viscountess Ravenel, and in course of time Countess of Luxmore?' To which John Halifax replies: 'I believe it would. Her mother and I would rather see our little Maud lying beside her [dead] sister Muriel than see her Countess of Luxmore.' (pp. 399–400) Halifax further invokes his version of honor as a barrier to the union as he mentally considers 'what a foul, tattered rag, fit to be torn down by an honest gust, was that flaunting emblazonment, the so-called "honour" of Luxmore!' when 'contrasted with the unsullied dignity of the tradesman's life, the spotless innocence of the tradesman's daughter.' The essence of honor has become love and home, things that have been corrupted by the aristocracy. But love and home and bourgeois honor thrive in the pristine atmosphere surrounding the successful tradesman – the 'unsullied dignity' of his life, the 'spotless innocence' of his child.

Ravenel's ultimate fate dramatizes the absolute demise of the aristocratic model of honor and of its moral authority. While Ravenel the aristocrat cannot be a gentleman and cannot marry into the family of a gentleman like John Halifax, he is completely rehabilitated when he forsakes his wealth and title for bourgeois status. Ravenel persuades his dying father to cut off the entail of his estate, so that on the Earl's death the property becomes available to settle his immense debts. Ravenel's life and character are then recast in the image of John Halifax; he becomes a penniless vagrant, traveling to America to find work, humbly accepting the role of a subordinate. Unbeknownst to John and Ursula, Ravenel becomes the employee – and after proving his mettle, the partner – of their eldest son, Guy, who has sought refuge in America from the unfortunate effects of a broken heart and a brief but disastrous fling with high living on the continent. Ravenel then becomes to Guy what John had been to Abel and Phineas Fletcher. Guy describes his anonymous partner to his father as a willing, diligent worker, and a faithful, compassionate friend:

> 'He knew nothing whatever of business when he offered himself as my clerk; since then he has worked like a slave. In a fever I had he nursed me; he has been to me these three years the best, truest friend. He is the noblest fellow. Father, if you only knew – '
>
> 'Well, my son, let me know him. Invite the gentleman to Beechwood.' (pp. 430–1)

John recognizes the attributes of a gentleman, which were no part of Lord Ravenel but which now define the man who has become 'only Mr. William Ravenel', whose willing renunciation of rank, fortune, and love 'for the sake of duty or of honour' has at last made him worthy of the hand of the daughter of an honest tradesman.

John Halifax, Gentleman mediates the transition of the complete tradesman into the complete gentleman. But for all the overt repudiation of aristocratic values inherent in this celebration of *homo mediocris* as the model of integrity and leadership, the complete gentleman ends up as an odd hybrid, inheriting many of the attributes of his noble predecessor, Sir Charles Grandison. Despite a childhood of hunger and destitution, John Halifax is, like Sir Charles, a tall, strong, and commanding figure, exuding virtue and dignity from every pore. Despite his lack of formal education, John acquires a wide range of practical and academic knowledge in astronomy, mechanics, and the classics to complement his innate business sense; he is even quite inexplicably a fine horseman. Most importantly, John Halifax's actions are guided by his Christian principles and like Sir Charles he demonstrates his moral superiority by refusing to fight with a belligerent churl. When struck in public by Richard Brithwood, John restrains his anger and responds: 'I am a Christian. I shall not return blow for blow.' (p. 179) But whereas gentlemanly status in *Sir Charles Grandison* is determined by birth and confirmed by character, in Craik's novel character is the only legitimate criterion, and that character is defined by bourgeois values.

By the middle of the nineteenth-century, the moral authority that Sir Charles's commanding figure originally conferred upon bourgeois values has become the indisputable jurisdiction of the middle class. The conflicting assumptions that inform the bitter irony of Sealand's comments in *The Conscious Lovers*, that merchants are 'as honourable, and almost as useful, as ... landed Folks' and that 'Industry is dishonourable' are in conflict no longer: industry and honor have become synonymous and entrepreneurs have no need to call themselves 'a Species of Gentry' to validate their status. It is now the bourgeois gentleman who determines the nature of gentility; it is John Halifax who dubs plain William Ravenel a gentleman. The metamorphosis of the gentleman from an aristocrat into a bourgeois entrepreneur is complete. The fictional representations that constitute the gentleman's progress from Grandison to Halifax, from mid-eighteenth-century to mid-nineteenth-century ideals, mediate the transition of British society from aristocratic to bourgeois hegemony and in the process generate an important cultural by-product – the literary conventions for representing middle-class characters.

2
The Literary Evolution of the Lower Middle Class: *The Natural History of the Gent* to *Little Dorrit*

> 'How is it that some people can't understand that your social position is like your digestion, or the nose on your face, you're never aware of either, unless there's something wrong with it.'
>
> May Sinclair, *The Divine Fire*

The gentleman, as Daniel Defoe recognized, is a cultural construction, the 'exalted Creature of our own forming'. Fictional characters are no less cultural constructions, shaped as much by the values and assumptions of the society for which they are created as by the author who creates them. The cultural values of intensely class-conscious nineteenth-century Britain accordingly dictated that fictional characters must have a class identity, and indeed, a character's class is arguably a more fundamental personal attribute than gender in the novels of this period. Consider, for example, the androgyny of many omniscient narrators, especially George Eliot's, for while narrators, strictly speaking, are not characters, they are nevertheless constructed fictional identities, albeit often incomplete ones. The narrator of *Middlemarch*, while dis-embodied, has so distinct a personality that one critic has been prompted to attribute the pervasive wisdom and discernment of the narrative voice to middle-aged sagacity rather than omniscience.[1] More fundamental, but perhaps less obvious, is that narrator's middle-class sensibility. It is indeed the unobtrusiveness of his/her class position that makes the narrator undeniably middle-class; the narrator of *Middlemarch* is the normative voice *par excellence* of the nineteenth-century British novel, the classic bourgeois genre.

The less this voice is overtly class-positioned within the world of the novel, the more it is middle-class.

The essence of the bourgeois character in nineteenth-century British novels is interiority, the strong sense of a personal and integrated identity that is formed and controlled by the individual consciousness. The representation of middle-class characters is accordingly predicated on the construction of internal rather than external attributes, on Grandisonian-style integrity rather than on fencing skills. The middle-class identity is both sustained and defined by the myth of progress embodied in the nineteenth-century bourgeois novel. This progress is typically highly personal and individualistic, involving a process of coming to understand the self. The middle-class identity, in other words, becomes the normative one in nineteenth-century novels, the standard by which fictional characters are implicitly judged and given relative social positions.[2] Not surprisingly, protagonists are generally middle-class or, like John Halifax, Pip, and Oliver Twist, in the process of *embourgeoisement*, especially in the works of the major male Victorian novelists. The Brontës, Elizabeth Gaskell, and George Eliot are somewhat less constrained and attempt to create protagonists like Jane Eyre and Felix Holt, who rebel against accepted social norms, or ones like John and Mary Barton, working-class protagonists whose very conception challenges novelistic conventions. The provocativeness of Jane Eyre's and Felix Holt's unconventionality is vitiated, however, by the fact that their stories ultimately conform to standard middle-class expectations of marriage and domestic felicity. In *Mary Barton*, Gaskell is more successful in resisting middle-class models for presenting a working-class story, and so comes closer to producing a convincingly working-class ethos. The dominant ethos of the nineteenth-century novel, however, remains middle-class, and is virtually indistinguishable from that of the typical protagonist.

The middle-class character, like his or her real-life counterpart, could not rely on the external or quantifiable attributes of identity available to the aristocrat – titles, lineage, family property – to define his or her worth or class position. The personal attributes of individualism, sensitivity, and intelligence alone make such a character engaging and make his or her inner life comprehensible within the ideology of the nineteenth-century novel. Characters who are reflective and self-critical, who suffer or agonize over moral dilemmas, and whose creators portray them with earnestness and sensitivity, embody the essence of the middle class. Within the circular logic of the bourgeois novel, the identity of the typical novelistic protagonist and the process by which that identity is formed thus become distinctly class-based. The essential characteristic of a middle-class protagonist, then, is that he or she has an inner life that reveals an intense subjectivity. Regenia Gagnier notes a similar unmistakably middle-class subjectivity in autobiographical writing, a 'strongly class-based' distinction 'between writers who do claim an autonomous introspective "self" and those who do not.' (Gagnier, p. 13) Working- class identity, by contrast, tended to be collective – as in Richard Hoggart's 'us against them' formulation in *The Uses of Literacy* (1957) – rather than individualistic, and often valued introspection less. The extent to which characters from other classes exhibit qualities similar to those that define the bourgeois protagonist reveals the extent to which they can be considered either worthy of compassion (in the case of such characters as Mary Barton, Sir Leicester Dedlock, or Stephen Blackpool) or, as with Pip, Oliver, and John Halifax, fit to rise to bourgeois status.

Once the middle-class identity and the ascendency of that identity within novelistic conventions had been established, bourgeois novelists could turn their attention to the representation of other classes, and to the ordering of the external world through those representations. The class placing of characters in Victorian novels is generally something the reader absorbs, rather than overtly takes note of. The narrator does not announce a character's class but instead reveals it through his or her dress and general appearance, language, and attitudes. But class, as Raymond Williams has demonstrated, is essentially relational,[3] and the class position of characters is most tellingly represented through their interaction with other characters; the degree to which a character is commanding or deferential in social situations registers his or her social status. Beyond the relational component of a character's representation, class stereotypes work to define both social position and personal worth: the more a character exhibits the most extreme conventional shortcomings of his class – that is, the extent to which he or she deviates from the middle-class norm – the more unworthy he or she is. An aristocratic character will accordingly be, to a greater or lesser extent, idle, haughty, vain, extravagant, and, in the worst cases, debauched; young men especially tend to be supercilious, debt-ridden, and port-sodden. The super-refined manners of aristocratic characters typically betray affectation, a concern with forms and social niceties over personal integrity; as a result, aristocratic males are not truly 'manly'.

The overwhelming social and economic determinism of nineteenth-century working-class poverty dictated that, in any fiction purporting to be realist, working-class characters must be rough in speech and dress.[4] A fashionably dressed member of the working class would be immediately suspect.[5] The extent to which the inevitably coarse clothing of a working-class character is clean or dirty, orderly or dishevelled, however, indicates the level of his or her merit. The coarseness of lower-class speech is typically rendered in dialect, the relative comprehensibility of which, for readers more than for other characters, represents the relative distance of a particular character's experience and sensibility from the norms of bourgeois life; this is the technique Holcroft uses to contrast the gentlemanliness of Frank Henley with the coarseness of his father in *Anna St. Ives*. Like their aristocratic counterparts, working-class characters are frequently debt-ridden – but from the effects of improvidence rather than extravagance – and drunk. Working-class drunkenness typically leads to, or is a metonym for other kinds of intemperance, especially violence and sexual incontinence. If working-class characters are not ungodly and superstitious – or, worse yet to the Victorian bourgeois mind, Roman Catholic – they demonstrate an alarming propensity to Methodism or to even more distressing forms of collectivism, such as Chartism.

The traits that define the aristocrat and the laborer are, of course, inversions of the qualities that define the middle-class character: restraint and sobriety in dress and demeanor, honest and forthright expression, sexual continence, religious conformity, and, last but certainly not least, financial solvency. And just as characters outside the middle class demonstrate their relative moral worth to the extent that they temper their class-determined failings with countervailing bourgeois virtues, so too do middle-class characters reveal their unworthiness to the extent that they deviate from the path of bourgeois orthodoxy. Guy Halifax's brief fling with continental high living, inevitably accompanied by debt, accordingly constitutes more than an excusable youthful indiscretion; rather, it constitutes a fall from grace that requires the purification of a prolonged exile in America. This class coding of personal attributes also makes it possible to create a character like John

Halifax, whose overt class position is at odds with his 'real' or 'natural' position. His meteoric rise from beggar to gentleman comes as no surprise to the reader, and not only because the novel's title announces his ultimate destiny. Rather, his destiny – like that of Oliver Twist before him – is manifest in his character from the outset, in his grammatical Queen's English and in a dignified bearing that makes him respectful of rank but never servile.

The class coding of personal attributes also represents the class system as stable and just, for John Halifax's class mobility is in fact more apparent than real. As a vagrant, he has no predetermined class position within the town in which he settles, and while the town's inhabitants initially respond to his outward appearance – his ragged clothes – they soon acknowledge his innate superiority with their increasingly deferential treatment of him: John is still in his teens when the other workers in the tan-yard begin to call him 'sir'. Thus while ostensibly the quintessential self-made man, John Halifax can fulfil his destiny only because he demonstrates his suitability by conforming to the cultural characteristics of the class for which he is ordained. Moreover, Phineas's claim that John 'was indebted to no forefathers for a family history' and that his story 'commenced with himself, and was altogether of his own making' is far from accurate. John Halifax is not, in fact, entirely without pedigree and the credentials to prove it. The documentation and validation of his status are contained in his one cherished possession, the Greek Testament inscribed with his father's name.[6] John's sole asset accordingly incorporates a dense conflation of symbols of the mandatory values and accomplishments of the middle-class gentleman: classical education, Christian orthodoxy, and literacy. The Testament, moreover, like the family Bible of all good Victorian middle-class households, contains a genealogy, albeit a rudimentary one; it records the marriage of Guy Halifax and the birth of his son. 'Guy Halifax, gentleman' accordingly begets *John Halifax, Gentleman*.

The creation of the illusion of class stability is a crucial component of the politics of literary representation in the English novel during the middle years of the nineteenth century. The specter of aristocratic dominance had been largely laid to rest over the course of the previous century, as the bourgeoisie wrested moral authority from the aristocracy by redefining the gentleman. The aristocracy retained its prestige and the aura of glamour, but bourgeois respectability had displaced gentility as the basis for social and moral leadership, and so the aristocracy no longer posed a serious threat to bourgeois cultural hegemony. The middle class accordingly turned its attention to defining and stabilizing its relationship to those on the lower end of the social scale.[7] It is this shift of emphasis from the politics of achieving dominance to the politics of exercising domination that produces the parallel literary shift from the novel of manners to the social or industrial novel, from Austen's narrow focus on three or four families in a country village to Dickens's densely populated recreations of urban life. Furthermore, the relative political significance of the upper and lower classes in the bourgeois imagination is reflected in a cultural mythology that views the aristocratic drunk as merely contemptible, but the working-class drunk as a threat to social stability.

The conventional stereotypes of the working class that develop in the first half of the nineteenth century are of course strongly influenced by Malthusian economic philosophy, by the gloomy vision of unavoidable poverty and human misery being the inevitable result of the irresistible pressures of natural drives. The idea that want could be the only effective restraint on the theoretically unlimited fecundity of the species, combined with Malthus's widely endorsed contention that 'dependent poverty ought to be held disgraceful',[8] formed the philosophical basis for the New Poor Law of 1834, which made public charity in the form of the workhouse more degrading and humiliating than the meanest employment and the most grinding 'independent' poverty.[9] While Malthus, as Gertrude Himmelfarb points out, is at pains to emphasize the universality of the 'laws of nature' that dictate the inevitable misery of the poor, he also implies that the peculiar vulnerability of the poor is the consequence of their primitiveness. The masses, '[l]ike the infant and the savage', needed to be 'goaded ... by necessity' before they would be willing to work; leisure and prosperity were likely to lead them to evil and degradation.[10] Influenced by Malthusian doctrine, the Victorian bourgeoisie came to regard the lower classes as the potentially delinquent children of their social family, in need of guidance and, when recalcitrant, punishment.

The notion of latent atavism among the lower classes played on the imaginations of the middle class during a period of rapid social change and apparent political instability.[11] The specter of the French Revolution continued to haunt the public imagination, and the fear of violence and insurrection was fostered by continuing uprisings on the continent throughout the first half of the century. The Luddites, Peterloo, the Swing Riots, and Chartism seemed to confirm the worst nightmares of the middle class, that the propensity for political restiveness and violence among the lower classes had spread to England. The lower classes were perceived to be less civilized, and so more animal-like and predatory – especially sexually – than the 'respectable' classes. Dirt, disease, and squalor were often interpreted as the cause, rather than the result, of poverty, and in the most reductive formulations of middle-class social mythology, the lower classes figured as a collective of morally weak beings in need of control and guidance, who presented a more or less overt threat to social stability.

The unease that plagued the consciousness of the bourgeoisie, while fostered by fears of political unrest, was also inspired, I would argue, by the sheer size and diversity of the 'masses' that comprised the lower classes – the masses that had to be placed within the map of the bourgeois social world before they engulfed it. The categorizing impulse inherent in the class system itself, which comes into full flower in this period, reflects the need to order and stabilize an apparently unstable society. It is this same impulse that drives Henry Mayhew's obsessively detailed classifying of the London poor, a typically Victorian attempt to bring order out of chaos that produces the illusion of having control over an alien world. The undifferentiated 'lower classes', the sprawling and spawning 'masses', seem less overwhelming when subdivided. Vice could then be contained within the 'dangerous' or 'criminal' classes and left to fester within the confines of the infamous Seven Dials. Middle-class attention and solicitude could then focus on the further compartmentalized laboring classes, on the employed and the unemployed, the deserving (i.e., those perceived as espousing bourgeois values and morality) and the undeserving poor.

The vice-ridden dangerous classes are the subject of much early nineteenth-century sensational fiction, but the horror induced by the violent and degraded exploits of thieves, murderers and prostitutes in William Ainsworth's *Rookwood* (1824) and *Jack Sheppard* (1839), and in G. W. M. Reynolds's *The Mysteries of London* (1845–8) is titillating rather than disturbing in a broad social or political sense.[12] Vice is either self-destructive or subject to the law: Dick Turpin and Jack Sheppard are hanged for their crimes. In *Oliver Twist*, Fagin, too, is executed, while Bill Sikes accidentally hangs himself. But even when crime evades the law, it exists in a nightmare world that is distanced from the substantial and material 'reality' of the bourgeois social realm. Therefore crime and vice, while deplorable, pose no substantial threat to the integrity of society or to the stability of the class system. Accordingly Nancy, though far less corrupt than Bill or Fagin, is doomed by a different order of crime – the transgression of the boundary between the criminal and respectable worlds. But Nancy's fate represents a further containment of the world of vice: her murder at the hands of Sikes demonstrates that the criminal world is policed from within.

The integrity and stability of the bourgeois vision of the world thus come to rest, in the middle decades of the century, on the ability of the middle class to order and control society through the manipulation of images and representations of the working class. In the industrial novel of the mid-nineteenth century, the working class becomes the repository of all the perceived lower-class virtues and failings, of humility, loyalty, and diligence as well as of shiftlessness, intemperance, and restiveness. In his comprehensive study of the working classes in Victorian fiction, P. J. Keating notes that the two most common types of working-class characters are the virtuous poor and the debased. The virtuous poor character is '[u]nskilled, often illiterate, poor through no fault of his own, [and the] ... object of social pity. He is usually shown to possess a high standard of morality and good-neighbourliness.' The debased character 'is defined in terms of drunkenness, brutality or moral viciousness. These are really character traits and the debased working man is distinct from the criminal whose anti-social activities are to some extent rationalized.'[13] The general Victorian cultural associations of poverty with drink, idleness, and violence would, however, suggest that the virtuous, subject as always to Malthusian determinism, might at any time slide down the slippery slope of indigence into a slough of degradation and violence. As the industrial novel develops, however, the most skilled of its producers, Elizabeth Gaskell and Charles Dickens, develop techniques for interpreting and representing the culture of working-class poverty that imaginatively tame the lion of working-class violence and maintain order within the bourgeois vision of society.

In their industrial novels, Gaskell and Dickens attempt to expose the injustices of the factory system and inspire sympathy for the working classes by focusing on the plight of the virtuous poor, on characters like Stephen Blackpool. At the same time, they try to play down or rationalize the activism and potential violence of the working class. In *Mary Barton*, Gaskell portrays the Barton family as representatives of the deserving poor – working people who lead orderly lives and who try to grapple with ethical problems rather than give in easily to the temptations of violence and sexual licence. However, as a character who embodies both the best and the worst of working-class traits – as a man who is a responsible and devoted father, but who nevertheless commits murder in the cause of working-class rights – John Barton is a problematic figure. Raymond Williams maintains that the difficulty of reconciling middle-class sympathy to violence and murder undermines both the characterization of John Barton and the artistic and emotional integrity of the novel. Williams contends that Barton becomes 'a very shadowy figure' after committing the murder, suggesting that the crime has put him 'not only beyond the range of Mrs Gaskell's sympathy (which is understandable), but, more essentially, beyond the range of her powers.' Williams claims, furthermore, that the 'imaginative choice of the act of murder and then the imaginative recoil from it have the effect of ruining the necessary integration of feeling in the whole theme.'[14]

John Barton, according to Williams, is 'a dramatization of the *fear of violence* which was widespread among the upper and middle classes at the time'. But John Barton is also a dramatization of the problems inherent in the representation of working-class characters in the nineteenth-century novel: there is the same 'gap between ideology and experience' noted by Gagnier in many working-class autobiographies that attempt to follow a middle-class model, a gap that leads to the disintegration of both narrative and identity. (Gagnier, p. 46) The working-class identity, which tended to be collective rather than individualistic, was incompatible with the kind of intense subjectivity demanded of the protagonist of a conventional nineteenth-century novel; and the motives of a John Barton are neither comprehensible nor justifiable in terms of bourgeois ideology. In other words, the characterization of working-class figures like John Barton is doomed to failure not because murder or other rash and violent acts place them beyond the author's sympathy or powers, but because such actions place them beyond the conventional novel's range of sympathy or powers. It is likely that this limitation of the conventional novel contributed to Gaskell's recourse to the 'formal eclecticism' noted by Catherine Gallagher, the distracting conflation of tragedy, melodrama, and domestic fiction within the structure of *Mary Barton* that distorts the characterizations and the stories of its working-class protagonists.[15]

The solution to this problem of representation, however, could not be simply to write only about the virtuous poor – who would by definition be politically uninvolved – because this would sidestep the problem of working-class activism and the possibility that otherwise trustworthy individuals could be driven to desperate action. The most successful novelistic representations of the working class under duress are, accordingly, those in which the virtuous and activist aspects of the working-class identity are isolated and presented in different characters, who nevertheless interact. Thus in *Hard Times* Dickens develops sympathy for the misery of his representative working-class man, Stephen Blackpool, by presenting him not as an activist, but as a victim of both the murderous mad elephant of the factory system and the potential activism of other factory workers who ostracize him. His fellow workers cannot be fully blamed for their inhumanity or their restiveness, however, because they are never fully identified as the source of either. They remain faceless and inarticulate, while the voice of insurrection is housed in the person of Slackbridge, an outsider and parvenu who has no legitimate or permanent place in the workers' community. Through this maneuver, Dickens is able to displace the source of activism, to transfer it from the workers themselves to an unethical interloper. The workers are thus absolved of direct blame; their only sin is their weakness. They have the potential to become dangerous not because of inherent wickedness, but because without compassionate and responsible leadership from their middle-class employers and legislators, they are susceptible to Slackbridge's hollow but insinuating rhetoric.

Dickens also diminishes the threat posed by working-class drunkenness in *Hard Times* by representing it in a woman and making it another feature of Stephen's victimization. But while his wife's intemperance blights his life, the damage is contained within the domestic sphere; it does not make Stephen less effective or loyal as an employee. And although to Victorian sensibilities drunkenness may be more shocking and more reprehensible in a woman than in a man, it would also seem more anomalous. Moreover, Stephen's wife is a nameless outcast, with no permanent place in either the working-class community or the text. Her presence in the novel is as ethereal and ephemeral as Stephen's dream in which he imagines he has allowed her to take poison, for Stephen may not have disposed of her, but the novel does. She is not granted even an exit; she simply disappears from the story. Thus working-class sexuality and intemperance are figured in a single expendable character. Working-class feminine virtue, by contrast, is embodied in the more substantial form of Rachael who, in the committed celibacy of her relationship with Stephen, is represented as the epitome of female chastity and selfless devotion. Their relationship indeed demonstrates a level of self-control and personal integrity unmatched by any of the middle-class characters in the novel, and Stephen's love for Rachael drives him to an expression of passion that is not sexual, but reverential: he 'put[s] an end of her shawl to his lips.'[16]

In *North and South*, Gaskell similarly represents working-class virtue and working-class violence in separate characters. The Higginses, the novel's most prominent representatives of a working-class family, are honest and responsible, and within their household the potentially disruptive forces of passion and intemperance are either defused or displaced. Mr Higgins resists his desire to indulge in sporadic binges for the sake of his daughters, thus demonstrating both his rationality and the important influence of affective bonds. Sexual passion, however, finds no expression in this family, in which the mother is dead and the older sister is dying. Bessy's passion thus has no hope of physical expression, and is diverted into religious ardor, just as her father's passion is diverted into a fervent commitment to his family and to the plight of his fellow workers. But Higgins, though a crusty and argumentative activist, is opposed to violent action of any kind, while the potential for violence is located in the mutinous crowd of angry factory hands that gathers outside Thornton's house.

The action of the crowd poses a more direct and immediate threat to middle-class authority than anything that happens in *Hard Times*, but it is a threat that Gaskell is able to defuse by domesticating it. First she disrupts the potentially violent crowd action through the agency of a woman. By trying to shield Thornton from the crowd and receiving the blow of the stone hurled at him, Margaret Hale diverts the attention of both the characters and the reader from the issue of class conflict to issues of courage, chivalry, and propriety. The pale, bleeding, and unconscious figure of Margaret transforms the encounter between master and men into a symbolic violation of Victorian womanhood. The sight of Margaret's prostrate body alarms and unmans master and workers alike, making Thornton's solitary and implacable stand before his impassioned workers seem like so much bluster, and turning the defiance of the crowd into cowardly flight:

> [T]he retrograde movement towards the gate had begun – as unreasoningly, perhaps as blindly, as the simultaneous anger. Or, perhaps, the idea of the approach of the soldiers, and the sight of that pale, upturned face, with closed eyes, still and sad as marble, though the tears welled out of the long entanglement of eyelashes, and dropped down; and, heavier, slower plash than even tears, came the drip of blood from her wound. Even the most desperate – Boucher himself – drew back, faltered away, scowled, and finally went off, muttering curses on the master, who stood in his unchanging attitude, looking after their retreat with defiant eyes. The moment that retreat had changed into a flight (as it was sure from its very character to do), he darted up the steps to Margaret.[17]

The 'most desperate' member of the crowd, Boucher, is subsequently assigned the blame for the collective loss of control and for throwing the stone that wounds Margaret. Thus, in much the same way that political activism in *Hard Times* is identified with Slackbridge, the urge for violent action in *North and South* is transferred from the group and isolated in the motivations of a single individual – an individual, incidently, who, with a suspiciously French name and an Irish accent, is comfortingly un-English (and probably Catholic).

Boucher's motivations further depoliticize violence by domesticating its source: he is driven not by class animosity, but by despair and concern for his large and starving family. Working-class violence accordingly retains its conventional association with working-class sexuality, in this case with irresponsible reproduction – although Boucher is a sincerely loving and faithful husband and father. His violence and sexuality symbolically stand in for each other, and neither is represented as the uncontained or uncontrolled force that the middle class most feared. Boucher's violence is thus no more uncontrolled than his sexuality, which is contained within the legal bounds of marriage, the social bounds of domesticity and the home, and the moral and affective bounds of love. In the end, violence, like crime, proves to be self-destructive: Boucher destroys only himself, drowning while on the tramp in a desperate attempt to find work to feed his family. His family, however, seems better off without him, since the working-class community rallies round to comfort and provide for them. That Boucher probably did not in fact throw the stone seems to get lost in the complexities of his motivations for actions that are in the end only potentially violent. At the same time, the prime example of collective action in *North and South* is the response of the working-class community to the plight of Boucher's widow and children, action that is peaceful, charitable, nurturing, and responsible.

In thus creating sympathy for the plight of the working poor, Victorian fiction also worked to reassure the bourgeoisie, to present the working class as less violent and threatening than the middle class feared. But class stability was also threatened by infiltration; the notoriously fuzzy class boundaries were crossed frequently and with impunity in the nineteenth century by individuals of humble origin who had talent, ambition, or ruthlessness – individuals such as Charles Bradlaugh (who rose from errand-boy to member of Parliament) and Charles Dickens. Bourgeois commitment to personal industry and progress, to the ideology of self-help, indeed endorsed upward mobility. Any perceived threat to social stability that such social mobility might engender was mitigated by novelistic representations of characters who rise in status. Thus we have the infamous innate social and grammatical refinement and uncanny imperviousness to the vitiating influences of lower-class upbringings of characters like Oliver Twist and John Halifax. These characters are presented as having been in some sense 'born in exile'. Those without the fortunate pedigrees of Oliver and John and the engraved lockets and Greek Testaments to prove it – must also conform to the standards of the positions to which they aspire or be doomed to failure. Accordingly, Pip can rise to the status of a middle-class gentleman because he acquires the requisite intellectual sophistication and linguistic refinement. Bounderby, by contrast, betrays himself through his persistent coarseness, his 'brassy speaking-trumpet of a voice' and his overbearing manner as 'the Bully of humility',[18] and as a consequence he ultimately sinks to an appropriately low social level. This imaginative reformulation of class movement not only provided a model that was reassuring to the collective bourgeois consciousness, but also mapped out for lower-class aspirants to social position the terms of assimilation into the bourgeoisie.

THE CONSPIRACY OF DISPARAGEMENT: THE GENESIS OF LOWER-MIDDLE-CLASS MAN

The strategies thus far developed in the novel for imaginatively restructuring society focus on the reinterpretation of the stereotypes of existing classes – the aristocracy and the lower orders. And however ingenious and successful Victorian middle-class authors are in manipulating the stereotypes to suit their ideologies – to undermine the authority of the aristocracy or to bring a semblance of order to the unruly masses – the specters of older perceptions haunt the images of the new bourgeois social order: an aura of glamour and status lingers around even discredited aristocrats like Lord Ravenel in *John Halifax, Gentleman,* and the fear of and fascination with the degradation of characters like Fagin and Bill Sikes remains almost palpable. By comparison to the paradoxes thus often inherent in the portrayal of upper and lower-class characters, the representation of lower-middle-class figures seems, on the surface at least, to be unproblematic. In Victorian literature, lower-middle-class man – typically represented as a low-level office clerk or shopkeeper – is the embodiment of insignificance, and the class itself the repository of numbing mediocrity. Such characters pose no apparent threat whatever, possessing neither the disarming finesse of the aristocrat nor the disturbing physical presence of the manual laborer. While lower-middle-class characters are sometimes portrayed as flashy and vulgar, especially in early sketches in the periodical literature, they are more typically presented as pale, haggard, and dull, the pathetic and overworked but contemptible denizens of dusty, cramped offices. The physical conditions of the workplace, the stifling and confined atmosphere of offices and shops, become metonymically associated with other aspects of lower-middle-class life. Petty clerks and shopkeepers are depicted as intellectually and morally stifled as well, and the lower-middle-class home as insular and oppressively domestic, the breeding ground of shallow minds. The alternate term for lower-middle-class, *petit bourgeois*, is suggestive of the attitudes the class inspired. Generally pronounced – and indeed often spelled – 'petty' bourgeois, the term carried with it connotations of inferiority, diminutiveness, insignificance, and small-mindedness.

There is virtually nothing in Victorian literature that challenges the prevailing image of the lower middle class as the locus of all that is narrow and lackluster. Even members of the class concur with the unflattering bourgeois assessment of themselves and their fellows. A Liverpool office clerk, in an 1871 monograph analyzing the social and economic position of the members of his profession, endorses the opinion of 'thoughtful observers' who agree that clerks 'deserve the mingled pity and contempt with which other classes of society appear to regard them.'[19] Other lower-middle-class writers present the plight of the oppressed office-worker more sympathetically, and the clerk's lament for the misery of his position as impoverished, overworked, and unappreciated forms a small but significant sub-genre of nineteenth-century literature. The earliest and most impressive example is Charles Lamb's 'The Good Clerk', a stinging indictment of the self-serving entrepreneur who makes outrageous demands of employees whom he underpays and treats with contempt.[20] But the concentration in the laments on the meagerness of salaries, the cramped and unhealthy conditions in offices, and the monotony of the work does nothing to dispel the impression of life in the lower middle class as dull and dreary. The laments indeed draw on the unflattering stereotypes to elicit sympathy.

Because the literary stereotypes of the lower middle class develop at virtually the same historical moment that the class emerges, they have extraordinary suggestive power. There are no conflicting images to challenge the demoralizing portrayals generated in bourgeois literature, no ghosts of an earlier tradition to counteract the distortions of contemporary representations. The stereotypes accordingly become virtually irresistible and irrefutable, defining the outlines of the class from without and shaping the self-perception of those within it. The Victorian bourgeois conception of the lower middle class retains its force and influence to this day.

Present-day historical practice endorses the nineteenth-century perception of the class as insignificant. The lower middle class is conspicuously absent from all but passing references in most histories of the Victorian period. F. M. L. Thompson's chapter, 'Town and city', in *The Cambridge Social History of Britain 1750–1950*, is an exception. Thompson devotes several pages to the lower middle class, and argues for their importance in municipal politics in the late nineteenth and early twentieth centuries. But even this accomplishment Thompson presents as inadvertent, something that 'was thrust upon the lower middle class' by the 'retreat of the more substantial middle classes' from urban centers. Note that within the logic of Thompson's rhetoric the lower middle class remains an apparently unsubstantial group. Thompson similarly disparages the lower middle class in *The Rise of Respectable Society*, where he describes it as '[t]he weakest group' within Victorian society because it was 'the most purely imitative in its standards, the least capable of generating its own culture, and the most despised by those from whom its moral clothes were borrowed', although he does admit to the 'grittiness of its nonconformist sections'.[21] There was also a brief flurry of scholarly interest in the class twenty years ago when it featured in one article ('The Lower Middle Class as Historical Problem', by Arno Mayer) and a single collection of essays (*The Lower Middle Class in Britain 1870–1914*, ed. Geoffrey Crossick). Neither Mayer nor Crossick *et al.*, however, challenge the perception of members of the class as bland and unassertive; Mayer indeed fosters the general tone of disparagement by suggesting ironically that historians disdain the lower middle class because it is the class from which most of them come, and which they are trying to escape.[22] The class has stimulated even less of a response among literary scholars, who have paid little or no attention to the representation and possible significance of lower-middle-class figures in Victorian literature. As a consequence of this generalized academic indifference, the lower middle class has remained as marginal in recent scholarship as it apparently was in Victorian society.

   This sustained perception of the insignificance of the lower middle class represents a triumph of ideology over reality, and the Victorian bourgeoisie has managed to dupe posterity as well as its own society. A skeptical reading of nineteenth-century portrayals of the lower middle class suggests that the bourgeoisie was in fact protesting too much. The persistence of the denigration does not accord with the message contained in these portrayals. The intensity of the responses it inspired indeed suggests that the lower middle class was a more troubling presence than has previously been recognized. It was an unknown quantity, a potential loose cannon: not only was it a new constituent within the class system, but as the manpower for the bureaucracies that were supporting trade, industry, and empire, the lower middle class was also expanding as relentlessly as urbanization, commercialization, and imperialism. The class was undeniably a substantial component of England's power and prosperity and accordingly occupied an important strategic position in the power relations of the period. Despite insistent contemporary avowals to the contrary, the lower middle class was profoundly significant. Moreover, this burgeoning new class was positioned on the fringes of the middle class, and consequently was potentially far more disruptive to bourgeois hegemony than were individual transgressions of class boundaries like those represented by Pip and David Copperfield.

For the Victorian middle class, the insidious threat of the apparently unrestrainable growth of a large – not to mention contiguous and kindred – stratum of society required the development of a new kind of strategic reaction, a response quite distinct from that to the perceived threat to the stability of the class system posed by the lower classes. Especially galling and disturbing to members of the Victorian bourgeoisie was the encroachment on middle-class territory: lower-middle-class clerks, like their employers, lived in the suburbs and worked in the city; like their employers, they dressed in sober and 'respectable' black coats and they behaved with decorum. This new class had to be given a place within the existing system of middle-class hegemony and had to be kept in that place, and the urgency of this undertaking is evident in the hostility that colors the uniformly disparaging contemporary portrayals of clerks and shop assistants, although it was the clerk – the most visible and rapidly proliferating type – who bore the brunt of contemporary ill-will.[23] Disparagement is indeed a component of the imaginative strategy of control and containment that evolved during the nineteenth century, a strategy that restrains the potential power of the lower middle class by feminizing it and defining the domestic sphere as its natural habitat. Victorian authors accordingly represent lower-middle-class figures – almost always male – as diminutive, obsessed with dress and appearance, and, while perhaps virtuous in their way, endowed with only limited vision and intellectual capacities; in other words, the lower-middle-class figure is largely sketched from the blueprint of the conventional Victorian woman. Such characters, unlike their middle-class counterparts, cannot effectively bridge the gap between the spheres of business and the home. They appear dwarfed and slightly ridiculous in the world of trade and commerce, which remains the dominion of the bourgeoisie.

The conventions for representing the lower middle class have their genesis in periodical literature in the 1830s and 1840s, more than a decade before the term 'lower middle class' appeared in print.[24] Disparaging portrayals of petty clerks and shop assistants, often in the guise of 'Gents', appeared in virtually every major periodical not devoted exclusively to serious debates on religion, academics, or politics.[25] A variety of marginal social and occupational types populate the comic sketches of the *New Monthly Magazine* and *Bentley's Miscellany* – grocers, apothecaries, hack journalists, booksellers, various kinds of shop assistants. *Punch*'s cartoons and sketches tended to focus on the genus rather than on individual representative characters, as in a sketch titled 'The Clerk' in the series 'Punch's Guide to Servants' (1845). In addition to numerous individual sketches, *Blackwood's* featured a series about a 'tallow-faced counter-jumper' called Tittlebat Titmouse in 1839, while Thackeray's Samuel Titmarsh first graced the pages of *Fraser's* in 1841. Titmarsh became something of a regular in *Fraser's*, resurfacing in subsequent series in 1844 and again in 1846. The names of these characters alone, with their play on the names of insignificant small animals, speak volumes about popular attitudes toward the marginal social types they represent.

The earlier of these sketches tend to portray the widest variety of occupational groups, with shopkeepers of one kind or another figuring prominently. In a very early sketch in the *New Monthly Magazine* (1824), for example, a grocer by the name of Snooks has hopes of upward mobility.[26] In the later sketches, however, the lower middle class is most often represented by one of two figures: the bumbling clerk or the Gent. Inept and unprepossessing clerks repeatedly stumble into preposterous and often humiliating scrapes. Malachi Meagrim struggles through a night of terrifying nightmares after having overindulged in tea,[27] and Julius Nosebody makes a fool of himself after having been plied with punch by a couple of upper-class pranksters.[28] Alfred

Stokes, an excessively punctilious clerk, almost loses his girl because of his obsession for meticulous penmanship.[29] Jeremiah Fubkins, an unimpressive young man of the utmost thrift and excessively 'regular habits', falls prey to the machinations of a wily young seamstress and her flashy cousin who use Fubkins to help finance their evening of drinking and spooning.[30]

Lower-middle-class man as bumbling but inoffensive clerk might have fared better in the collective Victorian consciousness had it not been for his association – within that collective consciousness – with the Gent. Gents, too, are initially associated with trade rather than with office work, appearing first as "prentices' and then as shop assistants and low-level clerks. Their occupations, however, are not necessarily specified, their non-status as Gents apparently being sufficient to place them. The Gent is both degraded dandy and degraded gentleman, often simultaneously. The association of the Gent with the dandy is pejorative in several ways. The dandy embodied what the Victorian middle class most envied and most deplored in the aristocracy, the glamour of elegant deportment and social finesse, coupled with an absolute want of principles, of moral or intellectual commitment. The dandy was all form and no substance, an exterior with no discernible interior consciousness. As a cheap and nasty incarnation of the dandy, the Gent is inevitably denied an interiority and is defined by what he wears and by his lack of social graces. The Gent as depicted in the periodical press dresses with an excess of care and extravagant bad taste, and attempts to cut a fine figure by being cocky and obstreperous. One of the elements of mock-dandyism that appears in the portrayals of the Gent is diminutiveness, a parodic parallel to the suggestion of spareness in the traditional style of the dandy, in the elegance of the trim figure and the uncluttered, impeccably tailored clothing.[31] At the same time, as a diminutive form of 'gentleman', the term 'Gent' explicitly suggests an association with cherished middle-class ideals that the bourgeoisie would have been anxious to undermine by emphasizing the disparity between both the terms and what they represent.

Initially, diminutiveness is not unduly emphasized, and indeed seems to be a component either of the author's parodic reworking of the dandy as Gent, or of the Gent's attempt to ape the refinement of his genteel prototypes. Accordingly, Mr Robert Bolton, a self-styled 'gentleman connected with the press' who appears in *Bentley's Miscellany* in 1838, may be 'a short, spare man', but his stature is only a secondary feature of his debased dandyism, a travesty of graceful slimness that accords perfectly with the travesty of style represented by his clothes.[32] Diminutiveness is also a relatively muted component of a sardonically fulsome description of tailors' advertisements which feature Gents 'in such attitudes as may display their figures and little boots to best advantage' that appears in *Punch* in 1842; here the Gent is assumed to draw attention to his trim figure and elegant small foot, although the writer is clearly not impressed.[33]

Diminutiveness also suited the other personal characteristics of the conventional Gent, who was typically a young clerk of small accomplishments or a draper's assistant, uncommonly well. Given that the real-life counterparts of the fictional figures would then have been impoverished, undernourished, and very young indeed – probably in their late teens – the transference of features of the Gent onto the reedy young clerk or linen-draper was inevitable. This move further disempowered the lower-middle-class figure by removing all lingering hints of glamour or sexuality associated with any version of the dandy. A pair of *Punch* cartoons from 1847 registers this maneuver. The first shows a Gent, or 'fast man', being mocked by a street urchin (Fig. 2.1). This Gent may be the butt of a joke, but his overdressed figure, with its full bosom, nipped waist, and small but erect stick, is nevertheless highly – if somewhat ambiguously – eroticized. The second cartoon (Fig. 2.2) shows a smooth-talking salesman trying to sell an unsuitably large top-hat to a diminutive version of the Gent, a young man whose angularity bespeaks adolescent gawkiness, with no hint of anything that could be mistaken for elegance or sexual potency.

These variations and combinations of the clerk and the Gent flourish in the periodical press throughout the 1840s, and indeed remain endemic throughout the century. E. J. Milliken's comic creation 'Arry', for example, a low level commercial clerk with a cockney accent, a flamboyant wardrobe, and a taste for cheap drink, cheap cigars, and the music halls, features in a series of sketches in *Punch* that runs from 1877 until the 1890s.[34] But it is Albert Smith's *The Natural History of the Gent* that initially brings this social type into sharper focus. *The Natural History of the Gent*, which comprises

Little Boy. "OH, MY EYE! THERE GOES EIGHTPENCE OUT OF A SHILLING."

Figure 2.1 Cartoon accompanying 'A Piece of Poetry by Our Fast Man.' *Punch* 13 (1847): 148.

an expanded version of Smith's comic sketches from *Punch* and *Bentley's* from this period, not only defines in exhaustive detail exactly who and what a Gent is, but it also defines the purpose of representing these figures in print – to foster contempt for them. In the preface, Smith attests to having 'laboured, for three or four years, to bring the race of Gents into universal contempt' by means of 'direct attacks in *Punch* and *Bentley's Miscellany*', augmented by 'side-wind blows through the medium of our esteemed friend John Parry, certain burlesques at the Lyceum, and various other channels.'[35] Smith was only one voice, if a

SHOPKEEPERS AND THEIR CUSTOMERS.

'THERE'S A 'AT, SIR! A STYLE ABOUT THAT 'AT, SIR!! JUST BECOMES YOUR STYLE OF FACE, SIR!!!'

Figure 2.2 'Shopkeepers and their Customers.' *Punch* 13 (1847): 230.

particularly persistent and strident one, in a growing and influential conspiracy of disparagement whose members, Smith's fears notwithstanding, were entirely successful in bringing 'the race of Gents into universal contempt', and who were increasingly turning their attention to the emerging class of which this 'race' formed a part. By the time the class was established, so was its association with the self-important nonentity – the popular stereotype of the low level clerks and office workers who formed the most visible and numerous components of the lower middle class.

By presenting his book as a mock-anthropological study, Smith is able to turn his comic sketches into a veritable handbook for the identification and social placement of a particular segment of society. As he acknowledges in his preface, 'we determined upon reconsidering all we had ever propounded on the subject, and publishing it in the form now presented to the reader, that all might clearly see who the Gents were, and shun them accordingly.' (p. vii) Like Smith's detailed descriptions of the Gent, the representations of lower-middle-class man in comic sketches and in fiction during this period are in part instruction for the reader: they demonstrate how to tell the soberly dressed middle-class employer and his soberly dressed clerk apart, how to distinguish the gentleman from the cheap imitation. As the strutting Gent modulates into the pretentious clerk, the emphasis on physical appearance remains dominant, and what ultimately develops is a semiotics of dress, a set of indicators that mark the lower-middle-class man as inferior – frayed collars and cuffs, shiny pants, shabby boots, a tattered umbrella, and any signs of careful mending or patching.[36] Once he has been identified, the conventions of representation define his personal and social limitations. His intellectual inadequacy is exemplified by his stilted speech, as the comically inflated diction often used to describe Gents is transformed into the ludicrously inflated diction of the clerk or shop assistant trying to impress his 'superiors'.[37] The suggestion of effeminacy in the descriptions of the Gent's preening and posing also colors the representation of lower-middle-class man, but while the Gent's boldness tends to counterbalance this aspect of his characterization, the unassertiveness of the clerk, for all his supposed pretensions, tends to reinforce his lack of manliness. Moreover, while the Gent seems to exist only in public venues, lower-middle-class man is represented as an essentially domestic creature; he always ends up seeking refuge at home after his public humiliations.

The greatest sin of the Gent, as outlined by Smith in his attack on the type, is his attempt to imitate middle-class style and manners, which constitutes an assault on the cherished bourgeois cultural symbol of the gentleman. The Gent, Smith laments, 'copies the gentleman, but sees, as usual, every thing through a wrong medium. In fact, his reflection is that of a spoon, in more senses than one: making the most outrageous images of the original, distorting all the features, but still preserving a strange sort of identity.' (pp. 75–6) It is perhaps this lingering identity that most alarms those who wish to preserve the exclusivity of the gentlemanly ideal, and which prompts Smith to characterize the Gent as the 'species of the human race . . . of all others the most unbearable, principally from an assumption of style about him – a futile aping of superiority that inspires us with feelings of mingled contempt and amusement, when we contemplate his ridiculous pretensions to be considered "the thing".' (pp. 1–2). This aping is most readily apparent in the Gent's dress, many aspects of which become distinguishing features of the lower-middle-class figure. The flashiness is quintessentially an attribute of the Gent, but the obvious cheapness of the clothes, the obsessive attention to dress, and the ubiquitousness of the stick or the cheap umbrella become associated with clerks and shop assistants. It is, indeed, this talisman of class – the umbrella – that the lower-middle-class clerk, Leonard Bast, loses and must retrieve from the middle-class Schlegels more than sixty years later in E. M. Forster's *Howards End*. The diminutiveness that becomes a supposedly natural attribute of the office worker or shop assistant also figures prominently in *The Natural History of the Gent*; the stick becomes a 'little stick', and Gents sport 'Lilliputian boots' and 'tiny gloves.' (pp. 6, 13–14) The littleness of the gloves demonstrates the deliberate strategy of minimizing lower-middle-class figures in this type of representation: in the original sketch in *Bentley's*, the emphasis is on the cheapness of the gloves, which are accordingly not small, but 'large-sized' and 'awkwardly cut'.[38] The lower-middle-class white collar worker inherits from the Gent, along with a rusty version of his wardrobe, the sin of social pretentiousness. In the eyes of middle-class Victorian commentators, clerks and shop assistants are, in their own inept way, also guilty of trying to imitate the style and manners of their social superiors.

Interestingly, Smith characterizes the 'race' of Gents as 'an offensive body, of more importance than you would at first conceive' (p. viii), and while his essentially comic approach would seem to favor an ironic reading of this apparent overstatement, there is a hostile edge to his treatment of the Gent, as there is in virtually all the literary representations of the lower middle class, that suggests that Smith, like his contemporaries, was alarmed by the masses of people accumulating on the fringes of the middle class. This animosity, given the apparent inadequacies of Gents and clerks, seems hard to fathom. Smith's own anxiety, however, is not difficult to explain. He had been a poor medical student – one of the marginal 'types' most mercilessly lampooned in *Punch*. As Ellen Moers points out, he 'must surely have been something of a Gent himself.' Moreover, the other staff members at *Punch* considered him 'low' and according to R. G. G. Price, 'they did not feel inclined to put up with the vulgarity and bumptiousness of Albert Smith.'[39] Smith's hostility appears to be an attempt to distance himself from his roots and to define himself against the Gent by attacking him.

The situation of the middle class as a whole could be seen as analogous to Smith's. At mid-century, the bourgeoisie was still the upwardly mobile upstart of the class system. Members of the bourgeoisie had successfully defined themselves against the aristocracy, to their own advantage, as morally superior and industrious. When the parvenu appears, bourgeois identity is threatened because of the overall similarity of the two classes, a problem that is exacerbated by the rapid growth of the lower middle class. By adopting a strategy similar to Smith's, by disparaging and literally belittling the lower middle class, members of the Victorian middle class could define themselves against it and at the same time aggrandize themselves.

VIRTUE DOMESTICATED: DICKENS AND THE LOWER MIDDLE CLASS

The first great novelist to focus substantially on life in the lower middle class was Charles Dickens. He was also an active agent in the development of the conventions for representing the class, being both a contributor to periodical publications in the 1830s and the first editor of *Bentley's Miscellany*. Dickens's first portrayals of clerks and Gents in *Sketches by Boz*, written when he was in his early twenties, are relatively tame, and lack some of the distinguishing characteristics of the types and the point and flair of Dickensian style that are evident in his later works. In 'Thoughts About People', the dress and the antics of London apprentices clearly mark them as Gents, but also as mildly amusing and innocuous: '[W]ere there ever such harmless efforts at the grand and magnificent as the young fellows display!'[40] (The mature Dickens, by contrast, declared in *Household Words* in 1853 that he considered 'a mere gent' to be 'the lowest form of civilisation'.[41]) In the same sketch, Dickens describes an impecunious middle-aged clerk in terms of barely restrained pathos, rather than humor: 'Poor, harmless creatures such men are; contented but not happy; broken-spirited and humbled, they may feel no pain, but they never know pleasure.' (p. 217) The archetypal man of diminished means in 'Shabby-Genteel People', with his 'depressed face, and timorous air of conscious poverty' is even more pitiful and not very engaging. Nevertheless, Dickens uses him to make a satirical jab at established élites, a move that anticipates his mature style. This pathetic figure, Boz comments, 'will make your heart ache – always supposing that you are neither a philosopher nor a political economist.' (p. 263) Dickens's satire is more effective, however, in 'Horatio Sparkins', where it is combined with his already impressive comic powers. Sparkins – alias Samuel Smith, shop assistant – temporarily succeeds in passing himself off as a young man of means and social distinction. Whatever humiliations he might suffer when the ruse is discovered are glossed over, however, in favor of contemplating the mortifications of the pretentious Maldertons, a family of vulgar and snobbish social-climbers who have cultivated Sparkins's friendship on the assumption that he might be an aristocrat.

The young Dickens is obviously alert to the developing stereotypes, and begins to incorporate into his lower-middle-class characters some of the conventional attributes assigned to such figures by other writers. He exploits the theme of diminutiveness with peculiarly Dickensian excess, for example, in the portrayal of the parish clerk Pipkin in one of the interpolated tales in *The Pickwick Papers* (1836–7). Pipkin is a 'little man' who lives in a 'little house' in the 'little high street' close to the 'little church' in the 'little town' where he teaches 'a little learning to the little boys'.[42] The focus on dress, which is more descriptive than judgmental in *Boz*, has become the conventional means of implicit ridicule in 'Mr. Robert Bolton'. (*Bentley's* 1838) The shabby-genteel man's yellowing linen and tattered garments identify him as pitiable because of his situation, but they do not define his character. Similarly, the humorously incongruous get-ups of the 'prentices in 'Thoughts About People' is something Boz finds harmless, 'a little occasional foolery' that elicits a smile. (p. 219)

Bolton's pretentiousness, by contrast, is implicit in the inflated diction the narrator uses to describe him and his dress. Bolton wears not simply clothes, but 'habiliments', consisting of ink and mud besmattered trousers and a 'high black cravat, of the most tyrannical stiffness', while 'the mysteries of his interior dress' remain '[s]acred to the bare walls of his garret'.[43] The narrator's comically grandiloquent description suggests not only the disparity between Bolton's version of style and the genuine thing, but also Bolton's self-importance. Bolton is simultaneously exposed, judged, and condemned by means of the inflated rhetoric that deflates his ludicrous pomposity.

Dickens rapidly gains mastery over the conventions, and becomes a virtuoso in the representation of the lower middle class, for a number of reasons. The most obvious is that the essentially comic conventions used to portray lower-middle-class characters are particularly well suited to Dickens's style. But Dickens also had an indefinable affinity for the ethos of the class, which is confirmed by his contemporaries. In his critical biography of Dickens, George Gissing, himself a member of the lower middle class, observes that '[t]o the lower middle class, a social status so peculiarly English, so rich in virtues yet so provocative of satire, he by origin belonged; in its atmosphere he always breathed most freely, and had the largest command of his humorous resources.'[44] While Dickens was anxious to distance himself from his humble beginnings, his ability to create memorable lower-middle-class characters did likely owe something to his youthful experience as a member of that class. His father was a clerk in the Navy Pay Office who, Micawber-like, was incapable of living within his income, and was briefly incarcerated in the Marshalsea prison for debt. The sense of shame and degradation that young Charles felt when he was subsequently forced to leave school and work in a blacking factory is well known, as is his early white-collar experience in journalism. Whatever adverse effects his early life had on Dickens, it also provided him with an intimate knowledge of the lower middle class. Dickens was also the standard by which other authors' portrayals of the class were measured; in praising what he felt was H. G. Wells's outstanding accomplishment in the realistic representation of the lower middle class, Henry James compares Wells's achievement favorably to that of Dickens.[45]

Dickens's portrayals of the class in his novels and stories draw on the existing comic stereotypes, but also incorporate significant alterations. Like Albert Smith and other satirists, Dickens depicts lower-middle-class figures as humorous, but rather than presenting them as the objects of scorn or ridicule, as the butts of jokes, he presents them as inherently comical, and he treats them with affection. Mr Wilfer in *Our Mutual Friend* (1864–5), for example, has as 'the modest object of his ambition' a goal which might seem worthy of one of Smith's Gents: 'to wear a complete new suit of clothes, hats and boots included, at one time.' But Mr Wilfer is portrayed as mildly quixotic, in a material way, rather than as vain or pretentious; he is indeed so retiring that he is 'unwilling to own to the name of Reginald', which he finds 'too aspiring and self-assertive'.[46] Mr Wilfer is thus not an exemplar of degraded style, but a comic illustration of the marginality of the lower-middle-class figure living in obscurity on the edge of poverty and respectability. The conventional flamboyance of the flashy Gent is modulated by Dickens into the comic excesses of caricature in characters like Wemmick, with his portable property and miniature castle, or Mr Bagnet, whose attempts to maintain a military bearing fail to mask his essential domesticity – his soft heart and his complete submission to the benevolent rule of 'the old girl', his wife. Dickens's treatment of unappealing lower-middle-class characters is likewise governed by the conventions of humor or of controlled exaggeration. Accordingly, the Smallweeds' home is a parody of lower-middle-class domesticity, and Uriah Heep is an excessively unctuous and sinister version of the insinuating clerk.

Dickens thus develops and expands the conventions for representing the lower middle class, especially in the rich diversity of characters that he portrays as inhabiting it. But the kind of ambivalence to his origins that Gissing betrays in characterizing the lower middle class as 'rich in virtues' but 'provocative of satire' is everywhere apparent in Dickens's work, in his conflation of affectionate parodies and sympathetic condescension. For all their comic or villainous excess, these figures remain smaller-than-life; they retain a characteristic diminutiveness that signifies their social insignificance and marginality. Thus for all the sympathy inherent in the often affectionate humor of his treatment of the lower middle class, Dickens also belittles them, as surely as the journalists belittle them through condescension. He consigns these characters to the margins of their fictional worlds, as surely as real-life members of the lower middle class were consigned to the margins of Victorian society. While Dickens betrays his ambivalence to his lower-middle-class roots in his fiction, he appears to have been scarcely more comfortable with the middle-class world into which he had risen, and as he grew older, he became increasingly disillusioned with bourgeois society. As Edmund Wilson observes, Dickens developed a 'mounting dislike and distrust of the top layers of that middle-class society with which he had begun by identifying himself'; as a result, Dickens's 'ideal of middle-class virtue was driven down to the lower layers.'[47] Dickens's later fiction registers this disillusionment in its increasingly critical assessments of bourgeois society and its values – in the probing of the concept of the gentleman in *Great Expectations*, and in the sounding of the hollow tones of the 'voices of society' in the Veneerings' dining room in *Our Mutual Friend*. It is in *Little Dorrit*, however, that Dickens attacks the class system and bourgeois values most directly and comprehensively. Peter Ackroyd calls *Little Dorrit* Dickens's 'single most ferocious onslaught against England and English society'; Bernard Shaw describes it as 'a more seditious book than *Das Kapital*'. Roger Lund observes that '[i]n no other Dickens novel is the Victorian preoccupation with respectability and social position made to seem so odious, so dangerous, or so grotesquely ridiculous.'[48] And in no other Dickens novel is class identity more problematic. The evils of Victorian bourgeois commercialism make the middle class an unappealing habitat for Arthur Clennam, who can subsist in that world only with great difficulty and uneasiness. Other characters, too, are misfits in their social class. Fanny Dorrit, for example, feels out of place in the lowly station of daughter of an imprisoned debtor, but admirably suited to the superficiality of fashionable society. Dickens thus constantly undermines assumptions about social position and class boundaries in *Little Dorrit*.

To feel the full force of his social critique, however, it is essential to factor in Dickens's treatment of the lower middle class and lower-middle-class characters as constituents of class politics. Lower-middle-class characters in *Little Dorrit* are, as Pam Morris argues for working-class figures in Dickens's fiction in general, part of a dialogic structure that produces 'complex internal polemics'.[49] It is in a dialogism of conflicting class identities –

specifically in the manipulation of middle-class and lower-middle-class identities, and in the consequent destabilizing of class stereotypes – that Dickens is most daring in *Little Dorrit*. He uses the means of social control – the disparaging conventions for representing the lower middle class – against the class that developed them, and uses them more directly and with more devastating effects than he had done before or would do in subsequent novels.

The lower-middle-class figures in *Little Dorrit* initially seem to fit the established class stereotypes, two seemingly classic examples being John Chivery and Mr Pancks. As the son of the Marshalsea turnkey and assistant to his mother in the family tobacco shop, Young John is very much a marginal figure. His person is suitably diminutive, and while apparently inoffensive, he provokes the narrator's satire:

> Young John was small of stature, with rather weak legs and very weak light hair. One of his eyes (perhaps the eye that used to peep through the keyhole) was also weak, and looked larger than the other, as if it couldn't collect itself. Young John was gentle likewise. But he was great of soul. Poetical, expansive, faithful.[50]

Despite his unprepossessing physical appearance, Young John tries to cut an elegant figure when he sets out to propose to Little Dorrit. He dons a costume of such exaggerated magnificence that the flashiest of Gents would pale beside him – plum-colored coat, embroidered vest and neckerchief, striped pants, and 'a cane like a little finger-post' (pp. 180–1) – and addresses Little Dorrit with a fulsome imitation of genteel discourse:

> Miss Amy, I know very well that your family is far above mine. It were vain to conceal it. There never was a Chivery a gentleman that ever I heard of, and I will not commit the meanness of making a false representation on a subject so momentous. Miss Amy, I know very well that your high-souled brother, and likewise your spirited sister, spurn me from a heighth. What I have to do is to respect them, to wish to be admitted to their friendship, to look up at the eminence on which they are placed, from my lowlier station – for, whether viewed as tobacco or viewed as the lock, I well know it is lowly – and ever wish them well and happy. (p. 183)

The characterization of John Chivery thus begins as the quintessential affectionate parody; he is one of the lovable but absurd inhabitants of the lowliest levels of the lower middle class.

Mr Pancks first appears as a less likable character than Young John. As Mr Casby's clerk, Pancks is better educated and socially more adroit and mobile than John Chivery. His manners may not be the best, but he dines with his middle-class employer and discusses business affairs with some intelligence, if without Young John's 'greatness of soul'. His intimacy with the Casby family and the rigor with which he 'squeezes' the rent from the tenants of Bleeding Heart Yard suggest that Pancks is another Uriah Heep, a representation of the meanness of the cramped lower-middle-class spirit. But Pancks's assiduity in the collection of rents is not a function of his own ruthlessness; it is a function of his complete subservience to his employer. 'I belong body and soul to my proprietor', he tells Little Dorrit. (p. 240) This complete submission of will and eradication of personal scruples in the execution of duties constitute the great flaw in Pancks's character, but it is precisely what middle-class employers expected of their lower-middle-class employees. As a result, what appears to be the petty vice of a lower-middle-class character is in fact a displacement of the larger vice of his bourgeois employer; Casby's pose as benevolent patriarch masks his blatant exploitation of power and influence.

Pancks's public exposure of this charade reveals the perverse distortions of class stereotypes. While the class identities of Pancks and Casby remain fixed, conventional class attributes are transposed from one to the other. Casby is identified with shabbiness – not the shabbiness of mere dress, but of morals; he is, Pancks reveals, 'the shabbiest of all the lots'. Moreover, in figuratively cutting Casby down to size – diminishing him – by exposing his spiritual meanness and then literally trimming his 'sacred locks', Pancks transforms him from a figure that inspires veneration into one that inspires ridicule. The white-haired patriarch metamorphoses into a 'bare-polled, goggle-eyed, big-headed, lumbering personage . . . not in the least impressive, not in the least venerable', who ignites 'the sound of laughter in Bleeding Heart Yard'. (pp. 668, 669–70) Pancks, meanwhile, emerges as the voice of truth and justice – traditional preserves of the middle class.

The reedy figure of John Chivery, too, stands up to challenge class stereotypes, but with Young John the issue at stake is not the benevolence of the bourgeois patriarchy, but the notion of honor and the status of the gentleman. In the closing chapters of the novel, John's unrequited love for Little Dorrit, no longer the subject of comedy, proves to be not only enduring, but selfless and honorable. He alone is able to discern the secret of her heart, that she is in love with Clennam, and when Clennam is imprisoned in the Marshalsea, John demonstrates his magnanimity by revealing this secret to his rival. Moreover, he is faithful in his promise to Little Dorrit never to forsake Clennam in his need; with the forthrightness supposedly characteristic of all classes of Englishmen but his own, John offers Clennam his loyalty and passes on Little Dorrit's message of undying love. After executing his painful mission with feeling and dignity, John deferentially asks Clennam for the bourgeois seal-of-approval on his conduct: 'Have I been honorable, sir?' (p. 636).

While honor can thus survive on the margins of society in *Little Dorrit*, in the murky atmosphere of the Marshalsea, the conversation between Blandois and Mrs Clennam that immediately follows this scene in the prison reveals the extent to which the concepts of honor and gentlemanliness have been corrupted at the core of bourgeois society. With none of John's agonized forthrightness, Blandois and Mrs Clennam engage in a circumlocutory discussion of her past treacheries and his present intent to blackmail her, while nevertheless affirming the honor of the Clennam house and of Blandois's word. Blandois smugly assures himself that he has 'lived a gentleman' and 'will die a gentleman.' (p. 656)

Within the ethos of commercialism and greed that the novel depicts as dominating society, Blandois's cynical confidence in his gentlemanly status within that society is not misplaced. But Blandois's chilling self-affirmation is immediately followed in the text by the appearance of a quietly dignified figure that displaces the false image of the gentleman with a true one. As Mrs Clennam rushes from her home and from Blandois in search of the Marshalsea and Little Dorrit, a young man rescues her from a jeering rabble that has deemed her mad:

> A short, mild, quiet-looking young man, made his way through to her, as a whooping ensued [from the crowd] . . . and said: 'Was it the Marshalsea you wanted? I'm going on duty there. Come across with me.'
> She laid her hand upon his arm, and he took her over the

way; the crowd, rather injured by the near prospect of losing her, pressing before and behind and on either side, and recommending an adjournment to Bedlam. After a momentary whirl in the outer courtyard, the prison-door opened, and shut upon them. In the Lodge, which seemed by contrast with the outer noise a place of refuge and peace, a yellow lamp was already striving with the prison shadows.

'Why, John!' said the turnkey who had admitted them. 'What is it?'

'Nothing, father; only this lady not knowing her way, and being badgered by the boys. Who did you want, ma'am?' (p. 657)

The quiet-looking young man is, of course, John Chivery, stripped of the comic flourishes of caricature. John is still small, but he no longer provokes satiric comment about his weak legs and weak light hair, or about his pretensions to greatness of soul. He has, after all, proved his greatness of soul, and everything about his conduct in this passage suggests the bearing of a gentleman – his quiet demeanor, his consideration for a stranger in distress, his composure in maneuvering through the unruly crowd, his courteous but dignified treatment of his flustered charge, and his controlled and uninflated diction. In the society in which he lives, John's class position may preclude the general acknowledgment of his true merit, but the readers of *Little Dorrit* must recognize that John's own earlier observation that 'there never was a Chivery a gentleman that ever ... [he] heard of' should now be revised.

The only locus of apparently unsullied middle-class virtue in *Little Dorrit* would appear to be the home of the Meagleses. But here again, Dickens blurs class boundaries and class identities. The Meagleses clearly enjoy a middle-class income, but for the most part they appear to live below their income and they espouse lower-middle-class values. Their home is a haven of the temperate, insular – even dull – but comfortable domesticity of the lower middle class; their standard of entertainment is not the grand dinner party of the Merdles, but a quiet evening with two or three friends. Their traveling is prompted by concerns for Pet – for her health before her marriage and for her happiness after – rather than by any interest in the grand tour for its own sake. Mr Meagles is not above petty snobbery, but he and his wife are not comfortable with Pet's choice of a vain and selfish husband, despite his social connections. The Meagleses genuinely desire their daughter to be happy, rather than socially prominent or successful. For all his financial success, Mr Meagles remains essentially unpretentious, good-hearted, and a little vulgar. Even his misguided but well-intentioned bungling of the family's relationship with Tattycoram betrays a quintessentially lower-middle-class inability to relate to domestic help, to adopt an appropriate and workable balance between familiarity and formality. Mr Meagles accordingly has more in common with Mr Pooter than with Mr Merdle, and Dickens treats him with the conventional affectionate parody he usually reserves for lower-middle-class characterization.

It is no accident, therefore, that Clennam, so uncomfortable in his middle-class milieu, should be drawn to the Meagleses, even after his disappointment in his love for Pet. Dickens's characterization of Clennam, however, conforms to the conventional representation of a middle-class figure. There is no hint of parody or caricature; Clennam is portrayed as intelligent, well-spoken, humane, serious, and introspective. Nevertheless, there are subtle dissociations of Clennam from his class. His heritage, we eventually learn, is as ambiguous as his class identity is ambivalent. He is illegitimate, the offspring of passion rather than of propriety; and while his father was middle-class, his mother is impossible to place. She was an orphan and worked as a singer – a profession of questionable respectability – under the sponsorship of Little Dorrit's uncle. Clennam remains unaware of his own dubious origins, but he is curiously lacking in the self-assurance usually associated with middle-class males; he is as colorless and ineffectual as the dustiest of bank clerks. In social relations, he is frequently awkward or uncomfortable, and he is a perennial failure in both love and business – fit, he eventually comes to believe, only for a subservient, lower-middle-class position. As he insists to his solicitor, Mr Rugg, when the financial ruin of his firm is imminent, Clennam intends to have his own share in the business revert to his partner, Doyce, while 'he himself, at as small a salary as he could live upon, would ask to be allowed to serve the business as a faithful clerk.' (p. 598) As the text of *Little Dorrit* endlessly reiterates, in bourgeois society and business, Arthur Clennam is a 'nobody', just as Mr Pooter will be after him.

* * *

Dickens's savage critique of middle-class society is thus dramatized through the generalized class confusion that characterizes the social world of his novel. But this overt attack on the bourgeoisie incorporates an implicit and subtle validation of the lower-middle-class ethos, at the heart of which is Little Dorrit. She is untainted by any explicit class identification, a conjuring trick made possible in part by the context of slippery class distinctions and misleading class stereotypes within the novel, but also by her sex. A lower-middle-class male character would have to conform to the conventional patterns of representation in order to be recognized and accepted as inhabiting his class. But in the mid-nineteenth century, conventions for representing lower-middle-class women were not well established, mainly because such characters were seldom represented at all. Lampoons in the periodical literature were directed at the visible part of the class – at the men whose work brought them to the city to hover around the fringes of the commercial world, not at their wives and daughters who stayed at home. Because they were less visible in the public sphere, lower-middle-class women were less likely to be perceived as destabilizing entities within class politics. Dickens goes so far as to claim, in 'Shabby-Genteel People', that women cannot be placed in the equivocal category defined by the sketch's title. '[A] woman', Boz maintains, 'is always either dirty and slovenly in the extreme, or neat and respectable, however poverty-stricken in appearance' (262), a claim that verges on placing women outside class designations altogether. Moreover, the strategy of feminization used to disempower lower-middle-class men would be meaninglessly redundant in the construction of female characters. In the mid-Victorian period, lower-middle-class women typically appear only as the wives of their husbands, tied to the domestic hearth, cooking Christmas dinner like Mrs Cratchit, or washing greens like Mrs Bagnet.

 In his creation of Little Dorrit, Dickens exploits the tangled class and gender associations that had become part of the representation of the lower middle class. In so doing, he is able to finesse the issues of class perception and class biases, and succeeds in constructing a character who resists categorical class placement. The domestic role, whatever its class variations, is gender-specific, rather than class-specific – bourgeois feminization of the lower middle class notwithstanding. And the domestic role is the one that Little Dorrit most assuredly fulfils. She is indeed the quintessential domestic woman, the Victorian 'angel in the house', no matter what sort of dwelling she may inhabit. Domestic comfort and security abide with her wherever she may be, whether in the Marshalsea, the cold night streets of London, the fashionable hotels of Italy, or the secluded corners of the Clennam and Casby homes where she sits sewing. But Little Dorrit is never really a part of the worlds or fragments of worlds through which she moves, nor is she a part of any of the classes associated with them. She is clearly too virtuous to belong in a prison, too honest and artless to be a success in society, too intelligent and refined to be a simple seamstress. She inhabits instead a singularity, an aristocracy of virtue that transcends the bondage of class or of iron bars, a rank of which she is the sole member.

In this symbolically exalted position of combined privilege and humility, the values that Little Dorrit embodies become unassailable. And while it would be too much to say that the aristocracy of virtue that I claim as Little Dorrit's natural habitat is really the lower middle class in disguise, there are nevertheless important ways in which Little Dorrit is identified with the lower middle class. It is also true, of course, that she is endowed with a number of typically middle-class characteristics. She is both intelligent and capable, and even more significantly, her speech is articulate and her manners refined; while she is excessively shy, she has none of the awkwardness of John Chivery, nor the pretentious pomposity of her father. But if her bearing thus marks her as a meek but refined *bourgeoise*, her diminutiveness makes of her a decidedly *petite bourgeoise*. She is so tiny and retiring that she seems more a child than a woman, as Arthur Clennam notes when he sees her in his mother's house:[51]

> Arthur found that her diminutive figure, small features, and slight spare dress, gave her the appearance of being much younger than she was. A woman, probably of not less than two and twenty, she might have passed in the street for little more than half that age. Not that her face was very youthful, for in truth there was more consideration and care in it than naturally belonged to her utmost years; but she was so little and light, so noiseless and shy, and appeared so conscious of being out of place among the three hard elders, that she had all the manner and much of the appearance of a subdued child. (pp. 44–5)

Little Dorrit's dress also features the distinguishing mark of lower-middle-class attire – genteel shabbiness. '[I]t must needs have been very shabby to look at all so', the narrator comments, 'being so neat.' (p. 45) For all her remarkable dignity in the unenviable position into which she was born, Little Dorrit remains an inconspicuous figure, and her childlike bearing suggests an undeveloped sexuality similar to the virtual asexuality of lower-middle-class male figures. She is, indeed, so insignificant that she is initially invisible in the text. We learn of her being in the room with Arthur and Mrs Clennam only after the fact, when Arthur responds to her presence as an afterthought. When he questions Affery about her, he seems not even to be sure that she was there at all. 'It was a girl, surely, whom I saw near you – almost hidden in the dark corner?' he tentatively suggests. 'Oh! She? Little Dorrit?' responds Affery, apparently astonished that Arthur has noticed her, '*She's* nothing.' (p. 33)

If Little Dorrit is nothing, it is partly because she belongs nowhere. As the 'child of the Marshalsea', born inside its walls, a space beyond the pale of bourgeois society, she has no real home and no clear class position in the world outside the prison. Her heritage, too, is problematic. Her father's position before entering prison is not clearly defined; we know, however, that his 'affairs . . . were perplexed by a partnership, of which he knew no more than that he had invested money in it.' (p. 50) From Mrs Clennam's confession, we also learn that his brother, Frederick, in the days when the Dorrits were prosperous, was sufficiently wealthy to entertain and even sponsor aspiring singers and other performers. (p. 650) Apparently, the Dorrits were middle-class in origin, and indeed the lower middle class would not have existed as such at the time of Mr Dorrit's arrest (circa 1825). But Rugg's advice to Clennam, when he is about to be arrested for debt, indicates that the Marshalsea was the prison for petty debtors. Rugg counsels Arthur not to allow himself to be taken at the instigation of one of his smaller creditors, on some 'insignificant matter', but 'to keep up appearances' by being 'taken on a full-grown one'. (p. 599) 'If you should be taken on the little one, sir', he warns, 'you would go to the Marshalsea.' (p. 600)[52] Thus as an inmate of the Marshalsea, Mr Dorrit cannot even maintain the questionable dignity of being a significant debtor, and if he is able to affect a superior air in prison, it is only because his associates – a plasterer, a dancing instructor, and a seamstress, to mention a few – are of a very inferior social class indeed. Mr Dorrit, like the conventional lower-middle-class figure in Victorian literature, is only a poor and distorted reflection of a bourgeois gentleman, maintaining a ludicrous pretense of status in his cramped and squalid milieu.

Mr Dorrit accordingly represents what the middle class views as the deplorable, if venial, sins of the lower middle class. He is ineffectual, shabby, and pretentious. As he condescends to the 'Collegians', accepting the 'tributes' he feels are his due, he is like an inferior version of Mr Casby standing in Bleeding Heart Yard surrounded by his 'suitors', the paupers off whom he lives. It is only Little Dorrit who recognizes the degradation inherent in confusing alms with homage, in interpreting the exploitation of others as a right, when she implores Clennam not to respond to the subtle solicitations of her father. Through the characterization of Mr Dorrit, whose perverted values allow him to fit smoothly into bourgeois society when he leaves the Marshalsea, Dickens suggests that in formulating the conventional image of the lower middle class, the Victorian bourgeoisie is simply projecting its own faults onto those below them on the social scale. Mr Dorrit's pretentiousness, his assumption of moral and social superiority over his fellow prison inmates, parallels the bourgeoisie's perception of itself within the Victorian class hierarchy. The bourgeoisie is in fact as pretentious and absurd as it would claim the lower middle class is; the absurdity, Dickens suggests, is inherent not in class position, but in the baseless assumption of superiority.

Little Dorrit, on the other hand, embodies the lower middle class's largely unsung virtues. She is unassuming and compassionate as she quietly fulfils her domestic and nurturing roles, acting as a dutiful daughter and patient sister to an undeserving family, and as surrogate mother to ungainly and pathetic Maggie. Even unassertiveness, a characteristic traditionally scorned as a feature of lower-middle-class weakness and subservience, emerges in the diminutive Little Dorrit as a form of gentle strength. By contrast, the unassertiveness of Clennam seems forgivable but unfortunate, while the apparent forcefulness of Pancks emerges as a manifestation of his weakness. But Little Dorrit's gentleness and virtue make her unfit for bourgeois society, unfit for its pretentiousness and hypocrisy. Accordingly, the text of *Little Dorrit* challenges the smug assumptions of the Victorian bourgeoisie by subverting its version of the relationship between class and character. *Little Dorrit* questions the validity of the bourgeoisie's cherished notions of the collective moral and intellectual superiority of its members. Moreover, the conventional image of the lower middle class is exposed as unjust. It is an image imposed from without, based on an exterior view which the middle class interprets as a poor reflection of itself. In this reflection, the middle class sees not the reality of the lower middle class, but its own warts – it is a reflection in which the middle class sees Mr Dorrit. But it is Amy Dorrit who embodies the domestic heart of the lower middle class, who represents its unsung soul and inner life.

In *Little Dorrit*, it is at the interstices of class, and most significantly of the middle and lower middle classes, that Dickens most effectively dramatizes the hypocrisy and smugness of the Victorian bourgeoisie and the commonplace but not insignificant virtues of the unremarkable – and largely unremarked – people living on the margins of bourgeois society. As traditional class attributes cross class boundaries, and the vices and virtues of one class become the virtues and vices of the other, Dickens not only exposes the corruption of bourgeois commercialism, but also calls into question the assumptions that dictate Victorian class discrimination and snobbery. Accordingly, at the conclusion of the novel, while Clennam is reinstated as Doyce's partner and so is restored to his position in the middle class, his future with Little Dorrit is destined to be shaped not by the stilted and hollow notions of middle-class respectability, but by the underrated values that she and the lower middle class represent: they will enter 'a modest life of usefulness and happiness'. (p. 688)

Little Dorrit thus ends on a muted note and in a minor key, which is perhaps inevitable in a nineteenth-century social critique that endorses – it cannot be said to extol – lower-middle-class values. The novel is ultimately more vociferous in its condemnation of corruption than it is in its validation of quiet virtues. Moreover, in his representation of lower-middle-class virtue, Dickens has been forced to compromise. To the Victorian reader, the essentially domestic lower-middle-class virtues that Dickens exalts would not have seemed particularly commendable in the conventional lower-middle-class character, who would have been male. Furthermore, such virtues would have seemed unremarkable and not especially laudable in their natural setting of a suburban home. For these virtues to seem appropriate to the character representing them, Dickens had to embody them in a woman; for these virtues to seem noteworthy, Dickens had to embody them in a figure who is dissociated from the standard conventions for representing the lower middle class and who is physically dislocated from the quiet and humble hearth. The icon of lower-middle-class virtue, accordingly, is a woman who is never seen in her natural setting but is placed first in a prison and then in fashionable society, for it is only in such foreign and jarring backgrounds that her diminutive figure can stand out in high relief. Her descent into the noisy street at the end of the novel is also her descent into the anonymity of the modest life that lies before her. In that setting, it is doubtful that Lionel Trilling would have canonized her as the 'Paraclete in female form'.[53]

The problems that Dickens was unable to overcome in *Little Dorrit* – that is, the problems inherent in any attempt to develop a serious representation of a commanding lower-middle-class male – also influence Elizabeth Gaskell's characterization of John Thornton in *North and South*. Gaskell, like Dickens, plays with the conventions of class representation to alter the readers' and the characters' response to Thornton. Gaskell does not present Thornton anonymously, as Dickens does with John Chivery, to undermine class biases and change the perception of a lower-middle-class figure. Rather, she suggests Thornton's personal unsuitability for the social position to which he has risen as a middle-class manufacturer through the other characters' inability to 'read' him and place him in his class. When asked to characterize Thornton, Margaret Hale has difficulty responding. 'I hardly know what he is like', she says. She finds 'nothing remarkable' about him, and socially damns him by observing that he is 'not quite a gentleman'.[54] Thornton, who began his working career as a draper's assistant, may not have that most typical lower-middle-class attribute – diminutive stature – but neither is he a commanding figure; he is nondescript and unprepossessing. Margaret's brother Frederick, too, does not recognize Thornton as middle-class when he sees him, and tells Margaret that he 'took him for a shopman, and he turns out to be a manufacturer.' (p. 257)

During the course of the novel, however, Thornton's bearing – or the characters' and narrator's perceptions of it – changes.

As his good qualities, his honesty and perseverance, come to be known and understood, and as his stern and uncompromising approach to his workmen is tempered by Margaret's softening influence, he emerges as a true captain of industry. His size and bearing, which have made him seem awkward in the past, now contribute to a dignified and noble carriage that somehow seems innate and natural. At the end of the novel, Margaret watches as Thornton enters the room, seeing in him a man who bears no resemblance to the unremarkable man she met a year before, although Thornton has by this time gone bankrupt:

> His fine figure yet bore him above the common height of men; and gave him a distinguished appearance, from the ease of motion which arose out of it, and was natural to him; but his face looked older and care-worn; yet a noble composure sate upon it, which impressed those who had just been hearing of his changed position, with a sense of inherent dignity and manly strength. (p. 429)

Having been tried and proven true, Thornton is finally recognizable as a middle-class gentleman, despite the loss of status that his financial setbacks would entail. His loss indeed adds to his aura of dignity, and his 'distinguished appearance' magically becomes 'natural', an apparently innate quality that can only now be discerned.

The magic of Thornton's transformation differs from that which allows John Halifax to acquire the attributes of a gentleman, despite his destitution and initial lack of social status, or which allows Little Dorrit to escape class categorization – the magic of symbolism and abstraction. John Halifax carries with him the symbolic validation of his innate gentility – his Greek testament – while Little Dorrit is given an idealized status outside conventional hierarchies. By contrast, Gaskell does not move outside realism in her attempt to alter Thornton's class designation. Thornton has neither the accent nor the grace of a 'gentleman', and his interest in learning classical languages seems quixotic; moreover, he cannot, like John Halifax, teach himself, but requires the help of Mr Hale. The criticism of the class system implicit in his transformation is accordingly potentially more radical than the similar criticism in *Little Dorrit*. In the alteration of the narrator's and the characters' responses to Thornton, Gaskell suggests that class placement in Victorian society is based less on inner qualities than on conventional readings and misreadings of purely external signs like dress, personal appearance, and accent. It is thus the response of the observers, the alteration of their reading of Thornton, that produces the magical transformation.

Dickens's manipulation of class stereotypes in *Little Dorrit* had no immediate effect either on contemporary perceptions of the lower middle class or on the literary conventions for representing it. The conventions which he himself had helped to develop were simply too powerful for him to overthrow. Similarly, Gaskell's characterization of Thornton, for all its subversive implications, does nothing to alter the conventions of representation, and consequently it does not ultimately alter the class stereotypes. The re-reading of Thornton at the end of *North and South* involves reinterpreting his various attributes according to the conventions for representing a middle-class character, rather than representing the lower middle class as having merit. Throughout the nineteenth-century, in fiction as in life, the lower middle class was doomed to remain a marginal group, only marginally middle-class and marginally respectable. Its centrality to Dickens's critique of Victorian society in *Little Dorrit* is nevertheless a powerful testament to the significance of the lower middle class within the power politics of nineteenth-century England. And while neither Gaskell's nor Dickens's reassessments of lower-middle-class stereotypes had an immediate and radical effect on either Victorian culture or literature, they did point the way for a new generation of writers, lower-middle-class novelists like H. G. Wells and Arnold Bennett, who would challenge the class stereotypes more directly.

3
Voices from the Margins: Dickens, Wells and Bennett

> To pay his way, to lie in bed an hour later on Sundays; an outing on Bank holidays, a fine fortnight in the summer – he asks no more. And because he asks for so little he generally fails to get it. The clerk's summer fortnight in the country is notoriously wet.
>
> Alice Dudeney, *The Wise Woods* (1905)

> It is a pathetic thing, this suburban life, when viewed through non-suburban eyes. Yet there is much happiness in the suburbs; and that is perhaps the most pathetic thing of all.
>
> A review of *The Wise Woods*, *Contemporary Review* 88 (1905):455

Perhaps the most famous lower-middle-class figure of the late Victorian period is Mr Pooter, who first appeared in *Punch* in the 1890s in a series of illustrated comic sketches by George and Weedon Grossmith. The sketches subsequently appeared in book form with the telling title of *The Diary of a Nobody* (1892). The Grossmiths' portrayal of an earnest and loyal but intellectually and socially limited clerk is very much in the tradition of Dickens's affectionate parodies of lower-middle-class figures. Mr Pooter is mocked by the junior clerks in his office, scorned by tradesmen and cab-drivers, and undermined by his charwoman, who uses pages from his diary, in which he professes to have invested 'much pride' and 'a great deal of pains', to light the fire.[1] Pooter's exaggerated sense of his own dignity and his oversensitivity to the indifference he never fails to inspire in others betray the kind of lower-middle-class pretentiousness deplored by bourgeois observers. But Pooter's petty pretensions are born of naïvety rather than of pomposity or social ambition. By the end of *The Diary of a Nobody*, Pooter has indeed reached what seems to be the pinnacle of his ambitions with his promotion to senior clerk, which he celebrates in typically Pooterish fashion with a bottle of grocers' champagne. He is completely satisfied with his modest life and endearingly blind to its limitations.

What makes Mr Pooter remarkable is the survival – even the expansion – of his popularity after the initial publication of the book. *The Diary of a Nobody* has been reprinted numerous times throughout the hundred years since its first appearance, and each new edition includes an introduction that lovingly details both Pooter's absurdity and his merit. The successful conjunction of these two qualities is indeed the basis of Pooter's special charm and, in the assessment of one of the introductions, of his creators' special genius. '[I]t is a particular triumph of the authors', John Squire attests, 'that, although they make him so superbly silly, they leave us with an admiration of his "sterling worth".'[2] This apparently sincere but nevertheless rather condescending affection for Pooter and the values he represents is coupled in the introductions with the extraordinary conviction that *The Diary of a Nobody*, while comic, is realism at its best. Squire claims that 'while we are laughing at the Pooters and their friends we are also fascinated by the verisimilitude, the stark, unannotated realism of the events of the dialogue'; the *Diary of a Nobody*, he maintains, is a 'transcript from life' that is 'destined to a perennial popularity amongst the discriminating.' (p. 18)

A generation later, another introduction makes even more extravagant claims for the realism of *The Diary of a Nobody*:

> Many besides Hilaire Belloc have valued it as 'one of the half-dozen immortal achievements of our time'. It is 'a slice of life', a social document, and no conscientiously realistic novel, however grim, has come nearer to presenting with absolute, literal truth the life which it sets out to portray. In particular the Nobody himself, the honest, obtuse, child-like Mr Pooter, who is Platitude personified, appears in his habit as he lived, completely self-revealed by his own unsparing chronicle of trivialities.[3]

Such claims are patently ridiculous, although it can be argued that much of the humor of *The Diary of a Nobody* is effected through touches of realism – through apparently inconsequential but carefully observed detail, such as Pooter's mentioning in his description of his 'nice little back garden' that it 'runs down to the railway.'

(p. 27) If the entire portrait of Pooter were to be accepted as 'absolute, literal truth', however, then we would have to believe that Victorian suburbs were populated by and Victorian bureaucracies run by harmless but ineffectual fools. What is realistic about *The Diary of a Nobody* is not the characterization of the Nobody but the attitudes toward him as an exemplar of his class that the characterization expresses. As the embodiment of the ethos of the lower middle class, Pooter appears not 'in his habit as he lived' but in the habit of entrenched attitudes and conventions of representation. He is comic not because, as Squire claims, the 'Grossmiths held the mirror up to nature, and there was a comic face in the glass' (p. 18), but because for the purposes of fictional representation the only mirrors held up to the lower middle class were ones from the fun house.

Mr Pooter is indeed 'one of the half-dozen immortal achievements' of the late Victorian period; he is the crowning achievement of bourgeois class propaganda, lower-middle-class man so reassuringly tamed – so laughable in his pretensions, so outmoded in his dress, so unsophisticated in his tastes, and so utterly domesticated in all things – that he and his entire class seem no more threatening than the family dog. Little wonder that the 'unsparing chronicle of trivialities' that constitutes his diary – and his life – continues to be popular with 'discriminating' readers who no doubt feel how distanced their sensibilities are from his. Not that the rest of us fail to smile affectionately – and condescendingly – at Mr Pooter's foibles, but we also tend to squirm when his humiliations sometimes seem so similar to our own and thus we, too, feel the pall of Victorian class discrimination. To blush for Mr Pooter on occasion, instead of laugh at him, is to come to some kind of dim realization of how powerfully the conventions of representation could influence self-perception. A moment of identification with Mr Pooter, however fleeting, is not empowering.

The tradition of the affectionate parody of lower-middle-class man that Pooter epitomizes is countered during the same period by the survival of the tradition from which the conventions that created Pooter had derived – the denigration of the clerk and the vilification of the Gent that had originated in comic sketches in the periodicals during the 1830s and 1840s. Nonfictional accounts in newspapers and in the periodical press intensify the disparagement of the lower middle class by moving the conventional portrayal of the pretentious would-be gentleman outside the realm of parody and humor. In a *Cornhill Magazine* article, James Fitzjames Stephen accordingly brands the clerk, and with him all his class, as inferior to the laborer because of his affectations of speech, one of the attributes of the Gent deplored by Albert Smith. While Smith's obvious and sometimes ill-natured exaggerations of these affectations are censorious, they are laughable; in Stephen's sober argument, they become the outward manifestation of inner moral weakness. In Stephen's assessment the laborer, because of his earthy but forthright manner of speech, is closer in character than the clerk to the true gentleman, since '[t]he great characteristic of the manners of a gentleman, as we conceive them in England, is plain, downright, frank simplicity. It is meant to be, and to a great extent it is, the outward and visible sign of the two great cognate virtues – truth and courage.' By implication, the clerk or shopkeeper who 'constantly tries to talk fine' condemns himself as false and pusillanimous.[4]

What is only suggested by Stephen – that the clerk and his type are morally deficient – becomes more explicit in many subsequent assessments of the lower middle class. In a series of letters in the Liverpool *Courier*, for example, a curmudgeon who signs himself Benjamin Battleaxe repeatedly attacks clerks for their obsessive concern with dress and status, for their 'absurd display' that betrays inappropriate '[a]mbition and vanity'. Battleaxe's bombastic rhetoric soon escalates the misdemeanor of dressing in a black coat and white shirt into a veritable crime. 'But *must* a clerk indulge in more display than an artisan?' Battleaxe feelingly implores. 'By what strange impulse is he driven to spend more than he makes? Why does not his honourable and manly pride consist in humility and honesty? There is more true grandeur in a saint afoot than in a swindler on horseback.'[5] An equally indignant anonymous observer complains that '[n]owadays your attorney's clerk – apparently struck by some "leveling-up" theory of democracy – is dissatisfied unless he can dress as well as the son of a duke'. The writer himself is committed to quite another theory than a democratic one and surmises that if such young men 'could be stripped of their sham finery ... and if they could be clad in rough blue homespun, and sent to serve a couple of years before the mast, they might be woke up to something like manhood. As they are, they are nothing but pitiful cheats, who have not even succeeded in deceiving themselves.'[6] These analyses of the clerk and his deficiencies clearly replay the same themes that dominated the comic denigrations of Gents and clerks a generation earlier. The clerk, according to observers circa 1870, is unmanly, obsessed with dress, and deluded about his social status. The imminent threat of democracy and the justification it might give to clerks to see themselves as in any way equal to their employers is no doubt what gives these particular commentaries their especially acrimonious edge. The writers seem anxious to establish that the true affinity of the clerk and the lower middle class should be with the classes below, with artisans and laborers, not with the classes above.

By the end of the century, writers were devoting entire volumes to satirical expositions on the moral and intellectual infirmities of the lower middle class. Walter Gallichan – a prolific author who was prepared to hold forth on a wide range of unrelated topics, from fishing in Scotland to women's sexuality – published just such a volume, entitled *The Blight of Respectability*, in 1897. As the title suggests, Gallichan focuses on that most salient component of the lower-middle-class ethos, respectability, which he analyzes through the analogy of a disease. To label a man as respectable, Gallichan claims, is 'to blast ... [his] reputation as a tolerable specimen of the human race'. The respectable man is 'a sort of factory-made cheap line in humanity, with a few prim, precise little superstitions, no reasoned morals, and no intellectual or aesthetic needs.'[7] The most vituperative of the satirical attacks on lower-middle-class life appears in T. W. H. Crosland's *The Suburbans*, a mock anthropological study in the spirit of Albert Smith's *The Natural History of the Gent*. Crosland characterizes suburbia as the locus of 'everything on earth that is ill-conditioned, undesirable, and unholy', and as 'devoid of graciousness to a degree which appals'. He assesses the suburban spirit as 'inhuman', shaped by 'avarice and rapacity and cupidity'. Even the major, if often qualified, attractions of lower-middle-class life – the comforts of hearth and home – are interpreted negatively by Crosland. He describes the suburban husband as 'a hen-pecked, shrew-driven, neglected, heart-sick man' and lower-middle-class domesticity as a form of cold war: 'The married life of the suburb may appear to be tranquil and peaceful and undisturbed; really it is nothing of the kind. An armed neutrality, a cold resignation, is the best that can be said for it.'[8]

Not all nonfictional accounts of lower-middle-class life in the late nineteenth century were entirely negative. Stephen's comments are indeed a response to a largely sympathetic assessment of the character of the mercantile clerk in a speech made by the outspoken independent Member of Parliament, J. A. Roebuck. Roebuck compares clerks favorably to members of the working class, but only to argue for the civilizing effects of education. Moreover, the benefits of literacy enhance only the private and domestic aspects of the clerk's life: he 'reads his book' and 'occupies the mind of his family', but the brutish agricultural laborer, according to Roebuck, 'has the more ennobling occupation'.[9] Other contemporary endorsements of the lower middle class are similarly qualified. They portray the lower middle class as having an attenuated form of virtue, a desire to be moral and upright that can readily be eroded by dubious influences or unpropitious circumstances. One writer sees in 'the lower section of the middle class . . . a happy interspace of virtue', but goes on to characterize its weaker members as easy prey to the pernicious influence of novels, society journals, and the easy fraternizing typical of such apparently vicious venues as 'watering-places, hotels, skating-rinks, [and] lawn-tennis grounds'.[10] The ethical and intellectual marginality implied by such extreme susceptibility suggests that this 'happy interspace of virtue' is populated by a class of people with little moral fiber or integrity. A similar attitude of patronizing sympathy and concern colors a plea for better housing for single men of 'the clerk class', which presents the impecunious clerk as likely victim of the superior resourcefulness of both the classes above and below him. Exploited by his employer and cheated by his grasping landlord, the clerk, it seems, is doomed to a life that is devoid of comfort and that consequently predisposes him to the lures and baleful influences of a cheap and nasty nightlife: 'From the miseries of the cheap lodging-house he flies to the doubtful distractions of the public-house, the cheap play-house, or the night club. Thus many a promising career has been ruined.'[11]

The almost fatherly concern expressed in these sympathetic middle-class appraisals eventually gives way to a more balanced view of the lower middle class, or at least of its significance within the framework of society. By the early years of the twentieth century, the lower middle class is generally recognized as not just an unfortunate anomaly, a sort of adolescent social group that needs guidance, but as an integral and permanent part of the class system and of the social fabric of Britain. Writing in

Cornhill Magazine, G. S. Layard virtually inverts customary nineteenth-century views by claiming that 'the lower middle class... is the backbone of the commonwealth' and that '[t]here is not... much room for false pride on 150 *l*. a year.'[12] Noted author, politician, and social observer C. F. G. Masterman, in his assessment of the role of social classes within the larger concern of 'the condition of England', also attests to the importance of the lower middle class. Masterman states that the lower middle class forms, 'in conjunction with the artisan class below, from which it is so sharply cut off in interest and ideas, the healthiest and most hopeful promise for the future of modern England.'[13] Neither Layard's nor Masterman's analysis is completely free of condescension, however. Layard refers to the 'matters of small moment' that comprise lower-middle-class life (p. 662) and Masterman is hard pressed to describe the condition of England's 'most hopeful promise for the future' in positive terms. Most of his observations carry with them a sense of deep ambivalence to his subject. 'It is no despicable life which has... silently developed in suburban London (p. 74)', he writes, in a negative formulation that suggests that it is no particularly commendable life, either. Masterman indeed portrays this life as less than enviable. The suburban wife, he claims, 'is harassed by the indifference or insolence of the domestic servant', (has he been reading *The Diary of a Nobody?*) while her husband labors at a 'dismal sedentary occupation so many incredible hours a day' (pp. 71–3). Whatever promise they may represent for the future, Masterman's suburbans remain a pretty spineless and unimpressive bunch in the present: 'They are easily forgotten: for they do not strive or cry.... No one fears the Middle Classes, the suburbans; and perhaps for that reason, no one respects them.' (p. 68)[14]

The strained conflation of the old prejudices against the lower middle class and the new acknowledgment of their inevitable significance in the social structure of England produces an odd tension in Masterman's *The Condition of England*. Masterman apparently intends to challenge dismissive attitudes towards the lower middle class with the analysis he presents, but he seems to find his protégés difficult to promote successfully. This same attempt to mix the oil of old prejudices with the water of new social awareness produces an even stranger effect in an early sociological analysis of the British class system by F. G. D'Aeth, entitled 'Present Tendencies of Class Differentiation'. D'Aeth ranks categories of people in the new social order on a scale ranging from A (The Loafer) to G (The Rich). The bulk of the lower middle class falls into grade C or D. Grade C includes 'petty officers, clerks, smaller officials, etc.', along with skilled laborers, and grade D, which is almost exclusively lower-middle-class, comprises 'clerks, shopkeepers and tradesmen, commercial travellers, printers, engineers, etc., elementary school teachers, a few ministers'. D'Aeth assesses the members of grade C as being 'shrewd at times', as having 'a simple mind', and as following 'laborious procedures at business meetings'. He assesses grade D as follows:

> *Social customs* – furnish their houses; entertain visitors; some have a young servant: *Ability* – varied; either a high degree of technical skill; or a little capital and managing a business; shrewd in small matters; read magazines; express superficial opinions freely upon all subjects.[15]

D'Aeth is clearly striving for a factually based, objective analysis of society but he produces instead an analysis that is a parody of itself: it is mock-scientific, its note-like style and highly organized system of classification completely at odds with its largely subjective content. But even D'Aeth's version of the lower middle class indicates something of an advance over older attitudes in its recognition of the class as a viable and significant social group. Nevertheless, the view from outside remains prejudicial. D'Aeth effectively condemns all of the lower middle class to a life constrained by intellectual limitations. Class is both natural and cultural, determined not just by 'social custom' but also by 'ability', which in the case of the lower middle class includes such designations as 'a simple mind' and 'shrewd[ness] in small matters'.

It remains for members of the lower middle class itself to change perceptions of what the people who make up this large and significant group are really like. But members of the class were sometimes its harshest critics. In his analysis of the situation of his fellow clerks in Liverpool in 1871, B. G. Orchard, for example, dismisses the most common complaint of his peers – that they are underpaid – as 'egregiously absurd'. In Orchard's opinion, 'clerks, as a class, have singularly overstrained conceptions of the part they perform in the great drama of commercial enterprise.'[16] Less cynical assessments show more sympathy for white-collar workers and criticize employers who demand high levels of education and performance from employees who are subjected to long hours and poor working conditions, and who are in return paid meager salaries. 'The practice of giving inadequate salaries', one writer complains, 'has the effect of disparaging mental attainment and respectability.'[17] Another lower-middle-class writer presents what he sees as the typical life cycle of the average clerk:

> Underpaid, with a great deal of laborious and monotonous work, in addition to heavy responsibilities and anxieties as his position gradually 'improves', his constitution frequently impaired (often ruined) by sedentary duties and confinement in ill-ventilated back offices, without either time or means to enjoy the recreation necessary to everyone so employed, he grows up an unhealthy, dissatisfied man.... [He must also face the] fear of losing his precarious situation, and, lastly the anxieties of home-life often destitute, as he increases in years, of the comforts which render middle-age enjoyable to other classes. He commences life as an ill-paid clerk, his ambitions are never encouraged, all the hopes of his manhood are thwarted, his employer can get numberless others to replace him at even less than he earns; and so he continues at the only calling he is capable of following and with nearly every feeling soured by adversity – he dies: a hard-worked, ill-paid clerk from beginning to end.[18]

This rather overwrought portrait is followed by impressive evidence of the exploitation of clerks in an unidentified railroad company, but however justified its melodrama, this portrayal inspires pity in the reader, not admiration or even indignation. In voicing the grievances of their peers, lower-middle-class writers do not break the mold into which their class has been cast by the bourgeoisie. In the scenarios of injustice these writers create, white-collar workers are unassertive victims who, however virtuous and exploited, are neither impressive nor memorable. It is only through fiction that lower-middle-class writers are able to challenge existing perceptions effectively.

DICKENS AND THE LOWER MIDDLE CLASS

The great strength of Charles Dickens's depiction of the lower middle class lies in the sheer number and variety of characters he portrays as inhabiting it. Dickens creates a gallery of saints and sinners and all grades of humanity in between: the homely and generous Bagnets and the grasping Smallweeds, the insinuating Mr Guppy and the sensitive Dick Swiveller, the distressingly efficient Sally Brass and the incomparably incompetent Wilkins Micawber. However exaggerated the characterization of these figures – however marked by 'the picturesque, the grotesque, the fantastic and romantic interference' that Henry James accuses Dickens's portrayals of the lower middle class of being 'so misleadingly . . . full'[19] – each one projects a vitality and an individuality that preclude the categorization of his or her character as a type or stereotype that simply represents the class or its features.

The lower-middle-class figures created by Dickens and other lower-middle-class authors are indeed shaped by the stereotype, which is subsequently undermined as the characterizations challenge or refute it. These characters' lives and personalities may in part be influenced by their class but their responses to their situations are the responses of individuals to particular circumstances. Two of the most striking features of lower-middle-class life – its narrow domesticity and its financial marginality – are accordingly manifested in Dickens's fiction in highly individualized ways in different characters. Thus financial marginality either directly or indirectly prompts the Bagnets to generosity, Sally Brass to meanness, and Wilkins Micawber to reckless extravagance. Similarly, the narrow domesticity of the Cratchits engenders warmth and intimacy, while that of the Smallweeds produces isolation and hostility.

Dickens also confronts the issue that elicited the most indignant response from the middle class – the apparent obsession of the lower middle class with dress. Middle-class observers interpreted lower-middle-class attempts to dress respectably as the outward and visible sign of pretentiousness and social ambition, as an attempt to make inroads into their territory. Many of Dickens's lower-middle-class characters do indeed betray a preoccupation with dress and personal display, as John Chivery does in the carefully orchestrated and completely outlandish outfit he wears when he sets out to propose to Little Dorrit, or as Mr Wilfer does with his 'ambition' to wear a complete new suit of clothes. But Dickens reveals the motivation behind this kind of display as something quite different from what the middle class was reading into it. Dress means both more and less than what the middle class assumed it did. The pride and slight awkwardness Peter

Cratchit feels in sporting his father's collar on Christmas Day, for example, suggests youthful flamboyance rather than self-aggrandizement. More significant, however, is the spirit in which Bob Cratchit has handed down this small but not inconsequential article of dress: the collar is 'Bob's private property, conferred upon his son and heir in honour of the day.'[20] In his choice of words and phrasing, Dickens here suggests that dress is heavily symbolic, that it plays a crucial role in class identity, and that the conferring of the collar is tantamount to a rite of passage. But neither the collar nor any other aspect of Bob Cratchit's dress represents an attempt on his part to ape the bourgeoisie; he does not wear a collar because he imagines himself to be the social equal of his employer. He is, indeed, sincerely deferential, even toasting Scrooge at Christmas dinner, to the chagrin of Mrs Cratchit.

The middle class was accordingly correct in recognizing dress as an issue of consuming interest to lower-middle-class man, but incorrect in associating it with vanity or social pretensions. In the increasingly anonymous milieu of an expanding commercial bureaucracy, the new Victorian white-collar worker would have had few apparent distinguishing features beyond his white collar, the uniform of respectable attire that identified him with his occupation. He had virtually no hope of accumulating the property or capital that provided prosperous members of the bourgeoisie with a sense of personal worth. He did not have even the artisan's 'capital' – the tools that were at once a modest form of investment and a concrete symbol of specialized training and skill. Mr Wilfer's ambition to own a respectable suit of clothes is thus not frivolous; it is the most significant acquisition, both materially and symbolically, to which he can aspire. And there is more than just comic flourish in Dickens's reference to the Cratchit family collar as 'Bob's private property': it is the only asset Bob has to pass down to 'his son and heir'. Dickens thus uses collars and suits to demonstrate that lower-middle-class concern with dress appears to be inappropriate only when viewed through the distorting lens of other class values. At the same time, he exposes the absurdity of middle-class misgivings about lower-middle-class ambitions by having collars and suits represent the limited nature of the 'property' that members of the class could realistically aspire to owning.

Dickens dramatizes the circumscribed nature of lower-middle-class life most deftly, most provocatively, and most memorably in the character of Wemmick in *Great Expectations*. The defining features of the lower middle class – financial marginality, the significance of the domestic sphere, diminutiveness, and limited prospects – are crystallized in his person, his miniature castle, and his 'portable property'. Wemmick is in no way a debased version of middle-class man, nor does he aspire to higher status. His 'Castle', by virtue of its very diminutiveness, does not represent self-aggrandizement but is instead a celebration of the domestic merits of hearth and home. It is not pretentious, but endearing. The Castle is, moreover, an emblem of Wemmick's resourcefulness and prudence. As he tells Pip, he is his own engineer, carpenter, plumber, gardener, and Jack of all Trades. The Castle is also a freehold – that jewel in the lower-middle-class domestic crown that Pooter attains through the agency of his employer two generations later – as a result of Wemmick's own thrift: 'I have got hold of it, a bit at a time. It's a freehold, by George!'[21]

Wemmick accepts with equanimity the difference in social status between himself and his employer, which he indicates in a discussion with Pip about Pip's forthcoming dinner engagements with Jaggers and himself: 'Well, . . . he'll give you wine, and good wine. I'll give you punch, and not bad punch.' (p. 199) And Wemmick's assets, like Bob Cratchit's, are forms of apparel – mourning rings and brooches, mementoes of departed former clients, with which he adorns his person in a most un-middle-class manner, and which he freely acknowledges to Pip are both peculiar and trifling:

> 'I always take 'em. They're curiosities. And they're property. They may not be worth much, but, after all, they're property and portable. It don't signify to you with your brilliant look-out, but as to myself, my guiding-star always is, Get hold of portable property.' (p. 199)

Wemmick's 'property', being of both limited consequence and questionable taste, is completely unlike the substantial financial assets of the solid middle class. Moreover, in wearing his 'portable property', Wemmick becomes a walking parody of the pretensions – both social and sartorial – which other classes ascribed to the lower middle class.

While Wemmick does not, like John Chivery, metamorphose into the arguably truest representative of gentlemanliness in the novel, there are nevertheless in Wemmick's character implicit points of comparison with middle-class norms, which eventually work out in his favor. Wemmick, with his apparently ingrained impersonality, seems less sensitive than Pip, for example. When they visit Jaggers's clients together in Newgate, Wemmick's assumption of impartiality initially seems mechanical, like a bureaucratic prerequisite of his profession. He affirms too programmatically, it would seem, the innocence of the client he is on his way to see, when asked by Pip if the man has committed the crime of which he has been charged: '"Bless your soul and body, no," answered Wemmick, very dryly. "But he is accused of it. So might you or I be. Either of us might be accused of it, you know".' (p. 256) Pip feels 'contaminated' by the 'soiling consciousness of Mr. Wemmick's conservatory', while Wemmick himself remains indifferent. (p. 261) The great irony, of course, is that Pip is especially apprehensive about Newgate contamination because he is on his way to see Estella, whose true history is as yet unknown to him. Wemmick's impartiality in fact allows him to feel more true compassion for the inmates of Newgate than Pip can because, like the legal system he serves, Wemmick does not assume guilt in those who have only been accused. Thus while Wemmick's impartiality produces understanding, Pip's sensitivity eventually emerges as a form of self-deception. Similarly, Wemmick's apparent lack of intellectual capacity does not in the end prevent him from being a valuable advisor to Pip. Although Pip judges Jaggers to be 'a thousand times better informed and cleverer than Wemmick', he also acknowledges that he 'would a thousand times rather have had Wemmick to dinner.' (p. 288) Jaggers's stiff and forbidding bearing disqualifies him as confidant and counselor, while the essentially compassionate core of Wemmick's being – that part of himself that emerges only in the domestic setting – more than compensates for his intellectual limitations, making him the wiser, if not the cleverer, of the two.

While Wemmick is not an exemplar of virtue and right reason, some form of natural and therefore superior gentleman against which to measure the shortcomings of the bourgeois version, he nevertheless becomes the means for making such judgments because he functions not only as Pip's advisor, but in effect as the reader's advisor as well. Pip relies on Wemmick for advice in promoting Herbert's career and for guidance in trying to secure Magwitch's safety. Wemmick also subtly directs the responses of both Pip and the reader to other characters, noting that Jaggers is 'Deep . . . as Australia' and that Molly is 'a wild beast tamed.' (pp. 197, 199) Moreover, as N. C. Peyrouton points out, it is Wemmick's willingness to trust Pip, to allow him into the privacy of the Castle, that signals the beginning of Pip's regeneration, and that confirms that 'his genuine expectations to become a gentleman will be realized. . . . [I]t is more our respect for Wemmick's shrewdness and capacity to judge character than anything evidenced in Pip himself which advises us.'[22] Accordingly, Wemmick is a character who remains uncompromisingly lower-middle-class in status, bearing, and values but who nevertheless commands some measure of respect.

There is in the characterization of Wemmick, as there is in the characterization of many of the figures in *Little Dorrit*, an indirect challenge to middle-class values and to middle-class assumptions about the lower middle class. But with Wemmick, rather than manipulating the conventions for representing the lower middle class, Dickens has aggressively seized them and turned them to his character's advantage, making Wemmick's marginality not limiting, but extraordinary and unique. In doing so, Dickens has created a character who is vivid and memorable, but not one with whom the reader can or is meant to identify. Like his portable property, Wemmick is a curiosity. The challenge to bourgeois assumptions that he represents is limited by his marginal role, however serviceable, in the working out of Pip's great expectations. It is not until the 1890s, three decades after Wemmick's appearance, that lower-middle-class characters begin to have some expectations of their own.

WELLS AND BENNETT

The fortunes of the lower-middle-class character were at a low ebb in the years following Dickens's death, years when the British literary scene was dominated by writers with neither the class sympathies nor the comic vision suited to working with the conventions for representing such a figure. In the 1890s, however, two new literary aspirants appeared on the scene, young men whose class background and energetic humor made them natural advocates for the lower middle class – H. G. Wells and Arnold Bennett. Both men had come from lower-middle-class backgrounds. Wells's parents had left domestic service to set up business in a small china shop in Bromley, at that time a town outside London. The business was never successful and Wells's mother eventually left to be the housekeeper for her former mistress. Wells himself was apprenticed during his teens, twice as a draper's assistant and once as a pharmacist. Wells found the dreary routines and subservience of these apprenticeships soul-destroying, and he made a point of falling so short of his employers' demands and expectations that they were generally willing or even eager to release him from his indentures. Wells also worked with more enthusiasm, but no greater success, as a pupil-teacher before ill-health drove him to embark on a writing career to sustain himself.

Arnold Bennett's youth was not as difficult as Wells's. Bennett's father, unlike Wells's, was a man of drive and ambition who had raised himself and his family above their impoverished origins before Arnold had reached his teens. While running a pawn shop in Burslem to support his family, the elder Bennett studied at night to qualify as a solicitor, which he succeeded in doing in 1876, at age thirty-four. Arnold then worked as a clerk in his father's firm in Burslem from the time he left school at sixteen until he set out for London five years later. In London, he continued to work as a solicitor's clerk while freelancing as a journalist in his spare time before turning his hand to fiction. In their fiction, both Wells and Bennett draw on their early experiences in lower-middle-class occupations, creating characters who feel trapped in their dreary and restricted lives and who long to escape. What is new about Wells's and Bennett's presentations of these figures is that, while they may be socially marginal, they are the central characters of the novels. They no longer exist simply to embellish someone else's story, but to draw the reader into the interests and complexities of their own stories.

It is this shift in focus that produces the enhanced sense of realism in Wells's treatment of the lower middle class that Henry James praised in a letter to Wells after the publication of *Kipps* in 1905:

> You have for the very first time treated the English 'lower middle' class, etc., without the picturesque, the grotesque, the

fantastic and romantic interference of which Dickens, e.g., is so misleadingly, of which even George Eliot is so deviatingly, full. You have handled its vulgarity in so scientific and historic a spirit, and seen the whole thing in its *own* strong light.[23]

Wells's characters are not, in fact, free of the kind of interference for which James criticizes Dickens and Eliot; it is most probably this 'interference' – mostly affectations of speech and dress – that produces the 'vulgarity' that James interprets as a scientific and historic fact. But Wells has not only seen the lower middle class 'in its own strong light', he has both trained the fictional spotlight on it and presented the rest of society from the perspective of the lower middle class's 'own strong light'. Lower-middle-class man in Wells's fiction is no longer defined exclusively by external features, by one kind of portable property or another. Wells's lower-middle-class characters have something previously granted only bourgeois protagonists: a highly developed inner life that is defined by hopes, dreams, drives, and ambitions. These characters, in other words, have an interiority in which they construct their own interpretations of the world. In this way, they also differ from Pooter who, as the central character of a series of sketches rather than of a novel, has a severely limited interiority.

The world presented in the lower-middle-class novel may seem trivial, however, when compared to the expansive social vistas presented in the novels of the mid-Victorian period. But this dwindling of the fictional world does not represent a shrinkage in the powers of the novelist or a trivialization of the nineteenth-century novelistic enterprise; it represents only the shift in perspective of both narrator and protagonist. The bourgeois mid-Victorian narrator portrays and regulates his or her fictional world from a position at the center, from a position of power. The social and class injustices he or she may deplore, implicitly or explicitly, are accordingly relatively distanced and impersonal, however vividly stigmatized lower-class characters and their suffering may be portrayed; the fate of these characters is finally only one element within the grand design. The shift of perspective to a view from outside the magic circle of bourgeois authority and confidence necessarily limits the scope of the fictional world presented in the lower-middle-class novel. And while these novels incorporate a questioning of class stereotypes not unlike that suggested by Dickens in *Little Dorrit* and Gaskell in *North and South*, the shift in perspective necessarily alters its nature and effect. Such questioning, coming from those who are denigrated and marginalized by the stereotypes, has a subjective intensity unattainable from the bourgeois perspective. For all their comic exuberance, lower-middle-class novels challenge class stereotypes and class assumptions with a new vigor and by means of a proven and time-honored imaginative strategy in the politics of literary representation: the transposition of class identities within the narrative. Authors of the lower-middle-class novel revamp and revitalize the technique used by Richardson to endorse middle-class values by means of the exemplary character of Sir Charles Grandison, the bourgeois aristocrat, and used by Dickens a century later to condemn bourgeois corruption and hypocrisy in *Little Dorrit*. Rather than work subtle realignments of class identity, as Richardson does, or artfully blur and confuse class divisions and attributes, as Dickens does, authors of the lower-middle-class novel are more direct – they generate the overt and complete reversal of conventional class identities within the narrative.

In a letter to Frederick Macmillan, Wells articulates the strategy of the social critique embodied in *Kipps* (1905). That novel, he affirms, 'is designed to present a typical member of the English lower middle class in all of its pitiful limitations and feebleness, and by means of a treatment deliberately kind and genial links a sustained and fairly exhaustive criticism of the ideals and ways of life of the great mass of middle-class English people.'[24] Although Wells's formulation of his design suggests that *Kipps* focuses on the faultiness of middle-class ideals, the novel in fact conveys a greater sense of the homely virtues of decidedly unpretentious lower-middle-class life. This strategy is also at work, and is indeed more overt, in Wells's first social novel, *The Wheels of Chance* (1896). The protagonist, Mr Hoopdriver, is an unprepossessing and impoverished draper's assistant, distinguished, if at all, by his utter conventionality, which the narrator is at pains to point out:

> Now if you had noticed anything about him, it would have been chiefly to notice how little he was noticeable. He wore the black morning coat, the black tie, and the speckled grey nether parts (descending into shadow and mystery below the counter) of his craft. He was of a pallid complexion, hair of a kind of dirty fairness, greyish eyes, and a skimpy, immature moustache under his peaked, indeterminate nose. His features

were all small, but none ill-shaped. A rosette of pins decorated the lapel of his coat. His remarks, you would observe, were entirely what people used to call cliché, formulae not organic to the occasion, but stereotyped ages ago, and learnt years since by heart.[25]

Hoopdriver embodies all the conventional characteristics of the lower middle class. He is literally colorless, with pale skin and grey eyes, and grey and black clothes. Smallness is the distinguishing component of his features and even of his 'skimpy' moustache. His conversation is pure affectation, the mouthing of clichés.

Mr Hoopdriver's undistinguished exterior, the only aspect of lower-middle-class man hitherto represented in fiction, contrasts with his highly romanticized interior life, in which he relieves the tedium of his drab existence by escaping into a dream world in which he casts himself in dashing and heroic roles. Mr Hoopdriver, the narrator tells us, is a 'poet', a 'romancer' who makes his 'absolutely uninteresting' life bearable by 'decorating his existence with imaginative tags, hopes and poses, deliberate and yet quite effectual self-deceptions; his experiences were mere material for a romantic superstructure.' (p. 42) Mr Hoopdriver's dreams accordingly are not an expression of lower-middle-class pretension or ambition – or even of hope. They are, rather, purely a form of escape. The 'little dramatic situations' that constitute Mr Hoopdriver's fantasies range from the relatively mundane – the glorious return of a nattily dressed Hoopdriver to his native village – to the highly romanticized – 'a gallant rescue of generalized beauty in distress from truculent insult or ravening dog.' (p. 44)

At this point in the novel, Mr Hoopdriver's apparently obsessive fixation on fantasy is itself rescued from becoming an irredeemably bathetic eccentricity by a skillfully crafted narrative intrusion that interprets the self-deceptive dream as a necessary and universal form of psychic defense:

> So many people do this – and you never suspect it. You see a tattered lad selling matches in the street, and you think there is nothing between him and the bleakness of immensity, between him and utter abasement, but a few tattered rags and a feeble musculature. And all unseen by you a host of heaven-sent

fatuities swathes him about, maybe, as they swathe you about. Many men have never seen their own profiles or the backs of their heads, and for the back of your own mind no mirror has been invented. They swathe him about so thickly that the pricks of fate scarce penetrate to him, or become but a pleasant titillation. And so, indeed, it is with all of us who go on living. Self-deception is the anaesthetic of life, while God is carving out our beings. (p. 44)

The switch to the second person in this paragraph initially aligns the reader's perspective with that of the narrator, producing the illusion of objective observers sharing confidences about their insights into the social condition. The alignment then alters, identifying the reader with the dreamers, the Mr Hoopdrivers, who then become exemplars of all humanity, 'all of us who go on living'. 'You see now', the narrator continues, 'how external our view has been; we have had but the slightest transitory glimpses of the drama within, of how the things looked in the magic mirror of Mr. Hoopdriver's mind'. The reader may not subsequently identify with Mr Hoopdriver, but he cannot subsequently disengage himself entirely from Hoopdriver's perspective.

The reader's perspective is also subtly aligned with Hoopdriver's in his anticipation of the one other form of escape that provides some respite from the dreariness of his life – the ten days' annual holiday when '[a]ll the dreary, uninteresting routine drops from you suddenly, your chains fall about your feet. All at once you are Lord of yourself, Lord of every hour in the long, vacant day; you may go where you please, call none Sir or Madam, have a lapel free of pins, doff your black morning coat and wear the colour of your heart, and be a Man.' (p. 12) On the particular holiday that is the subject of the novel, Hoopdriver takes to the road on a solitary cycling tour and the wheels of chance carry him into a romantic adventure as fantastic and improbable as his fondest dreams, and one that brings both him and the reader to fresh insights. Mr Hoopdriver becomes a knight-errant on a bicycle and he rescues a specific beauty from both a 'truculent insult' and a 'ravening dog'.

The specific beauty who is saved by Mr Hoopdriver is Jessie Milton, a seventeen-year-old middle-class girl who is trying to escape from the confines of conventionality. The ravening dog is Bechamel, an art critic and friend of Jessie's stepmother, who has offered to assist her in getting away. Because he bears a superficial resemblance to Bechamel, Hoopdriver is frequently mistaken for him and as a result is inadvertently drawn into the melodrama of Jessie's flight from her stepmother. Jessie and Bechamel are, like Mr Hoopdriver, using bicycles to pursue their adventure, but all three cherish very different visions of where their adventures will lead. Jessie dreams of personal liberty; Bechamel dreams of seducing Jessie; Mr Hoopdriver just dreams. And herein lies the first demonstration of Hoopdriver's superiority to the novel's middle-class characters: while his dreams may be fatuous, he is paradoxically a greater realist because he accepts these dreams as fantasies, rather than setting them up as specious goals as Jessie and Bechamel do. But the narrative demonstrates that it is the action of one set of dreams on another that produces reality. Thus Jessie's adolescent dreams are deliberately frustrated by Bechamel's sordid ones, as he maneuvers her into ever more compromising situations. Bechamel is in turn thwarted by Hoopdriver, whose sincere concern for Jessie's obvious distress temporarily transforms his fantasies into reality. He becomes Jessie's champion, protecting her from Bechamel by assisting her in a wild midnight escape on bicycles, an adventure that fosters all that is chivalrous and valorous in Hoopdriver's soul.

The similarities in appearance between Hoopdriver and Bechamel set up an overt comparison between lower-middle-class and middle-class man in the novel. The two men are of about the same stature and coloring, although Bechamel's bearing is, unlike Hoopdriver's, elegant and confident. Moreover, Hoopdriver's new cycling suit, of which he is inordinately proud, is an inferior version of the one Bechamel is wearing, a fact that contributes to the sense of Hoopdriver as a representation of marginal man attempting to mimic his social superiors in dress and bearing. This is certainly Bechamel's reading of the situation. 'Greasy proletarian', he mutters with obvious distaste when he first sees Hoopdriver. 'Got a suit of brown, the very picture of this. One would think his sole aim in life had been to caricature me.' (p. 32) This is the voice of the middle class, assuming its sartorial as well as its cultural centrality and assigning the stereotypical role of caricature to the lower-middle-class figure. Bechamel's comment encapsulates the absurdity of bourgeois misconceptions about lower-middle-class values and motivations. Mr Hoopdriver's delight in his brown cycling suit has nothing whatever to do with Bechamel, whom he has never seen before. His delight is a function of being on holiday, when he can 'wear the colour of . . . [his] heart'. And while Hoopdriver does imagine himself as cutting quite a fine figure, he does not imagine himself as being accepted as an equal by his social superiors. He fantasizes, rather, about the impression that he is making upon the rustics he passes on the road or that he would make upon his co-workers if they could see him. Hoopdriver may dream about being a hero, but not about being middle-class.

As *The Wheels of Chance* makes clear, it is only in appearance that Bechamel is the superior man. Mr Hoopdriver's affectations may be foolish, but they are harmless and are, moreover, largely the result of pressure from his employer. To be a draper's assistant, he tells Jessie, is '[t]o be just another man's hands, as I am. To have to wear what clothes you are told, and to go to church to please customers, and work.' (p. 164) Mr Hoopdriver's preoccupation with clothes and general deportment has been forced upon him by members of the middle class who then mock that same preoccupation. Bechamel's affectations are, by contrast, self-serving and dangerous: he pretends to be a man of honor willing to help Jessie, while in reality he is a cad who wants to deceive her. It is lowly Mr Hoopdriver who is the true man of honor, who honestly wishes to help and protect her. Jessie recognizes his unselfishness and his inner worth – previously the hallmark of the bourgeois protagonist – and responds with something like awe when he declares he would do anything for her:

> She caught at her breath. She did not care to ask why. But compared with Bechamel! – 'We take each other on trust', she said. (p. 99)

Jessie thus not only places trust and confidence in Hoopdriver but also compares him favorably to Bechamel, a comparison that she couches in suitably Romanticized terms: '"I have lost an Illusion and found a Knight-errant." She spoke of Bechamel as the Illusion.'

Bechamel seems to have been the last illusion that Jessie had to lose, at least as far as her assessment of the life and the people of the middle class is concerned. And Jessie's assessment of society and situations, however naïve it may seem, plays an important role in shaping the perceptions of both Mr Hoopdriver and the reader. She judges her stepmother and the members of her stepmother's social circle as unenlightened and hypocritical and sees her own life as dull and circumscribed – like being 'a thing in a hutch.' (p. 99) But Jessie's immaturity and inexperience severely limit her discernment. She does not understand the extent to which the conventionality that she seeks to escape defines her identity and even her rebellion. With her flight she is in fact only exchanging one set of middle-class conventions for another, the conventions of society for those of the New Woman novel – the kind of novel her stepmother writes.

At the same time, Jessie's inexperience allows her the insight and candor of innocence. Jessie accordingly sometimes blends preposterous errors with uncanny perceptiveness. She is unable to place Mr Hoopdriver's social position, for example, because he is neither in the right setting nor the right costume, and she decides he must be from South Africa. (She has recently read Olive Schreiner's *The Story of an African Farm*.) Hoopdriver initially welcomes the opportunity to hide his true identity and obligingly spins fictions about his life in the colonies. When he is finally overcome with shame and confesses to lying, Jessie is momentarily unable to reconcile the deception with her intuitive sense of his honesty. 'I don't know what to make of you', she tells him. 'I thought, do you know, that you were perfectly honest. And somehow.... I still think so.' After a moment's hesitation, she decides her intuition was right: '"Of *course* you are honest," she said. "How could I ever doubt it? As if *I* had never pretended! I see it all now."' (p. 166) And just in case the reader does not yet see it all, Wells has Jessie spell out the kind of middle-class prejudices that lead essentially honest souls like Hoopdriver to assume pretenses: '"You did it ... because you wanted to help me. And you thought I was too Conventional to take help from one I might think my social inferior.... I am sorry," she said, "you should think me likely to be ashamed of you because you follow a decent trade."' (p. 167)

The accuracy of Jessie's insight into people's inner worth is borne out in the characterizations of her stepmother and the men in her social circle. Mrs Milton responds to circumstances through a series of melodramatic poses that are as mannered as her novels. She elicits sympathy and help from her male friends by posing as the distraught mother concerned for the welfare of her daughter, when she is really only concerned about appearances and Jessie's ultimate marriageability. Three sorry examples of middle-class male ineptitude, Messrs Widgery, Dangle, and Phipps, quite literally fall all over themselves in their attempts to help her find Jessie. Their pursuit of the elusive cyclists degenerates into a parody of Hoopdriver's quixotic but valiant knight-errantry. Driven by a combination of personal antagonism and rivalry for Mrs Milton's favors, the three men pick up the trail of the cyclists only to allow, by dint of disorganization and incompetence, another escape. Weary and battle-scarred (a belligerent hostler has given Dangle a black eye), the 'Rescue Party' retreats to the town of Botley to regroup, at which point the narrator assesses their situation:

> It goes to my heart to tell of the end of that day: how the fugitives vanished into Immensity; how there were no more trains; how Botley stared unsympathetically with a palpable disposition to derision, denying conveyances; how the landlord of the 'Heron' was suspicious; how the next day was Sunday, and the hot summer's day had crumpled the collar of Phipps and stained the skirts of Mrs. Milton, and dimmed the radiant emotions of the whole party. Dangle, with sticking-plaster and a black eye, felt the absurdity of the pose of the Wounded Knight, and abandoned it after the faintest efforts. Recriminations never, perhaps, held the foreground of the talk, but they played like summer lightning on the edge of the conversation. And deep in the hearts of all was a galling sense of the ridiculous. Jessie, they thought, was most to blame. Apparently, too, the worst, which would have made the whole business tragic, was not happening. Here was a young woman – young woman, do I say? a mere girl! – had chosen to leave a comfortable home in Surbiton, and all the delights of a refined and intellectual circle, and had rushed off, trailing us after her, posing hard, mutually jealous, and now tired and weather-worn, to flick us off at last, mere mud from her wheel, into this detestable village on a Saturday night! And she had done it, not for Love and Passion, which are serious excuses one may recognize, even if one must reprobate, but just for a Freak, just for a fantastic Idea; for nothing, in fact, but the outraging of Common Sense. Yet withal, such was our restraint, that we talked of her still as one much misguided, as one who burthened us with anxiety, as a lamb astray, and Mrs. Milton, having eaten, continued to show the finest feelings on the matter. (pp. 137–8)

The middle-class characters are here exposed in all their commonness and hypocrisy. They are more out of place finding their way around the back roads of England than Mr Hoopdriver is, and no more successful at commanding the respect of the local townspeople, who regard them with 'palpable derision'. They also lack true compassion and the kind of honesty that Jessie recognized as so valuable in Hoopdriver. Mrs Milton subordinates the pangs of her heart to those of her stomach and her cavaliers call Jessie 'a lamb astray', while secretly blaming her – by their own admission 'a mere girl' – for the awkwardness of their present circumstances. Moreover, the three men care so little for Jessie's welfare that they are put out because she has apparently not succumbed to a seduction and thus dignified their role by casting them in a tragedy instead of a farce. But the manifest shabbiness of the morals of these middle-class characters becomes more than just a comic demonstration of their failings when Wells once again subtly realigns the narrative perspective. The passage opens in the first person singular, with the narrator ironically expressing his feelings about the plight of the Rescue Party, whose antics he casts in the third person. In the middle of the passage, however, he shifts the perspective to the first person plural with a collective 'us' that encompasses not just Widgery, Dangle, and Phipps but also the narrator. The collective first person even threatens to incorporate the reader who, after all, has also been forced to trail after Jessie. Even a momentary identification with these middle-class characters, who are 'posing hard' and 'mutually jealous', is something the reader is forced to resist. However problematic it may have been to identify with Hoopdriver, it is clearly preferable to being lumped in with the Rescue Party.

While the fortunes of the Rescue Party recover from this nadir, the credibility of its members never does. They may overtake Jessie and Mr Hoopdriver in the end, but only after they have made complete fools of themselves, overturning bicycles and losing control of carts drawn by unpredictable rustic nags. Their bombastic outbursts of indignation at what they assume Hoopdriver's role in Jessie's flight must have been are as hollow as their values. Their assumption of superiority is groundless, for as Jessie in her grave innocence understands, Hoopdriver's modesty makes him the wiser man. 'You're in front of them already in one thing,' she tells him. 'They think they know everything. You don't. And they know such little things.' (p. 169) And while Hoopdriver does not win the girl, he does win her respect and, more importantly, his own.

The tone and content of 'The Envoy' that follows the story suggests that Wells is not confident that the reader will respond as uncritically as Jessie does to the unimpressive figure of Mr Hoopdriver. 'The Envoy' is defensive, conciliatory, even apologetic and apparently unselfconsciously affirms the intention of the author: '[I]f you see how a mere counter-jumper, a cad on castors, and a fool to boot, may come to feel the little insufficiencies of life, and if he has to any extent won your sympathies, my end is attained. (If it is not attained, may Heaven forgive us both!)' (p. 195) The characterization of Hoopdriver as 'a mere counter-jumper, a cad on castors, and a fool to boot' is not entirely ironic. This may be Wells presenting the middle-class readership with an image of its own prejudiced assessment of such a character, but the gap between that assessment and his own is not as great as the gap between the stereotype and the reality within the story. Now that the story is over, Wells seems to feel that he has taken too great a liberty in forcing the reader into the consciousness of 'a mere counter-jumper'. Wells may feel on the one hand that it would be unforgivable not to sympathize with Hoopdriver, but on the other hand he seems ready to acknowledge that Hoopdriver really *is* 'a cad on castors'. Like Kipps, he is 'a typical member of the lower middle class [presented] in all of its pitiful limitations and feebleness'. Wells, like other successful writers from his class – including Dickens – is unable to free himself or his characters completely from the social and cultural preconceptions that marginalized and minimized members of the lower middle class. At the same time, the reader, like Wells himself, must certainly look on Hoopdriver with more favor than on any other character in the novel.

Besides the overall reversal of narrative and, to a certain extent, cultural roles of middle- and lower-middle-class characters, *The Wheels of Chance* also incorporates other distinctive features of what could be called the lower-middle-class novel of manners. Such novels are generally humorous, even when penned by such notoriously gloomy authors as George Gissing, whose two short novels about lower-middle-class life, *The Paying Guest* (1895) and *The Town Traveller* (1898), are comic. The typical male protagonist is young and badly educated and he speaks with a Cockney or provincial accent, represented orthographically with phonetic spelling and the ubiquitous dropped aitch. By middle-class standards, he is supremely unimpressive and unsuccessful. Moreover, he accepts and sometimes even enthusiastically embraces the humble life, as Artie Kipps does when, after inheriting and then losing a fortune, he retires in contentment to raise a family and run a bookshop.

Arnold Bennett's *A Man from the North* (1898) similarly endorses lower-middle-class life, albeit with some ambivalence. The protagonist Richard Larch, a relatively successful solicitor's clerk, has decided to abandon his dream of becoming a writer after numerous false starts and rejected manuscripts and becomes engaged to an ordinary but pleasant young woman. He has no romantic illusions, either professional or marital, and indeed sees in his fiancée's older married sister the first hint of the dowdy, content lower-middle-class matron both young women are destined to become. The novel closes with Larch's clear-sighted assessment of his past and of his future with Laura:

> He knew that he would make no further attempt to write. Laura was not even aware that he had had ambitions in that direction. He had never told her, because she would not have understood. She worshipped him, he felt sure, and at times he had a great tenderness for her; but it would be impossible to write in the suburban doll's-house which was to be theirs. No! In future he would be simply the suburban husband – dutiful towards his employers, upon whose grace he would be doubly dependent; keeping his house in repair; pottering in the garden; taking his wife out for a walk, or occasionally to the theatre; and saving as much as he could. He would be good to his wife – she was his. He wanted to get married at once. He wanted to be master of his own dwelling. He wanted to have Laura's kiss when he went out of a morning to earn the bread-and-cheese. He wanted to see her figure at the door when he returned at night. He wanted to share with her the placid, domestic evening. He wanted to tease her, and to get his ears boxed and be called a great silly. He wanted to creep into the kitchen and surprise her with a pinch of the cheek as she bent over the range. He wanted to whisk her up in his arms, carry

her from one room to another, and set her down breathless in a chair.... Ah! Let it be soon. And as for the more distant future, he would not look at that. He would keep his eyes on the immediate foreground, and be happy while he could. After all, perhaps things had been ordered for the best; perhaps he had no genuine talent for writing. And yet at that moment he was conscious that he possessed the incommunicable imaginative insights of the author.... But it was done with now.[26]

Framed as it is with indirect expressions of regret for the dreams he has abandoned, Larch's vision of the future captures the essence of lower-middle-class life; a life that derives meaning and satisfaction from an unpretentious domestic harmony that, in its 'suburban doll's-house' setting, places limits on aspirations and is in turn restricted by those limitations. The sense of inevitable and inescapable limitations and the touch of regret, with the vague ambivalence it expresses, prevent this picture of lower-middle-class life from degenerating into sentimentalism and make it instead a poignant tribute.

Although it fits most of the criteria of a typical lower-middle-class novel, *A Man from the North* is not comic. The characterization of Richard Larch is accordingly much closer to that of a middle-class protagonist than that of Hoopdriver is. But it was difficult for such a character to engage the sympathy or imagination of the reading public of the time. Lower-middle-class life, seen in all its ordinariness through the lens of realism, provides the reader with neither the thrill of decadence nor the delight and comforting reassurance of condescending humor. In the rather brutally forthright assessment of one contemporary reviewer, both Larch and the life he leads are unrelentingly banal:

> Granting that such a character is worth describing, it is well described. The writer is an uncompromising realist. He is master of all the little sordid details, the little sordid ambitions and loves and sorrows of lower middle-class existence; and he possesses the art of drawing lifelike portraits with a few touches. The subject is not a very attractive one, and the hero, it must be confessed, is a cold fish at the best. We have met him before in other walks of life. He has appeared in 'Hamlet' and 'Virgin Soil', but the problems which palsied the wills of the heroes of those tragedies were worth solving. The difficulties of Richard

Larch, we cannot but feel, might have been removed by a touch of vice. An English clerk, it is to be feared, would have solved them in this way.[27]

The bias of this review is clear. What makes Larch an unsuitable hero is not his character, but his class. The same character, in the guise of Hamlet, has difficulties that produce tragedy, but the 'ambitions and loves and sorrows' of the lower middle class are 'little' and 'sordid', without even some enlivening vice. What is most unforgivable, it seems, is blandness.

Blandness is not what Bennett saw when he looked at lower-middle-class life, but he is unable to convey the urgent sense of life that he feels is smouldering unnoticed in apparently quiet suburban settings, the sense of dramatic potential outlined in the novel by Mr Aked, Larch's mentor:

> [T]he suburbs, even Walham Green and Fulham, are full of interest, for those who can see it. Walk along this very street on such a Sunday afternoon as to-day. The roofs form two horrible, converging straight lines I know, but beneath there is character, individuality, enough to make the greatest book ever written. Note the varying indications supplied by bad furniture seen through curtained windows, like ours . . .; listen to the melodies issuing lamely from ill-tuned pianos; examine the enervated figures of women reclining amidst flower-pots on narrow balconies. Even in the thin smoke ascending unwillingly from invisible chimney-pots, the flutter of a blind, the bang of a door, the winking of a fox terrier perched on a window-sill, the colour of paint, the lettering of a name, – in all these things there is character and matter of interest, – truth waiting to be expounded. How many houses are there in Carteret Street? Say eighty. Eighty theatres of love, hate, greed, tyranny, endeavour; eighty separate dramas always unfolding, intertwining, ending, beginning, – and every drama a tragedy. No comedies, and especially no farces! (pp. 100–1)

Aked, a defeated and dying man, has failed to write the tragedy of the suburbs, just as Larch will fail. Bennett likewise has failed, largely because he has not had the courage to push his protagonist forward as an inherently interesting character, the result, as the reviewer observes, of his being too much of an 'uncompromising realist'. Bennett presents his protagonist as an unremarkable character in an unremarkable setting. Moreover, Bennett tells an unremarkable story that allows insufficient scope for developing the arresting paradox of a conventionally dull lower-middle-class setting – populated by 'enervated . . . women', 'ill-tuned pianos', and domesticated terriers – providing 'theatres of love, hate, greed, tyranny, endeavour'. The provocative juxtaposition of forsaken dreams and as yet unrealized reality at the close of the novel is poignant, but hardly tragic.

It is ironic, given Aked's injunction against comedies and farces, but perhaps inevitable, that Bennett creates his most popular and remarkable lower-middle-class protagonist in a farce: Denry Machin in *The Card* (1911). The conventions, as they existed, did not lend themselves to the creation of anything but comic lower-middle-class characters. Authors could successfully make clerks and shop-assistants central and even sympathetic characters, but if the comic conventions were absent, these characters simply would not work for Victorian readers – or writers. Victorian readers did not find such characters engaging and could not or would not accept them as believable. It is Mr Pooter, not Richard Larch, who survives as the most memorable representative of the late Victorian lower middle class and who strikes his readers as absolutely and starkly real. Humor works as an all-purpose cultural insulation: it confirms for middle-class readers that they need not take the problems of a 'cad on castors' too seriously; it protects the Hoopdrivers of literature from overly critical character analysis; and it safeguards the author against any sense he may feel or produce that he has presumed too much in inflicting the dull interiority of a lower-middle-class protagonist on his readers. The humor of the lower-middle-class novel is an apology for the subject matter. Accordingly, Denry Machin works supremely well because in his characterization Bennett, rather than dropping the comic conventions, has taken them to the extremes of absurdity. Denry is the culmination of the convention of lower-middle-class man rising above the limitations of his 'superiors'. Denry is also the personification of all the faults that the middle class ascribed to the lower middle class. He is vain, shallow, and pretentious – but writ large. Dismissal from his job as a solicitor's clerk fills him with joy. He sings and whistles as he contemplates starvation and revels in his freedom: 'No longer a clerk; one of the employed; saying "sir" to persons with no more fingers and toes than he had himself; bound by servile agreement to be in a fixed place at fixed hours! An independent unit, master of his own time and his own movements! In brief, a man!'[28]

The ambitions and pretensions that Denry cherishes go far beyond those usually ascribed to members of his class. He develops money-making schemes and aspires to nothing less than social pre-eminence in Bursley (a fictionalized version of Bennett's native Burslem). He is embodied affectation: he consciously adopts 'a worldly manner, which he had acquired for himself by taking the most effective features of the manners of several prominent citizens, and piecing them together so that, as a whole, they formed Denry's manner.' (p. 42) His ambitions and pretensions have a quality of pure fantasy, however, and their eventual realization does not produce a hackneyed image of the middle class's worst fears – lower-middle-class man attaining the bourgeois goal of affluence and respectability. On the contrary, Denry achieves success through Sloperesque flouting of all the accepted middle-class standards of behavior. He becomes rich through slightly questionable business schemes that require a minimum of effort on his part, and his social prominence is the by-product of his flamboyant public *faux pas*. It is the middle class that is mocked in *The Card*, as its members constantly find themselves beaten at their own games, disarmed by a mere wag in the venues of business and public affairs that they traditionally dominate. Their consternation over Denry's ability to secure the interest of the *crème de la crème* of Bursley society, the Countess of Chell, reveals a peculiarly bourgeois form of pretentiousness.

The Countess of Chell is representative of another important feature of lower-middle-class novels written by men and about men. In most of these novels, a woman, always of a class above that of the protagonist, plays an important symbolic role. Between her and the protagonist there is a bond, not of a romantic nature, but of some level of identification. Any notion of sexual interaction between the characters is indeed an impossibility, not just because of the class discrepancy, but more significantly because of the logic of literary representation. In the nineteenth-century novel, lower-middle-class males are virtually a different species from middle- and upper-class women. It would be unthinkable for Little Dorrit to marry John Chivery, for example, or for Wemmick to marry anything but another 'curiosity' like Miss Skiffins. The real shock value of Leonard Bast's relationship with

Helen Schlegel in *Howard's End* lies in the breaking of this literary and cultural taboo, and is undoubtedly lost on modern readers. A character like Mr Hoopdriver, moreover, is too innocuous to pose a sexual threat. Thus while he falls in love with Jessie as a romantic ideal, what is significant is their relationship during their flight. The flight creates a space where the constraints of class and reality are loosened, and where Jessie and Mr Hoopdriver meet on terms of equality, partly because they share a need to escape. 'I wanted to come out into the world', she tells him, 'to be a human being – not a thing in a hutch', a feeling he immediately comprehends.[29]

Denry's relationship with the Countess of Chell is less intimate, but he also in a sense rescues her. He is fortuitously at hand when her carriage breaks down and he gallantly, if not very elegantly, conveys her to a public appearance in his mule-drawn victoria. During the ride and a visit to a tea-shop after her public engagement, they share nothing more than pleasantries. Appearances are all, however, and his apparent familiarity with her empowers him as he becomes the driving force in the debunking of the myth of middle-class superiority. A comparable cross-gender, cross-class bond develops in *A Man from the North*. In that novel, the single interesting female character – the others are entirely conventional – is a young middle-class woman who makes a brief appearance as the nurse attending Mr Aked in his final illness. Like Richard Larch, she writes, and her poems have even been published. Unlike him, however, she is highly critical of her own work, and suspects that she has been successful not because her work has merit but because she happens to be the daughter of a famous novelist. She instinctively understands what Larch must learn, that lower-middle-class roles and professions – in her case, the profession of private nursing, which has none of the Romantic resonance of Florence Nightingale's sojourn in the Crimea – can be worthwhile and satisfying. She embraces a lower-middle-class role, as Larch eventually will, but with an assurance and conviction that he lacks. To his surprise, she insists that she prefers nursing to writing and indeed, she tells him, 'to anything in the world. That is why I am a nurse.'[30] She accordingly validates lower-middle-class identity more forcibly than Larch can.

The suggestion of a shared identity between women and lower-middle-class men that emerges in these novels is a natural result of the similarities in the literary conventions for representing both groups. This seemingly odd conjunction of class and gender is the effect of the essentially feminine and domestic roles that they both are assigned and constrained by. The urge to escape that is so much a part of these novels mirrors and expresses the author's urge to escape from the limitations of representational conventions, to feel free, as Wells does not, to present a lower-middle-class character as a protagonist without feeling an obligation to justify doing so, or to be free, as Bennett is not, to depict drama and tragedy under a suburban roof. These authors try, but fail to free the lower-middle-class protagonist from being, like Jessie in *The Wheels of Chance*, 'a thing in a hutch'. But a middle- or upper-class female character has one prerogative within the conventions of the standard nineteenth-century novel that a lower-middle-class male character lacks, which is that she may unapologetically be the central character. The identification of the lower-middle-class protagonist with a middle- or upper-class woman accordingly to some extent validates his claim to the reader's attention.

In the end, however, the lower-middle-class male remains trapped by the conventions, for while he may be able to turn middle-class males into comic figures, he cannot turn himself into a serious one. In the words of C. F. G. Masterman, he can 'only appear articulate in comedy.' (Masterman, p. 68) Thus it is only as a consummate comic, a 'card', that Denry Machin can make his way in the world. When he becomes mayor of Bursley someone asks, 'What great cause is he identified with?' The answer closes the novel: 'He's identified . . . with the great cause of cheering us all up.' And that, it would seem, would have remained the inevitable fate of the lower-middle-class male character, had it not been for the subtle alliance that was forming between women and lower-middle-class men. The first result of this alliance is that a lower-middle-class male novelist is able to play the role of Hoopdriver and rescue Jessie from her hutch: that is, he releases the nineteenth-century heroine from the constraints of literary and class conventions by making her lower-middle-class – George Gissing creates Rhoda Nunn.

4

Bachelor Girls and Working Women: Women and Independence in Oliphant, Levy, Allen and Gissing

> To obtain a firmer footing on the earth's broad surface, to acquire some weight in affairs, to be taken into some real account as the half of humanity, women must work, and so work as they have not done yet. The tricks of attraction – nay, the sobrieties of domestic sympathies, have been tried for centuries, and when has woman's condition been best? Not when she was loved, but when she was esteemed; not when she was idle and indulged, but when she was useful.
>
> From 'The Disputed Question,'
> *English Woman's Journal* 1:60 (1858)

At the end of Wells's *The Wheels of Chance*, Hoopdriver returns to his place behind the counter, and Jessie Milton returns to her hutch – the hutch of conventional Victorian womanhood. Like Hoopdriver, Jessie tries to escape the constraints imposed by her social position by entering the sphere of Romance. In doing so, however, she simply switches one set of defining conventions for another, and risks becoming an outcast in the process. As her unlikely knight errant, Hoopdriver can rescue her from seduction and social ruin, but he can do no more than return her unscathed to her former position as a marriageable middle-class girl. The typical Victorian fictional heroine follows a pattern not unlike Jessie's, exiting the Romance only to enter the domestic sphere: she is 'courted' and then marries. In all cases, her identity and her fate are defined and controlled by men – by fathers, husbands, or seducers. Moreover, like Dick Sparrow and other lower-middle-class anti-heroes from the comic sketches in midcentury periodicals, Victorian heroines must always return in the end to the domestic hearth, although few of them are permitted to venture very far from its security in the first place. In order to break free of restricting conventions, Victorian heroines, like their real life counterparts, had to do more than resist and complain – they had to work, and 'work as they had not done yet.' Victorian heroines and Victorian women had to exit the domestic sphere and enter the public sphere – they had to find liberation in lower-middle-class, white-collar work.

By the 1890s, conventional attitudes towards women and their role in society were under attack on several fronts. The cultural phenomenon of the New Woman was in full flower. She inspired a wide range of literary responses, including periodical essays, cartoons, novels, plays, and even a few poems. The New Woman met with resistance and hostility in the culture at large and suffered from unfavorable comparison with her anti-type, the 'womanly woman', a popular cultural throwback to traditional values. Wells, in having Jessie refer to herself as being like 'a thing in a hutch', was not the only free-thinker to liken these traditional ideals of Victorian womanliness overtly to a particularly lowly form of imprisonment usually associated with domestic animals. George Bernard Shaw similarly compares women's lot to that of caged parrots:

> If we have come to think that the nursery and the kitchen are the natural sphere of a woman, we have done so exactly as English children come to think that a cage is the natural sphere of a parrot: because they have never seen one anywhere else. No doubt there are Philistine parrots who agree with their owners that it is better to be in a cage than out, so long as there is plenty of hempseed and Indian corn there. There may even be idealist parrots who persuade themselves that the mission of a parrot is to minister to the happiness of a private family by whistling and saying Pretty Polly, and that it is in the sacrifice of its liberty to this altruistic pursuit that a true parrot finds the supreme satisfaction of its soul. I will not go so far as to affirm that there are theological parrots who are convinced that imprisonment is the will of God because it is unpleasant; but I am confident that there are rationalist parrots who can demonstrate that it would be a cruel kindness to let a parrot out to fall a prey to cats, or at least to forget its

accomplishments and coarsen its naturally delicate fibres in an unprotected struggle for existence. Still, the only parrot a free-souled person can sympathize with is the one that insists on being let out as the first condition of making itself agreeable. A selfish bird, you may say: one that puts its own gratification before that of the family which is so fond of it – before even the greatest happiness of the greatest number: one that, in aping the independent spirit of a man, has unparroted itself and become a creature that has neither the home-loving nature of a bird nor the strength and enterprise of a mastiff. All the same, you respect that parrot in spite of your conclusive reasoning; and if it persists, you will have either to let it out or kill it.

The sum of the matter is that unless Woman repudiates her womanliness, her duty to her husband, to her children, to society, to the law, and to everyone but herself, she cannot emancipate herself.[1]

Shaw follows this last apocalyptic pronouncement with an analysis of why duty is, as it were, a mere scutcheon. But even in the often iconoclastic 1890s, the absolute repudiation of duty was not a viable course of action for anyone, let alone for women, who had limited rights and who were legally dependent on those very persons and institutions from whom they were to withdraw their dutiful allegiance.

The juxtaposition of the parodic analogy of the parrot and the overzealous and unworkable vision of emancipation in this passage exemplifies the kind of impossible box in which independent-minded women found themselves at the end of the nineteenth century. The absurdity of traditional attitudes towards women is evident only through an analogy that is itself absurd. The reader experiences a shock of surprise in recognizing the blatant illogic of society's cherished notions of womanliness, when those same notions are applied to a parrot. But the effectiveness of the analogy lies in the fact that the parrot is anthropomorphic rather than gynomorphic. All the references to self-sacrifice and ministering to the needs of others, to the need for protection from cats and to the coarsening of 'delicate fibres' would take on a very different color if there were baby parrots hopping about in that cage. To the culturally indoctrinated, society's expectations of women appear to be absurd only when misapplied, when ascribed to anyone – or anything – other than a woman: her 'natural' attributes are denatured when transposed to parrots, especially parrots without a gender. The piquant humor of this passage moreover both masks and muffles Shaw's serious intent; his radical position is made palatable, but the joke is a little too clever and is more apt to elicit good-natured chuckles rather than serious reassessment of values, especially if such a reassessment entails anything like what Shaw then suggests about women's emancipation. If the only hope for liberty really *is* in the repudiation of all social and legal ties, then clearly there is no hope – Woman cannot free herself.

There was, however, a more practical means available for women's emancipation, and that was financial independence. Such independence was less radical in concept than Shaw's notion of the repudiation of social and legal ties, but it was still something of an impossible dream for women of the Victorian period. As Shaw's parrot analogy confirms, women were seldom seen outside the cage of conventional domesticity and were not readily accepted in roles that seemed to challenge traditional assumptions about feminine identity. To enter the public sphere, to adopt a public persona, would be another kind of radical repudiation – the repudiation of femininity.

There were avenues of financial independence open to women in the middle classes during the nineteenth century, but these were limited in number and in scope. Respectable women who had to make their own way in the world were generally restricted – in both the real and fictional worlds – to careers as governesses, schoolmistresses, or companions. None of these jobs was likely to suggest emancipation from conventional femininity, since they are all associated with the traditional female roles of the teaching and nurturing of children or of otherwise ministering to the needs of others. For this reason, Mary Barfoot, the grande dame of Victorian feminism in George Gissing's *The Odd Women*, spurns these 'womanish' occupations as detrimental to women's liberation from domestic bondage. 'An excellent governess, a perfect hospital nurse, do work which is invaluable,' she tells a group of young women she is training in clerical skills, 'but for our cause of emancipation they are no good; nay, they are harmful. Men point to them, and say: Imitate these, keep to your proper world.'[2] The position of the governess and the companion – the unsatisfactory occupations of two of the 'odd women' in Gissing's novel – was especially limiting; in both cases, the employee would be confined to a domestic sphere that was not even her own, allowing her virtually no control over her life and environment. The conventional escape route through marriage would seem not only attractive by comparison, but also, for a fictional heroine, inevitable.

The one career that did allow women self-sufficiency and self-determination was writing, which sometimes functions as the vocation or avocation of minor and often comic female characters, usually in novels written by men. Writing is not taken up by fictional heroines, however, and for good reason;[3] as a career, it presented both personal and professional difficulties for nineteenth-century women. To be a woman who wrote was in itself a challenge to Victorian conventions of womanhood and femininity. Virtually every attempt by a woman to write for publication was something of a heroic act – or, as both Cora Kaplan and Mary Poovey term it, an act of 'defiance' – demanding a strength of character that was in itself regarded as unwomanly.[4] As the authors of a late nineteenth-century survey and analysis of women's work lament, 'the pursuit of literature was considered to "unsex" a woman,' and '[o]nly natures in which genius is a compelling force can burst such iron bonds' as those imposed by Victorian gender biases.[5] It is debatable, however, if any woman writer in Victorian England ever did burst the iron bonds of conventional feminine roles. While its symbolic associations may have suggested immodesty, writing as practised by women in the Victorian period was almost as private and domestic as mothering. Certainly women authors combined their writing with their domestic roles: Elizabeth Barrett Browning, Margaret Oliphant, and Elizabeth Gaskell all did their writing in their homes, with their children playing around them; Charlotte Brontë wrote while caring for her ailing sisters and father.

Nineteenth-century women novelists create heroines who likewise struggle to burst the iron bonds of conventional femininity, but like lower-middle-class men in their attempts to escape the restrictive conventions of representation and perception, both the characters and the authors have limited success. The cultural constraints on fictional women are, if anything, even more restrictive than those on women in the real world. Feminine modesty notwithstanding, to be of any significance in a narrative a woman must be sexual; that is, she either must be fallen and outcast or she must marry, the standard happy ending for the heroine. To be a heroine, she must also conform to Victorian novelistic conventions of femininity: she must be domestic, subservient, and dependent, both financially and emotionally. As Nancy K. Miller argues, the literary representation of women is constrained by narrative orthodoxies that have been designed to accommodate male plot-lines and masculine fantasies. According to Miller, 'the maxims that pass for the truth of human experience, and the encoding of that experience in literature, are organizations, when they are not fantasies, of the dominant culture.'[6] In Victorian England, the dominant culture was bourgeois and male and the maxims that dictated what a woman must be did more for the middle-class male psyche than they ever did for women. However strong and independent the heroines created by women novelists may be, they almost invariably succumb to the constraints of convention and marry, like Brontë's Jane Eyre and Shirley Keeldar, or if sexually compromised die, like George Eliot's Maggie Tulliver. Victorian heroines, like middle-class Victorian women, are caught in a sexual trap – they have to marry to survive.

This necessity produced a dilemma for many women, who, with neither training for nor access to suitable kinds of employment, could be caught between the equally degrading alternatives of marrying for convenience or of becoming an unwanted spinster, a hanger-on and financial burden to some distant relative. Brontë explores this problem and produces a trenchant critique of the existing social conventions and their effect on young unmarried women in *Shirley* (1849). Interestingly, it is not through the character of the novel's unconventional and free-spirited eponymous heroine that this critique is voiced, but through Caroline Helstone, who is the embodiment of Victorian womanhood, of feminine virtue and modesty. As she ponders her own future, Caroline expresses the importance of useful employment for single women, her conviction that 'single women should have more to do – better chances of interesting and profitable occupation.' But while she can see the problem, she can formulate no solution. '[N]obody in particular is to blame', she concedes, 'for the state in which things are; and I cannot tell, however much I puzzle over it, how they are to be altered for the better; but I feel there is something wrong somewhere.'[7]

Caroline is indeed trapped within the prevailing concepts of femininity and the place of women in the social order, and she ultimately calls on men to rescue women from their existing plight:

Men of England! look at your poor girls, many of them fading around you, dropping off in consumption or decline; or, what is worse, degenerating to sour old maids, – envious, backbiting, wretched, because life is a desert to them; or, what is worst of all, reduced to strive, by scarce modest coquetry and debasing artifice, to gain that position and consideration by marriage, which to celibacy is denied. Fathers! cannot you alter these things? Perhaps not all at once; but consider the matter well when it is brought before you, receive it as a theme worthy of thought: do not dismiss it with an idle jest or an unmanly insult. You would wish to be proud of your daughters and not to blush for them – then seek for them an interest and an occupation which shall rise them above the flirt, the manoeuvrer, the mischief-making tale-bearer. Keep your girls' minds narrow and fettered – they will still be a plague and a care, sometimes a disgrace to you: cultivate them – give them scope and work – they will be your gayest companions in health; your tenderest nurses in sickness; your most faithful prop in age. (pp. 392–3)

Caroline thus exposes the contradictions inherent in the Victorian ideals of womanhood, in the ideology of purity that scorns the celibacy of the old maid and honors the cynical opportunism of the woman who marries for money and position. At the same time, however, Caroline's logic maintains the subordinate and nurturing role of women by assigning the power to transform women to fathers, and by asserting that the girl who has been blessed with 'scope and work' will be a superlative version of the ideal Victorian woman – a superior companion, nurse, and prop to men. Caroline is not the prototype of the independent woman: her deepest desire is, in fact, for marriage and domestic felicity. Her views on the plight of single women, so poignantly expressed, are little more than a cry in the wilderness, but they prepare the way for Gissing and other later writers.

Caroline's voice echoes throughout the polemics of women reformers until at least the end of the century. Anna Jameson was much impressed with Caroline's heartfelt soliloquy, and included a lengthy excerpt in a footnote in the printed version of her 'Sisters of Charity' lecture.[8] At the turn of the century, Clara Collet still finds 'Caroline Helstone's vision of her own future' to be 'the best picture of the middle-class woman's outlook on life'.[9]

The issue of women's employment that Caroline addresses indeed becomes more pressing as the century progresses. The social and economic climate was changing, forcing a change in attitudes towards the idea of women working. By the middle of the nineteenth century, the problem of 'redundant women' was gaining public attention. The number of unmarried middle-class women appeared to be growing rapidly, although, as Martha Vicinus points out, it was a growth in absolute numbers, rather than in a percentage of the female population, and the increasing visibility of these women made the situation appear worse than it was.[10] More problematic than their visibility, however, was their financial dependence. Middle-class women were redundant not only in terms of the marriage market, but in terms of the market for the traditionally acceptable 'respectable' occupations of governess or companion, for which many women, if not most, were neither suited nor inclined. It was their appreciation of economic necessity coupled with a desire to liberate middle-class single women from stifling and enforced idleness that inspired pioneers of the women's movement like Barbara Bodichon, Bessie Raynor Parkes and their associates in the Langham Place circle to establish the Society for Promoting the Employment of Women and its literary organ, the *English Woman's Journal* which, from its inception in 1858, provided a forum for exposing the hardships of women's plight and for disseminating progressive remedies.[11]

Much of the rhetoric and many of the proposals of these early activists suggest, however, that they, like women novelists, were not easily able to free themselves from some of the basic assumptions of Victorian ideals of womanhood. Anna Jameson, for example, in a stirring appeal for greater opportunities for women, advocated work and vocational training in the appropriately feminine fields of teaching, social work, and nursing. Jameson defines a woman's role in clearly orthodox Victorian terms as the nurturer and moral center of the family, whose proper function in society then becomes an extension of her domestic role:

> [s]he begins by being the nurse, the teacher, the cherisher of her home, through her greater tenderness and purer moral sentiments; then she uses these qualities and sympathies on a larger scale, to cherish and purify society.[12]

The continuing and pervasive influence of orthodox notions of femininity on what society in general would accept as suitable employment for 'respectable' women is similarly evident in the limited range of occupations that form the basis of Martha Vicinus's study of Victorian 'independent women'. As Vicinus points out, advocates for women's employment had to find a way 'to justify creating a new role for women in which they could be both public ... and feminine', both 'paid workers' and womanly.[13] The acceptable occupations discussed in *Independent Women* include those that developed women's supposedly innate abilities to serve or nurture and that translated economic necessity or ambition into altruism – careers as teachers, nurses, social workers, or deaconesses.

Despite the apparent conventionality of the roles they defined for women, the growth of these professions nevertheless undoubtedly opened up greater opportunities for women to be independent. These early victories in the struggle for liberation were made possible by a canny manipulation of the very assumptions about femininity that oppressed women, by the insistence on the part of reformers that the feminine skills and civilizing influence of middle-class women should be brought into the public sphere and so be allowed to benefit all of society; in the words of Jameson, women should be allowed to fulfil their natural role, 'to cherish and purify society.' But while women thus achieved some measure of liberation by symbolically representing certain kinds of work as feminine, such work could not function as symbolic of liberation, as one late nineteenth-century working-girl heroine confirms. When advised not to seek employment as a typist in a commercial firm, but to take up the 'higher work' of teaching, she vehemently protests: 'I should hate teaching.... I prefer freedom.'[14] With all its associations with domesticity, work such as teaching could not be taken up by a fictional heroine and be read as anything but a substitution for that supposedly still higher role of traditional marriage and motherhood. Nevertheless, the activism of the fledgling women's movement and the growth of job opportunities for women created a social and cultural climate in which novelists could explore the potential for work to liberate women from more than strictly financial dependence.

INDEPENDENT WOMEN AND WORK: OLIPHANT AND LEVY

The opening up of white-collar work to women in the late nineteenth century provided new opportunities for women, in fiction as in life. As symbolic liberation, lower-middle-class employment presented none of the problems that teaching, nursing, or being a companion did. It was work that had nothing to do with children or with nurturing and that was not done at home. Being, indeed, a new phenomenon, it had few associations with anything – for women, at least.[15] The conventional image of the lower-middle-class male, of course, had powerful associations with domesticity, and these associations may well have smoothed the way for 'respectable' Victorian women who wanted to work by making lower-middle-class jobs seem to some extent suitable for women, even though these jobs brought women into the public sphere. The anonymity of the urban setting and the unassertive nature of lower-middle-class jobs also worked against the interpretation of such work, even when done by women, as a form of exhibition or public performance – as being, like writing, tainted with immodesty.

For ordinary women, there was now at least the possibility of choosing between dependence and independence, the possibility of rejecting conventional feminine roles and even of rejecting marriage as the only fulfilling female destiny. By 1889, the *Girl's Own Paper* – which was, to quote Judith Walkowitz, 'a great defender and interpreter of domestic femininity to lower-middle-class and working-class girls' – was prepared to declare that 'the girl who by steady industry makes a living for herself need be in no haste to change her condition' (that is, to marry).[16] White-collar work has an even more liberating effect on women in fiction, who take up typing and shorthand with enthusiasm. 'Type-writer girls' and other white-collar 'bachelor girls' provide spirited and adventurous heroines for many novels of the 1890s and early 1900s, such as Grant Allen's *The Type-Writer Girl*, Keble Howard's *The Bachelor Girls and their Adventures in Search of Independence*, and George Gissing's *The Odd Women*, which develops the most impressive and successful of the working-woman heroines, Rhoda Nunn. The low pay and numbing routines that make clerical work soul-destroying for male characters – for Leonard Bast in E. M. Forster's *Howards End*, for example – do not discourage female characters, who find in such work the exhilarating means of escape from the even more restrictive confines of the Victorian domestic sphere.

Women (both fictional and real) are invigorated rather than enervated by clerical work because it provides the possibility of independence, and independence is an issue of such consequence that it eclipses that of class – no mean feat in the Victorian period. Most of the women who were willing and able to do low-level white-collar work were middle-class, and indeed clerical jobs for women in government bureaucracies such as the Post Office were initially (i.e. during the 1870s and 1880s) available only by nomination for a limited number of positions. Not only was the awarding of these positions thus restricted, but the women were often segregated from male employees and from the public in order to preserve their 'respectability'.[17] As the century progressed, more white-collar positions with less supervision and prestige became available to women, but the loss in class status that taking on such minimally respectable jobs entailed does not seem to have much concerned anyone, either in fiction or in reality. Feminist historian Meta Zimmeck in fact asserts that, while men in clerical jobs may have been faced with a constant erosion of status as the nineteenth century progressed, 'for middle-class women there was nowhere to go but up' – that is, to a position of greater parity with men in their field, an accomplishment that renders class considerations 'somewhat ephemeral'.[18]

It is doubtful, however, that women working in offices and shops during the late Victorian period felt as uniformly positive about their experience as their counterparts in literature do, although Zimmeck asserts that, for women clerical workers at least, 'the typewriter, the ledger, and the shorthandwriter's pad were instruments not of oppression but of liberation.' But Zimmeck's main support for this claim is evidence drawn from three novels, all written by men.[19] Nonfictional sources from the period suggest greater ambivalence, and indeed express many of the same frustrations with insalubrious working environments, long hours, poor pay and worse prospects that plagued men working at the same jobs. Concerns about dress and sensitivity to criticism about extravagance in their expenditure on clothes also loom large in the psyches of female clerks, just as they had in their male counterparts. In an 1898 essay in *The Economic Journal*, in which she examines the budgets of several working women,

Clara Collet addresses a number of essential, pragmatic issues – such as the inadvisability of an underpaid young woman risking her health by forgoing meals or holidays in order to save money – but devotes an inordinate amount of space to an apologia for the outlay on dress by working women.[20]

There is no doubt, however, that the gradual opening up of real employment and financial opportunities for women in the late nineteenth century opened up new narrative possibilities as well. The fact that women could support themselves respectably by working outside the home presented the truly independent woman – the woman whose story need not be determined by male fantasies – as a viable fictional option. In the 1890s, the image of the independent working woman was typically combined with that of the New Woman in fiction, although the two are not necessarily congruent. Much of the New Woman fiction, however, focused on the evils of traditional marriage and of the double standard in sexual mores, rather than on work or viable avenues of self-determination.

Writing within seemingly less radical parameters of theme and character, Margaret Oliphant arguably made a greater contribution than most of the celebrated New Woman novelists did in the struggle to liberate novelists and their heroines from the constraining conventions of orthodox Victorian femininity. Oliphant, unlike some later creators of independent women, does not explicitly probe the class implications of work for women in her novels. She does, however, explore the implications of both the psychological and practical needs of her female protagonists, needs that can in some cases only be satisfied if there is the opportunity for them to work.

Margaret Oliphant, unlike Brontë, does not openly address the issue of women's roles and their lack of independence as social or philosophical problems in her fiction. But as an author whose writing spans five decades – the 1850s through the 1890s – Oliphant provides through her novels a valuable commentary on the changing attitudes towards women during the second half of the nineteenth century and the effects these changes had on how a woman writer was able to represent women in her fiction. Oliphant is not an especially daring or innovative writer; her debt to Trollope is unmistakable, and she unabashedly uses all the melodramatic conventions of Victorian fiction – rogues compromising young girls, near-fatal illness and delirium leading to personal transformation, past indiscretions coming to haunt prominent social figures, and love stories that keep going astray until the last page. Like other women writing in the second half of the nineteenth century, Oliphant consistently tries to move beyond the stereotypes in her representations of women, without ever overturning the conventions. Susan Vincent, the sister of the protagonist of *Salem Chapel* (1863), for example, does not suffer the fate of most other virtuous young women whose reputations are compromised by cads – she does not die. But she is suitably prostrated by her experience, which is complicated by the fact that she is suspected of murdering her erstwhile fiancé, and she becomes dangerously ill. As in many Victorian novels, physical recuperation also denotes moral rehabilitation, and as Susan slowly recovers, the proofs and assurances of her innocence of both legal and moral offenses accumulate thick and fast. Susan's moral rehabilitation functions only figuratively, however, and while there is no death, there is a transfiguration. During her illness, she becomes an image of transcendent, deathlike purity as she lies 'stretched upon her white couch, marble white'. Once recovered, she remains distanced from the meagerness of the present and of reality, a 'grand figure, large and calm and noble like a Roman woman'.[21] As this quasi-classical figure, Susan commands attention and even awe, but she is no longer eligible to be a heroine or a wife within the restrictive codes of the Victorian novel. Moreover Susan, while larger than life, remains dependent. It is obvious in the text not only that she will never marry, but also that she must continue to live under the protection of her mother and her brother.

Oliphant creates a much more assertive woman, and a much greater challenge to the Victorian conventions of femininity, in the eponymous heroine of *Phoebe Junior* (1876). Phoebe is clearly a character whose drive and energy need an outlet; she cannot be contained within a restrictive domestic sphere. Admittedly the senior Phoebe, who appears in *Salem Chapel*, was almost as spirited as her daughter, but her energies were directed into overt and simpering flirtations aimed at securing the most advantageous match available to her in the limited social circle of Dissenting tradespeople in Carlingford. Superficially, Phoebe Junior's situation is similar; she, too, is anxious to make an advantageous marriage, but unlike her mother, she is emotionally self-aware and socially sophisticated. Phoebe may beguile, but she does not pursue her suitors. Moreover, while she may not be independent,

Phoebe is in control, both of herself and of her situation. In choosing rich but dim-witted Clarence Copperhead over Reginald May, she is not choosing money over a love-match, but a life of action over an idyllic domestic retirement. After carefully preventing Reginald from openly expressing his intentions, she mourns briefly for the kind of life and love she is thus denying herself:

> She cried, and her heart contracted with a real pang. He was very tender in his reverential homage, very romantic, a true lover, not the kind of man who wants a wife or wants a clever companion to amuse him, and save him the expense of a coach, and be his to refer to in everything. That was an altogether different kind of thing. Phoebe went in with a sense in her mind that perhaps she had never touched so close upon a higher kind of existence, and perhaps never again might have the opportunity.[22]

That she senses what she is losing 'in her mind', rather than in her heart, is typical of Phoebe; so is the rapid recovery that follows this sentimental interlude: 'before she had crossed the garden' her thoughts revert to Clarence and her doubts that he will be able to stand up to his parents' objections to her as his bride.

It would be easy to dismiss Phoebe as simply calculating, but the complexity of Oliphant's characterization demands a more subtle analysis. Phoebe is not, like Reginald, a romantic; nor is she, like Reginald's sister Ursula, the typical Victorian heroine who is unaware either of loving or of being loved, who is perpetually the pawn in other people's games. But neither is Phoebe completely unfeeling and selfish. Although appalled and embarrassed by their vulgarity, she demonstrates real affection and regard for her grandparents; and while she is not moved by 'actual love' for Clarence, she does feel 'a kind of habitual affection' for him. (p. 267) Moreover, Phoebe is loyal and honorable. She does not desert the Mays when financial disaster and dishonor threaten to destroy them, nor will she desert Clarence when his father threatens to disinherit him. Indeed, the doggedness and energy with which Phoebe embarks on her mission to save Mr May's reputation suggest that her virtues are not the traditional feminine ones of tenderness and subservience, but the supposedly masculine ones of action and command. It is hardly surprising, then, that she regards marriage not as the culmination of romantic dreams and the fulfilment of her feminine identity, but as a career:

> She did not dislike Clarence Copperhead, and it was no horror to her to think of marrying him. She had felt for years that this might be on the cards, and there were a great many things in it which demanded consideration. He was not very wise, nor a man to be enthusiastic about, but he would be a career to Phoebe. She did not think of it humbly like this, but with a big capital – a Career. Yes; she could put him into parliament, and keep him there. She could thrust him forward (she believed) to the front of affairs. He would be as good as a profession, a position, a great work to Phoebe. He meant wealth (which she dismissed in its superficial aspect as something meaningless and vulgar, but accepted in its higher aspect as an almost necessary condition of influence), and he meant all the possibilities of future power. Who can say that she was not as romantic as any girl of twenty could be? only her romance took an unusual form. It was her head that was full of throbbings and pulsings, not her heart. (p. 234)

The narrator is, of course, having a great deal of fun with Phoebe's notions of Clarence as Career, which are in their way as romantically inflated as the more traditional versions of 'living happily ever after'. It is even possible to see this passage as mocking the idea of women aspiring to careers outside of marriage, except that Phoebe so brilliantly succeeds whenever she goes against accepted customs or values, whether by wearing black to a ball or by destroying the evidence of Mr May's forgery. It is less Phoebe that is mocked than the conventions that contain an unsentimental, energetic, and intelligent heroine – the narrator asserts that she has 'more brains' than Clarence and her grandfather Tozer 'put together' (p. 316) – within the confines of domestic romance and of traditional feminine roles.

In *Phoebe Junior*, it seems that Oliphant strains as much as Phoebe does against the restrictions that limit the acceptable options for fictional heroines. And as Penelope Fitzgerald notes, it is not until late in her career, in *Kirsteen: The Story of a Scotch Family Seventy Years Ago* (1891), that Oliphant 'allowed herself a heroine who stays unmarried and opens a successful business.'[23] But in this apparent flouting of the conventions of domestic fiction, Oliphant is circumspect. She circumvents the provocative implications of having a heroine who becomes a successful businesswoman by setting the story back in time and in a culture recognizably foreign to late Victorian English readers. The sense of distance between the two cultures is heightened by the fact that Kirsteen herself moves between London and her home, Drumcarro House, which exists in a kind of time warp, dominated by her father who insists on living according to the highland customs of a generation earlier. That Kirsteen is driven to resist unreasonable patriarchal domination seems, under the circumstances, only just and reasonable.

The old laird of Drumcarro is indeed a thinly disguised parody of a Victorian patriarch. He overvalues his sons and has contempt for his daughters, whose only mission in life, he believes, should be to serve and obey him in all things. The daughters represent stock types of Victorian fiction: the eldest, Anne, has run away to marry a respectable and skilled young doctor, against the wishes of her tyrannical and unreasonable father who regards him as a 'commoner' and henceforth refuses to acknowledge either the marriage or his daughter; the second daughter, Mary, dutifully – even enthusiastically – marries an aging but wealthy Scottish lord; and Jeanie, the youngest, almost loses her virtue to the heir of a duke, but is ultimately won by a sensitive but dashing hero of the Peninsular Wars. The third of the four daughters is the rebellious Kirsteen, who runs away to avoid being forced to marry the lord whom Mary later accepts. While Kirsteen thus irredeemably disgraces herself in her father's eyes – and further degrades herself by becoming a mantua-maker – she functions in the text as an exemplar of honor and courage.

The lives of Kirsteen's sisters are, like those of all conventional Victorian heroines, defined and controlled by men. Even Anne's rebellion ultimately constitutes little more than a passage from the domination of her father to that of her husband. But Kirsteen herself, the narrator asserts, 'with her quick temper and high spirit and lively imagination' is not suited for a blank part. She is, rather, 'one of those who make a story for themselves'. (I: 65) In this regard she is like Phoebe, who will not let others take control of her life. But unlike Phoebe, Kirsteen yearns for an independent existence rather than a vicarious career. She wishes that she, like her brothers, could go 'out into the world' (I: 46) and once there she begins to realize the value of an occupation. Stopping briefly in Glasgow on her way to London, she sees 'a flock of mill-girls' on their way to a cotton factory:

Kirsteen's eyes followed them with a sort of envy. They were going to their work, they were carrying on the common tenor of their life, while she sat there arrested in everything. 'I wish,' she said, with a sigh, 'I had something to do.' (I: 220)

Accordingly, Kirsteen recognizes, just as Victorian feminists did, the importance of work in any attempt to effect independence and self-definition, in any attempt to seize control of her destiny and her story. The fact that the mill-girls are far below her in class status does not diminish them in her eyes. Their independence – undoubtedly more apparent than real – makes class issues 'somewhat ephemeral', just as it would for middle-class women working in offices in late nineteenth-century London.

Having just left her home, however, and with no clear plans for her future, Kirsteen is caught in a kind of limbo: she has escaped the direct interventions of her father's will, but not the psychological paralysis of patriarchal domination, a paralysis analogous to that which hampers novelists and so limits the narrative options available for Victorian heroines. Just as for women in general, financial self-sufficiency is only part of what is at stake for Kirsteen; she has to find 'something to do', has to establish a tenor for her independent life in order to free herself from the sense of being 'arrested in everything'.

While Oliphant thus takes Kirsteen one step further than Phoebe along the road to liberation, nothing in this novel suggests that either the author or her creation is a radical or even an unequivocal feminist. Despite her yearnings for an active life, Kirsteen leaves home only to escape being forced to marry, a not unconventional escape mechanism for a heroine in her situation. Marriage is distasteful to Kirsteen not because of any aversion to marriage itself or even to the proposed bridegroom, but because she has promised Ronald Drummond, who has set off for India with her brother, that she will wait for him. Accordingly, Kirsteen embarks on her working life with no sense that it will be her only and ultimate vocation. But the stories of her working life and of her personal life follow different trajectories, and indeed are played out in different venues. Her dressmaking business in London prospers. Her personal story, however, remains grounded in Scotland, her family, and her first and only love. It is a story, moreover, that develops in an almost *ad hoc* manner, moving not towards climax and closure, but through a series of disappointments and disheartening realizations. When she learns of Ronald's death, it is with a sense of sad resignation that she acknowledges that 'her life had taken the form and colour which it must now bear to the end. She had accepted it for his sake that she might be faithful to him, and now it was to be for ever, with no break or change.' The narrator's summation of Kirsteen's fate at this point indeed reads like a warning against radical change, against any thoughtless or irresponsible severing of personal or traditional bonds, including narrative ones: 'She was independent of all the world, and bound to that work for ever.' (II: 120) For Kirsteen, as for Oliphant, commitment to work does not satisfactorily replace personal commitment.

Perhaps for women of Oliphant's generation, and especially for Oliphant herself, who had had independence and the financial responsibility for her children thrust upon her by the untimely death of her husband, work and independence would inevitably bear the aspect of just another form of bondage. To a single woman of a younger generation, who was perhaps more attuned to the concept of the 'new woman', work and independence bore a more uniformly positive guise. In *The Romance of a Shop* (1888), Amy Levy, a young Anglo-Jewish author of poetry, fiction, and criticism, tells the story not of a Scotch family seventy years since, but of a contemporary English one.[24] Levy is much more daring than Oliphant, not only in the setting of her novel, but in the attitudes towards work she expresses through her characters. The four Lorimer sisters, who had been raised in comfortable middle-class circumstances, find themselves poor and homeless after the sudden death of their father and must face the prospect of being split up to live with various relatives. But the sisters are unwilling to be separated and dependent; they prefer to stay together and work. They consider and reject the kinds of work generally regarded as appropriate for middle-class women – becoming teachers or governesses;[25] Gertrude, the protagonist, even briefly considers a literary career. They finally hit on the rather unlikely idea of opening a photography business, thus following the injunction voiced in the *English Woman's Journal* that women must 'work as they have not done yet'.[26] And this work casts them headlong into the murky depths of the lower middle class. For the Lorimer sisters, however, a shop suggests growth and opportunity, not lower-middle-class limitations. 'Think of all the dull little ways by which women, ladies, are generally reduced to earning their living!' comments Gertrude. 'But a business – that's so different. It is progressive; a creature capable of growth; the very qualities in which women's work is dreadfully lacking.' (p. 63)

The creative promise of their prospective business indeed represents the romance of the age of commerce – the romance of a shop. Only Fanny, the eldest and most conventional of the sisters, sees such an enterprise as degrading: 'need it come to that – to open a shop?' she protests. But Fanny, as her sisters recognize and the narrator confirms, is 'behind the age,' a 'round, sentimental peg in the square scientific hole of the latter half of the nineteenth century'. 'Don't you know that it is quite distinguished to keep a shop?' Lucy asks her. 'That poets sell wall-papers, and first-class honour men sell lamps? That Girton students make bonnets, and are thought none the worse for doing so?' (p. 63) As they playfully try to cajole Fanny into accepting their plan, the other sisters suggest fanciful scenarios for their future as shopkeepers:

> 'Our photographs would be so good and our manners so charming that our fame would travel from one end of the earth to the other!' added Lucy, with a sudden abandonment of her grave and didactic manner.
>
> 'We would have afternoon tea in the studio on Sunday, to which everyone should flock; duchesses, cabinet ministers, and Mr. Irving. We should become the fashion, make colossal fortunes, and ultimately marry dukes!' finished off Gertrude. (p. 64)

Gertrude thus invokes the conventional happy ending as a joke. Money and marriage are not what this romance is supposed to be all about.

The girls courageously commit themselves to their communal destiny with a set of resolutions that confirms both their youthful optimism and their awareness of the inevitable hardships that await them in their 'romantic' adventure in business. They resolve to be happy, not to be cynical, and never to mention that they have seen better days. 'Thus, with laughing faces,' the narrator comments, 'they stood up and defied the Fates.' (p. 75) Defying the Fates, however, is a small matter compared with defying social conventions, especially as represented by the Lorimers' Aunt Caroline, Mrs Septimus Pratt, who denounces their plan as 'dangerous and unwomanly': 'She spoke freely of loss of caste; damage to prospects – vague and delicate possession of the female sex – and of the complicated evils which must necessarily arise from an undertaking so completely devoid of chaperones.' (p. 80) There is in this passage a troubled irony, the product of an apparent desire to undermine Mrs Pratt's prudery that is blunted by an acquiescence to the persistent power of Mrs Grundy and her minions. This conflict in principles continues to influence the Lorimers' responses to their aunt, whom they are willing to defy, but never to ignore or offend. They recognize that 'when all was said, Mrs Pratt's was not a presence to be in any way passed over', and Gertrude is sincerely 'distressed and disturbed' when her aunt later suggests that they are inviting scandal because of their irregular style of life. (pp. 105, 108)

Levy, too, repeatedly defers to the more stringent demands of convention, frequently emphasizing the femininity and moral delicacy of the Lorimers. She thus presents Gertrude, the driving force behind the business scheme, as being inspired less by their romantic adventure than by a desire to re-establish a home. When her friend suggests that they simply seek employment as assistant photographers, Gertrude responds, 'We want a home and an occupation, Conny; a real, living occupation. Think of little Phyllis, for instance, trudging by herself to some great shop in all weathers and seasons!' (p. 76). Their shop is thus more than a source of income, it is a refuge for the weaker sisters: for sentimental and utterly ineffectual Fanny, who takes up 'the vague duty of creating an atmosphere of home for her more strongminded sisters' (p. 89); and for physically – and, as it turns out, morally – frail Phyllis. The most damaging aspect of the Lorimers' situation in Mrs Pratt's eyes – the complete absence of chaperones – is, moreover, something that Gertrude is very conscious of and not entirely at ease with. When their neighbor, a young artist named Frank Jermyn, hires them to take a series of photographs in his studio, for example, Lucy and Gertrude hesitate to make the appointment for an unchaperoned business call: 'It was humiliating, it was ridiculous, but it was none the less true, that neither of these business-like young people liked first to make a definite suggestion for the inevitable visit to Frank's studio.' (p. 101)

Despite the practical and moral problems that their new life presents, the Lorimers embrace it with energy and pursue it tenaciously. 'Oh, Lucy,' Gertrude exclaims when they finally have the shop and their modest living quarters arranged, 'this is work, this is life. I think that we have never worked or lived before.' (p. 87) This ecstatic equation of work with life suggests that work gives them something else as well. Work gives them a special kind of freedom, the freedom to create their own destinies, their own stories; it gives them access to a self-determined life, not just to a conventional existence. But work and life also bring the Lorimers face to face with the harsh reality of running a shop, rather than with romance. Business is slow at first and money short, and the sisters become discouraged and disillusioned with their dreary and shabby conditions. The reality of down-at-the-heel lower-middle-class life – with that seemingly inevitable fixation on the common and the trivial so scorned by middle-class observers both inside and outside the realm of fiction – prompts Gertrude, in a moment of despair, to question the value of their cramped existence:

> Was this life, this ceaseless messing about in a pokey glass out-house [the photography studio], this eating and drinking and sleeping in the shabby London rooms?
> Was any human creature to be blamed who rebelled against it? Did not flesh and blood cry out against such sordidness, with all the revel of the spring-time going on in the world beyond?
> It is base and ignoble perhaps to scorn the common round, the trivial task, but is it not also ignoble and base to become so immersed in them as to desire nothing beyond? (pp. 124–5)

In a more tranquil mood some hours later, Gertrude looks back on their first troubled year in the shop, and recognizes that it is in the harshness and sordidness of reality that the value of their experience in fact lies:

> Her brief rebellious mood of the morning had passed away, and, looking back on the year behind her, she experienced a measure of the content which we all feel after something attempted, something done. That she had been brought face to face with the sterner side of life, had lost some illusions, suffered some pain, she did not regret. It seemed to her that she had not paid too great a price for the increased reality of her present existence. (p. 131)

Work has liberated Gertrude and her sisters from the protective but stifling cocoon of conventional middle-class femininity and the enforced idleness that comfortable spinsterhood would entail. In their faded dresses and worn boots, they may look more like moths than butterflies, but at least they can fly.

The dead hand of convention ultimately reasserts its authority over Levy and her characters in *The Romance of a Shop*. Levy is unable to sustain the realism of the shop, and concludes the novel by moving into the diluted romance of traditional love stories. Deborah Epstein Nord interprets this move as a failure on Levy's part. 'Levy's failure,' Nord argues, 'is precisely that she does not know what to do with her independent, idiosyncratic heroines – particularly Gertrude – and resorts to killing off the beautiful, "fallen" sister and marrying off the remaining ones.'[27] Certainly Levy falls back onto the most worn novelistic clichés, turning the Lorimer sisters into stock types of Victorian fiction, much as Oliphant does with the Douglas sisters but without Oliphant's ironic undercutting. Fanny's long-lost beau unexpectedly returns to marry her – 'like a person in a book', Phyllis quips (p. 143) – having made his fortune in Australia. Phyllis, morally compromised by a dalliance with a wealthy married cad, subsequently (and inevitably) dies of consumption. Lucy marries Frank Jermyn and Gertrude marries a learned and distinguished lord (with the unfortunate name of Watergate – how was Levy to know?). Perhaps Levy, for all her apparent commitment to female independence, had, like her protagonist Gertrude, an inveterate yearning for the domestic idyll, 'a feminine belief in love as the crown and flower of life'. (pp. 131–2) But a stronger influence is that of social and literary convention, of what is acceptable and what is expected of young ladies and heroines. Accordingly, when Phyllis falls prey to seduction, Gertrude comes to the unhappy conclusion that Aunt Caroline was right, if not in her moral philosophy then at least in her pragmatic assessment of social attitudes. 'It is the Aunt Carolines of this world who are right', Gertrude muses bitterly. 'I ought to have listened to her. She understood human nature better than I.' (p. 178) In light of this comment, it is inappropriate to read the ending of the novel simply as an artistic failure or to interpret Phyllis's death as Levy's 'revenge' on the beautiful sister, as Oscar Wilde and subsequent critics have done.[28] The novel ends the way it does because as Levy brings the stories of the Lorimer sisters to a conclusion, Aunt Caroline is sitting on her shoulder.

Levy is thus able to use work as symbolic of liberation and independence but only as a temporary condition, not as the satisfactory culmination of her characters' lives. The only lingering remnant of female self-definition through work survives in Lucy, whose role in both the business and the novel is second only to Gertrude's. Though less dominant and philosophical than Gertrude, Lucy is adaptable and optimistic, even finding advantages in their poverty and the consequent narrowing of their associations: 'That is the best of being poor', she affirms; 'one's chances of artificial acquaintanceships are so much lessened. One gains in quality what one loses in quantity.' (p. 131) Within this scant number of acquaintances, Lucy nevertheless has two suitors, and while she does marry, she chooses impoverished Frank over the wealthy brother of their fashionable friend Conny. More importantly, Lucy continues to work, even after becoming a mother. She gains distinction in her field, although the medals she wins are for her suitably feminine specialty of photographing children. But most satisfying for the advocates of working women is the rhetorical subordination of Frank's career to hers. 'Her husband', the narrator comments, 'is no less successful in his own line.' (p. 195)

Levy is thus, like Oliphant, unable to espouse lower-middle-class employment unequivocally as a positive end for middle-class women. But Levy does move her characters out of the confines of work that has traditional feminine associations. Kirsteen can find a means of subsistence and even of self-expression in the artistry of dressmaking, but the Lorimers find self-definition in the artistry of a new and relatively untried field, demonstrating a distinctly unfeminine (in Victorian terms) recklessness and pioneering spirit. But as the century progressed and new kinds of 'respectable' employment were increasingly open to women, employment without domestic associations, so too were writers increasingly able to imagine heroines who actively seek the experience and freedom of working in shops or offices. Indeed, the young woman who defies or rejects conventional roles by finding gainful employment in some segment of the lower middle class becomes a fairly common trope in turn-of-the-century British fiction. In a novel by Keble Howard with the revealing title of *The Bachelor Girls and their Adventures in Search of Independence*

(1907), for example, two respectable young women from the village of Chipping Bagot – one the daughter of the impecunious local vicar, the other of the equally impoverished village doctor – set off to find work in London. In becoming Bachelor Girls, they wish to escape unfulfilling feminine roles and the narrow rounds of domestic routine; they are 'sick of darning socks, sick of Chipping Bagot, sick of reading soft stories to ungrateful old women, sick of teaching in the Sunday School, sick of bread-puddings, and noisy meals, and all the rest of it.'[29] Like the Lorimer sisters before them, they must learn that independence entails the frustration of coping with mundane necessities and limited resources as well as the euphoria of freedom. And like the Lorimers, they eventually forgo their bachelor roles for marriage.

WOMEN AND WHITE-COLLAR WORK: ALLEN AND GISSING

Not all writers felt constrained finally to consign their spirited and independent young heroines to marriage, however. In two novels written in the 1890s, *The Woman Who Did* (1895) and *The Type-Writer Girl* (1897), Grant Allen explores the plight of women in late Victorian culture from divergent perspectives. Between them, these novels present a useful commentary on late Victorian attitudes towards class and on the conventions of representing women in fiction. What Herminia Barton, the heroine of the first novel, in fact does is eschew marriage, on the strictest of moral and philosophical grounds, in favor of a free union. Her attempt to free herself from social and cultural constraints is thus literal rather than symbolic. As in most of the New Woman novels, the issue is not work and independence but marriage and faulty sexual mores, although Herminia does work and must continue to work to support herself and her child after the untimely death of her free-union partner.[30] Herminia's chosen profession, however, is the approved middle-class feminine vocation of teaching. Once she has disgraced herself by having an illegitimate child, however, she is unemployable as a teacher and is reduced to the declassé vocation of journalism. Writing for publication is, of course, not an entirely proper line of work for a woman in the Victorian period and the symbolic undermining of Herminia's pristine femininity that this profession entails indeed prompts Allen to soften its implications. Through the narrator he reassures the reader that, outside of one serious attempt at a novel that is unappreciated by the public, her writing is of 'so commonplace and so anonymous [a kind] that she was spared that worst insult of seeing her hack-work publicly criticized as though it afforded some adequate reflection of the mind that produced it.'[31] Allen is clearly at pains to sustain the private and domestic dimensions of Herminia's character, her thoroughly conventional middle-class femininity.

Allen's characterization of Herminia indeed conforms to all the most cherished Victorian ideals of womanhood. She is dainty and beautiful, initially supports herself by the traditionally accepted career of teaching, and regards motherhood as 'the best privilege of her sex'. (p. 94) As Alison Cotes observes, 'Herminia, for all her liberated theories, remains an image of romantic womanhood, with the finest ideals of motherhood and femininity.'[32] Accordingly, Herminia is never free, and neither is her creator. Allen is trapped in a quagmire of clichés in what appears to be an attempt to raise his heroine to such a level of unassailable virtue that neither her motives nor her unconventional liaison can be questioned by any thoughtful reader. He invokes images of angels and martyrs, virginal purity and motherhood, but succeeds only in creating a heroine who is tedious and even perverse in her implacable commitment to self-sacrifice.

The Woman Who Did is less a novel than a treatise – a solemn, heavy-handed pronouncement against 'the leprous taint of that national blight that calls itself "respectability".' (p. 94) It was nevertheless immensely popular, running to twenty editions in one year despite uniformly bad reviews. And it was indeed the popularity of the book that some reviewers most deplored. Margaret Oliphant complained of the growing tendency towards sensationalism in novels and the cynical 'practical consciousness' among writers 'that it is profitable to shock', *The Woman Who Did* representing the most flagrant example of this phenomenon. 'The twenty editions of Mr Grant Allen are not a joke to be laughed at in society', she admonishes, 'but a shame to society, and a most dangerous precedent.'[33] Rather than setting a precedent, however, Allen's novel was the culmination of a subcategory of New Woman fiction dubbed 'the purity school'. And while unquestionably the worst novel of its kind, *The Woman Who Did*, Gail Cunningham notes, 'ultimately overshadowed all the rest and was remembered long after the works of . . . [Allen's] more sensible contemporaries had faded into oblivion.'[34] *The Woman Who Did* also spawned progeny at a prodigious rate. Within months, *The Woman Who Didn't* (by Victoria Cross) and two editions of *The Woman Who Wouldn't* (by Lucas Cleeve) were published, and *Punch* featured the story of 'The Woman Who Wouldn't Do'.[35]

A novel of such little distinction that was nevertheless so widely read, widely reviled, and widely parodied clearly hit a sensitive nerve in Victorian culture. Women in novels challenge conventions or engage in illicit sexual relations long before Herminia without drawing fire on such a grand scale. What most outraged – and apparently most titillated – the Victorian sensibility was her unrelenting and unrepentant stand against marriage. To Oliphant, *The Woman Who Did* is an instrument of 'the crusade against marriage', and the currency it gives its subject matter, which she finds 'painful' even 'to refer to', has an 'effect upon the general mind and conversation [that] is disastrous.'[36] It is, nevertheless, the shocking nature of its subject and of its polemics that makes the novel noteworthy, as another unenthusiastic reviewer admits. Millicent Garrett Fawcett assures her readers that, although 'feeble and silly to the last degree,' *The Woman Who Did* is worthy of comment because its author purports to support the enfranchisement of women, while in fact undermining their cause. Grant Allen, she asserts, 'is not a friend but an enemy, and it is as an enemy that he endeavours to link together the claim of women to citizenship and social and industrial independence, with attacks upon marriage and the family.'[37]

Even an attack on marriage, however, does not fully explain the furor that raged over Allen's novel, especially since his heroine's *outré* convictions and behavior lead her to a suitably miserable fate: poverty, rejection, and ultimately suicide. Moreover, other New Women in fiction – Ménie Muriel Dowie's Gallia, for example – question the morality of conventional marriage and inspire only mixed responses and respectable sales. Even Thomas Hardy's Sue Bridehead, while eliciting moral outrage from reviewers, did not turn *Jude the Obscure* into a wildly lucrative bestseller. What so fascinated and repelled Victorian readers about Herminia, I would argue, is the clash between ideal femininity and radical ideas in Allen's characterization of her. The New Woman virtually by definition does not conform to the Victorian ideal of womanhood – that is what makes her new and what makes Sue and Gallia less controversial than Herminia. Allen's use of the rhetoric of purity in recounting a tale of scandalous conduct is a potential threat to Victorian ideology, as Oliphant recognizes when she acknowledges the 'additional danger' in this 'dunghill [that] is constructed on the best sanitary principles' with 'no nastiness, scarcely even an evil smell to it.'[38] Herminia's greatest sin, accordingly, is not that she openly and unabashedly engages in fornication, but that she does so in the guise of the angel in the house, while endlessly mouthing her favorite scriptural text, 'the truth shall make ye free'. To the Victorian sensibility, she is a blasphemy, the Whore tricked out as the Madonna.

In *The Type-Writer Girl*, Allen creates a very different heroine, with a very different approach to her situation within the restrictive Victorian patriarchy. Herminia's challenge to established values and conventions is essentially retained within the private sphere. Sex and marriage are the salient issues, not work. The heroine of *The Type-Writer Girl*, by contrast, is defined by work from the outset in the title of the novel. Juliet, the orphaned daughter of a debt-ridden army officer, decides to learn typing and shorthand and the art of 'professional indigence'.[39] Through the voice of his heroine, as first-person narrator of this zany version of what was becoming a familiar plot, Allen lightheartedly mocks contemporary assumptions about women, work, and propriety. Reflecting on her choice of careers, for example, Juliet equates the supposedly genteel accomplishment of piano-playing with typing and compares them both unfavorably with traditionally feminine but decidedly working-class occupations. 'I did not then know that every girl in London can write shorthand', she comments, 'and that type-writing as an accomplishment is as diffused as the piano; else I might have turned my hand to some honest trade instead, such as millinery or cake-making.' (p. 20) Nevertheless office work, in Juliet's view, liberates her from the role of 'young lady', and the symbols and agents of her emancipation are her typewriter and her bicycle. And while Juliet's proud acknowledgment of her place in the lower middle class functions as a kind of declaration of independence, the same class position continues to suggest limitations for men. The law clerks with whom she works are as drab, spiritless, and unimaginative as the dry legal documents they draw up.

If Juliet is never weighed down by the mundane necessities of lower-middle-class life, it is in part because she never acknowledges reality, however freely she may acknowledge her class. Juliet translates the most ordinary people and events of her world into latter-day versions of characters and episodes from opera, classical literature, or Shakespearean drama, and she is anxious to cast herself in the role her name suggests. Her story could indeed be called 'the romance of an office', but it is nevertheless a romance with a peculiar twist that produces an ending truly liberated from the dictates of conventional romance. Alone and penniless in Venice at the conclusion of yet another unlikely escapade, Juliet confronts the death of romance as well as the more pragmatic issue of how to get back to London with an invocation to what could be interpreted as her patron saints: 'St. Nicholas, help! John Stuart Mill, stand by me!' (p. 255) As the allusions and the rhetoric suggest, Juliet is also confronting the conflicting ideologies that shape her character. She resolves the conflict in a most unconventional way: she gives up the man she has cast as her Romeo and returns to what might after all be the more daring and romantic role of type-writer girl.

The Type-Writer Girl thus ends on an optimistic note, with the heroine voluntarily remaining single and independent – and in the lower middle class. But *The Type-Writer Girl* did not generate the reaction that Allen's earlier novel had, and the example of *The Woman Who Did* and the furor it inspired make clear how restrictive Victorian novelistic conventions of femininity remain, even in the last decade of the century. To be of any significance in a narrative, a woman still has to be sexual and either marry or be fallen and outcast. If she is to elicit a sympathetic response she cannot, like Herminia, be represented as sexual but neither married nor fallen. And if she is to elicit any interest she cannot be an old maid, although she can, like Lucy Snowe or Kirsteen, end up 'widowed' before having the opportunity to solemnize a previously acknowledged commitment. Even the New Women generally conform to standard expectations and reluctantly submit to marriage and the prospect of living miserably ever after. It is unlikely that even spirited and comic Juliet would have been able to espouse the single life had there not been the example of a more impressive heroine before her, for it is only with the appearance of Rhoda Nunn in George Gissing's *The Odd Women* (1893), which predates both of Allen's novels, that a woman in fiction finally triumphs over the conventions and is able to opt for a career rather than for marriage to a handsome and eligible man. And in the end it is not truth, but lower-middle-class employment that sets this woman free.[40] More to the point, it is her ability to find fulfilment in a career rather than in a sexual relationship that frees her from the dominant conventions of Victorian femininity and traditional novelistic plot-lines.[41]

Rhoda actively rejects not only the role of wife, but also the most obvious of traditional 'feminine' employments, teaching. Her assessment of her brief career as a teacher echoes the objection voiced by contemporary feminists that single women, whether suited to such work or not, turned to teaching to support themselves simply because there were few if any other options that were socially acceptable. 'Half my teaching was a sham', she admits to a friend, ' – a pretence of knowing what I neither knew nor cared to know. I had gone into it like most girls, as a dreary matter of course.' Rhoda's decision to spend a year learning commercial skills – shorthand, bookkeeping, and commercial correspondence – frees her from a sense of worthlessness. Her health improves and she feels that she is now 'worth something in the world.'[42]

Rhoda is certainly 'worth something' in the eyes of the other characters, most of whom are in awe of her. The ineffectual Madden sisters, who scratch out a marginal existence in the traditional roles of governess and companion, are overcome by her strength and resourcefulness. 'She is *full* of practical expedients. The most wonderful person!' they report enthusiastically to their younger sibling, Monica. 'She is quite like a *man* in energy and resources. I never imagined that one of our sex could resolve and plan and act as she does!' (p. 57) Rhoda indeed seems more 'manly' than the typically diminutive and ineffectual lower-middle-class male characters in fiction during this period. Her strength of character, coupled with her imposing physical presence, also makes her a sexually potent figure who catches the attention of Everard Barfoot, the handsome middle-class suitor she eventually rejects. Nevertheless, Gissing does not represent Rhoda as either unfeminine or as a *femme fatale*. Her decision against marriage is one she struggles with, and her respect for the supreme feminine role – motherhood – is made clear in her gentle but heartfelt lecture to a despairing Monica near the end of the novel. She admonishes Monica to remember her responsibility to her unborn child, invoking all the time-honored values of Victorian womanhood: love, duty, and Nature. (p. 315)

It is indeed through the characterization of Monica that the significance of Rhoda's character and actions, and of Gissing's analysis of the position of women in late Victorian England, becomes clear. Rather than being just another rebellious New Woman, Rhoda becomes the thoughtful and intelligent woman who struggles to protect herself from the fate that destroys weak and passive women like Monica and her sisters. The lives of all three Madden sisters are described in terms of bondage. The experience of the older two working as companion or governess to a series of relatively unrefined families becomes service 'in one or the other house of bondage.' (p. 44) In a fruitless attempt to find an easy and comfortable life, Monica consigns herself to a series of other kinds of bondage, often psychologically self-induced. Having even less training and aptitude than her older sisters, she is unfit to attempt teaching, and so works as an apprentice in a draper's shop, where she is overworked and underpaid. Given the opportunity to begin vocational training under the guidance of Rhoda, she is almost paralyzed by fear of the older woman's energetic enthusiasm and her own ineptitude: 'To put herself in Miss Nunn's hands might possibly result in a worse form of bondage than she suffered at the shop; she would never be able to please such a person, and failure, she imagined, would result in more or less contemptuous dismissal.' (p. 63) Her loveless marriage to Widdowson, which she initially sees as a form of escape from misery and poverty, proves to be the worst bondage of all, one that prompts her to look back favorably on her life in the shop when she had at least some privacy in which to think or to grieve:

> She wished to be alone. The poorest bed in a servant's garret would have been thrice welcome to her; liberty to lie awake, to think without a disturbing presence, to shed tears if need be – that seemed to her a precious boon. She thought with envy of the shop-girls in Walworth Road; wished herself back there. (p. 212)

Monica's story provides a compendium of issues regarding class and gender in the late Victorian period.[43] Like so many heroines of the period – including Rhoda Nunn – Monica is an orphan who has been raised genteelly but left with few resources. But unlike Rhoda or any of the other bachelor-girl or typewriter-girl heroines, Monica has nothing of the New Woman about her. She is, instead, the ideal of passive femininity; she has 'native elegance' and 'no aptitude for anything but being a pretty, cheerful, engaging girl, much dependent on the love and gentleness of those about her.' (p. 41) Accordingly, she is unfit for any kind of gainful employment or for the demands of an independent life. The drudgery and long hours of the shop and the intellectual demands of learning clerical skills alike undermine her health, and while she seems eminently suited for a middle-class marriage, she is also unfit to endure the emotional strain of dealing with a jealous husband. She is finally unfit even for motherhood, too weak to withstand the physical and emotional rigors of pregnancy and childbirth. Accordingly, her death represents the withering of ideal Victorian femininity when confronted with the conditions of real life. But Monica's experiences also provide valuable insights into the operation of status within the lower middle class and other marginal groups in the late nineteenth century.

One of the hallmarks of Gissing's fiction is the subtlety with which he delineates the hierarchies within these marginal classes, and in *The Odd Women* his sensitivity to nuances of status is especially acute. The status of the various women in the novel is problematic, largely because they are 'odd women,' with neither fathers nor husbands whose class positions would automatically define those of their wives and daughters. Without the wealth necessary to retain middle-class status, there is no other single criterion for placing them and their relative class positions are complicated by the coexistence of several different systems of defining values. Despite their poverty, the older Madden sisters retain the status conferred by upbringing, a moderate level of education, and 'genteel' employment. Their bearing, if nothing else, sets them above 'vulgarity'. Virginia Madden, the narrator affirms, 'could not have been judged anything but a lady. She wore her garments as only a lady can (the position and movement of the arms has much to do with this), and had the step never to be acquired by a person of vulgar instincts.' (p. 46) The Madden sisters accordingly remain 'superior' to their more affluent employers, who have been 'more or less well-to-do families in the lower middle class, people who could not have inherited refinement, and had not acquired any, neither proletarians nor gentlefolk, consumed with a disease of vulgar pretentiousness, inflated with the miasma of democracy.' (p. 44) Monica, on the other hand, despite her 'native elegance,' loses status when she finds work 'in business'. As an apprentice to a draper, she has placed herself precariously on the boundary between the working class and the lower middle class, in an environment where she must fraternize with decidedly 'vulgar' young women from working-class backgrounds. Her refined speech and bearing nevertheless mark her as 'superior' to her co-workers, which they resent, and gain her the attentions of Edmund Widdowson. Her subsequent marriage to Widdowson, a former City clerk who has retired on the income from an inheritance, raises her once again to the upper reaches of the lower middle class, placing her on the fringes of the middle class into which she had been born.

As Mrs Widdowson, Monica is limited to her husband's class position, which is as problematic and interesting as her own. Widdowson's income of £600 a year raises him above the lower middle class financially, but the clerkly taint bars him from the ranks of the solid middle class. He fulfils Monica's basic wish for a companion who has 'nothing of the *shop* about him' (p. 58), but even with her limited experience, Monica recognizes that, while his clothes are 'such as a gentleman wears', his 'utterance' falls 'short of perfect refinement'. (p. 59) The characterization of Widdowson indeed conforms to all the conventions for representing lower-middle-class men. He dresses carefully, is inordinately bound to domestic existence, and is uncomfortable and awkward in society. His limitations are especially telling in his intellectual capacities; he is a 'man with small knowledge of the world', with fixed ideas that lodge themselves in 'the crannies of his mind'. (p. 245) Monica, on the other hand, has the capacity for growth, even if it is at the expense of suffering. The relative affluence and maturity that her unhappy marriage affords her allow Monica to move comfortably in the limited middle-class society she meets through Mrs Cosgrove. Under the influence of complementary domestic pressures – of the accommodations he must make to married life – Widdowson seems to shrink and calcify.

The status associated with working in shops and with teaching in *The Odd Women* is of particular interest, especially given the significance of both kinds of work in representations of women and femininity. Working in a shop has been demoted from a form of liberation, as it was in *The Romance of a Shop*, to a form of bondage. The reasons for this shift, I would suggest, are twofold. First Gissing, having been born and raised in the lower middle class, was more aware of the conditions of lower-middle-class employment than the other authors discussed here. It therefore would have been difficult for him to imagine the drudgery of such work as symbolically liberating, and so would not have accorded with the stark realism of his style and vision. Second, practice and organization in the retail trade were changing during the 1890s. The small family enterprise envisioned in *The Romance of a Shop* was giving way to the large emporium and the frankly exploitative system of apprenticeship so tellingly delineated in the works of H. G. Wells. Here was bondage indeed, complete with indentures, but without the sense of mutual responsibility and commitment between master and apprentice inherent (although, of course, not always realized) in the trade model. Like other white-collar workers, shop assistants were reluctant to organize, and so did not benefit from the improvement in hours and conditions for which industrial laborers had fought long and hard.[44] 'It is a significant fact', Clara Collet observes, 'that whereas large numbers of factory girls cannot be prevailed upon to give up their factory work after marriage, the majority of shop assistants look upon marriage as their one hope of release, and would, as one girl expressed it, "marry anybody to get out of the drapery business".'[45]

Gissing's representation of Monica's experiences as a draper's apprentice is indeed a minor exposé of the abuses of the system, and his acute understanding of status distinctions within the lower middle class prevents him from depicting such a debasing level of servitude as liberating, except in the clearly relative terms of Monica's despairing recognition of the even greater bondage of her marriage. Clerical work, however, offers Monica the opportunity for both social and moral rehabilitation. When she begins her studies of bookkeeping and typing, she experiences 'a growth of self-respect', despite her lack of commitment. 'It was much to have risen above the status of shop-girl', the narrator comments, 'and the change of moral atmosphere had a very beneficial effect upon her.' (p. 94) That the further rise in status afforded her by her marriage paradoxically reduces Monica's personal liberty to less than that of a shop-girl accordingly becomes a blistering condemnation of Victorian social mores and of the rigid imposition of conventional feminine roles.

Gissing's sensitivity to status distinctions also complicates his treatment of women and teaching. Initially he has Rhoda eschew teaching, and while he makes no overt connections between teaching and concepts of femininity, he has her characterize her early career as a teacher in much the same way that she might characterize marriages like Monica's – as something young girls do more as a matter of convention than of devotion: 'I had gone into it like most girls, as a dreary matter of course.' (p. 50) Rhoda's career in the commercial world, however, has been brief. She has been a cashier and a shorthand clerk, but even as she relates the story of her liberation, she has reverted to teaching, although neither she nor the narrator ever refers to her present work as such. She is described instead as residing with and being the 'assistant' of a woman of 'private means' who 'train[s] young girls for work in offices.' This would seem to be an ideological lapse in the characterization of Rhoda, which can be interpreted in several different ways. Perhaps Gissing views vocational training as categorically different from 'teaching'. Rhoda's coolly efficient and businesslike manner certainly dissociates her role as instructor from nurturing images of femininity or maternity; moreover, her pupils are young women, not children. Then again, perhaps Gissing is too steeped in the social and sexual ideologies he only appears to reject to be able to imagine a heroine who is completely unconventional. Certainly Rhoda's character is charged with conflicting drives, as one contemporary reviewer recognized, describing her as 'the strong, self-reliant, revolted woman, with the old womanly woman still restless underneath as she fights against the recognition of it.'[46] But Gissing is otherwise open about her duality, which is indeed what makes her so interesting and appealing both to the reader and to other characters. The narrator depicts her as 'something like an unfamiliar sexual type.' (p. 48), and the Maddens describe her enthusiastically as 'quite like a man'. At the same time she is both sexual and decorous in her relations with Everard Barfoot and very nearly relinquishes her independence to marry him. She is also compassionate in her responses to Monica and tender with Monica's baby.

The best explanation for Gissing's equivocal treatment of Rhoda as 'teacher' is one that takes into account the complex interrelationship of the ideologies of both class and gender in her characterization. Having Rhoda revert to teaching, in whatever guise, may indeed 'feminize' her character; it may smack of the falling back of other liberated heroines into conventionally feminine roles once their freedom has been symbolically effected. But teaching also protects Rhoda's independence and class status. Working in an office might free Rhoda from conventional feminine roles, but in the realistic world of a Gissing novel it would necessarily commit her to another kind of servitude, though a lesser one. But as Monica's experiences demonstrate, bondage is often relative, shaped by perceptions and conventions. In Rhoda's case, working virtually as a partner in a nonprofit enterprise frees her in other important ways – from both the taint of 'business' and the oppression of an employer's demands. Moreover, to teach young women the skills of office work is to teach them the skills of independence; it furthers the cause of women's emancipation and undermines sexually biased social and economic structures. At the same time, it ensures that Rhoda's class status and level of independence remain high. Rhoda indeed becomes an odd hybrid of feminine and lower-middle-class conventions that cancel out each other's disabilities. She is marginal in a way that is liberating rather than restrictive – she is as assured and as socially mobile as any middle-class woman, but escapes the constraining conventions; she is far too assertive and independent to be considered ladylike, but she has more wisdom and dignity than the 'genteel' Madden sisters.

Rhoda Nunn is arguably the ideal New Woman, a woman whose identity is defined by her own status and who is socially and financially independent. Most latter-day New Women who follow her pale by comparison, largely because they either lack or relinquish that fundamental independence. Barbara Undershaft, the spirited heroine of Bernard Shaw's *Major Barbara*, opts for a career in which she ministers to the needs of others and she is prepared to marry; H. G. Wells's Ann Veronica similarly marries. The early twentieth-century stage also supplies a fleeting but glorious revival of the New Woman as truly independent career woman in the person of Kate, a sprightly and businesslike typist in 'The Twelve-Pound Look,' a one-act play by J. M. Barrie. For all its brevity – the play would not take more than half an hour to perform – 'The Twelve-Pound Look' is a thoroughgoing exposé of the absurdities and meanness of bourgeois sexual politics. It is, in fact, almost allegorical, with Sir Harry representing assured and pompous patriarchal authority, strutting about in his sumptuous drawing-room, and Lady Sims representing submissive femininity, looking haggard and fluttering nervously. The elaborate stage directions begin by explicitly instructing the audience to identify with Sir Harry – that is, with the dominant cultural ideology: 'If quite convenient (as they say about cheques) you are to conceive that the scene is laid in your own house, and that Harry Sims is you.'[47] The audience is thus also being set up, along with Sir Harry, to be deflated by Kate. Sir Harry has engaged Kate through an agency to type some letters, and is appalled when he realizes that he has hired his former wife. He is even more appalled to learn that she had not, as he always thought, left him for another man, but to escape his 'suffocating' success. When Sir Harry boasts that he is 'worth a quarter of a million', Kate coolly responds, 'That is what you are worth to yourself. I'll tell you what you are worth to me: exactly twelve pounds.' (p. 731) Twelve pounds is the price of Kate's ticket to freedom, the price of the typewriter she uses to earn her living. Furthermore, Kate admonishes Sir Harry and all husbands to become alert to the restlessness stirring beneath the bland and spiritless exteriors of their wives' resigned submission. 'If I was a husband', she warns, ' – it is my advice to all of them – I would often watch my wife quietly to see whether the twelve-pound look was not coming into her eyes.' (p. 734) Sir Harry, swathed in the complacency of those confident in the invulnerability of their power, is nettled but otherwise unmoved. Lady Sims, however, comments that Kate 'looked so alive ... while she was working the machine' and closes the play by asking her husband, 'Are they very expensive? ... Those machines?' (p. 736) 'The Twelve-Pound Look' thus suggests independence and lower-middle-class employment not just as a refuge for single women, but as preferable to the accepted model of middle-class marriage that glorifies the husband's role and imposes subservience on the wife.

As Gail Cunningham notes, writers of New Woman novels were inspired at least in part by a 'desire to liberate English fiction', or as one contemporary commentator disapprovingly expressed it, by a desire 'for the emancipation of the English novelist from the yoke of the virgin.'[48] Ann Ardis more assertively makes claims for New Woman novelists as early modernists, arguing that they 'anticipate the reappraisal of realism we usually credit to early-twentieth-century writers.'[49] The New Woman novels were, in fact, only the last stage in a prolonged struggle waged at first by women writers to free their characters from the oppressive and comprehensive yoke of Victorian femininity.

It is a distressing irony that it was men, rather than women authors, who first succeeded in convincingly portraying women who freed themselves from the conventions of femininity. But it was, perhaps, inevitable. Women, like members of the lower middle class, had only a marginal status in Victorian culture; consequently, women who wrote felt themselves and the heroines they created too vulnerable to withstand the censure of the dominant social ideology and its orthodox code of femininity. Most women who wrote New Woman novels, for example, were so fixated on the oppressive sexual mores that constrained them and their characters that they were largely unable to recognize the true potential of otherwise unglamorous work for middle-class women. What Rhoda's situation dramatizes is that it is only from a position of material – financial – independence that woman is enabled to redefine the terms of her emotional and sexual relationship to man. Rhoda is accordingly able to 'retreat with honour' from her relationship with Barfoot at the end of *The Odd Women* not, as Ann Ardis argues, because she retreats from sexual determinism in the 'voluptuousness' that he, as a sexually knowing New Man, attempts to awaken in her;[50] rather, Rhoda retains her honor because, while she has been proved egregiously wrong about the suspicions regarding Barfoot's involvement with Monica that drove her to reject his initial proposal of marriage, she has not been wrong about the limitations of his character and of his love. Even he realizes that her 'love had been worth more than his.' (p. 322) Moreover, in their final encounter he is the one who desires traditional marriage, while Rhoda is still prepared to agree to a free union. It is she who sets the parameters of their relationship and his ultimate retreat into an apparently passionless and conventional middle-class marriage with Agnes Brissendon, not Rhoda's continued chastity, is the true repudiation of sexuality.

 The men who were able to liberate their female characters from restrictive conventions were, interestingly, marginal figures themselves. Gissing was lower-middle-class, and while he felt himself superior to his social origins, he never fitted into the middle class either. Barrie was born in Scotland, the son of a handloom weaver. After acquiring an MA at Edinburgh University, Barrie went on to gain wealth and distinction, but was very much an 'odd man': he remained single, but became emotionally dependent on the Llewelyn Davies family, adoring the wife and playing an avuncular role to the five sons, for whom he wrote the stories of Peter Pan. It was most probably their own marginality that made these men the ideal liberators of fictional women, that made them sensitive to the plight of women, anxious to champion the cause of a subjugated group, but free of the peculiar social and ideological constraints that hampered women themselves. And women, as we shall see, were willing to return the favor, for the most positive portrayals of lower-middle-class men come from the pen of a woman – May Sinclair.

5
Modern Prometheus Unbound: May Sinclair and *The Divine Fire*

> The perfect heroes and heroines of this myth of modernity were the petite bourgeoisie.
>
> T. J. Clark, *The Painting of Modern Life*

The sense of empathy and identity between women and lower-middle-class men that emerges in the novels of Wells, Bennett, and Gissing was not just a literary phenomenon. The common experience of social and cultural marginality fostered similar sympathies in real life, and there is at least one notable and documented example of a middle-class woman giving the kind of moral support to lower-middle-class men that Jessie Milton gives to Hoopdriver or that the Countess of Chell gives to Denry Machin. In the summer of 1890, members of the newly formed National Union of Clerks (originally the Clerks' Union) organized a mass meeting to support the expansion of their association. The meeting, according to a report in a short-lived periodical called *The Clerk*, attracted a 'small but enthusiastic attendance', including a handful of politicians – Rev. A. W. Jephson, a Fabian who had served on the London School Board; W. M. Thompson, an Irish journalist and lawyer with radical sympathies who was standing as Liberal candidate for Deptford; and J. Allanson Picton, radical M. P. for Leicester, who addressed the meeting. The other prominent public figure to address the assembly of clerks and speak out in their support was feminist activist Clementina Black, who was 'enthusiastically cheered by her gentleman audience.'[1]

The impact of the meeting and of Black's support seems to have been limited, the result at least in part of official suppression. The police forced the meeting to move from the steps of the Royal Exchange to South Place Chapel, a move that obviously diminished the effect of what was meant to be a public demonstration. The ostensible reason for forcing the move was to prevent traffic congestion, although, as *The Clerk* points out, there was no traffic problem around the Exchange at four o'clock on a Sunday afternoon, the time scheduled. The meeting was subsequently ignored by *The Times*, which nevertheless devoted almost a full half column to a meeting of van builders in Hyde Park on the same afternoon. The *Daily Telegraph* reported the event briefly and with great comic flourish – the same kind of deflationary humor always applied to things lower-middle-class. The *Telegraph* describes one clerk as proposing a resolution from the top of an omnibus as it passed the Exchange. Most of the report is devoted to the spurious drama of and responses to the relocation of the 'sparsely-attended' meeting. Picton's comments on the deplorable working conditions for many clerks and on the urgent need for unionization are summarized in a single sentence. Black's presence is barely noted: she and others 'took part.'[2] Black's speech was thus ultimately of considerably less public influence than were the words of another middle-class woman, May Sinclair, who spoke out in support of lower-middle-class man in a different forum – in the pages of a novel. Sinclair's best-selling *The Divine Fire* (1904) made a major contribution to the imaginative liberation of the lower-middle-class male by presenting him as a true hero, not as one who was comic or pathetic, but as one who could confront and overmaster the middle-class gentleman on his own turf.

May Sinclair was the youngest child and only daughter of a Liverpool ship owner who went bankrupt in 1870, when she was seven years old; her parents subsequently separated. Her father was a veritable parody of the Victorian *paterfamilias*, tyrannical yet morally weak. The family as a whole seemed to be plagued by the kind of frailties that were the staples of Victorian melodrama – sensuality, alcoholism, and constitutional weakness. Sinclair's father drank and womanized, and in his early fifties succumbed to cirrhosis of the liver and chronic nephritis. Her five brothers in turn were not known for their self-restraint and four of them died young of heart disease.[3] Sinclair felt some apprehension about her heredity, although she never exhibited any tendency to moral or physical frailty herself. She lived in genteel poverty with her mother – a woman of stern religious and moral rectitude – until the latter's death in 1901, and was assessed by Arnold Bennett as 'a prim virgin' with '[g]reat sense'.[4] Moreover, Sinclair was something of a latter-day blue-stocking. She attended Cheltenham Ladies College for a year at age eighteen, but her mother feared that this education was eroding the strict religious training she had imposed on her daughter and she withdrew May after one year. Sinclair continued to study on her own, however, and developed notable expertise in philosophy. She published two books on idealism, *The Defence of Idealism* in 1917 and *The New Idealism* in 1922.

Sinclair conformed outwardly to the role of repressed Victorian spinster, but behind the shy and restrained exterior of 'the prim virgin' was a lively and rebellious spirit. She rebelled inwardly against her mother's religious orthodoxy and had a strong interest in probing the nature of relations between the sexes, a subject she explored at length and with great candor in her fiction. She also incorporated the principles of psychology and of the as yet still morally suspect new discipline of psychoanalysis into the development of her characters. Moreover, Sinclair was outspoken in her support of other authors whose advanced ideas drew public censure. She denounced the suppression of D. H. Lawrence's *The Rainbow* and defended Wells's *The New Machiavelli* against complaints of its eroticism. She also encouraged young writers, especially poets, who were trying to break new artistic ground – writers like Robert Frost, Ezra Pound, and T. S. Eliot.[5] Her friends and correspondents indeed included most of the major literary figures of her time including, besides those already mentioned, George Gissing, Thomas Hardy, Ford Madox Ford, Henry James, Dorothy Richardson, Rebecca West, John Galsworthy, and Hilda Doolittle.

Sinclair's early fiction, including *The Divine Fire*, reflects her admiration for Henry James in its elaborate yet subtle prose style and in its concern for ethical and philosophical niceties. At the same time, she traces the implications and inevitable effects of the circumstances and personality traits of her characters with relentless naturalistic precision. It is ultimately with the lower-middle-class writers of her generation – Wells and Bennett – that she seems most attuned, however. Like them, she focused on lower-middle-class life in her stories and even modeled the lower-middle-class hero of one of her novels, *Tasker Jevons*, on Bennett himself. (Zegger, pp. 86–7) Like Wells, she was interested in exploring the problems of marital relations in fiction. The link that connected the middle-class 'prim virgin' with the lower middle class, and specifically with lower-middle-class man, was, I would argue, the shared sense of marginality, of exclusion from the intellectual and artistic mainstream, as Sinclair herself suggested in a letter to a friend. With reference to the novels of Gissing, Sinclair expressed certainty that there was more of Gissing himself in *Born in Exile* than in any of his other works. 'I think I was born in another sort of Exile', she continued, 'and that makes me understand.'[6]

Certainly Savage Keith Rickman, the hero of *The Divine Fire*, was born in a kind of exile akin to that of Gissing and his alter-ego Godwin Peak. Rickman is an intellectual and a literary genius – and the son of a lower-middle-class secondhand bookseller. That Sinclair nevertheless identified with her hero is unquestionable. Rickman's literary career closely parallels that of his author; his early attempts at poetry are literally hers. The poems that appear in the novel as Rickman's include three of Sinclair's own previously published sonnets, as well as fragments of her early unpublished verse. (Boll, p. 179) Rickman's literary rise culminates in the triumph of his verse drama, a genre that his creator also attempted, but with considerably less success. While Sinclair thus vicariously fulfils her poetic literary aspirations through Rickman, she also uses him to exorcize the demons of alcoholism and sensuality, tendencies that she feared she might have inherited. Rickman is never a real alcoholic or womanizer, as Sinclair's father was, but he does struggle with drink and has a penchant for forming unhappy alliances with voluptuous but unintellectual women. His ultimate union with the ethereal, refined, and socially superior Lucia Harden unites the opposing aspects of Sinclair's own identity.

Unlike Wells's and Bennett's novels about lower-middle-class characters, *The Divine Fire* opens on a scene from the world of upper-middle-class ease, the world from which Rickman is exiled by his lowly birth. The scene is indeed vaguely reminiscent of the opening of James's *The Portrait of a Lady*: it is afternoon in the garden of Court House, an English country estate, and the conversation between Lucia Harden and her cousin Horace Jewdwine is focused on an outsider whose life is about to become enmeshed in theirs. This outsider is not an extraordinary young woman from America but an extraordinary young man from the lower middle class. Jewdwine, an Oxford don and literary critic, has given Lucia a fragment of Rickman's neoclassical verse drama, *Helen in Leuce*, to read and assess. Even in the impersonal form of his writing, Rickman is out of place in this setting. Lucia hands the manuscript back to Jewdwine, saying, 'Take him away. He makes me feel uncomfortable', which prompts Jewdwine's painful disclosure of Rickman's major personal flaw: he is 'a little unfortunate in – in his surroundings':

> 'I found him in the City – in a shop.'
> She smiled at the rhythmic utterance. The tragedy of the revelation was such that it could be expressed only in blank verse.
> 'The shop doesn't matter.'
> 'No, but he does. You couldn't stand him, Lucia. You see, for one thing, he sometimes drops his aitches.'[7]

Some of the conventional patterns of representation are clearly at work, even in this brief passage. The sensitive middle-class woman is less rigid than her male counterpart in her response to someone whose social position is marginal: to her, the 'shop doesn't matter.' The lower-middle-class shopman is nevertheless defined both by the 'unfortunate surroundings' and by his speech, his dropped aitches. The whole situation is mildly comic and the ironic reference to tragedy underscores how far from tragedy the scene really is. Moreover, the 'tragedy' is not Rickman's, but Jewdwine's – the pain of the revelation that his latest literary 'find' is so socially *outré*.

The sense of identification between lower-middle-class male protagonists and women from higher classes that plays such an important role in the works of Wells and Bennett is also clearly at work in the relationship between Lucia and Rickman even before they meet. This identity becomes evident when Jewdwine asks Lucia to read some of *Helen in Leuce* aloud:

> She read, and in the golden afternoon her voice built up the cold, polished marble of the verse. She had not been able to tell him what she thought of Rickman; but her voice, in its profound vibrations, made apparent that which she, and she only, had discerned in him, the troubled pulse of youth, the

passion of the imprisoned and tumultuous soul, the soul which Horace had assured her inhabited the body of an aitchless shopman. Lucia might not have the intuition of genius, but she had the genius of intuition; she had seen what the great Oxford critic had not been able to see. (pp. 5–6)

Again, Rickman is present only in his writing, which represents the essence of his being and which Lucia is able to discern through intuition. When the soul of the aitchless shopman first speaks, it speaks through the voice of an upper-class woman. In this voice, which is free of the infelicities of his own accents and which resonates with 'profound vibrations', Rickman's story is translated into the tragic tones previously denied to him and his type. This is not the story of a 'mere counter-jumper', an 'aitchless shopman', but of 'the passion' of an 'imprisoned and tumultuous soul'.

Contrary to what this initial indirect introduction to Rickman might lead readers to expect, he has much in common with his lower-middle-class fictional antecedents. As is the case with Hoopdriver and Denry Machin, the enforced dullness and drudgery of his work define and limit his experience. We first see him in his father's bookshop, looking forward to the escape of a holiday. That he has completed his 'great classic drama, *Helen in Leuce*' and that several poems from his cycle, *Saturnalia*, are currently in print in an intellectually avant-garde periodical are of secondary concern to a young man who spends endless hours of every day trapped behind a counter. As he watches the clock, he is 'mainly supported by the coming of Easter' (p. 13) and by the carefully detailed plans he has made for the three days of freedom that lie ahead. At this point in his life – the story opens in 'the days of his obscurity' in 1892 (p. 10) – Rickman is, as the narrator attests, something less than Prometheus unbound: 'Savage Keith Rickman was a little poet about town, a Cockney poet, the poet not only of neo-classic drama, but of green suburban Saturday noons, and flaming Saturday nights, and of a great many things besides.' His 'engagements' for his holiday are not untypical of the amusements of a late nineteenth-century version of the Gent: some early morning cycling, an afternoon's excursion with Flossie Walker (a 'little clerk' from his boarding house), dinner with his journalist acquaintances, and late-night trysts with a rather commonplace variety actress with the unlikely name of Poppy

Grace. Sandwiched in between these prosaic delights, Rickman has slotted in 'ten hours at least of high Parnassian leisure, of dalliance in Academic shades'. (p. 15) 'In a world of prose', the narrator comments, 'it is only by such divine snatches that poets are made.'

Divine snatches are a far cry from the divine fire, and it is clear that the 'little poet about town' as yet lacks the stature of tragic hero. He is indeed an unsettling hybrid of types, someone who makes people feel uneasy. Lucia is uncomfortable in the presence of his writing and Jewdwine betrays mixed emotions in his physical presence. During a conversation between the two men, which turns to what Jewdwine finds an unsavory topic – Rickman's relationship with Poppy Grace – and in which Rickman's aitches are distinctly absent, Jewdwine's ambivalence to his protégé is painfully apparent: 'In Rickman the poet he was deeply interested; but at the moment Rickman the man inspired him with disgust.' (p. 26) Even his name – Savage Keith Rickman – suggests the incongruities of his character, a mixture of the seemingly prosaic 'Keith' and 'Rickman' with the unusual 'Savage' and all the connotations of the untamed and the aggressive that it entails.

In the first section of the novel, fittingly titled '*Disjecta Membra Poetae*', Sinclair plays on the incongruities of Rickman's character and on the connotations of Savage. The oddness of this human hybrid is indeed what makes him fascinating, as well as disturbing, at least to the gaggle of 'Junior Journalists' who frequent the bookshop for the express purpose of marveling at Rickman. The Junior Journalists comprise a group of ambitious and progressive young men of letters, three of whom – Stables, Maddox, and Rankin – form the intellectual core of *The Planet*, the weekly that publishes Rickman's poems. These young men respond to Rickman with a combination of condescension and awe:

> He [Rickman] was so glad to be talked to, so frankly, engagingly, beautifully glad, that the pathos of it would have been too poignant, the obligation it almost forced on you too unbearable, but for his power, his monstrous, mysterious, personal glamour.
> It lay partly, no doubt, in his appearance; not, no, not at all, in his make-up. He wore, like a thousand city clerks, a high collar, a speckled tie, a straight, dark blue serge suit. But in spite of the stiffness thus imposed on him, he had, unaccountably, the

shy, savage beauty of an animal untamed, uncaught. He belonged to the slender, nervous, fair type; but the colour proper to it had been taken out of him by the shop. His head presented the utmost clearness of line compatible with irregularity of outline; and his face (from its heavy square forehead to its light square jaw) was full of strange harmonies, adjustments, compensations. His chin, rather long in a front view, rather prominent in profile, balanced the powerful proportions of his forehead. . . . He had queer eyes, of a thick dark blue, large, though deep set, showing a great deal of iris and very little white. Without being good-looking, he was good to look at, when you could look long enough to find all these things out. He did not like being looked at. If you tried to hold him that way, his eyes were all over the place, seeking an escape; but they held *you*, whether you liked it or not. (p. 12)

The conventional packaging of the lower-middle-class clerk is at odds here with what it contains, creating some confusion about what constitutes his 'appearance' and what constitutes his 'makeup'. Typical of young men in his class as represented in fiction, he is 'slender, nervous, [and] fair' – indeed, rather washed-out by the shop – and dressed in the high collar and dark suit of 'a thousand city clerks'. The unaccountable and mysterious glamour, the 'beauty' at once 'shy' and 'savage', appears to emanate from the 'strange harmonies' of his unusual head and from his 'queer' and apparently hypnotic eyes, eyes that represent both the fear of domination and the power to dominate.

That there is a split in Rickman's identity – that he is at once the lower-middle-class clerk and the smouldering genius – is confirmed by his own sense of multiple selves: 'There were, as he sorrowfully reflected, so many Mr. Rickmans.' (p. 29) There are in fact seven, according to the narrator's inventory of Rickman's inner self: 'our Mr. Rickman' of the shop; 'Mr. Rickman the student and recluse, who inhabited the insides of other men's books'; 'Mr. Rickman the Junior Journalist, the obscure writer of brilliant paragraphs'; and 'Mr. Rickman the young man about town'. The man of 'serene and perfect intelligence' brings the number up to five. (p. 30) But these five 'identities' are in truth just facets of a single personality. Of more interest and significance are the last two Rickmans, the 'commonplace but amiable young man' and 'Mr. Rickman the genius', the same two identities at odds in the physical description above. These last two finally define and control the others:

> [U]nderneath these [five] Mr. Rickmans, though inextricably, damnably one with them, was a certain apparently commonplace but amiable young man, who lived in a Bloomsbury boarding-house and dropped his aitches. This young man was tender and chivalrous, full of little innocent civilities to the ladies of his boarding-house; he admired, above all things, modesty in a woman, and somewhere, in the dark and unexplored corners of his nature, he concealed a prejudice in favour of marriage and the sanctities of home. (p. 30)

This Mr Rickman is the image of conventional lower-middle-class man; he is a latter-day John Chivery, tender and chivalrous within his limited social bounds, committed to the 'sanctities of home'.

The final incarnation – 'Rickman the genius' – is not, like the commonplace young man, 'one with' the others (however 'damnably'), but a disconcerting 'visitation' upon them:

> There was no telling whether he would come in the form of a high god or a demon, a consolation or a torment. Sometimes he would descend upon Mr. Rickman in the second-hand department, and attempt to seduce him from his allegiance to the Quarterly Catalogue. Or he would take up the poor journalist's copy as it lay on a table, and change it so that its own editor wouldn't know it again. And sometimes he would swoop down on the little bookseller as he sat at breakfast on a Sunday morning, in his nice frock coat and clean collar, and wrap his big flapping wings round him, and carry him off to the place where the divine ideas come from. Leaving a silent and to all appearances idiotic young gentleman in his place. Or he would sit down by that young gentleman's side and shake him out of his little innocences and complacencies, and turn all his little jokes into his own incomprehensible humour. And then the boarding-house would look uncomfortable and say to itself that Mr. Rickman had been drinking. (pp. 30–1)

The visitation of the genius clearly has a more profound effect on the commonplace young man of the boarding-house than on the other Rickmans. The Rickman of vast ideas is completely incompatible with the restraining conventions of lower-middle-class stereotypes, with the 'nice frock coat and clean collar' and the society of the boarding-house, and with the intellectual diminutiveness of 'little innocences and complacencies' and 'little jokes'. The genius, born and living in exile, disdains to accept the restrictions placed upon him by his social class, although Rickman himself – which Rickman is not specified – considers that he is 'a fellow who could only be expressed in fractions, and vulgar fractions, too'.

Those who observe Rickman from the outside are no more capable of reconciling the oppositions in his character. Asked to describe what Rickman is really like to his companions at the Junior Journalists club, Jewdwine hesitatingly hazards an attempt:

> 'If' – said he, 'you can imagine the soul of a young Sophocles, battling with that of a – of a junior journalist, in the body of a dissipated little Cockney – '
> 'Can't', said Stables. 'Haven't got enough imagination.'
> 'The child of 'Ellas and 'Ollywell Street – innocent of – er – the rough breathing', suggested Maddox. (p. 20)

Unable to comprehend Rickman, the Junior Journalists make something of a joke out of him, playfully characterizing him in terms of the gentlemanly status he clearly does not hold. Maddox claims that, while Rickman is a 'bounder' when he is sober, 'he's a perfect little gentleman when he's drunk.' Maddox's companions take up the theme, characterizing Rickman as 'a true gentleman at heart', '[o]ne of Nature's gentlemen', and even, according to Jewdwine, '[o]ne of Art's gentlemen.' (pp. 20–1) Clearly not of the order of the socially constructed gentleman of birth, breeding, and education, Rickman is granted the consolation prizes traditionally awarded to men of special talent or integrity and inferior social position – those seemingly gracious epithets that acknowledge the personal merits while nevertheless stressing the social ineligibility. Jewdwine is even willing to grant that Rickman is a very fine specimen of Art's gentlemen – 'if you take him that way' – and has 'smuggled' him into the membership of the Junior Journalists club on the strength of his artistic abilities. (p. 16) But while other versions of Nature's gentleman – such as John Halifax – can be assimilated into polite society, Rickman is ineligible because, unlike Halifax, he does not speak with a refined accent. To the Junior Journalists, the only kind of gentleman that Rickman can really be is 'a perfect little gentleman', a diminutive, vulgarized (this is, after all, what he is when drunk), lower-middle-class version of the real thing.

The Junior Journalists have at this moment lost sight of the soul of the 'young Sophocles' and are so absorbed in the cleverness of their own ironic playfulness with the idea of the gentleman that they fail to notice that Rickman himself has quietly entered the room and sat down. Like Little Dorrit moving about unnoticed in the shadows of the Clennam house, Rickman is an 'unobtrusive presence', virtually invisible in the recessed corners of the room, until he stands up and is spotted and finally recognized by Jewdwine. The men are mortified at their gaffe and try vainly to recover their composure while Rickman behaves with the restraint of a perfect gentleman – as opposed to a perfect *little* gentleman – smiling quietly in response to their raillery. The Junior Journalists, Rickman's social superiors, have been completely outclassed by the former target of their playful condescension and feel suddenly ill at ease on what is supposed to be their turf. Rickman the insignificant outsider, though passive, is in complete command. He is aware, composed, mildly bemused but, most significantly, exquisitely refined in his subtle response, prompting Maddox to observe that '[h]e isn't a gentleman. He's something more.' Far beyond being one of 'Nature's gentlemen', Rickman is a natural master, 'a master the most superb' the narrator comments, 'because unconscious'. (pp. 21–2)

In these early pages of the novel, Sinclair is obviously playing with conventions, both social and literary, and especially with notions of gentlemanliness, with class stereotypes, and with the ways in which essentially trivial details like accents determine social position and even identity. And while her manipulations of these conventions are most clearly at work in the characterization of Rickman, they are also evident in the fun the narrator has at Jewdwine's expense. Jewdwine is the most conventional character in the novel, both in the sense that he is the creation of hide-bound literary conventions and that, as a character, he is steadfastly wedded to the social and class conventions that have served him and his class so well for generations. The narrator satirizes Jewdwine's over-refined proclivities mildly, but devastatingly. His 'type', the narrator affirms, has 'none of the uncertainty and complexity of Rickman's':

> He looked neither more nor less than he was – an Oxford don, developing into a London Journalist. You divined that the process would be slow. There was no unseemly haste about Jewdwine; time had not been spared in the moulding of his body and his soul. He bore the impress of the ages; the whole man was clean-cut, aristocratic, finished, defined. You instinctively looked up to him; which was perhaps the reason why you remembered his conspicuously intellectual forehead and his pathetically fastidious nose, and forgot the vacillating mouth that dropped under a scanty, colourless moustache, hiding its weakness out of sight. (pp. 23–4)

Encapsulated in this description is the personal heritage of Horace Jewdwine as well as the political heritage of the fictional middle-class male protagonist; it is the devolution of the gentleman from an aristocratic ancestry (Jewdwine's uncle, Lucia's father, is a baronet) to the commercialism of the modern journalist. The strengths and deficiencies of the 'finished' product are embodied in the various elements of his physical appearance. He has a commanding bearing: 'You instinctively looked up to him.' But while he is 'conspicuously intellectual', he also shares many of the limitations of conventional lower-middle-class man: he is 'pathetically fastidious', 'vacillating', 'colourless', and weak.

Jewdwine's conspicuous intelligence is compromised by his weakness, allowing his class biases to cloud his judgment and limit his ability to assess Rickman's genius. These prejudices, when coupled with artistic pretentiousness, indeed betray Jewdwine into frank absurdities in his attempts to evaluate Rickman's character:

> [Rickman's] soul [was] (in Jewdwine's opinion) a trifle too demonstrative in its hospitality to vagrant impressions. The Junior Journalists may have been a little hard on him. On the whole, he left you dubious, until the moment when, from pure nervousness, his speech went wild, even suffering that slight elision of the aspirate observed by some of them. But then, he had a voice of such singular musical felicity that it charmed you into forgetfulness of these enormities. (p. 23)

The narrator's perspective fuses with Jewdwine's consciousness in this passage, making attribution of the ironic tone problematic. The inflated diction of phrases like 'suffering that slight elision of the aspirate' and 'forgetfulness of these enormities' is certainly Jewdwine's, as is the disengenuousness of the thought that the dropped aitches were 'observed by some of them'. These 'enormities' were undoubtedly observed by all, and are particularly distressing to Jewdwine's 'pathetically fastidious' sensibilities. While the irony resides in the absurdity of describing trifles in such elaborate terms, and while Jewdwine is not incapable of Wildean self-parody, the target of the satire embodied in the passage is the pomposity of Jewdwine and his type. And given that Jewdwine is convention made manifest, the categorizing of dropped aitches as 'enormities' constitutes an indirect collective criticism of conventional responses and of a class whose members would in reality never let the 'musical felicity' of a voice drown out the supposed dissonance of an 'unrefined' accent.

The almost obsessive emphasis in the text on the dropped aitch – it is the dominant trope throughout the novel – thus undermines Jewdwine and conventions, rather than Rickman. Similarly, the recurrent theme of diminutiveness, the symbolic hallmark of lower-middle-class limitations, ultimately diminishes not Rickman's stature, but Jewdwine's. Initially, narrator and middle-class characters alike refer to Rickman in terms consistent with lower-middle-class stereotypes. He is the 'little poet about town' to the narrator, 'little Rickman' to Jewdwine, and 'a perfect little gentleman' to Maddox. In a scene late in the novel, however, the theme of diminutiveness surfaces in a conversation between Jewdwine and Rickman, but in the context of intellectual stature, the area in which Rickman decidedly stands above the crowd. His genius has indeed recently been endorsed by the leading contemporary poet, the aging Walter Fielding, who has gone so far as to acknowledge that Rickman is a greater poet than he is himself. Jewdwine, however, has by this time developed an animus towards Rickman, who is subtly and unconsciously threatening his mentor's sense of superiority, in much the same way that the emerging lower middle class threatened the ascendency of the bourgeoisie in the mid-nineteenth century. Jewdwine complains that the growth of modernity and democracy is destroying his role, the role of the discriminating critic. 'A critic only exists through the existence of great men', he tells Rickman. 'And there are no great men nowadays; only a great number of little men.' (p. 366) At the same time, according to Jewdwine, this profusion of nonentities demands even greater powers of discernment on his part: 'I assure you it means far more labour and a finer discrimination to pick out your little man from a crowd of little men than to recognize your great man when you see him.' Jewdwine then challenges Rickman to name 'one work of unmistakable genius published any time in the last five, the last ten years'. The pointed reference to five years, before expanding the time frame to ten, defines the reign of the 'little men' as precisely that period since Rickman's work first appeared in print.

Jewdwine's discourse on little men is obviously directed at Rickman as an unpleasant challenge to his literary status. It is indeed a personal affront, apparently triggered by Jewdwine's resentment and perhaps professional jealousy: he feels that Rickman 'was rather too obviously elated at the great man's [Fielding's] praise.' Rickman responds to the goading with serene silence, but Jewdwine realizes that he is hurt. The littleness accordingly emerges not as an element of Rickman's stature, literary or otherwise, but of Jewdwine's. Jewdwine is small-minded, unable to accept with grace either the intellectual superiority of a social inferior or the greater significance of Fielding's endorsement of poetic genius over his own. Even Jewdwine himself senses the pusillanimity of his response, feeling 'a miserable misgiving as to the worthiness of his own attitude to his friend'. Rickman, by contrast, is the man of intellectual power, struggling with dignity against class biases and social restrictions that wound him and that thwart him personally, professionally, and socially.

This direct role reversal seems straightforward enough, and not much of an advance, in artistic or culturally symbolic terms, over similar political moves in the fiction of Wells and Bennett. But *The Divine Fire* is not in any sense simple or straightforward. For one thing, its lower-middle-class hero has such finely-tuned scruples that he makes the likes of Isabel Archer and Lambert Strether seem gross by comparison and he accordingly finds himself caught in ethical quagmires no less problematic than theirs. The most overt conflict centers on the great Harden library, the property of Lucia's father, Sir Frederick Harden, who has unbeknownst to his family incurred massive debts. Sir Frederick is planning to sell the library and his agent, Dicky Pilkington, has promised first refusal to Rickman's father. But Rickman Sr has also quite inexplicably received a request from Court House to catalogue the library, a request he chooses not to question because of the enormous advantage doing such an inventory will afford him: detailed knowledge of the library's value before its sale, all nicely catalogued at the previous owner's expense instead of at his own. Accordingly, he dispatches his son with all haste to Court House before the members of the Harden family 'find out their mistake.' (p. 61) His son sets off with some misgivings, the result at this point not of his scruples, but of his dismay – intensified by the effects of a hangover – that his Bank holiday has been disrupted.

Rickman's departure for Court House closes the first section of the novel and his arrival there opens 'Lucia's Way'. As the title of this section suggests, Rickman is about to come under the transforming influence of a socially superior woman, just as his lower-middle-class fictional antecedents have done. Despite Lucia's intellectual maturity, she is as ingenuous as Jessie Milton and her unaffected openness with Rickman makes him as uncomfortable with his conflict of interest over the library as Hoopdriver was with the fictions about South Africa that he spun to impress Jessie. As it turns out, it was Lucia, unaware of her father's debts or of his intention to sell the library, who requested the cataloguing. As the alcoholic fog in his head clears, Rickman realizes just how compromising his situation is and his motives emerge as being as divided and complex as his character, driven at once by both utilitarian and idealist principles. To be serving his father's interests when Lucia is paying him and believes him to be serving hers becomes increasingly painful for Rickman, especially given Lucia's own openness. At the same time, he feels that he alone might be able to protect the library from the desecrating hands of Pilkington, whom he regards as a 'Vandal... about to descend like Alaric on the treasures of Rome.' (p. 62) He also believes that he owes his father filial loyalty and the use of his scholarly abilities, given that his father had financed his education with the express purpose of making him an asset in the bookselling trade.

All these feelings are further complicated by the almost reverential awe that the library inspires in Rickman as a scholar. It is a library of historic significance; its collection of fifteen thousand volumes includes many rare volumes and represents 'the work of ten generations of scholars'. (p. 66) Moreover, Sir Joseph Harden, the last of the Harden scholars and Sir Frederick's father, had frequented the Rickmans' secondhand bookstore during his lifetime, purchasing 'cartloads' of volumes for the library. Sir Joseph had taken an interest in the bookish young lad who had haunted the aisles of his father's shop, reading Homer, and Rickman is now 'devoted to Sir Joseph's memory.' (p. 60)

The mixture of responses Rickman has to the library, its cataloguing, and its probable sale, in part reflects his fragmented identity: they are the responses of the various Rickmans that form his being. Rickman the Junior Journalist, and more especially Rickman the young man about town, are both disinclined to leave London and the freedom of a holiday. But Rickman of the shop is prepared to do his job, while the student and recluse wants to protect the integrity of the library, perhaps against the commercial interests of the shop. Rickman the amiable young man responds in a more personal way to the library as the former prized possession of a man whose memory he reveres, while the serene and perfect intelligence recoils from the dishonor of accepting wages – and more significantly Lucia's gratitude – when he cannot do so without reserve. The poet, however, is unmoved by the library, and responds instead to what is beyond his reach: Lucia herself. The library – the actual room that is replete not only with books, but also with Lucia's aura – then becomes the crucible, heated by thwarted passion, in which the fragments of Rickman's character begin to fuse.

Rickman's passion is thwarted because he is unsuitable for the role of professed – or even unprofessed – lover of a woman of Lucia's rank. His unsuitability is not, of course, a matter of personal unworthiness. As he agonizes over the conflict of interest inherent in his position at the library, it is clear that his sense of honor and integrity is at least as refined as Lucia's. That his intellect exceeds hers, moreover, is obvious, despite the modest demeanor he maintains out of respect for both her and propriety. His unsuitability is nothing more nor less than a function of his social class and the conventions that define him as inhabiting it, a class bias that exists in other lower-middle-class texts as axiomatic. *The Divine Fire*, however, radically challenges class biases and conventions, first by exposing and undermining them in the first section, and then by allowing them to resurface in 'Lucia's Way'. However open and compassionate Lucia may be, her relations with Rickman are conditioned by social conventions, by her acute awareness of his social inferiority. A highly polished reserve governs her responses to him. When they are working together in the library – she has insisted on helping in order to speed up the cataloguing – she achieves a 'serene unconsciousness' of his presence. He seems as invisible to her as he was to the Junior Journalists in the club, and she conducts herself with 'a certain courtesy, which he gathered to be rather more finished than any she would have shown to a man of her own class.' This rigorous courtesy, Rickman senses, is 'not only finished', but 'final', creating an impenetrable barrier of delicacy between them: 'It was as if some fine but untransparent veil had been hung between him and her, dividing them more effectually than a barricade.' (pp. 82-3)

While the first section of the novel demonstrates the inappropriateness of defining Rickman according to class perceptions, the second section demonstrates that such a definition is ineluctable. The class biases and conventions that were initially mocked accordingly resurface to plague Rickman and to reassert their cultural power within the text. Moreover, no one in the novel is more aware of and responsive to the biases than Rickman himself. He feels acutely that 'the barrier of the counter' stands between him and Lucia, and that he is not 'what Miss Harden would call a gentleman.' (p. 115) The counter also stands as a barrier between Rickman and any real hope of escaping the limitations imposed upon him by his class. 'Most doors seem closed pretty tight', he laments, 'except the one marked Tradesman's Entrance.' (p. 151) But it is the elusiveness of his aitches that most troubles Rickman, that – in his own eyes as surely as it does in others' – utterly damns him. The 'fatal habits of his speech', he acknowledges to himself, are 'infinitely more disastrous, more humiliating' than any frailty of character could be:

> Take the occasional but terrific destruction of the aitch. It was worse than drink; it wrecked a man more certainly, more utterly beyond redemption and excuse. It was anxiety on this point that partly accounted for his reserve. He simply dared not talk about Aeschylus or Euripides, because such topics were exciting, and excitement was apt to induce this lapse. (p. 132)

It is, in other words, more ruinous to be branded with stereotypically *déclassé* lapses of speech than it is to be branded with the moral lapses traditionally assigned to the working class – unrestrained sexuality and drunkenness. But even more devastating is the tyranny of constraint exerted by lower-middle-class fear of conventional perceptions, a fear that produces in Rickman a kind of psychic and social paralysis that will not permit him to express himself freely, to discuss with others those things that most inspire him and raise him above class conventions. To do so would expose him to ridicule, to being perceived as a parody of a scholar, to being assigned labels like 'little gentleman' or 'little poet about town'.

The purely conventional nature of Rickman's linguistic deficiencies is emphasized by the fact that his Greek is flawless. In other words, when speaking the language of classical scholarship, rather than that of social discourse, his class position ceases to have significance. In an impromptu discussion with Lucia about Greek literature, during which Rickman's excitement betrays him into referring to Homer as 'Omer', he nevertheless quotes Sophocles with such musical perfection that the 'obscuring veil' of class bias is temporarily lifted:

> He began to quote softly and fluently, to her uttermost surprise. His English was at times a thing to shudder at, but his Greek was irreproachable, perfect in its modulation and its flow. Freed from all flaws of accent, the musical quality of his voice declared itself indubitably, marvellously pure.
>
> The veil lifted. Her smile was a flash of intelligence, the sexless, impersonal intelligence of the scholar. This maker of catalogues, with the tripping tongue that Greek made golden, he had touched the electric chain that linked them under the deep, under the social gulf. (p. 85)

The bond that connects Rickman and Lucia at this moment is one of pure intelligence, which seems at the same time to be a form of pure identity, 'sexless' and 'impersonal'; it is something that both transcends the conventions of gender and class and (as the metaphor of the electric chain under the gulf implies) charges the deepest and most essential levels of being.

The contradictions in this passage between the idea that it is pure intelligence that links Rickman and Lucia and the metaphor used to represent that idea are revealing and far-reaching in their implications. Intelligence, traditionally a masculine quality associated with light – not to mention class position no lower than middle-class – is here imaged as something that exists in depths and darkness, something that is, like electricity, highly charged. In other words, intelligence has been transformed into something symbolically feminine, something dark, mysterious, and dangerous. But the bond is also a chain; it not only bonds, but binds. The bond is not, in fact, intelligence, but that which disqualifies their intelligence, that which would deny the plausibility of anyone other than an educated upper-class man having the ability to speak or understand classical Greek. In other words, the chain is forged of those very conventions that the passage tries to deny. For Lucia, like Rickman, cannot fulfil her intellectual potential not because of who she is, but because of what she is – a woman.

As a woman, Lucia has been assigned a subordinate and largely decorative role within the privileged world of wealth and status that she inhabits, a world – like the novel – entirely regulated by tradition and conventions. The official chronicle of the family, which Rickman reads when he first arrives at the library, immortalizes the scholarly achievements of the Harden men, but notes that 'no woman had ever been permitted to inherit the Harden Library.' (p. 67) The history of the women is recorded in the portrait gallery, a record of images only, visual manifestations of woman as 'the irrational and mutable element in things': 'The portraits have immortalized their faces and their temperaments. Ladies of lax fibre, with shining lips and hazy eyes; ladies of slender build, with small and fragile foreheads.' This dichotomized family record accords with the Harden family tradition 'that its men should be scholars and its women beauties, occasionally frail':

> And scholarship, in obedience to the family tradition, ran superbly in the male line for ten generations, when it encountered an insuperable obstacle in the temperament of Sir Frederick. Then came Sir Frederick's daughter, and between them they made short work of the family tradition. Sir Frederick had appropriated the features of one of his great grandmothers, her auburn hair, her side-long eyes, her fawn-like, tilted lip, her perfect ease of manners and of morals. By a still more perverse hereditary freak the Harden intellect, which had lapsed in Sir Frederick, appeared again in his daughter, not in its well-known austere and colourless form, but with a certain brilliance and passion, a touch of purely feminine uncertainty and charm.
> The Harden intellect had changed its sex. It was Horace Jewdwine who had found that out, counting it as the first of

his many remarkable discoveries. Being (in spite of his conviction to the contrary) a Jewdwine rather than a Harden, he had felt a certain malignant but voluptuous satisfaction in drawing the attention of the Master of Lazarus [i.e., Lucia's grandfather, Sir Joseph] to this curious lapse in the family tradition. Now in the opinion of the Master of Lazarus the feminine intellect was simply a contradiction in terms. (pp. 103–4)

The tradition of the Harden family conforms in several ways to the conventions of the nineteenth-century novel. The aristocratic version of the gentleman, Sir Frederick, has become degenerate and feminized; his role as head of the family has been taken over by Jewdwine, the gentleman scholar with one foot firmly in the commercial world of lucrative journalism. Lucia, however, is not the perfect Victorian heroine. She is suitably refined and beautiful, but she is neither bourgeois nor domestic. There is no question that the servants, not Lucia, run the Harden household. When Lucia takes on a task, it is at once scholarly and bureaucratic – helping to catalogue the library.

Lucia is nevertheless imprisoned by the traditions and conventions which, like the Master of Lazarus, dismiss 'the feminine intellect as a contradiction in terms'. Even Jewdwine, though recognizing Lucia's intelligence, considers it to be intuitive rather than substantive: 'the genius of intuition' rather than 'the intuition of genius'. (p. 6) Thus family and social traditions cannot accommodate the fact that the Harden intellect has 'changed its sex', just as social conventions cannot accommodate the fact that in Rickman the divine fire has changed its class. And Lucia, too, is inspired by something like divine fire, the mysterious power of the feminine and its 'uncertainty and charm'. Her intellect accordingly has 'a certain [notice how uncertainty produces what is certain] brilliance and passion' that was lacking in the 'austere' and 'colourless' male line.

It is the spark of the divine fire that charges the metaphoric chain that links Lucia with Rickman, but the intellectual bonding is short-lived; it is short-circuited by the same issues it attempts to transcend – class and sexuality – which re-emerge in an incident immediately following the conversation in which Rickman burst out in musical Greek. He has been provided with a small but elegant tea in the library, and has his tea-cup to his lips as he gropes 'abstractedly' with his free hand in 'a dish of cream cakes'. At that moment, Lucia enters the room and her mere presence shatters his composure:

> He was all right; so why, oh, why, did he turn brick-red and dash his cup down and draw back his innocent hand? That was what he had seen the errand boy at Rickman's do, when he caught him eating lunch in a dark passage. He always had compassion on that poor pariah and left him to finish his meal in privacy; and with the same delicacy Miss Harden, perceiving his agony, withdrew. He was aware that the incident had marked him.
> He stood exactly where he stood before. Expert knowledge was nothing. Mere conversational dexterity was nothing. He could talk to her about Euripides and Sophocles till all was blue; he could not blow his nose before her, or eat and drink before her, like a gentleman, without shame and fear. (p. 87)

Thus while the fatal influence of his accent has briefly lost its potency, his social inferiority continues to stigmatize him in other, more subtle ways. In this case, a sense of awkwardness, a sense that it is somehow improper for him to be caught eating by a lady, marks him as a pariah, and disrupts the tenuous bond that so fleetingly 'linked them ... under the social gulf'.

There is more at issue in this scene than mere social niceties, however. The acuteness of Rickman's embarrassment suggests an impropriety verging on the sexual, that to be caught eating and drinking is to be caught in the act of being a physical animal, which Lucia's response to the incident confirms. 'Really, you'd have thought that taking afternoon tea was an offence within the meaning of the Act', she tells her friend Kitty. 'He couldn't have been more excited if I'd caught him in his bath. Mr. Rickman suffers from an excess of modesty.' (p. 102) In fact, Rickman's excess of modesty, along with Lucia's excess of courtesy, is an essential part of the social relations between a lower-middle-class male and a woman of superior rank. Decorum requires that they do not exist for each other as fully physical human beings.

Such punctiliousness is not an obvious feature of previous stories about lower-middle-class men, because they are essentially asexual. Hoopdriver is too innocent, Pooter too domesticated, and Denry too extravagantly comic to be sexually potent characters. Richard Larch does have some interest in sex, but he is too enervated to strike fear in the hearts of the bourgeoisie. Rickman, however, throbs. The intensity of his intellectual commitment is only one component of a manifestly passionate persona. As the initial description of Rickman quoted above on pages 163–4 emphasizes, he radiates a 'personal glamour' – a quality conspicuously missing in other representations of the lower middle class – despite the impediments of his situation and of his high-collared city clerk's uniform. The focus in this description on the head, the locus of the mind, and the eyes, the traditional mirror of the soul, indicates the intellectual and spiritual sources of Rickman's special glamour. The 'savage beauty of an animal untamed' and the deep-set hypnotic eyes in turn suggest not only that Rickman is intense, but also that he exudes a powerful and overt sexuality. And it is this facet of Rickman's character that most troubles Jewdwine and makes him reluctant to endorse his protégé fully. For Jewdwine assures himself that, 'provided he was sure of the genius', he is prepared to go to 'almost any length' to support Rickman's career – any length, that is, 'short of introducing him to the ladies of his family.' (p. 26) Jewdwine has at this point, it must be remembered, already witnessed Lucia's intuitive response to the power of Rickman's anonymous manuscript.

The power of Rickman's poetic voice is finally pitted against the destructive power of his 'afflicting accent' when Lucia comes to the realization that the young man she has hired to catalogue the library is not only the same obscure boy who had captured her grandfather's imagination, but is also none other than her cousin Horace's 'find'. A gust of wind blows a sheet of paper off Rickman's desk in the library while he is out, and Lucia, picking it up to replace it, notices that it is the first page of *Helen in Leuce*, no longer anonymous, but signed 'S. K. R.':

> Was it possible that her grandfather's marvellous boy had grown into her cousin's still more marvellous man? Horace, too, had made his great discovery in a City shop. *Helen in Leuce* and a City shop – it hardly amounted to proof; but, if it did, what then? Oh then, she was still more profoundly sorry for him. For then he was a modern poet, which in the best of circumstances is to be marked for suffering. And to Mr. Rickman circumstances had not been exactly kind.
>
> A modern poet, was he? One whom the gods torment with inspired and hopeless passion; a lover of his own 'fugitive and yet eternal bride', the Helen of Homer, of Aeschylus and

Euripides, the Helen of Marlowe and Goethe, the Helen of them all. And for Rickman, unhappy Mr. Rickman, perdition lurked darkly in her very name. What, oh what, must it feel like, to be capable of eliding the aitch in 'Helen' and yet [be] divinely and deliriously in love with her? (p. 109)

The incongruities that constitute Rickman confound Lucia in her musings here, just as they have confounded her cousin and the Junior Journalists. She cannot reconcile Helen with the City shop, nor the young man who elicits her pity with the poet she places in the company of Homer, Aeschylus, Euripides, Marlowe, and Goethe – tormented immortal geniuses whose inspiration was their love for the divine ideal. But most of all, she cannot reconcile the divine ideal with the missing aitch.

This inability to reconcile Rickman's silent poetic voice with his audible speaking voice reifies the contradiction of the binding chain. Lucia's affinity with the poetic voice is incontestable; she becomes one with that voice in the early pages of the novel, when she reads *Helen in Leuce* aloud to Jewdwine. But Rickman's speaking voice cannot invoke the muse; it can call up only the warden, the internalized enforcer of the social and class conventions that hold him apart from Lucia. Rickman himself addresses the problem of voices provocatively in a conversation with Lucia about the Romantic poets, whom he accuses of having sentimentalized Nature beyond redemption, while at the same time identifying himself with them:

> 'We've done our work, and it can't be undone. We've given Nature a human voice, and now we shall never – never hear anything else.'
> 'That's rather dreadful; I wish you hadn't.'
> 'Oh, no, you don't. It's not the human voice you draw the line at – it's the Cockney accent.'
> Lucia's smile flickered and went out, extinguished by the waves of her blush. She was not prepared to have her thoughts read – and read aloud to her – in his way; and that particular thought was one she would have preferred him not to read.
> 'I dare say Keats had a cockney accent, if we did but know; and I dare say a good many people never heard anything else.'
> 'I'm afraid you'd have heard it yourself, Miss Harden, if you'd met him.' (p. 122)

While Lucia was perfectly comfortable reading Rickman's inner voice aloud – the voice of *Helen in Leuce* – she is disconcerted when the tables are turned and Rickman reads *her* inner voice aloud. To have her thoughts read 'in his way' is not only to hear his perspective, but it is also to give her thoughts a Cockney accent. It is to confront the arbitrariness of class prejudices that make people deaf to the humanity of the voice, deaf to the feelings and ideas expressed, and responsive only to a secondary feature of that voice – its accent. Society has given accents a class, and now it can never hear anything else; the accent, rather than the medium, is the message. The example of Keats illustrates both the power and the folly of these ingrained class biases. As Rickman's final comment makes evident, Lucia can acknowledge that Keats had a Cockney accent with equanimity only because it is something she has never actually heard. She has never had to look into Chapman's 'Omer, or contemplate the fall of 'Yperion.

Once Rickman begins to speak to Lucia about what he has written and the experience of writing it, however, the resonance of the poetic voice muffles the 'afflicting accent' of the shopman: 'Lucia no longer heard the Cockney accent in this voice that came to her out of a suffering so lucid and so profound. She forgot that it came from the other side of the social gulf.' (pp. 124–5) They cannot always be talking poetry, of course, but she increasingly hears and responds to the poet rather than to the shopman, to 'the wonderful voice' that covers 'its own offences with exquisite resonances and overtones'. She even fashions a fanciful apologia for his dropped aitches:

> If he dropped his aitches it was not grossly as the illiterate do; she wouldn't go so far as to say he *dropped* them; he slipped them, slided them; it was no more than a subtle slur, a delicate elision. And that was only in the commoner words, the current coin of his world. He was as right as possible, she noticed, in all words whose acquaintance he had made on his own account. And his voice – his voice pleaded against her prejudice with all its lyric modulations. (pp. 147–8)

Lucia's prejudice seems to have 'lyric modulations' as profound as those of Rickman's voice. The aitch becomes the ultimate sliding signifier, no longer the marker of his class but of his natural refinement in the subtlety and delicacy with which he elides it.

All this is nonsense, of course, and if Lucia doesn't quite realize it, Sinclair does. On the very next page, as Rickman talks to Lucia not in 'the current coin of his world' but about his plans for concluding *Helen in Leuce* with a 'Hymn to Pallas Athene', Sinclair lets him drop the aitch in 'Hymn' with a big thud. Lucia and Rickman are equally dismayed as she averts 'her ardent gaze before the horror in his young blue eyes.' (p. 149) The rules of class prejudice had previously marked Rickman, when he was too self-conscious to drink tea in front of Lucia. But in their exquisite mutual self-consciousness in this scene, the dropped aitch now marks them both; it marks the man who strives to speak in the voice of the poet that transcends class and it also marks the woman who strives to hear that poetic voice.

By this time, Lucia has also been marked in another way, by her reading of all of the existing manuscript of *Helen of Leuce*, of which she had previously seen only a fragment. The manuscript radiates with the brilliance and passion of divine fire, as all the Promethean allusions in the description of Lucia's response to it emphasize:

> Rickman's Helen was to the Helen of Euripides what Shelley's Prometheus is to the Prometheus of Aeschylus. Rickman had done what seemed good in his own eyes. He had made his own metres, his own myth and his own drama. A drama of flesh and blood, a drama of spirit, a drama of dreams. Only a very young poet could have had the courage to charge it with such a weight of symbolism; but he had contrived to breathe into his symbols the breath of life; the phantoms of his brain, a shadowy Helen and Achilles, turned into flesh and blood under his hands. It was as if their bodies, warm, throbbing, full-formed, instinct with irresistible and violent life, had come crashing through the delicate fabric of his dream. (p. 138)

The overt and implicit Promethean allusions in this passage overlap in complex ways and include Mary Shelley's *Frankenstein* as well as her husband's *Prometheus Unbound*. Rickman is clearly assigned the role of a Modern Prometheus, breathing life into the 'phantoms of his brain', which in turn breathe passion into Lucia, who feels herself 'in the grasp of a new power, a new spirit': 'There were passages (notably the Hymn to Aphrodite in the second Act) that brought the things of sense and the terrible mysteries of flesh and blood so near to her that she flinched. Rickman had made her share the thrilling triumph, the flushed passion of his youth.' Lucia's perception of both herself and Rickman is profoundly altered by her experience of reading *Helen in Leuce*. She thinks of Rickman and feels abashed that 'this was the man she had had the impertinence to pity.... As she stood contemplating the pile of manuscript before her, Miss Lucia Harden felt (for a great lady) quite absurdly small.' (p. 139)

The passion that permeates this passage – in the ardor of Rickman's poetry, in the emphasis on 'flesh and blood' and on 'bodies, warm, throbbing', and in the intensity of Lucia's reaction – is clearly sexual and mutual. It is the moment when Rickman and Lucia become metaphorically one flesh, a union that is consecrated and indelibly recorded with Lucia's tears, as they fall 'upon Rickman's immaculate manuscript, where their marks remain to this day.' This figurative union works on several levels, many of which are unredeemably trite. Lucia becomes Rickman's muse, his Helen, the focus of the love that 'of all his passions... is the nearest akin to the divine fire.' (p. 425) Within the conventions of the lower-middle-class novel, she has also been the woman of higher status whose temporary and limited intimacy with the protagonist helps him to gain some insight into himself and his situation. Lucia assuredly does that; when Rickman leaves her and Court House to return to London, he is no longer a man of seven identities. He is a man of genius and honor, whose mission is to prove his worth to himself, to Lucia, and to the world. He accordingly rejects the shop and its commercialism; he rejects the charms of Poppy Grace and 'flaming Saturday nights'; and he integrates those roles – journalist, scholar, and intellectual – that serve his larger purpose.

This is the point at which the other lower-middle-class novels end, with the protagonist accepting his role and his life – Hoopdriver returning to the shop with modest ambitions for improving his knowledge, Richard Larch anticipating the role of suburban husband, and Denry Machin devoting himself to the great cause of being a card. And while this is where the story of the lower-middle-class 'little poet about town' ends, it is not where the story of Savage Keith Rickman ends. Rickman also returns to

Modern Prometheus Unbound 183

his lower-middle-class life, but not with a sense of acceptance. On the contrary, he increasingly experiences that life as a form of bondage. At the same time, as his miseries mount he also begins to escape the conventions of the lower-middle-class story; his story becomes what other lower-middle-class stories could not, what the text of the *Divine Fire* indeed denies through ironic undercutting in its early pages – a tragedy.

Rickman leaves the painful ecstasy of 'Lucia's Way' to enter the even more painful miseries of 'The House of Bondage'. The house is literally his lower-middle-class boarding-house, but the bondage is multivalent – it is the bondage of life within his class, including the bondage of an unsuitable (but temporary) engagement to a hopelessly limited lower-middle-class girl; it is the bondage of the social perceptions and conventions that continue to shape people's responses to him; and it is the bondage of the dilemma that his work in the library has precipitated. This last form of bondage is one to which he in part consigns himself because of his commitment to honor. He had felt compromised by the commission to catalogue the library from the beginning, by accepting Lucia's trust as well as her money while he plays the role of his father's spy. The twists of the plot complicate his situation. Sir Frederick dies suddenly, and Lucia finds out what Rickman had always known – that the library must be sold and that his father will be the one to benefit. In an agony of remorse, Rickman refuses to accept pay for his work and tries to thwart the sale of the library by writing to Jewdwine and begging him to buy it from Lucia before Pilkington can close his deal. When Jewdwine stalls, Rickman tries to convince his father to offer Lucia a fair price for the library, which would allow her to pay Pilkington the money due her father's creditors and still escape complete financial ruin. Rickman fails in all these efforts and is further pained when he learns that Lucia has been forced to become music mistress at a women's college in order to maintain herself. When his own father subsequently dies, Rickman feels that he is 'heir, not only to his father's estate, but to that very considerable debt of honour which Isaac had left unpaid' – that is, the debt to Lucia. (pp. 453–4) The library remains largely intact, but the bookshop – and its inventory, which includes the Harden volumes – is heavily mortgaged to Pilkington, who is thus about to gain possession of the Harden library once more. Rickman gets Pilkington to extend the mortgage for three years, during which time he almost starves to death in order to pay it and so redeem the library and his honor.

As with many of the lower-middle-class characters created by lower-middle-class male authors, Rickman proves more honorable than his class 'superiors'. He is certainly more honorable than Horace Jewdwine, whose ambivalence toward Rickman leads him to subvert rather than promote the career of his great 'find'. Jewdwine moreover subverts the relationship between Rickman and Lucia by withholding all letters and messages she gives him to pass on to Rickman. In the end, Jewdwine, in his excessive concern to preserve his own position and to promote his own career, subverts even himself. He has slavishly devoted himself to conservative journalistic policies – to praising the works of the prominent and powerful and dismissing or ignoring the efforts of the promising but obscure – policies that serve the commercial rather than the artistic interests of the periodical he edits. This commitment to maintaining the status quo, he finally realizes, leads not to personal and professional security, but to decline:

> In the interminable watches of the night Jewdwine acknowledged himself a failure; and a failure for which there was no possible excuse. He had had every conceivable advantage that a man could have. He had been born free; free from all social disabilities; free from pecuniary embarrassment; free from the passions that beset ordinary men. And he had sold himself into slavery. He had opinions; he was packed full of opinions, valuable opinions; but he had never had the courage of them. He had always been a slave to other people's opinions. Rickman had been born in slavery, and he had freed himself. When Rickman stood before him, superb in his self-mastery, he had felt himself conquered by this man, whom, as a man, he had despised. Rickman's errors had been the errors of one who risks everything, who never deliberates or counts the cost. And in their repeated rivalries he had won because he had risked everything, when he, Jewdwine, had lost because he would risk nothing. (pp. 583–4)

The freedom that Jewdwine was born into, as a man and as a fictional character, is the freedom granted by class privilege: the freedom, in other words, conferred by social and literary conventions. But this freedom presents the classic problem of 'freedom from' versus 'freedom to'. Jewdwine is free from various social and personal 'disabilities', but the very advantages of his position paradoxically enslave him because he dares not act on his 'valuable opinions'. The most important of these opinions is his original assessment of Rickman, who ultimately recognizes in Jewdwine's inertia a subtle kind of treachery: Rickman understands that 'he had been sacrificed to a prejudice, a convention, an ineradicable class-feeling on the part of the distinguished and fastidious don.' (p. 389) Jewdwine thus forfeits the opportunity to forge an individual identity in favor of the security of 'other people's opinions'. He accordingly becomes a cipher, and his failure constitutes the failure of the bourgeois gentleman. As a cultural symbol, he has been emptied of meaning and the void is sustained with vain opinions; it is 'packed full' of more emptiness.

Rickman, by contrast, struggles to establish an identity, as an artist and as a man, unfettered by convention. And Sinclair uses textual commentary about Rickman's iconoclastic artistic endeavors to announce her own intentions in creating him. A striking non sequitur in an exchange between Lucia and her friend Kitty, when Rickman is still working in the library, reveals the extent to which Sinclair conflates Rickman's purposes with the purposes of her characterization of him. 'Poor darling', Kitty comments, 'he has dressed himself with care.' And Lucia replies, 'He always does. He has broken every literary convention.' (p. 158) Dressing with care is a conventional lower-middle-class trait that would seem to be a contradiction of the iconoclasm of both Rickman and Sinclair. But the very incongruity of the exchange calls attention to its implications, to the defining power of conventions and to the fact that Rickman is breaking the literary conventions not only as an artist within the story, but also as a character in a novelistic text.

A similarly metafictional moment occurs near the end of the novel, after Rickman's close brush with death. His former friends, after neglecting him because they thought his physical decline was the result of dissipation rather than of starvation, rush him to a hospital and await news of the end they fear is inevitable:

> But Rickman did not die. As they said, it was not in him to take that exquisitely mean revenge. It was not in him to truckle to the tradition that ordains that unfortunate young poets shall starve in garrets and die in hospitals. He had always been an upsetter of conventions, and a law unto himself. (p. 540)

It is by virtue of this combined ability of character and creator to upset the conventions that Rickman, the lower-middle-class man, is able to win out over Jewdwine, the gentleman, in their professional and personal rivalries. Most significantly, Jewdwine has failed to prevail as the hero of his own or of the novel's story. *The Divine Fire* had opened with what promised to be the conventional nineteenth-century hero and heroine, gentlemanly Jewdwine and ladylike Lucia, but ends with Lucia and Rickman in a passionate embrace. In other words, it has opened in the decorous world of the nineteenth-century novel – the story indeed opens in 1892 – and has ended in the passionate turmoil of early twentieth-century modernism.

The union of Rickman and Lucia at the end of *The Divine Fire* constitutes more than the resolution of the novel's plot. Rickman and Lucia represent the kinds of exile that Sinclair lived as a woman and as a scholar and writer whose gender placed her on the margins of intellectual life, exile that Sinclair recognized as similar to that of Gissing's Godwin Peake. Their union thus also represents, on one level, the integration of May Sinclair's identity, the union of the refined woman disinherited of her class security by a profligate father with the writer and scholar born in the exile created by social discrimination. The union also confirms both the liberation of the lower-middle-class male from restrictive stereotypes and the significance of the bond between women and lower-middle-class men, for Lucia, the symbol of refined and idealized (though decidedly not domestic) womanhood, explicitly switches her allegiance in the course of the novel. It is, moreover, Lucia's identity as much as Rickman's that is empowered by the change. She turns away from the middle-class gentleman, her cousin Horace with whom she shared 'the bond of kindred and caste' (p. 564), to embrace Rickman, who is 'bound to her by an immaterial, intangible' – but obviously more powerful – 'link.' (p. 168) The essence of the link is articulated by Rickman, who recognizes that '[h]e was hers by right of her perfect comprehension of him; for such comprehension was of the nature of possession.' (p. 303)

That the link is also in part sexual is undeniable. Moreover, the bourgeois gentleman is sexually diminished by comparison with the new masculine potency of his lower-middle-class rival. Lucia has envisioned love with Horace as 'a great calm light rather than a flame. There was no sort of flame about Horace.' But her heart 'beat faster at the very thought of . . . [Rickman], after Horace Jewdwine.' (p. 564) Her relationship with Rickman awakens in her a sexual potential of which she had previously been unaware. Initially, the narrator tells us, 'her attitude to his manhood [was] profoundly unconscious. She had preserved a formidable innocence. There had been nothing in Horace Jewdwine's slow and well-regulated courtship to stir her senses or give her the smallest inkling of her own power that way.' (p. 157) Lucia has thus progressed from the ideal of Victorian womanhood – 'formidable innocence' and 'profoundly unconscious' sexuality – to the sexual awareness of early modernism. The sexuality of the heroine has been released from the constraints of restrictive domesticity, propriety, and procreativity and can now be explicitly acknowledged as an expression of power and passion.

The novel, as I have argued throughout this study, played a vital role in the evolution of class relations in eighteenth- and nineteenth-century England. The code of honor that sustained the authority of the aristocratic gentleman by insuring the exclusivity of his rank and privilege was successfully challenged by Sir Charles Grandison and his fictional heirs. The code of representational conventions subsequently preserved the authority of the bourgeois gentleman by normalizing the social configuration of nineteenth-century class society. It required the combined force of those exiled from positions of cultural authority – of writers from the ranks of women and of lower-middle-class men – to overcome the power of the social and literary conventions and to create startlingly different characters who could successfully flout the accepted norms: Rhoda Nunn who is 'something like an unfamiliar sexual type',[8] and Savage Keith Rickman who is 'a law unto himself.' (p. 540)

The union of Rickman and Lucia at the end of *The Divine Fire* thus marks an important moment in the history of the novel and of its role as a device for disseminating and normalizing bourgeois social ideology. Their union marks a signal victory in the struggle to free lower-middle-class man from restrictive stereotypes, a struggle that had begun almost simultaneously with the formation of the conventions of representation that defined the stereotypes. The pertinacity of the conventions was undoubtedly an effect of the centrality of their role in maintaining the social equilibrium of the Victorian class system and the privileged status of the bourgeoisie. To destabilize the conventions was accordingly to undermine bourgeois hegemony. The union of Rickman and Lucia thus has profound significance, not only because it is a marriage that breaks a novelistic taboo in transgressing a virtually sacrosanct class boundary, but also because it denies the primacy of the union of the bourgeois gentleman and the domestic woman that had constituted the ideological foundation of the nineteenth-century novel.

The union of Rickman and Lucia nevertheless sustains the interdependence of the sexes and of gender roles in the formation of an identity that has social and cultural authority. Just as their marriages confirmed the 'rightful' positions of Coelebs and of John Halifax as complete bourgeois gentlemen, so Rickman's union with Lucia consecrates his position as the protagonist of a serious story and indeed as its hero. To end the story with the anticipated marriage of the hero and heroine would seem to be a falling back to the standard happy ending, the conventional nineteenth-century plot resolution. But the plot of *The Divine Fire* both incorporates and undermines various nineteenth-century novelistic conventions as it traces the progress of Rickman from a socially and culturally marginal figure to fictional hero. The novel begins with Rickman as mildly comic and recognizably, if somewhat problematically, lower-middle-class. The 'tragic' potential of his story is initially mocked by characters and narrator alike, only to be fulfilled as consummate tragedy by Rickman's intense suffering in 'the house of bondage'. The ultimate 'resolution' then itself becomes a travesty of the conventions: the aitchless shopman sets the literary world on its ear and gets the girl. The resolution, moreover, is not complete, because of Rickman's and Lucia's positions as exiles of class and gender. To be, as they are, *born* in exile precludes the possibility of affirming their place in the established social order. To be born in exile is to have no rightful place, no established subject position to return to. They accordingly emerge at the end of the novel not as the conventional hero and heroine but as classless and iconoclastic modern individuals.

Conclusion

In the last decade of the nineteenth century, lower-middle-class male writers struggled to free themselves and their creations from the restrictions of Victorian novelistic conventions, much as middle-class women writers had been doing since the middle of the century. The attempts by both groups to break the bonds of gender and class conventions have a formative influence on modernism, constituting a social and cultural component of its development that has been largely overlooked. Only relatively recently have studies of New Woman novels argued convincingly for their influence on the development of the novel and/or for their claims to a place under the rubric of modernism; moreover, these arguments generally focus on thematic issues rather than on form and conventions.[1] Whether writing about the New Woman or not, women authors throughout the second half of the nineteenth century tended to resist plot closure, since the only acceptable novelistic resolutions consign their heroines either to death or to domestic subservience in marriage. Accordingly, Charlotte Brontë writes *Villette*, which ends ambiguously with Lucy Snowe awaiting news of Paul Emmanuel's fate; and George Eliot writes *Daniel Deronda*, in which the hero and heroine can never marry because of his Judaism, and in which Gwendolen's disastrous marriage and widowhood are uncomfortably balanced by Daniel's blissful union with Mirah. Both women and lower-middle-class male writers resist the constraints imposed by the conventions of representation on the individualism of their characters and on the opportunities open to them within the world of fiction. In so doing, these writers prepare the way for stories that do not resolve neatly, for protagonists who are socially insignificant, for wives and mothers who find their lives unsatisfying, for women who can flout sexual norms and still look forward to living happily ever after – for Leopold Bloom, Mrs Ramsay and Mrs Dalloway, and Connie Chatterley, as well as for a host of characters created by writers whose works have long been neglected, writers such as Hilda Doolittle, Dorothy Richardson, and Alice Dudeney. This is not to say, of course, that domestic heroines and pathetic clerks disappear from the pages of English novels – Maggie Verver and Leonard Bast are notable survivors – but options become available to writers to create characters whose personal attributes and careers are not necessarily predetermined by their class and gender.

The novel has thus continued to be a forum in which social and cultural configurations could be registered and influenced. Its importance to the development and maintenance of nineteenth-century bourgeois class society is unquestionable. But the novel was also open to the forces of resistance that ultimately were able to use it to promote the principles of democratization by effecting the literary enfranchisement of socially and culturally marginalized groups. The most uniformly denigrated of these groups – the lower middle class – should now be granted full critical and historical enfranchisement as well. The significance of the lower middle class to power relations in Victorian class culture demands greater attention than it has received from historians. The significance of the lower middle class in fiction has gone virtually unnoticed by literary critics. This study has, I hope, begun to redress this imbalance between the perceived and the actual importance of the lower middle class, especially in the literature of the nineteenth century.

A full understanding of the lower middle class, both as it existed and as it was perceived, must change how we read and interpret late nineteenth-century and early twentieth-century literature. Sensitivity to what a character like Leonard Bast, with his tattered umbrella and his limited intellectual pretensions, would represent to the imagination of the upper-middle-class characters in *Howards End* and to its upper-middle-class author, for example, necessarily alters how we perceive Leonard's role in the story. Similarly, the character of Phillotson, the schoolmaster in *Jude the Obscure*, takes on new significance. As the representative and mouthpiece of conventionality within that novel, Phillotson plays a role whose symbolic and thematic relevance becomes clear only when he is recognized for what he is – a man whose intellectual and emotional limitations are preordained by his position in the lower middle class.

The ability to apprehend the subtext of subtle class allusions and fine class subdivisions also dramatically enriches the reading of novels from the mid-Victorian period. This is especially true not only of the works of Dickens discussed in earlier chapters, but also of the works of a writer like Anthony Trollope, who continually focuses on the character and the social role of the gentleman. Trollope's most explicit treatment of gentlemanly conduct, false and true, is *The Three Clerks*. To comprehend fully the relevance of Charley Tudor – a low-level clerk and Gent – to the theme and design of the novel requires an understanding of Victorian perceptions of the lower middle class. Knowledge about prejudices against the lower middle class and lower-middle-class employment also clarifies the implications of Hugh Stanbury's decision to become a journalist earning a salary, rather than a lawyer earning a professional income, in *He Knew He Was Right*.

The persistent disparagement of the lower middle class has also led to the underestimation of the fiction of writers like H. G. Wells, Arnold Bennett, and May Sinclair.[2] The value of these authors' social novels should not go unrecognized. The lower-middle-class novel of manners, which they created, provides a unique entrée into the inner life of a large and otherwise silent segment of society whose perception of the world must be apprehended by those who wish to attain a complete appreciation of the Victorian period and of its literature.

Notes

INTRODUCTION

1. Ian Watt, 'Serious Reflections on *The Rise of the Novel*', *Novel* 1:3 (Spring 1968), 215–16.
2. As Jane Tompkins argues with reference to American fiction, literary texts are (at least in part) 'attempts to redefine the social order'. I would argue that they can also attempt to define and entrench the social order. *Sensational Designs: the Cultural Work of American Fiction 1790–1860* (Oxford & New York: Oxford University Press, 1985), p. xi.
3. Harold Perkin, *The Origins of Modern English Society* (London & Boston: Ark, 1985), p. 273; rpt London: Routledge, 1969.
4. Michael McKeon, *The Origins of the English Novel 1600–1740* (Baltimore: Johns Hopkins University Press, 1987), p. 21.
5. For a recent discussion of the complexities of the concept of class and the dubiousness of any application that posits a notion of class that is unproblematic see William M. Reddy, 'The concept of class', in *Social Orders and Social Classes in Europe since 1500: Studies in Social Stratification*, ed. M. L. Bush (London & New York: Longman, 1992), pp. 13–25. See also John Seed, 'From "Middling Sort" to Middle Class in late eighteenth- and early nineteenth-century England', in Bush, pp. 114–35, and Geoffrey Crossick, 'From Gentleman to the Residuum: Languages of Social Description in Victorian Britain', *Language, History and Class*, ed. Penelope J. Corfield (Oxford: Blackwell, 1991), pp. 150–78. Seed discusses the intersecting social institutions of family, church, and the public sphere (clubs and other secular organizations) and their role in defining social and class boundaries (pp. 129–35). Crossick examines the interplay of the terminology of class and of other kinds of social and cultural categorization in nineteenth-century Britain, including not only value-laden terms like 'gentleman' and 'the residuum' (the morally and economically destitute members of the lower classes) but also occupational terms like 'dock labourer, clerk, lawyer – [which] stood for a great deal more than the simple description of a job.' (p. 166) Two older but valuable and relevant discussions of class are E. P. Thompson, 'Eighteenth-Century English Society: Class Struggle without Class?' *Social History* 3:2 (May 1978), 133–65, and Asa Briggs, 'The Language of "Class" in Early Nineteenth-Century England', *Essays in Labour History*, eds A. Briggs and J. Saville (London: Macmillan, 1967); rpt *Essays in Social History*, eds M. W. Flinn and T. C. Smout (Oxford: Clarendon, 1974), pp. 154–77.
6. For a comprehensive examination of the values and ideas of the English bourgeoisie from the late eighteenth to the mid-nineteenth century, see Leonore Davidoff and Catherine Hall, *Family Fortunes:*

Men and Women of the English Middle Class, 1780–1850 (London: Hutchinson, 1987). Davidoff and Hall stress in particular the importance of gender and of Evangelical and Dissenting religion in the evolution of middle-class precepts and practices.

7. Coleridge was apprehensive about precisely this effect of leisure reading on the minds of the public at large. He refers with contempt to 'the devotees of the circulating libraries', whose '*pass-time*, or rather *kill-time*' he refuses to dignify 'with the name of *reading*. Call it rather a sort of beggarly daydreaming', he continues, 'during which the mind of the dreamer furnishes for itself nothing but laziness and a little mawkish sensibility; while the whole *material* and imagery of the doze is supplied *ab extra* by a sort of mental *camera obscura* manufactured at the printing office, which *pro tempore* fixes, reflects and transmits the moving phantasms of one man's delirium, so as to people the barrenness of an hundred other brains afflicted with the same trance or suspension of all common sense and all definite purpose.' This kind of passive absorption of impressions Coleridge classifies with mindless activities such as 'swinging, or swaying on a chair or gate; spitting over a bridge; smoking; snuff-taking'. Samuel Taylor Coleridge, *Biographia Literaria*, eds James Engell and W. Jackson Bate (Princeton: Princeton University Press, 1983), vol. I, 48–9; Coleridge's note. Carlyle expressed similar reservations about the passivity of reading, with specific reference to Scott's Waverley novels, which created a 'beatific land of Cockaigne and Paradise of Donothings', a world in which 'there was no call for effort on the reader's part. . . . The reader, what the vast majority of readers so long to do, was allowed to lie down at his ease, and be ministered to. . . . The languid imagination fell back into its rest; an artist was there who could supply it with high-painted scenes, with sequences of stirring action, and whisper to it, Be at ease, and let thy tepid element be comfortable to thee.' 'Sir Walter Scott', *Critical and Miscellaneous Essays*, 6 vols (London: Chapman & Hall, 1869), V, 251–2; first appeared in *London and Westminster Review* 12 (1837), as a review of the first six volumes of Lockhart's *Life of Sir Walter Scott*.

8. Mary Poovey, *Uneven Developments: the Ideological Work of Gender in Mid-Victorian England* (Chicago: University of Chicago Press, 1988); Nancy Armstrong, *Desire and Domestic Fiction: a Political History of the Novel* (New York & Oxford: Oxford University Press, 1987). Subsequent references to both works are in the text.

9. Donna T. Andrew, 'The Code of Honour and its Critics: the Opposition to Duelling in England, 1700–1850', *Social History* 5:3 (October 1980), 415.

10. For a detailed discussion of the variety of models of the gentleman see David Castronovo, *The English Gentleman: Images and Ideals in Literature and Society* (New York: Ungar, 1987). See also Robin Gilmour, *The Idea of the Gentleman in the Victorian Novel* (London: Allen & Unwin, 1981).

11. Anthony Trollope, *He Knew He Was Right*, ed. John Sutherland (Oxford & New York: Oxford University Press, 1985), p. 908.

12. Thomas Hardy, *A Pair of Blue Eyes* (London: Macmillan, 1965), p. 156. K. C. Phillipps quotes this passage and others from Victorian fiction to demonstrate the equivocal nature of the term in the late nineteenth century in his *Language and Class in Victorian England* (Oxford: Blackwell, 1984), pp. 6–7. Crossick contends that Phillips 'exaggerates the rapidity of the decline [of the meaning of "gentleman"], for the term remained precise in the setting of the landed country elites.' ('From Gentlemen to the Residuum', p. 164).
13. Raymond Williams, *Marxism and Literature* (Oxford & New York: Oxford University Press, 1977), pp. 112–13.
14. Arno Mayer, 'The Lower Middle Class as Historical Problem', *Journal of Modern History* 47:3 (September 1975), 409, 411. Subsequent references are in the text.
15. Ibid., and Geoffrey Crossick, 'The Emergence of the Lower Middle Class in Britain', *The Lower Middle Class in Britain 1870–1914*, ed. Geoffrey Crossick (London: Croom Helm, 1977), pp. 11–60. Subsequent references are in the text.
16. George Gissing, *Charles Dickens: a Critical Study* (London: Gresham, 1903), p. 42.
17. George Gissing, *Will Warburton* (London: Hogarth, 1985), p. 237.
18. George Gissing, *In the Year of the Jubilee* (London: Lawrence and Bullen, 1895); rpt Rutherford, NJ: Fairleigh Dickinson University Press, 1976, p. 443.
19. See H. J. Dyos, *Victorian Suburb: a Study of the Growth of Camberwell* (Leicester: Leicester University Press, 1966), pp. 191–2.
20. Alice Dudeney, *The Maternity of Harriott Wicken* (London & New York: Macmillan, 1900), p. 81.

1 'A KIND OF A SORT OF A GENTLEMAN': THE GENTLEMAN'S PROGRESS FROM SIR CHARLES GRANDISON TO JOHN HALIFAX

1. Thomas Smith, *The Commonwealth of England: and the Manner and Governement thereof* (London, 1609; originally published in 1583); cited in *The Past Speaks*, ed. Walter Arnstein (Lexington, MA.: Heath, 1981), p. 192.
2. Ruth Kelso, 'Sixteenth-Century Definitions of the Gentleman in England', *Journal of English and Germanic Philology* 24 (1925), 370–82.
3. Peter Earle, *The Making of the English Middle Class: Business, Society and Family Life in London, 1660–1730* (Berkeley & Los Angeles: University of California Press, 1989), pp. 5–9. Subsequent references are in the text.
4. John Loftis, *Comedy and Society from Congreve to Fielding* (Stanford: Stanford University Press, 1959), p. 1.
5. Richard Steele, *The Conscious Lovers*, in *The Plays of Richard Steele*, ed. Shirley Strum Kenny (Oxford: Clarendon, 1971), pp. 295–382; IV. ii., 50–7.
6. Laura Brown, *English Dramatic Form, 1660–1760: an Essay in Generic History* (New Haven & London: Yale University Press, 1981), pp. 180–1. Subsequent references are in the text.

Notes

7. George Lillo, *The London Merchant*, in *The Dramatic Works of George Lillo*, ed. James L. Steffensen (Oxford: Clarendon, 1993), pp. 149–209; I.i., 21–2.
8. William H. McBurney traces the history of the productions, editions, and nineteenth-century variations of the play in his 'Introduction', *The London Merchant* (Lincoln: University of Nebraska Press, 1965), pp. ix–xxv.
9. For a detailed discussion of the theme of gentility in Defoe's *oeuvre*, see Michael Shinagel, *Daniel Defoe and Middle-Class Gentility* (Cambridge, MA: Harvard University Press, 1968).
10. Daniel Defoe, *The Complete English Tradesman*, 2nd edn with supplement, 2 vols (London: Rivington, 1727; rpt New York: Kelley, 1969), I, 15. Subsequent references are given in the text by volume and page number.
11. This avenue of social advancement is indeed acknowledged by the eighteenth-century economist and divine Josiah Tucker (1712–99), who stated that the self-made man of business 'may not always meet with Respect equal to his large and acquired Fortune; yet if he gives his Son a liberal and Accomplished education, the Birth and calling of the Father are sunk in the Son; and the Son is reputed, if his Carriage is suitable, a Gentleman in all Companies'. R. E. Schuyler, ed., *Josiah Tucker: A Selection of his Economic and Political Writings* (New York, 1931), p. 264; as quoted by Nicholas Rogers, 'A reply to Donna Andrew' (to Andrew's 'Alderman and Big Bourgeoisie of London Reconsidered') *Social History* 6 (1981), 367. Tucker himself had risen from being the son of a small Welsh farmer to becoming the dean of Gloucester.
12. Daniel Defoe, *The Compleat English Gentleman*, ed. Karl D. Bülbring (London: David Nutt, 1890), p. 13. Subsequent references are in the text by page number.
13. G. J. Barker-Benfield, *The Culture of Sensibility: Sex and Society in Eighteenth-Century Britain* (Chicago & London: University of Chicago Press, 1992), pp. 37–103. The controversy over dueling, discussed below, also played a part in the reformation of male manners.
14. Samuel Richardson, 'Preface' to *Sir Charles Grandison*, ed. Jocelyn Harris (London & New York: Oxford University Press, 1972), p. 4. Subsequent references are in the text by volume and page number.
15. Donna T. Andrew, 'The Code of Honour and its Critics: the Opposition to Duelling in England, 1700–1850,' *Social History* 5:3 (October 1980), 413. Subsequent references are in the text. For more detailed histories of the practice of dueling, see V. G. Kiernan, *The Duel in European History: Honour and the Reign of Aristocracy* (Oxford: Oxford University Press, 1988) and Robert Baldick, *The Duel* (London: Chapman & Hall, 1965). See also J. C. D. Clark, *English Society 1688–1832: Ideology, Social Structure and Political Practice during the Ancien Régime* (Cambridge & New York: Cambridge University Press, 1985), pp. 109–18.
16. Kiernan observes that the duel 'grew into a ritual, as formal as a church service' (ibid., p. 135). The duel also conforms to the criteria

for 'secular ritual' – such as its explicit purpose, use of explicit symbolism, and involvement of specific social roles and identities – outlined by Sally F. Moore and Barbara Myerhoff in 'Secular Ritual: Forms and Meanings', in *Secular Ritual*, eds Sally F. Moore and Barbara G. Myerhoff (Assen/Amsterdam: Van Gorcum, 1977), pp. 3–24. Such rituals, they argue, can 'lend authority and legitimacy to the positions of particular persons, organizations, occasions, moral values, view of the world, and the like' (p. 4). They further argue that ritual is 'an attempt to reify the man-made. That which is postulated and unquestionable may but need not be religious. It may but need not have to do with mystical forces and the spirit world. Unquestionability may instead be vested in a system of authority or a political ideology' (p. 22).

17. This is not to say that the example of Sir Charles is necessarily opposed to aristocratic ideals, especially those embodied in the courtesy literature. However, as John Edward Mason notes, these ideals were often at odds with social practice: 'With regard to the relation of the courtesy books to the social life of their time, it may fairly be said that the author's attitude often represents an ideal rather than an actual condition.' Hence Richardson's emphasis on Sir Charles's actual conduct in social situations, on his 'acting uniformly well'. Mason's comment is from his *Gentlefolk in the Making* (Philadelphia: University of Pennsylvania Press; London: Oxford University Press, 1935), pp. 292. Subsequent references are in the text.
18. Clark, p. 94.
19. For comprehensive treatments of the debate over dueling, see Andrew (passim) and Kiernan, pp. 165–84. David Castronovo provides a brief but incisive account of the duel and resistance to it in *The English Gentleman: Images and Ideals in Literature and Society* (New York: Ungar, 1987), pp. 21–5. W. Lee Ustick discusses the increasing emphasis on the 'good man' and the opposition to dueling in early conduct manuals for gentleman, especially Brathwait's *The English Gentleman* (1630), in 'Changing Ideals of Aristocratic Character and Conduct in Seventeenth-Century England', *Modern Philology* 30:2 (November 1932), 147–66; see especially 154–61. Lawrence Stone discusses early attempts to control dueling in *The Crisis of the Aristocracy 1558–1641* (Oxford: Clarendon, 1965), pp. 242–50. Stone argues that the development of the 'code of the duel' was initially beneficial to society because it reduced faction fighting and local blood-feuds. He also suggests that the duel acted as a social leveler, 'blurring the distinction between gentry and nobility' because the wealthy nobleman, surrounded by his retainers, could no longer 'insult a mere gentleman with impunity' (p. 245). Thus the duel played a significant role both in the transition from a society controlled by the high nobility to one dominated by a broader based aristocracy, and in the later transition from aristocratic to middle-class hegemony.
20. For Addison and Steele's treatment of the duel, see *The Tatler* nos 25 (7 June 1709), 26 (9 June 1709), 28 (14 June 1709), 29 (16 June 1709), 31 (21 June 1709), 38 (7 July 1709), 39 (9 July 1709), 162 (22

April 1710) and *The Spectator*, nos 84 (6 June, 1711), 97 (21 June 1711), and 99 (23 June 1711). In 'On Good Manners and Good Breeding', Jonathan Swift makes a brief but caustic comment: 'I can discover no political evil in suffering bullies, sharpers, and rakes, to rid the world of each other by a method of their own, where the law has not been able to find an expedient'; *The Prose Works of Jonathan Swift*, ed. Herbert Davis, 14 vols (Oxford: Blackwell, 1957), IV, 214. In 'The Duel of Lord Mohun and the Duke of Hamilton', *Review* 1:34 (29 Nov. 1712), Defoe makes a strong statement against dueling as a response to the most notorious duel of the period: 'I call the Quarrel Unjust and Dishonourable, not as to the Cause of the Quarrel, which I have nothing to do with, but as to the Manner of Duelling, which I undertake to be Unjust and Dishonourable, because Illegal and Unchristian.' See also Jeremy Collier, 'Of Duelling,' in *Essays upon Several Moral Subjects*, 2nd edn (London: Sare & Hindmarch, 1697) and William Jackson, 'On Riches, Cards, and Duelling', in *Thirty Letters on Various Subjects*, 2nd edn (London: Cadell & Thorn, 1784). Those who argue against dueling far outnumber those who argue in favor. Bernard Mandeville presents the pro-dueling position, without endorsing it, in *An Enquiry into the Origin of Honour, and the Usefulness of Christianity in War* (1732) and in *The Fable of the Bees* (1729). Samuel Johnson's position on dueling is similarly ambiguous.

21. Anna Laetitia Barbauld, 'Life of Samuel Richardson, with Remarks on his Writings', in *The Correspondence of Samuel Richardson*, ed. Anna Laetitia Barbauld, 6 vols (London: Phillips, 1804; rpt New York: AMS, 1966), I, cxxvii. Margaret Anne Doody and, more recently, Gerard A. Barker, similarly criticize Sir Charles. See Doody, *A Natural Passion: a Study of the Novels of Samuel Richardson* (Oxford: Clarendon, 1974), p. 263 and Barker, *Grandison's Heirs: the Paragon's Progress in the Late Eighteenth-Century English Novel* (Newark: University of Delaware Press; London & Toronto: Associated University Presses, 1985), p. 133.

22. The stage is another obvious venue where the duel could have been, and was, represented visually. The performance of the duel in eighteenth-century plays, however, is generally perfunctory, and typically functions as an integral part of a classical setting, as in Joseph Addison's *Cato* and Nicholas Rowe's *The Fair Penitent*, thus circumventing the issue of dueling in contemporary society. Richard Steele, however, attacks the morality of dueling in *The Lying Lover* and *The Conscious Lovers*, both of which have contemporary settings. But the protagonist in *The Lying Lover* questions that morality only after having apparently killed his friend. The protest against dueling in *The Conscious Lovers* is more focused and explicit; Steele in fact claims that 'the whole was writ for the sake of the Scene of the Fourth Act, wherein Mr. *Bevil* evades the Quarrel with his Friend', with the hope that 'it may have some Effect upon the *Goths* and *Vandals* that frequent the Theatres' (see 'The Preface' to *The Conscious Lovers* in *The Plays of Richard Steele*, loc.cit, p. 299). As with Sir Charles, Bevil Junior's opposition to dueling is part of his virtue, but he lacks Grandison's supreme self-assurance and conviction in his resistance

to 'Tyrant Custom' (IV, i, 114). Moreover, Bevil avoids the duel through the dubious expedient of showing to his challenger a letter he has been implored to keep secret. Contemporary dramatic conventions, as discussed above, no doubt limited the extent to which dueling could be deconstructed on the stage, whether verbally or visually. The novel proves to be the ideal medium for the visual reinterpretation of the duel, not just because of the genre's suitability for bourgeois expression, but more importantly because it allows the author greater control over what can indeed be 'seen' and how it is interpreted.

23. Terry Eagleton, *The Rape of Clarissa: Writing, Sexuality and Class Struggle in Samuel Richardson* (Oxford: Blackwell, 1982), p. 100.
24. Elizabeth Inchbald, *A Simple Story*, ed. J. M. S. Tompkins (Oxford & New York: Oxford University Press, 1988), p. 329.
25. Despite finding both the novel and its hero to be failures, Eagleton acknowledges that Richardson played a major role in the class struggle between the aristocracy and the bourgeoisie and that *Sir Charles Grandison* is 'the logical culmination of Richardson's ideological project, a necessary move in the whole middle-class cultural enterprise' (p. 95).
26. Jane Austen, *Pride and Prejudice*, eds James Kinsley and Frank W. Bradbrook (Oxford & New York: Oxford University Press, 1980), p. 124.
27. Women writers in this period indeed often belittle dueling. Austen, for example, has Elinor sigh over Colonel Brandon's 'fancied necessity' of calling Willoughby out. Jane Austen, *Sense and Sensibility*, ed. Claire Lamont (London & New York: Oxford University Press, 1970), p. 184. And only the empty-headed Mrs Bennet imagines that her husband might duel with Wickham after his elopement with Lydia (*Pride and Prejudice*, p. 259). Maria Edgeworth completely undermines the duel as an enactment of manliness and honor by featuring a farcical female duel between the scandalous Lady Delacour and Mrs Luttridge in *Belinda* (1801).
28. Thomas Holcroft, *Anna St. Ives*, ed. Peter Faulkner (London & New York: Oxford University Press, 1970), p. 120. Subsequent references are given in the text by page number.
29. Hannah More, *Coelebs in Search of a Wife: Comprehending Observations on Domestic Habits and Manners, Religion and Morals*, 2 vols, 7th edn (London: Cadell & Davies, 1809), II, p. 426.
30. Henry James, 'A Noble Life', *Nation* 2:35 (1 March 1866), 276.
31. Dinah Mulock Craik, *John Halifax, Gentleman* (London & Glasgow: Collins, 1954), p. 22. Subsequent references are given in the text by page number.
32. Sally Mitchell, *Dinah Mulock Craik* (Boston: Twayne, 1983), p. 41.
33. Patrick Brantlinger, *The Spirit of Reform: British Literature and Politics, 1832–1867* (Cambridge, MA & London: Harvard University Press, 1977), p. 121.
34. James, loc. cit. Robin Gilmour rather less elegantly calls John Halifax 'the Sir Charles Grandison of the cotton-mills', in *The Idea of the Gentleman in the Victorian Novel*, (London: Allen & Unwin, 1981), p. 101.

35. The characterization of Ursula, as well as that of Anna in *Anna St. Ives*, undercuts Nancy Armstrong's claim that 'through marriage to someone of a lower station, the male but not the female of the upper gentry can be redeemed.' See Armstrong, *Desire and Domestic Fiction: a Political History of the Novel* (Oxford & New York: Oxford University Press, 1987), p. 113.

2 THE LITERARY EVOLUTION OF THE LOWER MIDDLE CLASS: THE NATURAL HISTORY OF THE GENT TO LITTLE DORRIT

1. See Kerry McSweeney, *Middlemarch* (London & Boston: Allen & Unwin, 1984), pp. 73–4.
2. The extent to which the nineteenth-century British novel embodies a middle-class ideology is most obvious in the ways in which it proves problematic for the mediation of the values of other classes, or for the representation of the stories of characters whose lives do not conform to essentially bourgeois novelistic structures. As Regenia Gagnier points out, the middle-class 'plot' that shapes both nineteenth-century autobiographies and novels traces 'ordered progress', from education to career and family life for men, or from life with father to life with husband for women. According to Gagnier, the structure and ideology inherent in this plot – or cultural 'master narrative' – is often unworkable for the self-representation of working-class writers. Working-class authors who do adopt the middle-class plot are frequently frustrated in telling their stories, or even in sustaining their identities because the 'gap between ideology and experience leads not only to the disintegration of the narrative the writer hopes to construct, but . . . to the disintegration of personality itself.' Regenia Gagnier, *Subjectivities: a History of Self-Representation in Britain, 1832–1920*, (Oxford & New York: Oxford University Press, 1991), pp. 6, 44–6. Subsequent references are in the text.
3. See Raymond Williams, *Marxism and Literature* (Oxford: Oxford University Press, 1977).
4. J. M. Jefferson posits the reverse case, that the representations of working-class poverty in nineteenth-century 'Condition of England' novels have produced misconceptions about industrialization by exaggerating the social ills and ignoring the benefits to the working class of the steadily increasing prosperity. See J. M. Jefferson, 'Industrialisation and Poverty: in Fact and Fiction', *The Long Debate on Poverty: Eight Essays on Industrialisation and 'the Condition of England'* (London: Institute of Economic Affairs, 1972), pp. 187–238. Jefferson argues aggressively, if not convincingly, that these novels have had an insidious influence on public opinion, fostering unfavorable views of industrialism and its effects that have persisted into the twentieth century.
5. Charlotte Brontë draws attention to the suspiciousness of inappropriate dress in *Jane Eyre*. When Jane is reduced to destitution after fleeing from Rochester, her attempt to exchange her gloves and

handkerchief for bread immediately elicits mistrust in the shopwoman she approaches. As Jane recognizes, 'an ordinary beggar is frequently an object of suspicion; a well-dressed beggar inevitably so.' *Jane Eyre*, ed. Richard J. Dunn, 2nd edn (New York & London: Norton, 1987), p. 289.
6. Robin Gilmour posits that the inscription and the emphasis on 'gentleman in the novel's title suggest 'a recovered as well as an achieved rank'. *The Idea of the Gentleman in the Victorian Novel* (London & Boston: Allen & Unwin, 1981), p. 101.
7. T. B. Tomlinson goes so far as to describe 'the nature of the middle class, from pre-1832 days onwards', as 'in part that of a defensive alliance' of 'conflicting interests' that set itself 'not so much against Tory landowners or the big industrialists, as against the working class'. See T. B. Tomlinson, *The English Middle-Class Novel* (London: Macmillan, 1976), p. 14.
8. Thomas Malthus, *An Essay on the Principle of Population*, ed. Philip Appleman (New York: Norton, 1976), p. 40.
9. Malthusian doctrine also influenced the self-perception of at least some members of the working classes, such as Charles Shaw, who bitterly identified his place in the socio-economic structures of his youth as 'a part of Malthus's "superfluous population".' Charles Shaw, *When I Was a Child* (1893; rpt East Ardsley, Wakefield: SR Publishers, 1969), p. 97. Quoted in Gagnier, p. 42.
10. Gertrude Himmelfarb, *The Idea of Poverty: England in the Early Industrial Age* (New York: Random House, 1983; rpt New York: Vintage, 1985), p. 107.
11. Himmelfarb stresses the effects that the 'anxiety and insecurity generated by the rapidity of change' had on attitudes to poverty and the poor during the 1830s and 1840s. Ibid., pp. 137–44.
12. Himmelfarb suggests that Ainsworth glamorized the dangerous classes, while Reynolds engaged in a 'pornography of violence'. Ibid., pp. 434, 441.
13. P. J. Keating, *The Working Classes in Victorian Fiction* (New York: Barnes & Noble, 1971), p. 27.
14. Raymond Williams, *Culture and Society* (London: Hogarth, 1982), pp. 89–90.
15. Catherine Gallagher, *The Industrial Reformation of English Fiction: Social Discourse and Narrative Form 1832–1867* (Chicago & London: University of Chicago Press, 1985), p. 67. Gallagher argues that Gaskell 'seeks refuge' in formal multiplicity because of 'an ambivalence about causality' that resulted from the influence of conflicting Unitarian philosophies. 'A dominant impulse in *Mary Barton*', Gallagher maintains, 'is to escape altogether from causality, to transcend explanation. *Mary Barton* expresses both stages of the Unitarianism of the 1840s; it was inspired by both the "Religion of Causality" that Harriet Martineau advocated and the "Religion of Conscience" that her brother eloquently preached.'
16. Charles Dickens, *Hard Times*, eds George Ford and Sylvère Monod, 2nd edn (New York & London: Norton, 1990), p. 70.

17. Elizabeth Gaskell, *North and South*, ed. Angus Easson (Oxford & New York: Oxford University Press, 1982), p. 180.
18. Dickens, *Hard Times*, p. 17.
19. B. G. Orchard, *The Clerks of Liverpool* (Liverpool: Collinson, 1871), p. 49. Orchard's own contempt for clerks, it transpires, had recently been confirmed by the failure of the Provident and Annuity Association, a self-help group for clerks of which he had been secretary.
20. Charles Lamb, 'The Good Clerk', *Reflector* 4 (1812). Later versions of the clerk's lament include J. S. Harrison, *The Social Position and Claims of Clerks and Book-Keepers Considered* (London: Hamilton Adams, 1852); Charles Edward Parsons, *Clerks: their Position and Advancement* (London [Provost], [1876]); and *The Clerk's Grievance*, anon., (London: Pole, 1878).
21. F. M. L. Thompson, 'Town and city', *The Cambridge Social History of Britain 1750–1950*, ed. F. M. L. Thompson, 3 vols (Cambridge & New York: Cambridge University Press, 1990), I, 63–7; and *The Rise of Respectable Society: a Social History of Victorian Britain 1830–1900* (Cambridge, MA: Harvard University Press, 1988), p. 360. Local government – school boards and town councils – was also the political venue that opened up to women from 1870 onward. See Patricia Hollis, *Ladies Elect: Women in English Local Government 1865–1914* (Oxford: Clarendon, 1987). Another recent historical examination of a segment of the lower middle class is Christopher P. Hosgood's analysis of the culture of the commercial traveller, 'The "Knights of the Road": Commercial Travellers and the Culture of the Commercial Room in Late-Victorian and Edwardian England', *Victorian Studies* 37:4 (Summer 1994), 519–47. For relevant earlier studies of clerks, see Gregory Anderson, *Victorian Clerks* (Manchester: Manchester University Press, 1976) and the introduction and first chapter of David Lockwood, *The Blackcoated Worker: a Study in Class Consciousness* (London: Allen & Unwin, 1958). For historical background on the expansion of white-collar work in the nineteenth century, see R. M. Hartwell, 'The Service Revolution: the Growth of Services in Modern Economy', *The Fontana Economic History of Europe: the Industrial Revolution* (London: Collins, 1973), III, 358–96.
22. Arno Mayer, 'The Lower Middle Class as Historical Problem', *The Journal of Modern History* 3 (September 1975), 409–36; Geoffrey Crossick, ed., *The Lower Middle Class in Britain 1870–1914* (London: Croom Helm, 1977). In a later essay, Crossick argues, much as Thompson does, that the petite bourgeoisie was influential in urban politics in the nineteenth century. Crossick emphasizes, however, that he is referring to the 'classic petty bourgeoisie of small businessmen – primarily shopkeepers and small manufacturers', and not the white-collar workers who manned the growing bureaucracies that were servicing industry and formed the 'new' lower middle class. See Geoffrey Crossick, 'Urban Society and the Petty Bourgeoisie in Nineteenth-Century Britain', *The Pursuit of Urban History*, eds Derek Fraser and Anthony Sutcliffe (London: Edward Arnold, 1983), pp. 307–26. Crossick also argues for the importance of the petite bourgeoisie to

the economic development of Britain, in 'The Petite Bourgeoisie in Nineteenth-Century Britain: the Urban and Liberal Case', *Shopkeepers and Master Artisans in Nineteenth-Century Europe*, eds Geoffrey Crossick and Heinz-Gerhard Haupt (London & New York: Methuen, 1984), pp. 62–94. Unlike the 'new' lower middle class, the 'classic' petite bourgeoisie had a history and tradition to draw on and to give its members some sense of collective identity, something that white-collar workers seemed to lack. The petite bourgeoisie has received greater attention by historians of continental Europe, especially in France and Germany, and is perceived to be a more significant entity. See, for example, the essays in *Shopkeepers*. Art historian T. J. Clark goes so far as to describe the members of the petite bourgeoisie of late nineteenth-century Paris as the 'perfect heroes and heroines' of the 'myth of modernity'. *The Painting of Modern Life: Paris in the Art of Manet and his Followers* (Princeton: Princeton University Press, 1984), p. 258.
23. See Richard N. Price, 'Society, Status and Jingoism: the Social Roots of Lower Middle Class Patriotism, 1870–1900', *The Lower Middle Class in Britain 1870–1914*, ed. Geoffrey Crossick (London: Croom Helm, 1977), pp. 89–112. Price concentrates on the clerk as the 'representative example of the lower middle classes'. Clerks, he affirms 'are universally recognized to be archetypal lower middle class workers, and they were, perhaps, the fastest growing occupational group of the period' (pp. 97–8).
24. According to the *Oxford English Dictionary*, the first appearance in print of the term 'lower middle class' was in 1852, in a letter from Harriet Martineau to G. J. Holyoake; '*petit bourgeois*' and its variations appeared around the same time, the first recorded instance being in Charlotte Brontë's *Villette* (1853).
25. Mary Cowling notes that artists and cartoonists, as well as authors, take up the representation of the Gent, commenting that 'from about 1840 he had received constant attention from both writers and artists'. *The Artist as Anthropologist: The Representation of Type and Character in Victorian Art* (Cambridge: Cambridge University Press, 1989), p. 274.
26. James Smith, 'The Hebdomadary of Mr. Snooks, the Grocer', *New Monthly Magazine and Literary Journal* 11 (1824), 436–40.
27. Paul Pindar, 'Malachi Meagrim, the Teatotaler', *Bentley's Miscellany* 11 (1842), 228–32.
28. 'Davus , 'A Passage in the Life of Mr. Nosebody', *Bentley's Miscellany* 11 (1842), 378–83.
29. J. B. Buckstone, 'The Man in the Mackintosh Cape', *New Monthly Magazine and Literary Journal* 50 (1837), 265–71.
30. 'Regular Habits', anon., *Bentley's Miscellany* 14 (1843), 393–401.
31. Moreover, the original dandy, Beau Brummell, was a small man. See Ellen Moers, *The Dandy: Brummell to Beerbohm* (New York: Viking, 1960; rpt Lincoln & London: University of Nebraska Press, 1978), p. 17.
32. [Charles Dickens], 'Mr. Robert Bolton', *Bentley's Miscellany* 4 (1838), 204–7.

33. 'Concerning the Gent', anon. but probably Albert Smith *Punch* 3 (1842), 60–1.
34. Gareth Stedman Jones discusses 'Arry as the quintessential cockney 'swell' of the later nineteenth century in 'The "Cockney" and the Nation, 1780–1988', *Metropolis London: Histories and Representations since 1800*, eds David Feldman and Gareth Stedman Jones (London and New York: Routledge, 1989), pp. 288–94.
35. Albert Smith, *The Natural History of the Gent* (London: Bogue, 1847), pp. vi–vii. It is not clear whether Albert Smith is the only writer contributing to this volume. He uses the editorial 'we' in his preface in a most awkward manner, suggesting that some of the material he uses may be from a *Punch* contributor who wishes to remain anonymous, or even that Smith is plagiarizing. Plagiarism eventually lost him his berth at *Punch*; see R. G. G Price, *A History of Punch* (London: Collins, 1957), p. 41. Some of the material in *The Natural History of the Gent* originally appeared in a sketch by Smith called 'The Gent' in *Bentley's Miscellany* 19 (1846), 316–22, but several passages appeared earlier and unsigned in *Punch*. The book was well received; although only one edition was ever published, all two thousand copies sold out in one day. John Parry was a popular singer and entertainer who performed at the Lyceum and in concert rooms. Some of the songs he performed were written expressly for him by Smith. See the entries on Smith and Parry in the *Dictionary of National Biography*.
36. In the Victorian period, as in our own, details of dress were often used to identify specific groups within anonymous urban settings in which styles of dress were increasingly uniform. In her autobiography, Mary Somerville describes how, by dressing in a particular way, she inadvertently identified herself as an Evangelical. Note also the significance of the style of speech:

> [A new acquaintance] came to ask me to go and drive in the Park with her, and afterwards dine at her house, saying, 'We shall all be in high dresses.' So I accepted, and on entering the drawing-room, found a bishop and several clergymen, Lady Olivia Sparrow, and some other ladies, all in high black satin dresses and white lace caps, precisely the dress I wore, and I thought it a curious coincidence. The party was lively enough, and agreeable, but the conversation was in a style I had never heard before – in fact, it affected the phraseology of the Bible. We all went after dinner to a sort of meeting at Exeter Hall, I quite forget for what purpose, but our party was on a kind of raised platform. I mentioned this to a friend afterwards, and the curious circumstance of our all being dressed alike. 'Do you not know', she said, 'that dress is assumed as a distinctive mark of the Evangelical party! So you were a wolf in sheep's clothing!'

Mary Somerville, *Personal Reflections* (Boston: Roberts Brothers, 1874), pp. 220–21.

37. The supposed self-conscious striving of members of the lower middle class to speak with refinement becomes a fixed idea in late Victorian culture. James Fitzjames Stephen's assessment of lower-middle-class speech expresses an attitude toward clerks and shop assistants typical of his class. The commercial clerk, according to Stephen

> constantly tries to talk fine. He calls a school an academy, speaks of proceeding when he means going, and talks, in short, much in the style in which the members of his own class write police reports and accounts of appalling catastrophes for the newspapers. The manners of a sailor, a non-commissioned officer in the army, a gamekeeper, or of the better kind of labourers ... are much better in themselves, and are capable of a far higher polish, than the manners of a bagman or a small shopkeeper.

[James Fitzjames Stephen], 'Gentlemen', *Cornhill Magazine* 5:27 (March 1862), 337.
38. 'The Gent', 317.
39. Moers, p. 216; R. G. G. Price, p. 40.
40. Charles Dickens, *Sketches by Boz* (London: Oxford University Press, 1957), p. 218. Subsequent references are in the text by page number.
41. Charles Dickens, 'The Noble Savage', *Household Words* 7 (11 June 1853), 337. Dickens does rank the Gent above a savage in this send-up of the notion of the 'noble savage'.
42. Charles Dickens, *The Pickwick Papers*, ed. James Kinsley (Oxford & New York: Oxford University Press, 1988), pp. 206–7.
43. 'Mr. Robert Bolton', 205.
44. George Gissing, *Charles Dickens: a Critical Study* (London: Gresham, 1903), p. 42.
45. See Henry James's letter to H. G. Wells, 19 November 1905, in *Henry James and H. G. Wells: a Record of their Friendship, their Debate on the Art of Fiction, and their Quarrel*, eds Leon Edel and Gordon N. Ray (Urbana: University of Illinois Press, 1958), p. 105.
46. Charles Dickens, *Our Mutual Friend*, ed. Michael Cotsell (Oxford & New York: Oxford University Press, 1988) p. 32.
47. Edmund Wilson, 'Dickens: The Two Scrooges', in *The Wound and the Bow: Seven Studies in Literature* (Cambridge, MA: Houghton Mifflin, 1941), pp. 1–104; pp. 32–3. Edgar Johnson similarly comments that in his later years Dickens 'found himself deeply and bitterly skeptical of the whole system of respectable attitudes and conventional beliefs' and that he 'despised the subservient snobbery of the middle class'. See *Charles Dickens: His Tragedy and Triumph*, 2 vols (New York: Simon & Schuster, 1952), II, 858.
48. Peter Ackroyd, *Dickens* (New York: HarperCollins, 1990), p. 758; George Bernard Shaw, 'Preface' to *Great Expectations* by Charles Dickens (Edinburgh: Clark, 1937), p. xi; Roger D. Lund, 'Genteel Fictions: Caricature and Satirical Design in *Little Dorrit*', *Dickens Studies Annual* 10 (1982), 47.

49. Pam Morris, *Dickens's Class Consciousness: a Marginal View* (London: Macmillan, 1991), p. 14.
50. Charles Dickens, *Little Dorrit*, ed. Harvey Peter Sucksmith (Oxford & New York: Oxford University Press, 1982), p. 178. Subsequent references are given in the text by page number.
51. Alexander Welsh, in his influential *The City of Dickens* (Oxford: Clarendon, 1971), sees Amy Dorrit, in her littleness, as one in a series of Dickens's child/women heroines, like Florence Dombey (pp. 153–4). As William Myers argues, however, Little Dorrit 'is not a child; on the contrary Dickens is repudiating very subtly his earlier faith in immaturity. . . . Amy [Dorrit] may have a childish form, but she has an adult personality.' Myers goes on to point out that Little Dorrit is frequently described as 'womanly'. In 'The Radicalism of "Little Dorrit"', *Literature and Politics in the Nineteenth Century*, ed. John Lucas (London: Methuen, 1971), pp. 77–104; p. 101.
52. The Marshalsea and the lower middle class are indirectly associated elsewhere in Dickens's work. Micawber – a figure who, incidentally, 'turns up' repeatedly in lower-middle-class memoirs later in the century as representative of the class's financial marginality – is taken to the Marshalsea in *David Copperfield*. See Frederick Willis, *Peace and Dripping Toast* (London: Phoenix House, 1950), p. 29 for an example of a lower-middle-class invocation of Micawber. Dickens's own father was imprisoned in the Marshalsea at the instigation of a baker, for a sum owing of forty pounds. See Ackroyd, p. 69 and Johnson, I, 34.
53. Lionel Trilling, '*Little Dorrit*', rpt 'Introduction' to *Little Dorrit* (London, 1953), *The Dickens Critics*, eds George H. Ford and Lauriat Lane, Jr. (Ithaca: Cornell University Press, 1961), p. 293.
54. Gaskell, *North and South*, op. cit., p. 64. Subsequent references are given in the text by page number.

3 VOICES FROM THE MARGINS: DICKENS, WELLS AND BENNETT

1. George and Weedon Grossmith, *The Diary of a Nobody* (London: Dent; New York: Dutton, 1940), pp.113–14. Subsequent references to this edition are given in the text by page number.
2. John Squire, 'Introduction' to *The Diary of a Nobody*, ibid., p. 14.
3. 'J. H.', 'Introduction' to *The Diary of a Nobody*, by George and Weedon Grossmith (London: Folio Society, 1969), p. 10.
4. [James Fitzjames Stephen], 'Gentlemen', *Cornhill Magazine* 5:27 (March 1862), 336.
5. Letters to the Editor, *Courier*, Liverpool: n.d.; rpt B. G. Orchard, *The Clerks of Liverpool* (Liverpool: Collinson, 1871), pp. 40, 44.
6. 'Our Music-Halls', anon., *Tinsley's Magazine* 4 (April 1869), 216, 218.
7. Walter Gallichan, *The Blight of Respectability* (London: University of London Press, 1897), p. 4.
8. T. W. H. Crosland, *The Suburbans* (London: Long, 1905), pp. 8, 46, 50, 76–7.

9. J. A. Roebuck, address to the Salisbury Literary and Scientific Institution, 19 January 1862; as reported in *The Times* (20 January 1862).
10. H. Anstruther White, 'Moral and Merry England', *Fortnightly Review* n.s. 38 (1885), 775–6.
11. Robert White, 'Wanted: A Rowton House for Clerks', *Nineteenth Century* (October 1897), 596.
12. G. S. Layard, 'A Lower-Middle-Class Budget', *Cornhill Magazine* 10 n.s. (1901), 656, 663.
13. C. G. F. Masterman, *The Condition of England* (London: Methuen, 1909), p. 95. Subsequent references are given in the text by page number.
14. Like many writers around the turn of the century, including Gallichan and Crosland, Masterman generally uses 'middle classes' to designate that segment of society that earlier and later writers call 'lower middle class'.
15. F. G. D'Aeth, 'Present Tendencies of Class Differentiation', *Sociological Review* 3:4 (1910), 270.
16. Orchard, pp. 26, 37.
17. J. S. Harrison, *The Social Position and Claims of Clerks and Book-Keepers Considered* (London: Hamilton, Adams, 1852), p. 17.
18. Charles Edward Parsons, *Clerks: Their Position and Advancement* (London: [Provost], [1876]), p. 9. For another version of the clerk's lament, see *The Clerk's Grievance*, anon. (London: Pole, 1878).
19. Letter from Henry James to H. G. Wells, 19 November 1905, *Henry James and H. G. Wells: a Record of their Friendship, their Debate on the Art of Fiction, and their Quarrel*, eds Leon Edel and Gordon N. Ray (Urbana: University of Illinois Press, 1958), p. 105.
20. Charles Dickens, *A Christmas Carol* in *Christmas Books* (London: Oxford University Press, 1954), p. 44.
21. Charles Dickens, *Great Expectations*, ed. Margaret Cardwell (Oxford & New York: Oxford University Press, 1994), p. 206. Subsequent references are given in the text by page number.
22. N. C. Peyrouton, 'John Wemmick: Enigma?' *Dickens Studies* 1 (January 1965), 42.
23. Henry James to H. G. Wells, 19 November 1905, *Henry James and H. G. Wells*, p. 105.
24. Quoted in David C. Smith, *H. G. Wells: Desperately Mortal* (New Haven & London: Yale University Press, 1986), p. 201.
25. H. G. Wells, *The Wheels of Chance* in *The Wheels of Chance* and *The Time Machine* (London: Dent; New York: Dutton, 1935), p. 4. Subsequent references are given in the text by page number.
26. Arnold Bennett, *A Man from the North* (New York: Doran, 1911), pp. 263–4; ellipses in the original. Subsequent references are given in the text by page number.
27. Anonymous, 'Review', *Manchester Guardian* (15 March 1898), 4; rpt James Hepburn, ed., *Arnold Bennett: the Critical Heritage* (London & Boston: Routledge, 1981), p. 145. Several contemporary reviews were positive, but they were written by Bennett himself, his younger brother, and his friends. See pp. 139–44 of *The Critical Heritage*.
28. Arnold Bennett, *The Card* (Harmondsworth: Penguin, 1975), p. 31.

Subsequent references are given in the text by page number.
29. Wells, p. 99.
30. Bennett, *A Man from the North*, p. 155. Linda R. Anderson also observes the significance of the nurse's role in the novel, seeing her as a foil for Aked's enervated devotion to 'Art' in her 'choice of an active social role [that] is both healthy and health-giving'. Bennett, *Wells and Conrad: Narrative in Transition* (London: Macmillan, 1988), p. 55.

4 BACHELOR GIRLS AND WORKING WOMEN: WOMEN AND INDEPENDENCE IN OLIPHANT, LEVY, ALLEN AND GISSING

1. George Bernard Shaw, 'The Womanly Woman', *The Quintessence of Ibsenism* in *Major Critical Essays* (London: Constable, 1932), pp. 39–40. First published in 1891.
2. George Gissing, *The Odd Women*, ed. Arlene Young (Peterborough, ON: Broadview, 1998), p. 152.
3. Diana Merion in George Meredith's *Diana of the Crossways* (1885) is, of course, an interesting exception, but her unconventionality and the difficulties she encounters being accepted in society more or less prove the general rule. Miss Bunion in *Pendennis* (1848–50) and Lady Carbury in *The Way We Live Now* (1875) are more typical of female authors in fiction. Blanche Amory is, of course, neither a minor nor an entirely comic character, nor does she have the other common dispensations of being old and homely, like Miss Bunion, or of being a widow in need of support, like Lady Carbury. But Blanche's writing, along with her other affectations, is arguably part of what makes her unsuitable as a true heroine and unfit to become Pen's bride. In the 1890s, the New Woman sometimes takes up writing – typically journalism – but usually only as a more or less unpalatable means of survival – Herminia Barton in Grant Allen's *The Woman Who Did* (1895), for example, and Mary Erle after failing as an artist in Ella Hepworth Dixon's *The Story of a Modern Woman* (1894).
4. See Cora Kaplan, 'The Indefinite Disclosed: Christina Rossetti and Emily Dickinson', *Women Writing and Writing About Women*, ed. Mary Jacobus (New York: Barnes & Noble; London: Croom Helm, 1979), p. 65; and Mary Poovey, *The Proper Lady and the Woman Writer* (Chicago & London: University of Chicago Press, 1984), p. xv. 'Writing for publication', Poovey notes, 'jeopardizes modesty, that critical keystone of feminine propriety; for it ... cultivates and calls attention to the woman as subject, as initiator of direct action, as a person deserving of notice for her own sake' (p. 36). Dorothy Mermin observes that '[a]ny venture into public life [including writing] by a woman risked being greeted as a highly sexualized self-exposure'; *Godiva's Ride: Women of Letters in England, 1830–1880* (Bloomington: Indiana University Press, 1993), p. xiv.
5. A. Amy Bulley and Margaret Whitley, *Women's Work* (London: Methuen, 1894), p. 3.

6. Nancy K. Miller, 'Emphasis Added: Plots and Plausibilities in Women's Fiction', *PMLA* 96:1 (January 1981), 46.
7. Charlotte Brontë, *Shirley*, eds Herbert Rosengarten and Margaret Smith (Oxford & New York: Oxford University Press, 1981), p. 390. Subsequent references are given in the text by page number.
8. Anna Jameson, *'Sisters of Charity, Catholic and Protestant' and 'The Communion of Labor'* (Boston: Ticknor & Fields, 1857; rpt Westport CT: Hyperion, 1976), pp. 33 ff. Subsequent references are in the text by page number.
9. Clara Collet, 'Through Fifty Years: The Economic Progress of Women', *Frances Mary Buss Schools' Jubilee Magazine* (November 1900); rpt *Educated Working Women: Essays on the Economic Position of Women Workers in the Middle Classes* (London: King, 1902), p. 134.
10. Martha Vicinus, *Independent Women: Work and Community for Single Women 1850–1920* (Chicago & London: University of Chicago Press, 1985), pp. 3, 27.
11. For a discussion of the growth and influence of the women's movement in Britain in the nineteenth century, see Philippa Levine, *Victorian Feminism 1850–1900* (Tallahassee: Florida State University Press, 1987) and Lee Holcombe, *Victorian Ladies at Work: Middle-Class Working Women in England and Wales 1850–1914* (Hamden CT: Archon, 1973), pp. 3–20. The problem of overcrowding in the teaching profession was the subject of the very first article – 'The Profession of the Teacher' – in the first number of the *English Woman's Journal* (1 March 1858).
12. Jameson, p. 29.
13. Vicinus, p. 12.
14. Grant Allen (pseud. Olive Pratt Raynor), *The Type-Writer Girl* (London: Pearson, 1897), p. 125.
15. That many white-collar jobs – such as typist – were new phenomena was also what made them available to women, because these jobs, unlike most civil service clerkships, were not seen as well-established male preserves. See Rosalie Silverstone, 'Office Work for Women: An Historical Review', *Business History* 18:1 (January 1976), 101, 105. Gregory Anderson discusses the opening up of clerical work to women and the resulting feminization of that sector of the work force in 'The White-Blouse revolution', *The White-Blouse Revolution: Female Office Workers since 1870* (Manchester & New York: Manchester University Press, 1988), pp. 1–26.
16. Judith R. Walkowitz, *City of Dreadful Delight: Narratives of Sexual Danger in Late-Victorian London* (Chicago: University of Chicago Press, 1992), pp. 72–3; Nanette Mason, 'How Working Girls Live in London', *Girls' Own Paper* 10 (1889): 422, as quoted in Walkowitz.
17. See Margaret E. Harkness, 'Women as Civil Servants', *Nineteenth Century* 10: 55 (September 1881), 369–81; and Silverstone, passim.
18. Meta Zimmeck, 'Jobs for the Girls: the Expansion of Clerical Work for Women, 1850–1914', in *Unequal Opportunities: Women's Employment in England 1800–1918*, ed. Angela V. John (Oxford: Blackwell, 1986), p. 170.

19. Ibid., pp. 164–5. The novels cited by Zimmeck are George Gissing's *The Odd Women* (1893), Grant Allen's *The Type-Writer Girl* (1897), and Tom Gallon's *The Girl Behind the Keys* (1903).
20. Clara Collet, 'The Expenditure of Middle Class Working Women', *Economic Journal* 8 (1898), 543–553. See also Harkness, p. 375 and Edward Cadbury, M. Cécile Matheson, and George Shann, *Women's Work and Wages* (London: Unwin, 1908), pp. 184–8 for additional discussions of the problem of working conditions for women in offices.
21. Margaret Oliphant, *Salem Chapel* (London: Virago, 1986), pp. 343, 458.
22. Margaret Oliphant, *Phoebe Junior* (London: Virago, 1989), p. 272. Subsequent references are given in the text by page number.
23. Penelope Fitzgerald, 'Introduction', *Phoebe Junior*, ibid., p. viii. The resemblance of *Kirsteen*'s full title to Sir Walter Scott's *Waverley; or, 'Tis Sixty Years Since* is undoubtedly intentional. As Fitzgerald notes, Oliphant indirectly acknowledges her debt to Trollope – the obvious parallels between her Chronicles of Carlingford and his Chronicles of Barsetshire – by having Phoebe read *Barchester Towers*. Similarly, Oliphant playfully acknowledges her debt to Scott not only in the title of *Kirsteen*, but by having Miss Jean read *Waverley* aloud in the seamstresses in her workroom. See *Kirsteen: the Story of a Scotch Family Seventy Years Ago*, 2 vols (Leipzig: Tauchnitz, 1891), II: 90. Subsequent references are given in the text by volume and page number.
24. Levy does use the expedient of temporal and cultural distance in her iconoclastic representations of women in poems like 'Xantippe' and 'Medea', dramatic monologues in which, according to Isobel Armstrong, Levy 'deconstructs feminine roles' and 'questions conventional paradigms'. Isobel Armstrong, 'Victorian Poetry', *Encyclopedia of Literature and Criticism*, eds Martin Coyle, Peter Garside, Malcolm Kelsall, and John Peck (London: Routledge, 1990), pp. 292–3.
25. The resistance to teaching as an acceptable option as a career is manifested later in the novel by the appearance of an 'ex-Girtonian without a waist, who taught at the High School for girls hard-by'. She drifts silent and phantom-like through the text, seen by the Lorimers from the window of their shop. The sisters 'indulged in much sarcastic comment on her appearance; on her round shoulders and swinging gait; on the green gown with balloon sleeves, and the sulphur-coloured handkerchief which she habitually wore.' The Lorimers' unfair aversion to the ex-Girtonian is supposed to be the result of her having taken over the rooms previously occupied by their friend Frank Jermyn, but on another level is a further rejection of one of the roles that convention would have imposed on them had they been conformists. Amy Levy, *The Romance of a Shop* in *The Complete Novels and Selected Writings of Amy Levy 1861–1889*, ed. Melvyn New (Gainesville: University Press of Florida, 1993), p. 164. Subsequent references are given in the text by page number.
26. 'The Disputed Question', anon., *English Woman's Journal* 1:60 (August 1858), 364.

27. Deborah Epstein Nord, *Walking the Victorian Streets: Women, Representation, and the City* (Ithaca & London: Cornell University Press, 1995), p. 202. Nord feels that the last third of the novel 'begins to resemble a shoddy *Pride and Prejudice*, with all four sisters searching for an appropriate mate'.
28. See Melvyn New, 'Introduction' to *The Complete Novels and Selected Writing of Amy Levy*, p. 10. New quotes Wilde's comments from *Woman's World* 2 (1889), 224. Both New and Nord appear to concur with Wilde.
29. John Keble Bell (pseud. Keble Howard), *The Bachelor Girls and their Adventures in Search of Independence* (London: Chapman & Hall, 1907), p. 3.
30. Ann Ardis interprets Herminia's situation – a single mother living in a London boarding house and working in the public sector as a journalist – as a challenge 'not only [to] bourgeois Victorian sexual ideology but also [to] the related ideology of domesticity, the normalization/standardization of both the nuclear family and the independent middle-class household.' *New Women, New Novels: Feminism and Early Modernism* (New Brunswick, NJ & London: Rutgers University Press, 1990), p. 14. I feel that this is giving Allen credit for progressive social principles that he did not espouse. Herminia's situation after the death of her affluent lover is the curse visited upon the philosophically pure heroine by an unenlightened society; it is what she is reduced to, not what she or her creator would embrace as a progressive or even satisfactory option.
31. Grant Allen, *The Woman Who Did* (Oxford & New York: Oxford University Press, 1995), p. 101. Subsequent references are given in the text by page number.
32. Alison Cotes, 'Gissing, Grant Allen and "Free Union"', *Gissing Newsletter* 19:4 (October 1983), 9.
33. Margaret Oliphant, 'The Anti-Marriage League,' *Blackwood's Magazine* 159 (1896), 136, 145.
34. Gail Cunningham, *The New Woman and the Victorian Novel* (New York: Barnes & Noble, 1978), p. 59.
35. 'The Woman Who Wouldn't Do', *Punch* 108 (March 1895), 153. Both authors of the novelistic spin-offs, incidentally, used pseudonyms. Victoria Cross was in reality a man, Vivian Cory, and Lucas Cleeve was a woman, Adelina Georgina Isabella Kingscote.
36. 'The Anti marriage League', pp. 144–5.
37. Millicent Garrett Fawcett, '"The Woman Who Did"', *Contemporary Review* 67 (1895), 629–30.
38. 'The Anti-Marriage League,' p. 142.
39. Grant Allen, *The Type-Writer Girl*, op. cit., p. 19. Subsequent references are given in the text by page number. For an insightful discussion of the problematic sexual and cultural role of the typewriter girl in the late nineteenth century see Christopher Keep, 'The Cultural Work of the Type-Writer Girl', *Victorian Studies* 40:3 (Spring 1997), 401–26.
40. Vivie Warren, in George Bernard Shaw's play, *Mrs. Warren's Profession*, makes a similar choice, although there is no truly tempting

suitor to divert her from her commitment to a career. Shaw's play was written in the same year that *The Odd Women* was published, but was not as palatable to Victorian tastes. It was not published until five years later, and was prohibited from being performed, ostensibly because of the nature of Mrs Warren's profession, although I suspect that Vivie's assertiveness and complete inability to find anything appealing in what were seen as normal feminine interests, along with her declaration that she liked to relax with whisky and a cigar, were equally offensive to the censors.

41. Most New Woman novels – and as a result most criticism of the New Woman novel – focus on sexuality and the perversity of Victorian sexual mores to the virtual exclusion of other themes. For insightful discussions of these novels and themes see Ann Ardis, op. cit., and Lyn Pykett, *The 'Improper' Feminine: the Women's Sensation Novel and the New Woman Writing* (London & New York: Routledge, 1992).
42. George Gissing, *The Odd Women*, op.cit., p. 50. Subsequent references are given in the text by page number.
43. Sally Ledger also argues for the fundamental significance of Monica to the social ideologies at play in *The Odd Women*, specifically to 'the masculine domination of the city', observing that 'the main New Woman figures in the novel' challenge that domination 'far less dramatically than does Monica Madden'. *The New Woman: Fiction and Feminism at the* fin de siècle (Manchester & New York: Manchester University Press, 1997), pp. 162–3.
44. For a contemporary account of the deplorable working conditions in shops in the 1890s, see Bulley and Whitley, pp. 49–65. See also the report to the Royal Commission on Labour, 'The Employment of Women' (1893), especially the section by Clara Collet on shop assistants. Poor working conditions in shops was also the topic of a lengthy study a decade earlier: Thomas Sutherst, *Death and Disease Behind the Counter* (London: Kegan Paul, Trench, 1884).
45. Collet, ibid., p. 89.
46. Unsigned review, *Pall Mall Gazette* (29 May 1893), p. 4.
47. J. M. Barrie, 'The Twelve-Pound Look', *The Plays of J. M. Barrie* (London: Hodder & Stoughton, 1929), p. 719. Subsequent references are given in the text by page number.
48. Cunningham, p. 58; *Nation* (17 May 1894), pp. 369–70, as quoted in Cunningham.
49. Ardis, p. 3.
50. Ibid., pp. 86–90, 110–11.

5 MODERN PROMETHEUS UNBOUND: MAY SINCLAIR AND *THE DIVINE FIRE*

1. 'The Clerks' Mass Meeting' and 'Chit-Chat for Our Lady Clerks', *The Clerk* 1:4 (1 August 1890), 61–2. *The Clerk* disappears after the 1 August issue, although a publication of the same name reappears in

1908 as the official organ of the National Union of Clerks. See Gregory Anderson, *Victorian Clerks* (Manchester: Manchester University Press, 1976), pp. 115–17.
2. 'The Clerks' Union', *Daily Telegraph* 23 June 1890, p. 4.
3. Theophilus E. M. Boll, *Miss May Sinclair: Novelist* (Rutherford, N.J.: Fairleigh Dickinson University Press, 1973), pp. 25–6. Subsequent references are in the text.
4. Arnold Bennett, journal entry for 22 May 1911, *The Journals of Arnold Bennett*, 3 vols, ed. Newman Flower (London: Cassell, 1932), II, 7.
5. Hrisey Zegger, *May Sinclair* (Boston: Twayne, 1976), pp. 77, 55, 23–5. Subsequent references are in the text. Zegger also claims that Sinclair's writing, both in fiction and philosphy, influenced the work of Lawrence and Eliot. See pp. 77 & 141.
6. Letter to Morley Roberts, 28 April 1906, as quoted by Boll, op. cit., p. 79.
7. May Sinclair, *The Divine Fire* (New York: Henry Holt, 1904), pp. 3–4. Subsequent references are given in the text by page number.
8. George Gissing, *The Odd Women*, ed. Arlene Young (Peterborough, ON: Broadview, 1998), p. 48.

CONCLUSION

1. See Ann Ardis, *New Women, New Novels: Feminism and Early Modernism* (New Brunswick and London: Rutgers University Press, 1990); Lyn Pykett, *The 'Improper' Feminine: the Women's Sensation Novel and the New Woman Writing* (London and New York: Routledge, 1992) and *Engendering Fictions: the English Novel in the Early Twentieth Century* (London: Arnold; New York: St. Martin's, 1995), pp. 1–76.
2. Although there has been an upsurge of scholarly interest in Wells in the last ten to fifteen years, most of the attention has focused on his utopian and science fiction novels. This critical bias is especially evident in special issues of *Cahiers Victoriens et Edouardiens* 46 (October 1997) and *English Literature in Transition* 30:4 (1987) devoted to Wells. See also David Y. Hughes, 'Recent Wells Studies', *Science-Fiction Studies* 11:1 (March 1984), 61–70.

Bibliography

Ackroyd, Peter. *Dickens*. New York: Harper Collins, 1990.
Allen, Grant (pseud. Olive Pratt Raynor). *The Type-Writer Girl*. London: Pearson, 1897.
—— *The Woman Who Did*. Oxford & New York: Oxford University Press, 1995.
Anderson, Gregory. 'The White-Blouse Revolution'. *The White-Blouse Revolution: Female Office Workers since 1870*. Manchester & New York: Manchester University Press, 1988, pp. 1–26.
—— *Victorian Clerks*. Manchester: Manchester University Press, 1976.
Anderson, Linda. *Bennett, Wells and Conrad: Narrative in Transition*. London: Macmillan, 1988.
Andrew, Donna T. 'The Code of Honour and its Critics: the Opposition to Duelling in England, 1700–1850'. *Social History* 5:3 (October 1980), 409–434.
Anonymous. 'Chit-Chat for Our Lady Clerks'. *Clerk* 1:4 (1 August 1890), 61–2.
—— *The Clerk's Grievance*. London: Pole, 1878.
—— 'The Clerks' Mass Meeting'. *Clerk* 1:4 (1 August 1890), 61.
—— 'The Clerks' Union'. *Daily Telegraph* (23 June 1890), p. 4.
—— 'Concerning the Gent'. *Punch* 3 (1842), 60–61.
—— 'The Disputed Question'. *English Woman's Journal* 1:60 (August 1858), 361–367.
—— 'Fashions for the Fast Man'. *Punch* 13 (1847), 190.
—— 'An Impudent Monkey'. *Bentley's Miscellany* 7 (1840), 358–361.
—— 'Our Music-Halls'. *Tinsley's Magazine* 4 (April 1869), 216–23.
—— 'The Profession of the Teacher'. *English Woman's Journal* 1:1 (March 1858).
—— 'Regular Habits'. *Bentley's Miscellany* 14 (1843), 393–401.
—— 'Review' (of *The Odd Women*). *Pall Mall Gazette* (29 May 1893), 4.
—— 'Shopkeepers and their Customers'. *Punch* 13 (1847), 230.
—— 'The Woman Who Wouldn't Do'. *Punch* 108 (March 1895), 153.
Ardis, Ann. *New Women, New Novels: Feminism and Early Modernism*. New Brunswick, NJ & London: Rutgers University Press, 1990.
Armstrong, Isobel. 'Victorian Poetry'. *Encyclopedia of Literature and Criticism*. Eds Martin Coyle, Peter Garside, Malcolm Kelsall and John Peck. London: Routledge, 1990.
Armstrong, Nancy. *Desire and Domestic Fiction: a Political History of the Novel*. Oxford & New York: Oxford University Press, 1987.
Arnstein, Walter, ed., *The Past Speaks*. Lexington, Mass.: Heath, 1981.
Austen, Jane. *Pride and Prejudice*. Eds James Kinsley and Frank W. Bradbrook. Oxford & New York: Oxford University Press, 1980.
—— *Sense and Sensibility*. Ed. Claire Lamont. London & New York: Oxford University Press, 1970.

Baldick, Robert. *The Duel*. London: Chapman & Hall, 1965.
Barker, Gerard A. *Grandison's Heirs: the Paragon's Progress in the Late Eighteenth-Century English Novel*. Newark: University of Delaware Press; London & Toronto: Associated University Presses, 1985.
Barker-Benfield, G. J. *The Culture of Sensibility: Sex and Society in Eighteenth-Century Britain*. Chicago & London: University of Chicago Press, 1992.
Barrie, J. M. 'The Twelve-Pound Look'. *The Plays of J. M. Barrie*. London: Hodder & Stoughton, 1929, pp. 717–36.
Bell, John Keble (pseud. Keble Howard). *The Bachelor Girls and their Adventures in Search of Independence*. London: Chapman & Hall, 1907.
Bennett, Arnold. *The Card*. Harmondsworth: Penguin, 1975.
—— *The Journals of Arnold Bennett*. 3 vols. Ed. Newman Flower. London: Cassell, 1932.
—— *A Man from the North*. New York: Doran, 1911.
Birkin, Andrew. *J. M. Barrie and the Lost Boys: the Love Story that Gave Birth to Peter Pan*. New York: Clarkson Potter, 1979.
Boll, Theophilus E. M. *Miss May Sinclair: Novelist*. Rutherford, NJ: Fairleigh Dickinson University Press, 1973.
Brantlinger, Patrick. *The Spirit of Reform: British Literature and Politics, 1832–1867*. Cambridge, MA & London: Harvard University Press, 1977.
Briggs, Asa. 'The Language of "Class" in Early Nineteenth-Century England'. *Essays in Labour History*. Eds Asa Briggs and J. Saville. London: Macmillan, 1967. Rpt *Essays in Social History*. Eds M. W. Flinn and T. C. Smout. Oxford: Clarendon, 1974, pp. 154–177.
Brontë, Charlotte. *Jane Eyre*. Ed. Richard J. Dunn. 2nd edn. New York & London: Norton, 1987.
—— *Shirley*. Eds Herbert Rosengarten and Margaret Smith. Oxford & New York: Oxford University Press, 1981.
Brown, Laura. *English Dramatic Form, 1660–1760: an Essay in Generic History*. New Haven & London: Yale University Press, 1981.
Buckstone, J. B. 'The Man in the Mackintosh Cape'. *New Monthly Magazine and Literary Journal*. 50 (1837), 265–71.
Bulley, A. Amy and Margaret Whitley. *Women's Work*. London: Methuen, 1894.
Cadbury, Edward and M. Cécile Matheson, and George Shann. *Women's Work and Wages*. London: Unwin, 1908.
Carlyle, Thomas. 'Sir Walter Scott'. *Critical and Miscellaneous Essays*. 6 vols. London: Chapman & Hall, 1869. V, 211–286.
Castronovo, David. *The English Gentleman: Images and Ideals in Literature and Society*. New York: Ungar, 1987.
Clark, J. C. D. *English Society 1688–1832: Ideology, Social Structure and Political Practice during the Ancien Regime*. Cambridge & New York: Cambridge University Press, 1985.
Clark, T. J. *The Painting of Modern Life: Paris in the Art of Manet and his Followers*. Princeton: Princeton University Press, 1984.
Coleridge, Samuel Taylor. *Biographia Literaria*. Eds James Engell and W. Jackson Bate. Princeton: Princeton University Press, 1983.
Collet, Clara. 'The Employment of Women'. Report to the Royal Commission on Labour. London: 1893.

—— 'The Expenditure of Middle Class Working Women'. *Economic Journal* 8:32 (1898), 543–553.
—— 'Through Fifty Years: the Economic Progress of Women'. *Frances Mary Buss Schools' Jubilee Magazine* (November 1900). Rpt *Educated Working Women: Essays on the Economic Position of Women Workers in the Middle Classes*. London: King, 1902, pp. 134–43.
Collier, Jeremy. *Essays upon Several Moral Subjects*. 2nd edn. London: Sare & Hindmarsh, 1697.
Cotes, Alison. 'Gissing, Grant Allen and "Free Union"'. *Gissing Newsletter* 19:4 (October 1983), 1–18.
Cowling, Mary. *The Artist as Anthropologist: the Representation of Type and Character in Victorian Art*. Cambridge: Cambridge University Press, 1989.
Craik, Dinah Mulock. *John Halifax, Gentleman*. London & Glasgow: Collins, 1954.
Crosland, T. W. H. *The Suburbans*. London: Long, 1905.
Crossick, Geoffrey. 'The Emergence of the Lower Middle Class in Britain'. Ed. Geoffrey Crossick. *The Lower Middle Class in Britain 1870–1914*. London: Croom Helm, 1977, pp. 11–60.
—— 'From Gentleman to the Residuum: Languages of Social Description in Victorian Britain'. *Language, History and Class*. Ed. Penelope J. Corfield. Oxford: Blackwell, 1991, pp. 150–78.
—— 'The Petite Bourgeoisie in Nineteenth-Century Britain: the Urban and Liberal Case'. *Shopkeepers and Master Artisans in Nineteenth-Century Europe*. Eds Geoffrey Crossick and Heinz-Gerhard Haupt. London & New York: Methuen, 1984, pp. 62–94.
—— 'Urban Society and the Petty Bourgeoisie in Nineteenth-Century Britain'. *The Pursuit of Urban History*. Eds Derek Fraser and Anthony Sutcliffe. London: Edward Arnold, 1983, pp. 307–326.
Cunningham, Gail. *The New Woman and the Victorian Novel*. New York: Barnes & Noble, 1978.
D'Aeth, F. G. 'Present Tendencies of Class Differentiation'. *Sociological Review* 3 (1910), 269–76.
Davidoff, Leonore and Catherine Hall. *Family Fortunes: Men and Women of the English Middle Class, 1780–1850*. London: Hutchinson, 1987.
'Davus'. 'A Passage in the Life of Mr. Nosebody'. *Bentley's Miscellany* 11 (1842), 378–383.
Defoe, Daniel. *The Compleat English Gentleman*. Ed. Karl D. Bulbring. London: David Nutt, 1890.
—— *The Complete English Tradesman*. 2nd edn with supplement. 2 Vols. London: Rivington, 1727. Rpt New York: Kelley, 1969.
—— 'The Duel of Lord Mohun and the Duke of Hamilton'. *Review* 1:34 (29 Nov. 1712), pp. 67–8.
Dickens, Charles. *Christmas Carol. Christmas Books*. London: Oxford University Press, 1954.
—— *Great Expectations*. Ed. Margaret Cardwell. Oxford & New York: Oxford University Press, 1994.
—— *Hard Times*. Eds George Ford & Sylvère Monod. 2nd edn. New York & London: Norton, 1990.
—— *Little Dorrit*. Ed. Harvey Peter Sucksmith. Oxford & New York: Oxford University Press, 1982.

—— [Pub. anon.] 'Mr. Robert Bolton'. *Bentley's Miscellany* 4 (1838), 204–207.
—— 'The Noble Savage'. *Household Words* 7 (11 June 1853), 337–339.
—— *Our Mutual Friend*. Ed. Michael Cotsell. Oxford & New York: Oxford University Press, 1988.
—— *The Pickwick Papers*. Ed. James Kinsley. Oxford & New York: Oxford University Press, 1988.
—— *Sketches by Boz*. London: Oxford University Press, 1957.
Doody, Margaret Anne. *A Natural Passion: a Study of the Novels of Samuel Richardson*. Oxford: Clarendon, 1974.
Drabble, Margaret. *Arnold Bennett*. Harmondsworth: Penguin, 1985.
Dudeney, Alice. *The Maternity of Harriott Wicken*. London & New York: Macmillan, 1900.
Dyos, H. J. *Victorian Suburb: a Study of the Growth of Camberwell*. Leicester: Leicester University Press, 1966.
Eagleton, Mary and David Pierce. *Attitudes to Class in the English Novel*. London: Thames & Hudson, 1979.
Eagleton, Terry. *The Rape of Clarissa: Writing, Sexuality and Class Struggle in Samuel Richardson*. Oxford: Blackwell, 1982.
Earle, Peter. *The Making of the English Middle Class: Business, Society and Family Life in London, 1660–1730*. Berkeley & Los Angeles: University of California Press, 1989.
Edel, Leon and Gordon N. Ray. *Henry James and H. G. Wells: a Record of their Friendship, their Debate on the Art of Fiction, and their Quarrel*. Urbana: University of Illinois Press, 1958.
Escott, T. H. S. *Transformations of the Victorian Age*. New York: Scribner's, 1897.
Faber, Richard. *Proper Stations: Class in Victorian Fiction*. London: Faber 1971.
Fawcett, Millicent Garrett. '"The Woman Who Did"'. *Contemporary Review* 67 (1895), 625–631.
Fitzgerald, Penelope. 'Introduction'. *Phoebe Junior*. By Margaret Oliphant. London: Virago, 1989.
Gagnier, Regenia. *Subjectivities: a History of Self-Representation in Britain, 1832–1920*. Oxford & New York: Oxford University Press, 1991.
Gallagher, Catherine. *The Industrial Reformation of English Fiction: Social Discourse and Narrative Form 1832–1867*. Chicago & London: University of Chicago Press, 1985.
Gallichan, Walter. *The Blight of Respectability*. London: University of London Press, 1897.
Gaskell, Elizabeth. *North and South*. Ed. Angus Easson. Oxford & New York: Oxford University Press, 1982.
Gilmour, Robin. *The Idea of the Gentleman in the Victorian Novel*. London: Allen & Unwin, 1981.
Gissing, George. *Charles Dickens: a Critical Study*. London: Gresham, 1903.
—— *In the Year of the Jubilee*. London: Lawrence & Bullen, 1895. Rpt Rutherford, NJ: Farleigh Dickinson University Press, 1976.
—— *The Odd Women*. Ed. Arlene Young. Peterborough, ON: Broadview, 1998.

—— Will Warburton. London: Hogarth, 1985.
Gordon, Robert C. 'Heroism Demilitarized: the Grandison Example'. San José Studies 15:3 (Fall 1989), 28–47.
Grossmith, George and Weedon. The Diary of a Nobody. London: Dent; New York: Dutton, 1940.
Hardy, Thomas. A Pair of Blue Eyes. London: Macmillan, 1965.
Harkness, Margaret E. 'Women as Civil Servants'. The Nineteenth Century 10:55 (September 1881), 369–381.
Harrison, J. S. The Social Position and Claims of Clerks and Book-keepers Considered. London: Hamilton Adams, 1852.
Hartwell, R. M. 'The Service Revolution: the Growth of Services in Modern Economy'. The Fontana Economic History of Europe. 4 vols. Ed. C. M. Cipolla. London: Collins, 1972–3. III, 145–157.
Hepburn, James. Arnold Bennett: the Critical Heritage. London & Boston: Routledge, 1981.
Himmelfarb, Gertrude. The Idea of Poverty: England in the Early Industrial Age. New York: Random, 1983. Rpt New York: Vintage, 1985.
Holcombe, Lee. Victorian Ladies at Work: Middle-Class Working Women in England and Wales 1850–1914. Hamden, CT: Archon, 1973.
Holcroft, Thomas. Anna St. Ives. Ed. Peter Faulkner. London & New York: Oxford University Press, 1970.
Hollis, Patricia. Ladies Elect: Women in English Local Government 1865–1914. Oxford: Clarendon, 1987.
Hosgood, Christopher P. 'The "Knights of the Road": Commercial Travellers and the Culture of the Commercial Room in Late-Victorian and Edwardian England'. Victorian Studies 37:4 (Summer 1994), 519–547.
Hughes, David Y. 'Recent Wells Studies'. Science Fiction Studies 11:1 (March 1984), 61–70.
Inchbald, Elizabeth. A Simple Story. Ed. J. M. S. Tompkins. Oxford & New York: Oxford University Press, 1988.
J. H. 'Introduction'. The Diary of a Nobody. By George and Weedon Grossmith. London: Folio Society, 1969, pp. 7–10.
Jackson, William. Thirty Letters on Various Subjects. 2nd edn. London: Cadell & Thorn, 1784.
James, Henry. 'A Noble Life'. Nation 2:35 (1 March 1866), 276.
Jameson, Anna. 'Sisters of Charity, Catholic and Protestant,' and 'The Communion of Labor'. Boston: Ticknor & Fields, 1857. Rpt Westport, CT: Hyperion, 1976.
Jefferson, J. M. 'Industrialisation and Poverty: in Fact and Fiction'. The Long Debate on Poverty: Eight Essays on Industrialisation and 'the Condition of England'. London: Institute of Economic Affairs, 1972.
Johnson, Edgar. Charles Dickens: His Tragedy and Triumph. 2 vols. New York: Simon & Schuster, 1952.
Jones, Gareth Stedman. 'The "Cockney" and the Nation, 1780–1988'. Metropolis London: Histories and Representations since 1800. Eds David Feldman and Gareth Stedman Jones. London & New York: Routledge, 1989, pp. 288–94.
—— Languages of Class: Studies in English Working-Class History, 1892–1982. Cambridge: Cambridge University Press, 1983.

Kaplan, Cora. 'The Indefinite Disclosed: Christina Rossetti and Emily Dickinson'. *Women Writing and Writing about Women*. Ed. Mary Jacobus. New York: Barnes & Noble; London: Croom Helm, 1979, pp. 61–79.
Keating, P. J. *The Working Classes in Victorian Fiction*. New York: Barnes & Noble, 1971.
Keep, Christopher. 'The Cultural Work of the Type-Writer Girl'. *Victorian Studies* 40:3 (Spring 1997), 401–26.
Kelso, Ruth. 'Sixteenth-Century Definitions of the Gentleman in England'. *The Journal of English and Germanic Philology* 24 (1925), 370–382.
Kiernan, V. G. *The Duel in European History: Honour and the Reign of Aristocracy*. Oxford: Oxford University Press, 1988.
Lamb, Charles. 'The Good Clerk'. *Reflector* 4 (1812).
Layard, G. S. 'A Lower-Middle-Class Budget'. *Cornhill Magazine* 10 n.s. (1901), 656–666.
Ledger, Sally. *The New Woman: Fiction and Feminism at the fin de siècle*. Manchester & New York: Manchester University Press, 1997.
Levine, Philippa. *Victorian Feminism 1850–1900*. Tallahassee: Florida State University Press, 1987.
Levy, Amy. *The Romance of a Shop. The Complete Novels and Selected Writings of Amy Levy, 1861–1889*. Ed. Melvyn New. Gainesville: University Press of Florida, 1993.
Lillo, George. *The London Merchant. The Dramatic Works of George Lillo*. Ed. James L. Steffensen. Oxford: Clarendon, 1993, pp. 149–209.
Lockwood, David. *The Blackcoated Worker: a Study in Class Consciousness*. London: Allen & Unwin, 1958.
Loftis, John. *Comedy and Society from Congreve to Fielding*. Stanford: Stanford University Press, 1959.
Lund, Roger D. 'Genteel Fictions: Caricature and Satirical Design in *Little Dorrit*'. *Dickens Studies Annual* 10 (1982), 45–66.
Malthus, Thomas. *An Essay on the Principle of Population*. Ed. Philip Appleman. New York: Norton, 1976.
Marks, Sylvia Kasey. *Sir Charles Grandison: the Compleat Conduct Book*. Lewisburg: Bucknell University Press; London & Toronto: Associated University Presses, 1986.
Mason, John Edward. *Gentlefolk in the Making*. Philadelphia: University of Pennsylvania Press; London: Oxford University Press, 1935.
Masterman, C. F. G. *The Condition of England*. London: Methuen, 1909.
Mayer, Arno. 'The Lower Middle Class as Historical Problem'. *Journal of Modern History* 3 (September 1975). 409–436.
McBurney, William H. 'Introduction'. *The London Merchant*. By Goerge Lillo. Lincoln: University of Nebraska Press, 1965, pp. ix–xxv.
McKeon, Michael. *The Origins of the English Novel 1600–1740*. Baltimore: Johns Hopkins University Press, 1987.
McSweeney, Kerry. *Middlemarch*. London & Boston: Allen & Unwin, 1984.
Mermin, Dorothy. *Godiva's Ride: Women of Letters in England, 1830– 1880*. Bloomington: Indiana University Press, 1993.
Miller, Nancy K. 'Emphasis Added: Plots and Plausibilities in Women's Fiction'. *PMLA* 96:1 (January 1981), 36–48.
Mitchell, Sally. *Dinah Mulock Craik*. Boston: Twayne, 1983.

Bibliography

Moers, Ellen. *The Dandy: Brummell to Beerbohm*. New York: Viking, 1960. Rpt Lincoln & London: University of Nebraska Press, 1978.

Moore, Sally F. and Barbara G. Myerhoff, eds, *Secular Ritual*. Assen/Amsterdam: Van Gorcum, 1977.

More, Hannah. *Coelebs in Search of a Wife: Comprehending Observations on Domestic Habits and Manners, Religion and Morals*. 2 vols. 7th edn. London: Cadell & Davies, 1809.

Morris, Pam. *Dickens's Class Consciousness: a Marginal View*. London: Macmillan, 1991.

Myers, William. 'The Radicalism of "Little Dorrit"'. *Literature and Politics in the Nineteenth Century*. Ed. John Lucas. London: Methuen, 1971, pp. 77–104.

New, Melvyn. 'Introduction'. *The Complete Novels and Selected Writings of Amy Levy, 1861–1889*. Ed. Melvyn New. Gainesville: University Press of Florida, 1993, pp. 1–52.

Nord, Deborah Epstein. *Walking the Victorian Streets: Women, Representation, and the City*. Ithaca & London: Cornell University Press, 1995.

Oliphant, Margaret. 'The Anti-Marriage League'. *Blackwood's Magazine* 159 (1896), 135–149.

—— *Kirsteen: The Story of a Scotch Family Seventy Years Ago*. 2 vols, Leipzig: Tauchnitz, 1891.

—— *Phoebe Junior*. London: Virago, 1989.

—— *Salem Chapel*. London: Virago, 1986.

Orchard, B. G. *The Clerks of Liverpool*. Liverpool: Collinson, 1871.

Parsons, Charles Edward. *Clerks: Their Position and Advancement*. London: [Provost], [1876].

Perkin, Harold. *The Origins of Modern English Society*. London: Routledge, 1969. Rpt London & Boston: Ark, 1985.

Peyrouton, N. C. 'John Wemmick: Enigma?' *Dickens Studies* 1 (January 1965), 39–47.

Phillips, K. C. *Language and Class in Victorian England*. Oxford: Blackwell, 1984.

Pindar, Paul. 'Malachi Meagrim, the Teatotaler'. *Bentley's Miscellany* 11 (1842), 228–232.

Poovey, Mary. *The Proper Lady and the Woman Writer*. Chicago & London: University of Chicago Press, 1984.

—— *Uneven Developments: the Ideological Work of Gender in Mid-Victorian England*. Chicago: University of Chicago Press, 1988.

Price, Richard N. 'Society, Status and Jingoism: the Social Roots of Lower Middle Class Patriotism'. *The Lower Middle Class in Britain 1870–1914*. Ed. Geoffrey Crossick. London: Croom Helm, 1977, pp. 89–112.

Price, R. G. G. *A History of Punch*. London: Collins, 1957.

Pykett, Lyn. *The 'Improper' Feminine: the Women's Sensation Novel and the New Woman Writing*. London & New York: Routledge, 1992.

Reddy, William M. 'The Concept of Class'. *Social Orders and Social Classes in Europe since 1500: Studies in Social Stratification*. Ed. M. L. Bush. London & New York: Longman, 1992, pp. 13–25.

Richardson, Samuel. *The Correspondence of Samuel Richardson*. 6 vols. Ed. Anna Laetitia Barbauld. London: Richard Phillips, 1804. Rpt New York: AMS, 1966.

—— *Sir Charles Grandison*. Ed. Jocelyn Harris. London & New York: Oxford University Press, 1972.
Roebuck, J. A. Address to the Salisbury Literary and Scientific Institution. 19 January 1862. As reported in *The Times* (20 January 1862).
Rogers, Nicholas. 'A Reply to Donna Andrew'. *Social History* 6 (1981), 365–9.
Seed, John. 'From "Middling Sort" to Middle Class in Late Eighteenth- and Early Nineteenth-Century England'. Ed. M. L. Bush. *Social Orders and Social Classes in Europe since 1500: Studies in Social Stratification*. London & New York: Longman, 1992, pp. 114–135.
Shaw, George Bernard. 'Preface' to *Great Expectations*. Charles Dickens. Edinburgh: Clark, 1937.
—— 'The Womanly Woman'. *The Quintessence of Ibsenism. Major Critical Essays*. London: Constable, 1932, pp. 32–41.
Shinagel, Michael. *Daniel Defoe and Middle-Class Gentility*. Cambridge, MA: Harvard University Press, 1968.
Silverstone, Rosalie. 'Office Work for Women: an Historical Review'. *Business History* 18:1 (January 1976), 98–110.
Sinclair, May. *The Divine Fire*. New York: Henry Holt, 1904.
Smith, Albert. 'The Gent'. *Bentley's Miscellany* 19 (1846), 316–322.
—— *The Natural History of the Gent*. London: Bogue, 1847.
Smith, David C. *H. G. Wells: Desperately Mortal*. New Haven & London: Yale University Press, 1986.
Smith, James. 'The Hebdomadary of Mr. Snooks, the Grocer'. *New Monthly Magazine and Literary Journal* 11 (1824): 436–440.
Smith, Thomas. *The Commonwealth of England: and the Manner and Governement thereof*. London: 1609.
Somerville, Mary. *Personal Reflections*. Boston: Roberts Brothers, 1874.
Squire, John. 'Introduction'. *The Diary of a Nobody*. By George and Weedon Grossmith. London: Dent; New York: Dutton, 1940, pp. 9–18.
Stedman Jones, Gareth. 'The "Cockney" and the Nation, 1780–1988'. *Metropolis London: Histories and Representations since 1800*. Eds David Feldman and Gareth Stedman Jones. London & New York: Routledge, 1989, pp. 272–324.
Steele, Richard. *The Plays of Richard Steele*. Ed. Shirley Strum Kenny. Oxford: Clarendon, 1971.
Stephen, James Fitzjames. 'Gentlemen'. *Cornhill Magazine* 5:27 (March 1862), 327–342.
Stone, Lawrence. *The Crisis of the Aristocracy 1558–1641*. Oxford: Clarendon, 1965.
Sutherst, Thomas. *Death and Disease Behind the Counter*. London: Kegan Paul, Trench, 1884.
Swift, Jonathan. 'On Good Manners and Good Breeding'. *The Prose Works of Jonathan Swift*. 14 vols. Ed. Herbert Davis. Oxford: Blackwell, 1957. IV, 213–18.
Thompson, E. P. 'Eighteenth-Century English Society: Class Struggle without Class?' *Social History* 3:2 (May 1978), 133–65.
Thompson, F. M. L. 'Town and City'. *The Cambridge Social History of Britain, 1750–1950*. Ed. F. M. L. Thompson. 3 vols. Cambridge & New York:

Bibliography

Cambridge University Press, 1990. I, 1–86.
—— *The Rise of Respectability: a Social History of Victorian Britain 1830–1900*. Cambridge, MA: Harvard University Press, 1988.
Tomlinson, T. B. *The English Middle-Class Novel*. London: Macmillan, 1976.
Tompkins, Jane. *Sensational Designs: the Cultural Work of American Fiction 1790–1860*. Oxford & New York: Oxford University Press, 1985.
Trilling, Lionel. 'Little Dorrit'. Rpt 'Introduction' to *Little Dorrit*. By Charles Dickens. London: 1953. *The Dickens Critics*. Eds George H. Ford and Lauriat Lane, Jr. Ithaca: Cornell University Press, 1961, pp. 279–93.
Trollope, Anthony. *He Knew He Was Right*. Ed. John Sutherland. Oxford & New York: Oxford University Press, 1985.
Ustick, W. Lee. 'Changing Ideals of Aristocratic Character and Conduct in Seventeenth-Century England'. *Modern Philology* 30:2 (November 1932), 147–166.
Vicinus, Martha. *Independent Women: Work and Community for Single Women 1850–1920*. Chicago & London: University of Chicago Press, 1985.
Walkowitz, Judith R. *City of Dreadful Delight: Narratives of Sexual Danger in Late-Victorian London*. Chicago: University of Chicago Press, 1992.
Watt, Ian. 'Serious Reflections on *The Rise of the Novel*'. *Novel* 1:3 (Spring 1968), 205–218.
Wells, H. G. *Experiment in Autobiography*. London: Cresset, 1934.
—— *The Wheels of Chance*. *The Wheels of Chance* and *The Time Machine*. London: Dent; New York: Dutton, 1935.
Welsh, Alexander. *The City of Dickens*. Oxford: Clarendon, 1971.
White, H. Anstruther. 'Moral and Merry England'. *Fortnightly Review*. n.s. 38 (1885), 768–779.
White, Robert. 'Wanted: a Rowton House for Clerks'. *Nineteenth Century* (October 1897), 564–601.
Whitehead, Charles. 'Dick Sparrow's Evening "Out"'. *Bentley's Miscellany* 18 (1845), 498–505.
Williams, Raymond. *Culture and Society*. London: Hogarth, 1982.
—— *Marxism and Literature*. Oxford & New York: Oxford University Press, 1977.
Willis, Frederick. *Peace and Dripping Toast*. London: Phoenix House, 1950.
Wilson, Edmund. 'Dickens: the Two Scrooges'. *The Wound and the Bow: Seven Studies in Literature*. Cambridge, MA: Houghton Mifflin, 1941.
Winstanley, Michael J. *The Shopkeeper's World, 1830–1914*. Manchester: Manchester University Press, 1983.
Zegger, Hrisey. *May Sinclair*. Boston: Twayne, 1976.
Zimmeck, Meta. 'Jobs for the Girls: the Expansion of Clerical Work for Women, 1850–1914'. *Unequal Opportunities: Women's Employment in England 1800–1918*. Ed. Angela V. John. Oxford: Blackwell, 1986, pp. 153–77.

Index

Ackroyd, Peter, 73
Addison, Joseph, 23
   Cato, 197
Ainsworth, William
   Jack Sheppard, 51–2
   Rookwood, 51–2
Allen, Grant
   The Type-Writer Girl (under pseud. Olive Pratt Raynor), 128, 142, 145–6
   The Woman Who Did, 8, 142–5, 146, 207
Andrew, Donna T., 5, 22, 23
the Angel in the House, 7, 80, 145
apprentices, 17, 18, 63, 70, 148, 150, 151
Ardis, Ann, 154, 210
aristocracy, 5, 14, 15, 17, 21, 43–4, 46, 47, 58, 69, 168, 176, 187
   degeneracy of, 40–2, 176
   see also code of honor, gentleman, lady
Armstrong, Nancy, 4
artisans, 10, 11, 90, 91, 93, 97
Austen, Jane, 30, 36, 50
   Emma, 31, 32
   Persuasion, 32, 198
   Pride and Prejudice, 32, 198

Barbauld, Anna Laetitia, 24
Barker, Gerard, 30
Barker-Benfield, G. J., 21
Barrie, J. M., 155
   The Twelve-Pound Look, 153–4
Battleaxe, Benjamin, 90
Bell, John Keble (pseud. Keble Howard)
   The Bachelor Girls and their Adventures in Search of Independence, 8, 128, 141–2
Benjamin, Walter, 30

Bennett, Arnold, 86, 100–1, 157, 159–60, 161, 170, 191
   A Man from the North, 112–15, 117
   The Card, 115–18, 157, 162, 182
Bentley's Miscellany, 62, 64–5, 69
Berkeley, George, 23
Black, Clementina, 157–8
Blackwood's Magazine, 62
Bodichon, Barbara, 126
bourgeoisie, 2, 6, 14, 15–22, 36, 37–8, 40–53 *passim*, 57–8, 61, 63, 67, 69, 75–6, 82–3, 89, 97, 102–3, 169, 187–8, 190
   see also gentleman, middle class, respectability
Bradlaugh, Charles, 57
Brantlinger, Patrick, 14, 38
Brontë, Charlotte, 123, 130
   Jane Eyre, 46, 124, 199–200
   Shirley, 124–6
   Villette, 146, 189
Brown, Laura, 16, 18
Browning, Elizabeth Barrett, 123
Burney, Fanny, 31, 32, 36
   Evelina, 32

Carlyle, Thomas, 6, 38
Chaucer, Geoffrey
   The Book of the Duchess, 6
Clark, J. C. D., 23
Clark, T. J., 157, 202
class, 3, 4, 8, 35, 79, 80, 82, 83, 89, 92, 94, 102–3, 114, 116–18, 129, 142, 145, 146, 148–50, 152–3, 167–91 *passim*, 170, 171–3
   boundaries, 9, 12, 15, 52, 61, 73, 77, 83, 150, 188
   stability, 2, 9, 49, 61, 79
   identity, 40, 47, 73–5, 77, 78, 97, 103

Index

identity of lower middle class, 58–9, 70, 77, 80, 86
  see also aristocracy, bourgeoisie, lower middle class, middle class, working class
class stereotypes, 7, 8, 45–51, 54–8, 70, 74, 75, 79, 86, 96, 102–3, 107, 161,166–70, 173
  and speech, 39, 47, 49, 67, 71, 74, 90, 104, 150, 161–81 passim, 188
  and dress, 39, 47, 61–2, 63–4, 67, 68, 69, 70–1, 74, 86, 90, 91, 96–7, 103–4, 107, 108, 111, 129–30, 150, 161–6 passim, 178
  see also lower middle class – conventions for representing
The Clerk, 157–8
clerks, 11, 38, 58–9, 61, 62, 63, 64, 67, 68, 78, 87, 90–2, 94–5, 101, 112, 114, 115, 129, 145, 150, 152, 157–8, 164, 178, 189, 191
National Union of Clerks, 157
  see also lower middle class
code of honor, 5, 22–4, 42, 187
  in *Sir Charles Grandison*, 22–31
  in *Anna St. Ives*, 33–4
  and the law, 23, 31
Coleridge, Samuel Taylor, 193
Collet, Clara, 125, 129–30, 151
companion, 122, 125, 126, 147–8
Cornhill Magazine, 93
Cotes, Alison, 143
Courier (Liverpool), 90
Cowling, Mary, 202
Craik, Dinah Mulock
  John Halifax, Gentleman, 7, 8, 14, 37–44, 46, 48–9, 57, 58, 85
Crossick, Geoffrey, 9–11, 60, 192, 194, 201
Crosland, T. W. H.
  The Suburbans, 91
Cunningham, Gail, 143–4, 154

D'Aeth, F. G., 93–4
The Daily Telegraph (London), 158
dandy, dandyism, 63–4
Davidoff, Leonore, 192–3

Defoe, Daniel, 6, 23, 45, 197
  The Compleat English Gentleman, 20–2, 45
  The Complete English Tradesman, 8, 18–20
  Moll Flanders, 19–20
  Robinson Crusoe, 5, 19
Dickens, Charles, 50, 57, 87, 102, 190
  representation of the working class, 52–3
  representation of the lower middle class, 69–72, 95–8
  Bleak House, 47, 72, 96
  A Christmas Carol, 96–7, 98
  David Copperfield, 61, 71, 72, 75, 96
  Great Expectations, 8, 17, 36, 46, 47, 57, 61, 72, 73, 97–100, 116
  Hard Times, 47, 53, 54–5, 56–7, 58
  Little Dorrit, 73–86, 96, 99, 100, 102–3, 116, 161, 162, 167
  'Mr. Robert Bolton', 63–4, 70–1
  The Old Curiosity Shop, 96
  Oliver Twist, 46, 47, 49, 52, 57, 58
  Our Mutual Friend, 72, 73, 96–7
  The Pickwick Papers, 70
  Sketches by Boz
    'Horatio Sparkins', 70
    'Shabby-Genteel People', 70
    'Thoughts About People', 69–70
Dixon, Ella Hepworth
  The Story of a Modern Woman, 207
domestic sphere, 5, 61, 98, 119–20, 123, 129, 131
  see also home
domestic woman, 4, 5, 6, 36, 40, 188
domestication, 2, 56–7, 89
domesticity, 3, 7, 40, 67, 77, 79, 82–3, 92, 96, 98, 113, 118, 124, 127, 128, 150, 177, 187
Doolittle, Hilda, 159, 189
Dowie, Ménie Muriel
  Gallia, 144–5

draper's assistants, 64, 84, 101, 103, 107, 148, 150
Dudeney, Alice, 189
  The Maternity of Harriott Wicken, 12–13
  The Wise Woods, 87
dueling, *see* code of honor

Eagleton, Terry, 28, 30, 198
Earle, Peter, 15
Edgeworth, Maria
  Belinda, 198
Eliot, George, 30, 102
  Daniel Deronda, 189
  Felix Holt, 46
  Middlemarch, narrator in, 45–6
  The Mill on the Floss, 124
Eliot, T. S., 159
English Woman's Journal, 119, 126, 136

Fawcett, Millicent, Garrett, 144
femininity, *see* gender
feminism, Victorian, 122, 135, 147
Fielding, Henry, 18
Fitzgerald, Penelope, 133
Ford, Ford Madox, 159
Forster, E. M.
  Howards End, 68, 116–17, 128, 190
Frost, Robert, 159
Foucault, Michel, 8, 9
Fraser's Magazine, 62
free union, 142, 155

Gagnier, Regenia, 47, 53, 199
Gallagher, Catherine, 54, 200
Gallichan, Walter
  The Blight of Respectability, 8, 91
Galsworthy, John, 159
Gaskell, Elizabeth, 52–3, 123
  Mary Barton, 46, 53–4, 200
  North and South, 55–7, 84–6, 102
gender, 2, 4, 5, 8, 45, 79, 116–18, 122, 123, 148, 152, 174–6, 186–90
  femininity, 8, 122–4, 127, 128,
    130–1, 137–8, 140–1, 142–4, 146, 147, 148, 152, 154–5
  manliness, masculine sexual potency, 24, 25, 28–9, 41, 64, 67, 90–1, 177–8, 186
  see also lower middle class – feminization; women – and lower-middle-class men
Gent, 62–70, 89–90, 91, 162, 191
gentleman, 4–7, 8, 11, 14–44 *passim*, 45, 49, 57, 63, 67, 74, 76, 77, 82, 85, 90, 99, 150, 165–9, 185, 186, 187, 188
Gilmour, Robin, 198, 200
Girl's Own Paper, 128
Gissing, George, 10, 71, 72, 125, 155, 157, 159, 160
  Born in Exile, 160
  The Odd Women, 118, 122, 128, 146–53, 155, 187
  The Paying Guest, 111
  The Town Traveller, 111
  Will Warburton, 11
  In the Year of the Jubilee, 11–12
Godwin, William
  Caleb Williams, 30–1
governess, 122, 126, 136, 147–8
Gramsci, Antonio, 9
Grossmith, George and Weedon
  The Diary of a Nobody, 78, 87–9, 93, 98, 102, 115

Hall, Catherine, 192–3
Hardy, Thomas, 159
  Jude the Obscure, 144–5, 190
  A Pair of Blue Eyes, 6–7
heroine, Victorian, 119, 127, 133, 142, 152, 155
  and conventions, 119–20, 123–4, 134–5, 140, 187
  see also gender – femininity
Himmelfarb, Gertrude, 50, 200
Hoggart, Richard, 47
Holcroft, Thomas
  Anna St. Ives, 8, 32–6, 48
home, 10, 42, 57, 59, 67, 77, 83, 91, 98, 138, 161
Household Words, 70
Hume, David, 23

Index

Inchbald, Elizabeth
   A Simple Story, 30–1
interiority, 4, 46, 63, 102, 104, 115

James, Henry, 37, 38, 71, 96, 101–2, 159
   The Ambassadors, 170
   The Golden Bowl, 190
   The Portrait of a Lady, 160, 170
Jameson, Anna, 126–7
Jefferson, J. M., 199
Jephson, A. W., 157
Johnson, Edgar, 204
Joyce, James
   Ulysses, 189

Kaplan, Cora, 123
Keats, John, 179–80
Keating. P. J., 52
Kelso, Ruth, 15

lady, 5, 6, 7, 13, 140, 149, 153
Lamb, Charles, 59
Lawrence, D. H., 159
   The Rainbow, 159
   Lady Chatterley's Lover, 189
Layard, G. S., 93
Ledger, Sally, 211
Levy, Amy
   The Romance of a Shop, 136–42, 150–1
Lillo, George
   The London Merchant, 16–18
Loftis, John, 16
lower middle class, 2–3, 6, 7–8, 9–13, 19, 58–86, 87–118 *passim*, 119–20, 123, 128, 136, 139, 145, 147, 149, 150–1, 155, 157–91 *passim*
   academic indifference to, 60, 190
   conventions for representing, 7, 58–73 *passim*, 77, 89, 115, 117–18, 158, 161, 172, 178, 185–6, 187
   definition, 9–13
   diminutiveness, 59, 61–4, 68, 70, 72, 74, 84, 98, 104, 147, 166–7, 169
   disparagement of, 2, 61–2, 66–9, 74, 89, 103, 158, 167
   and education, 92, 94–5
   feminization, 8, 61–2, 64, 67, 79
   perceived insignificance of, 58–61
   pretentiousness, 68, 82, 87, 89, 96–7, 98, 104, 108, 115–16, 149
   and property, 97–8, 100, 102
   see also domesticity, marginality, respectability, suburbs
Lund, Roger, 73

Macmillan, Frederick, 103
Malthus, Thomas, 50, 52
marginality, marginalization, 2–3, 62, 69, 72–3, 74, 83, 86, 92, 96, 98, 100, 101, 103, 111, 149, 153, 155, 157, 160, 186, 188
marriage, 29, 36–7, 40–1, 57, 91, 112, 119, 123, 124, 125, 127, 130, 132–3, 135, 137, 140, 142, 144–5, 146, 147, 148–9, 150, 151, 152, 153–4, 155, 188, 189
Martineau, Harriet, 202
Marshalsea Prison, 71, 74, 76, 81, 82, 205
masculinity, *see gender*
Mason, John, 23, 196
Masterman, C. F. G., 93, 118
Mayer, Arno, 9–11, 60
Mayhew, Henry, 51
McKeon, Michael, 2
Meredith, George
   Diana of the Crossways, 207
Mermin, Dorothy, 207
middle class, 1–23 *passim*, 36–53 *passim*, 60–3, 69, 73–86 *passim*, 96–112 *passim*, 122, 124–6, 136, 150, 174, 186–7
   see also gentleman, bourgeoisie, respectability
Miller, Nancy K., 124
Milliken, E. J., 64
Mitchell, Sally, 38
modernism, 154, 186–7, 189
modernity, 157, 169
Moers, Ellen, 69

Index

More, Hannah
  Coelebs in Search of a Wife, 36–7, 188
Morris, Pam, 73
Myerhoff, Barbara, 196
Myers, William, 205

New Monthly Magazine, 62–3
New Woman, 108, 120, 130, 142–5, 146, 148, 149, 153, 189
Nightingale, Florence, 117
Nord, Deborah Epstein, 140
the novel, 1, 2, 3, 6, 7, 8, 18, 19, 20, 30, 131, 147, 175, 176, 177, 187–91
  and class stereotypes or conventions, 45–58 *passim*, 101–3, 107
  industrial, 50, 52–3
  lower-middle-class, 111, 116–18, 160, 172, 177, 182–3, 191
  New Woman, 108, 130, 142–5, 146, 154–5, 189
  realism in, 3, 24, 30–1, 48, 85, 88, 154
  sensation, 51–2
nurse, 117, 122, 125, 126–7, 128

Oliphant, Margaret, 123, 130–1, 143–5
  Kirsteen, 133–6, 140, 141, 146
  Phoebe Junior, 131–3, 135
  Salem Chapel, 131
Orchard, B. G., 59, 94, 201
office work and workers
  see white-collar work

Parkes, Bessy Raynor, 126
Parry, John, 65
Peacham, Henry, 21
periodical literature, 3, 62–4, 69, 79, 89–90, 119–20
Perkin, Harold, 1
Peyrouten, N. C., 100
Phillipps, K. C., 194
Picton, J. Allanson, 157–8
Mr. Pooter
  see Grossmith, George and Weedon
Poovey, Mary, 4, 5, 6, 123, 207

Pound, Ezra, 159
Price, R. G. G., 69
Price, Richard, 202
Punch, 17, 62, 64–5, 69, 144

Reddy, William, M., 192
respectability, 2, 6, 10, 12, 50, 51, 78, 83, 86, 91, 95, 122, 126, 127, 128, 129, 130, 141, 143
Reynolds, G. W. M.
  The Mysteries of London, 51
Richardson, Dorothy, 159, 189
Richardson, Samuel, 6
  Clarissa, 19–20, 27–8, 30
  Pamela, 19–20, 28, 30
  Sir Charles Grandison, 6, 7, 22–31, 32, 37, 38, 43, 103, 187
Roebuck, J. A., 92
Rowe, Nicholas
  The Fair Penitent, 197

Schreiner, Olive
  The Story of an Africa Farm, 108
Seed, John, 192
Shaw, George Bernard, 73, 120–2
  Major Barbara, 153
  Mrs. Warren's Profession, 210–11
Shelley, Mary
  Frankenstein, 181
Shelley, Percy, Bysshe
  Prometheus Unbound, 181
Sheridan, Frances, 30–1
shop assistant, 11, 62, 63, 67, 68, 70, 115, 151
shopkeepers, 58–9, 90, 94
Sinclair, May, 156, 158–60, 191
  The Defence of Idealism, 159
  The Divine Fire, 8, 45, 158, 159, 160–88
  The New Idealism, 159
  Tasker Jevons, 160
Smith, Albert
  The Natural History of the Gent, 64–9, 72, 90, 91
Society for Promoting the Employment of Women, 126
Somerville, Mary, 203
Stedman Jones, Gareth, 203

Index

Steele, Richard, 23
  The Conscious Lovers, 16, 43, 197–8
  The Lying Lovers, 197
Stephen, James Fitzjames, 90, 204
suburbs, 12, 87, 89, 91, 93, 112–14, 118, 162
Swift, Jonathan, 23, 197

teaching, 122, 126–7, 128, 136, 142–3, 147, 150, 151–3
Thackeray, William Makepeace, 62
  'George de Barnwell', 17
  Pendennis, 36, 207
Thompson, E. P., 4
Thompson, F. M. L., 60
Thompson, William, 157
The Times (London), 158
Tomlinson, T. B., 200
tradesmen, 11, 13, 18–21, 42, 43
Trilling, Lionel, 84
Trollope, Anthony, 130, 190–1
  He Knew He Was Right, 6, 191
  The Three Clerks, 191
  The Way We Live Now, 207
Tucker, Josiah, 195
type-writers, 128–9, 145–6, 148–9, 151, 153–4

Ustick, W. Lee, 196

Vicinus, Martha, 127

Walkowitz, Judith, 128
Watt, Ian, 1, 3
Wells, H. G., 71, 86, 100–3, 151, 157, 159–60, 161, 170, 191
  Ann Veronica, 153
  Kipps, 101, 103, 111, 112
  The Wheels of Chance, 103–11, 113, 115, 118, 119, 157, 162, 171, 182
Welsh, Alexander, 205
West, Rebecca, 159
white-collar work, 8, 128–9, 147, 151, 153
workers, 10, 58–9, 68, 94, 120
Wilde, Oscar, 140
Williams, Raymond, 4, 8–9, 47, 53
Wilson, Edmund, 73
working class, 10, 11, 46, 47, 50–8, 90, 91, 92, 97, 128, 150, 151, 173
women, 4, 29–30, 54–5, 56, 62, 79, 84, 116–18, 121, 119–56, 161, 174–5, 186
  and independence, 122, 130, 135–6, 140–1, 145, 153, 155, 157–8, *see also* New Woman
  and lower-middle-class men, 2–3, 116–18, 157–62, 171, 177, 182, 186–7
  single, 124–6, 140, 146, 147, 154, 160
  and writing, 123, 130–1, 142–3, 189
  and work, 119–29, 123, 124, *see also companion, governess, nurse, teaching, type-writer*
Woolf, Virginia
  Mrs Dalloway, 189
  To the Lighthouse, 189

Zimmeck, Meta, 129